DELILAH

DELILAH

A Novel

INDIA EDGHILL

St. Martin's Press
New York

This is a work of fiction. All of the characters, organizations, and events portrayed in this novel are either products of the author's imagination or are used fictitiously.

www.stmartins.com

Map by Jackie Aher

Library of Congress Cataloging-in-Publication Data

Edghill, India.
    Delilah / India Edghill.—1st ed.
        p. cm.
    ISBN 978-0-312-33891-6
    I. Delilah (Biblical figure)—Fiction.   2. Samson (Biblical judge)—
Fiction.   3. Bible. O.T.—History of Biblical events—Fiction.   I. Title.
    PS3555.D474D45 2009
    813'.54—dc22   2009024138

First Edition: December 2009

10   9   8   7   6   5   4   3   2   I

Dedicated to Constance Helen Foster,

March 1, 1951–March 17, 2006.

A woman of great heart, noble spirit, and high courage.

She was a true woman of valor.

Two gates the silent house of Sleep adorn:
Of polished ivory this, that of transparent horn:
True visions through transparent horn arise;
Through polished ivory pass deluding lies.

—John Dryden, *Aeneid,* 6.1235–38

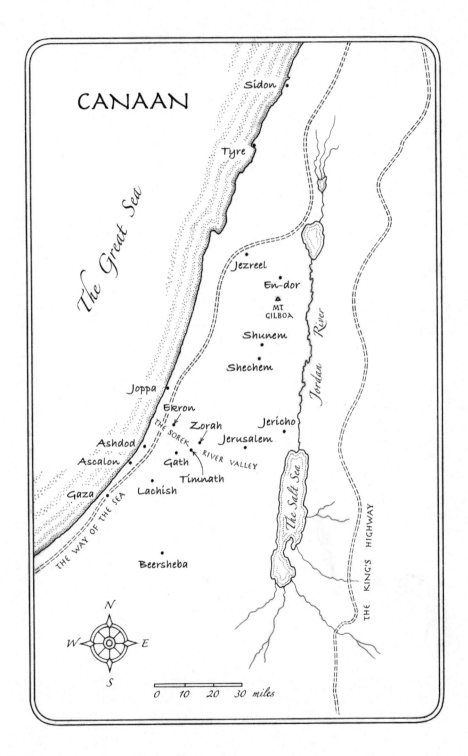

CANAAN

The Great Sea

Sidon

Tyre

Jezreel

En-dor

△ MT GILBOA

Shunem

Shechem

Joppa

Ekron

Zorah

Jericho

THE SOREK

Jerusalem

Jordan River

Ashdod

RIVER VALLEY

Ascalon

Gath

Timnath

Gaza

Lachish

THE WAY OF THE SEA

Beersheba

The Salt Sea

THE KING'S HIGHWAY

N
W   E
S

0   10   20   30 miles

DELILAH

Prologue

The Gate of Ivory

Although he knew many songs, he was famed for only one. Once that song had been his alone; now many sang it, but that did not matter to him. The song only he could sing truly remained his. No matter what else he sang, no matter how late the night grew, never would men or women—and as he grew older, he preferred to sing to the women—release him until he had sung that tale.

Always different, suited to the hearts and minds of his audience. Always the same, in the end.

And as the stars burned overhead, he would yield to those who listened, Hebrew or Philistine or strangers upon the endless road.

"Listen and hear of the deeds of Samson, strong and bold. A man who slew many men, a man whom many women desired. A man who loved a woman named Delilah, a woman who brought him low. A woman who gave Samson into the hands of his enemies—"

And men or women, Hebrew or Philistine or stranger, they listened. For everyone had heard tales of Samson, and many knew that only Orev could offer them the truth. Had he not walked beside Samson, and seen with his own eyes the wonders he now sang to them?

Sometimes, as he sang, Orev marveled at his own tales. That golden time seemed long ago and far away now, and truth elusive as a ghost . . .

PART ONE

New Moon

Delilah

"Long ago and in another land lived a maiden dark as night. Night she was named and night she was. And this maiden served a goddess bright and burning as the sun—and soft as shadows and midnight . . ."

Once I blamed the gods for the pain I endured. Later I blamed Samson himself. Only now, too late, did I lay the blame for what came to pass at the feet of the one whose fault it truly was.

Mine.

Oh, it was the gods who began the game. Yes, all our joy and pain are no more than a game to them—what are men and women to those whose breath is the wind and whose eyes are stars, whose blood is Time itself? A jest drew them to my birth, urged them to bestow upon me their double-edged gifts. Jest and play to them, to lay such a boon upon a girl new-born, god-begotten daughter of chance.

I was named for that boon: Delilah. Night-Hair.

But that name never seemed to fit me well, despite my gleaming midnight hair. For always, from the moment I drew breath, I, night-born, was drawn to the day's light. To the sun.

That, then, is what began it, set my feet upon the path that led me to where I now stood. After all that had passed, all that I had paid in tears and in desire, I now stood alone—alone before a silver mirror, a keen-honed knife close to my waiting hand.

I was a child of the Grove, begotten on a full moon by a stranger upon the first and last night my mother ever spent in the Lady's Grove. To be conceived beneath the full moon was a blessing, a sign of Our Lady's favor. Not until I was a woman grown did it occur to me to wonder why a full-moon child had been named instead for moonless Night Herself. The Temple did not encourage such unruly thoughts; those of us who dwelt within its peace were meant to serve, not to question. And from the day I took my first steps, I dwelt in the Great House of Atargatis in Ascalon, Pearl of the Five Cities.

The Five Cities of Philistia ruled the rich land of Canaan; their laws governed all from the eastern hills to the sea that stretched beyond the sunset. Although a man or a woman governed each of the Five Cities, it was the City itself that was Lord or Lady. Decrees were made, laws proclaimed, and justice rendered in the name of Lord Gath or Lady Ascalon, Lord Ekron or Lady Ashdod, or Lord Gaza. By tradition, its highest ranking priestess wed each lordly city, and its highest-ranking priest became the consort of each Lady.

It was the mortal consort of the City who sat in judgment, who listened to the arguments and pleas of the council of nobles and merchants. Sometimes I dreamed of becoming Priestess-Queen to one of the Cities—but then I would have to leave Ascalon to dwell in Gath, or in Ekron, or in Gaza. I could not imagine ever abandoning Lady Ascalon; no, not even for another of the Five. I remembered no other home than Ascalon's Great Temple of Atargatis, for my mother had given me into the Lady's hands at Her own bidding.

"When I was fourteen, Delilah, I went to Our Lady's House, and the Oracle asked the sacred fish to look upon my future. I was told that Our Lady would grant me long life and many children in return for a jewel of great price. 'But I own no such jewel,' I said, and the Seer-Priestess looked again into the pool and watched as the fish swam, and said, 'The Lady will provide the prize she wishes you to surrender to her. When you hold it in your arms, you then must choose.'"

My mother sighed, then; she always did when she spoke those words to me. For she was permitted to visit me once each season, and each time she did, she retold the tale of my begetting, as if I might have forgotten it, or her. I always sat quiet, and let her talk—although my mother was little more to me than a half-remembered dream. She was a married woman now, wed to a wealthy, indulgent merchant who had fathered half a dozen hearty sons upon her. When she came to visit me, she always wore a gown of gold-fringed linen fine and soft as water, and gems glowed like small bright fires against her skin.

But despite all she had been granted, my mother still looked upon me with hungry eyes. For she had traded her firstborn daughter for her own future; never again did she bear a girl child. The bloodline of her mothers would die with her. Now that it was too late, she mourned that eternal loss.

"Still," my mother said, "you seem happy here, my daughter."

"I am not your daughter. I am Our Lady's daughter," I reminded her, prim and pious as a Temple cat, and my mother's eyes glinted bright with unspilled tears.

But her grief did not move my heart, not then. My mother had made her choice, and must live with the life she had created for herself. I wish, now, that I had been kinder to her.

"Of course," she said, and managed to smile. "And you are already grown so tall—and so graceful. You will dance well before Her, Delilah."

"That will be as Our Lady wills." Although love of the Dance sang in my blood, and already my body swayed easily to music, young priestesses were not encouraged to flaunt their beauties or their talents. Not until we were fourteen were we permitted to look upon our faces in a mirror. I would not be given that privilege for another four years. My studies consisted of learning how to read and to write, to know the uses of herbs and flowers, to create scented oils, to choose a true gem from a false.

How to please Our Lady in greater things would be taught later, when I passed at last through the Women's Gate.

I yearned for that far-off day—in that I was no different from all the other girls dedicated to the Temple. To walk through the Full Moon Gate into the Lady's Courtyard, to wear Her scarlet girdle clasped about my waist, to paint my face into Her image; these things would prove my status as one of the Lady's Beloveds, whom all the world desired . . .

"Delilah?" My mother's voice held an odd mixture of timidity and rebuke. Clearly I had not heard whatever words she had spoken to me. But it was not her place to chastise me—a fledgling priestess—for error, and we both knew it.

I did not look at her, and I did not speak. Instead, I gazed down at my hands as I twined the end of my long braid about my fingers, over and through, as if I played at cat's cradle with my hair. The scarlet cord that bound my dark, tight-plaited hair gleamed bright as blood in the sunlight. After a moment, I broke the silence between us with a question, one I suddenly knew I must ask, even if my mother did not answer. I lifted my head and stared into her eyes.

"If you had known you must give me away, would you still have asked Our Lady for the same boon?"

For the span of forty heartbeats, my mother did not speak. Then she said, "That is a hard question, Delilah." She slid her eyes away from mine, and I knew her next words would be lies. "How could I have given you up, had I known?"

You should have known. What else would be a jewel of great price that you would hold in your arms? I looked at my mother; she had turned her face away, staring at the painted flowers upon the courtyard wall so that I could not look into her eyes. But that told me what she never would admit in words. *You did not want to know.*

Pain clutched my heart for a moment, only to be swept away by anger. My mother had tricked herself, and now blamed everyone but herself for the price she had paid. *I will never do that,* I swore silently. *I will never deceive myself and then blame the gods for what I myself have done.*

"Yes," I said. "How?" And I rose to my feet, smoothing my skirt so I need not look upon my mother's face. That was cruel, but I was very young, and the young are very cruel, especially to those who have hurt their hearts. Still refusing to meet her eyes, I said, "It is time for me to help carry in the offerings. I must go."

"Of course," my mother said. She hesitated, and then set her hands upon my shoulders and kissed me on the forehead. Another pause, and then she added, "I am glad you are happy here."

"Yes," I said in a voice cool as the moon, "I am happy here."

Of course, I knew nothing else but Temple life, and no one here was unkind to me. No one here would bargain me away for her own gain— or so I believed then, when I was a child, and still trusting.

My mother slowly walked away, to the gate that led to the Outer Court, where all worshippers were welcome. At the gate itself she paused, and looked back; I saw this through my lashes, but refused to lift my head and let her look full upon my face. She opened the door in the gate and stepped through, out of the inner Temple. To my shame, I was glad to see her go.

She did not want me enough to guess what it was she must pay for her good marriage and her many children—all of them sons. I would have guessed. I would have struck a better bargain with Our Lady Atargatis.

And if I ever conceived and bore a daughter, no power on earth or in heaven would make me give her up—even to a goddess.

All this makes it sound as if I were unhappy living in the goddess Atargatis's Temple, unhappy in Her service. But I was not. Our Lady's House was a joyous one; She liked laughter and love about Her. A child given into Her care—any child, from peasant's daughter to princess— was tended as lovingly as a rose from far Cathay. Children were Her treasure. Girls reared within Her walls heard nothing but soft words and felt no touch that was not kind. Our Lady's discipline was that of love; we all longed to please Her.

But even so, a part of my heart yearned for my real mother—my mortal mother, the woman who had chosen to bear me beneath her heart for ten full moons, who had risked death to give me life.

And who had bartered me for riches, and for a good marriage, before I even was conceived.

And now she has not even one daughter to show for it. At least I had not spoken those cutting words aloud; at least my mother did not hear that ultimate cruelty. Nor did she look back again before she passed beyond the gate, or she might have seen how my lower lip trembled, and tears pricked behind my eyes.

"Delilah!" A rustle of flounced skirt, a chime of ankle-bells, soft-skinned arms wrapped about me. "What troubles you, little goddess? What makes you weep?"

Nikkal, the novice priestess everyone called Golden Bells for the sound of her laughter, hugged me close. Sweet as honey, soft as cream, and with a heart as kind as that of Atargatis Herself, Nikkal cosseted the younger priestesses as if she were their mother, and tended the older priestesses as if she were their only daughter. To most I would have denied being troubled, or weeping, but to remain in Nikkal's embrace, I willingly abandoned bravery.

"My mother is gone again," I said, and when I thought of how my mother had walked away, and how Nikkal held me to comfort me, too-easy tears slid down my cheeks. Of course the tears drew the kohl outlining my eyes after them, leaving night-shadows upon my skin.

"No, Delilah." Nikkal cupped my chin in her hand and lifted my face until I looked into her eyes. "Your mother is here. The woman who bore you no longer matters. Atargatis is your true mother. She is within your heart, always. Never doubt that."

Nikkal took the end of her crimson veil and wiped the tear-wet kohl from my cheeks. "There, now you look less like a wild badger. Now tell me truthfully, sweeting—how did your mother's words pain you? What did she say that made you cry?"

Already I could barely remember why I had wept, so I only shook my head. Then I leaned my cheek against Nikkal's smooth breast. Beneath my ear, I could hear and feel the beating of her heart. I sighed, and snuggled closer to that steady, measured rhythm. It was hard, now, to remember how miserable I had felt only moments before. What did it matter if my mortal mother abandoned me? I was Atargatis's Dove, a daughter of the goddess and sister to all who wore the goddess's scarlet girdle about their loins.

"Delilah?" Nikkal's soft voice coaxed me to tell her all my secrets.

I did not tell all of them, but my woeful recitation of my childish grievance revealed enough to Nikkal that I never saw my mother again—not in Our Lady's House, at any rate. Later, I learned that Nikkal had told my tale to those charged with the care of the New Moons, and my mother was forbidden to visit me anymore. And for all my hot grief that last day I saw her, I must confess I barely noticed that my mother no longer came to see me. I saw her again only when I had grown into one of the Temple's jewels, and her husband made a rich offering to the Temple so that I danced at my half brother's wedding.

But that was years later, and by then I had nearly forgotten my mother, nor did I care whether she loved me or not. The day I wept my woes to Nikkal, I unbound my pain and anger, and my bitter words burned to ash like freed embers of a long-banked fire. When I had finished speaking I felt lighter, having given up the weight of my grief into another's care.

Nikkal smoothed back my unruly hair and then laid her hand cool upon my cheek. "You see? You have only to remember that this is your home, that Our Lady is your mother, and we are all your sisters. Now run along and find something amusing to do until sunset."

At sunset all the priestesses, even the youngest, who were spared the midnight prayers, gathered upon the rooftop to sing welcome to the Evening Star. I liked singing, liked the thought that my small voice was heard by the stars themselves. I was fonder still of the dawn prayers, of singing the sun into the sky, until golden light spilled over the hills and glittered upon the sea beyond the city wall.

Yes, I best loved to sing until the sun burned away night's shadows, and revealed the vast city's beauty to the waiting day.

Nikkal had bidden me entertain myself until sunset, so I decided her words gave me leave to wander away from the courtyard of the New Moons, sanctuary of the youngest and newest of the Temple's ladies. The Court of the New Moons was bright and filled with things to both amuse and teach the small girls who dwelt there, but it had been my home as long as I could remember, and I wished to explore the world that lay beyond its high, protecting walls—without an elder's hand guiding my steps, facing me only towards what she wished me to see. Now, with Nikkal's unwitting permission, I ran hastily past the closed cedar gate and slipped through the small door set within the wall beside the impressive barrier.

Once out that door, I stood in the long corridor that led past the courts, ranked in the precedence of those who inhabited them. At the far end, nearest the kitchen wing and the gardens, was the Court of Service, where the women lived who desired to dwell within the peace the Temple offered but who were not called further. They served the Lady's earthly needs; even the gods require mortals' aid.

My home, the Court of the New Moons, lay between the Court of Service and the Court of the Rising Moons, those girls who had passed through the first initiation and chose to continue upon the Moonlight Path. That was my heart's desire: to dance the Path that led to Our Lady Herself. To someday be the High Priestess of the Great House of Atargatis, Goddess-on-Earth and Lady Ascalon Incarnate. I prayed daily and nightly to Our Lady that I might gain such honor, that I would be forever remembered, and begged Her to grant my fervent petitions.

I had not yet learned to be careful what I asked of the gods.

I ran lightly past the Rising Gate, the silver charms and carnelian amulets sewn into my skirt chiming to the rhythm of my bare feet upon yellow tiles. The Lady's Luck favored me, for the gates to the Full Moon and the Dark Moon courts also were closed. It was Tammuz, hottest month of the Season of the Sun, when the days stretched longest, and it was near midday, when most of those who dwelt within the Temple withdrew to shaded gardens or to terraces hung with wet reed curtains that caught and cooled summer breezes. No one saw me; I made my way unchecked to the Passing Gate that led from the private courtyards to the Temple courts beyond.

I had a goal: the shaded Court of Peace that lay between the High Priestess's own court and the inner Temple itself. I wished to gaze upon the oracular fish that swam in the sacred pool. I had never seen them, although of course we heard many pious tales of the wisdom imparted by the revered creatures.

But I did not gaze upon the Lady's Fish that day. For as I reached my hand to the moonstone-studded bar that held the Passing Gate closed, the pale bar lifted and the gate swung open. To my dismay, I found myself facing Chayyat, priestess in charge of the New Moons. I braced myself for a scolding, but to my surprise, Chayyat looked pleased to see me standing there at the Passing Gate, where I had no particular business being.

I remembered enough of my manners to fold my arms over my breast and bow my head. As I lifted my eyes to Chayyat's face, she inclined her head and touched two fingers of her left hand to her heart in response.

"And here is one of your new sisters now," Chayyat said, and pushed forward a girl who had been hidden behind the priestess's seven-tiered skirt. "Now stop weeping, child. Here you will soon learn to be happy." The priestess nodded to me and stepped back, leaving me staring at a girl perhaps a year older than I.

She was thin as a starved cat, and dirt dulled her skin. Hair that seemed the color of summer dust tangled in a mat at the nape of her neck. Her eyes glowed pale as a dawn sky. Tears hung upon her eyelashes like heavy raindrops.

"Aylah has just come to Our Lady's House," Chayyat said. "I give her into your care, Delilah. She is to be to you as a true sister. Take her to the Court of the New Moons and tell Meitilila to do all that must be done for her." A brief pause, during which the only sound was the new girl's sobbing breaths, then Chayyat added, "Summati bought her in the bazaar, so she comes to us with nothing."

It grieves me to say that my first thoughts, when I looked upon my new Temple sister, were cross and ungenerous. *Now I shall lose my day's freedom! Why should I have to share my hours with* her?

More, despite her hunger-sharp bones and her tangled hair, Aylah was beautiful. Even my jealous eyes could see that once she had been freed of dirt, and fed enough to smooth out the lines of bones too close beneath her skin, she would glow like a rare pearl. The Temple had accepted her as a New Moon with no dowry, no offering, save that untouched beauty. Or rather, the Temple had paid for the privilege of claiming her for Atargatis.

Now I faced what I wished I had been: a girl whose beauty unlatched doors closed to those less blessed by the gods. I looked upon Aylah and knew my dreams of becoming Goddess-on-Earth were as much a fantasy as my mother's dream of regaining my heart. Who would choose me when true beauty stood beside me, waiting?

"Delilah." Chayyat's tone reminded me that I was only one of the New Moons, not yet even a novice priestess—and that she commanded my obedience.

I forced myself to think of my anger and jealousy as two cords, one scarlet and one black. When I saw the cords as clearly as if they lay before me upon the cool stone floor, I bound them into a knot, imprisoning my unworthy emotions. Then I smiled and held out my hands to Aylah. "Welcome, sister," I said, and Chayyat's approving smile gave my words added warmth. "I am Delilah. Come, I will show you where you shall live now."

Silent, Aylah followed me as I led her into the Lady's House, past the closed gates to the Dark Moon and Full Moon courts. I tried to take her hand, but when my fingers closed about hers, she slid her fingers from my grasp. That first day, she was cold and elusive as winter wind.

But I did as Chayyat had bidden me; I took Aylah into my care. One cannot always choose one's sisters.

"This is the main corridor—if you go that way, it leads past all the courtyards to the doors into Our Lady's Temple. If you go the other way, you will find the gate to the Street of Songbirds. To pass that gate is forbidden to us. We are only New Moons; we are not permitted to leave the Temple." I glanced sidelong at Aylah, but still she said nothing.

It is hard to walk in silence beside a silent companion. To fill the empty air, I chattered away, my words coming swiftly as a hoopoe's cries. If Aylah listened, she knew all my life and all the history I knew of Ascalon's Great Temple before we had walked half the distance to the Court of the New Moons.

There we climbed the corner stairs to the second floor, and I showed Aylah my room, which I supposed would now also be hers. *As a true sister*, Chayyat had ordered; a sister would share my bedchamber.

Still Aylah said nothing, but her eyes widened. I later learned she had never seen a house of brick or of stone until she had been brought to Ascalon. Her own people dwelt in huts of earth, or in caves, if they could find some that had not been claimed by bears or wolves. She had never looked out of a window, either; when I beckoned her over to the opening and pushed aside the blue linen curtain, she peered out and then drew back like a startled fawn.

"It is all right," I told her. "No one can see us." The Temple ensured that no unhallowed eyes spied upon its priestesses. My window looked inward, not out—I saw only Temple roofs and the tops of fruit trees in the courtyard gardens. To see more than that, I had to go to one of the corner towers and climb to the rooftop. I told Aylah this, and her eyes grew round as moonstones. "Would you like to go up to the rooftop?" I asked, and after a long pause, she nodded. But still she did not speak; I wondered, now, if she were mute.

So I ceased trying to make her answer me in words and took her hand, cautiously and gently, as if she were fragile as the glass vial Nikkal kept her Egyptian perfume in. I was about to lead Aylah out of my room, take her up the tower stairs to the roof, when I realized her hand was cold as well as bone-thin. I truly looked at her, and saw the grime under her nails and the knots and tangles in her dust-dulled hair. And for once, I thought before I acted.

"You must have a bath, and food," I said, "and your hair—" I wondered if her dirt-matted hair could be combed out at all; I hoped it would not need to be shorn short. "And clothing, you must have something proper to wear."

The Lady only knew where the grubby length of cloth wrapped about Aylah's too-slender body had come from, or what had turned it that dull mud color. I only knew that until she was clean, my new sister was not sitting upon my cushions or lying in my bed.

"Come with me," I said, and, still silent, Aylah obeyed.

When she set eyes upon the Lady's newest Moon, Hattah, the woman in charge of the baths—not the ritual baths but those for the mere cleansing of the body—was horrified. "By Our Lady's Breasts, where did this stray cat come from? Well, I suppose it is up to me to turn her out of here sweet and clean as springwater." She studied Aylah disapprovingly, dismissed her garment as too filthy to trouble over, and eyed the knotted mass of her hair.

"Don't cut her hair!" I don't know why I was so insistent upon saving Aylah's hair. After all, shorn hair grew again.

"We'll see" was all that Hattah would promise.

My new temple-sister remained silent throughout the long process of scrubbing her clean enough to look like a human girl rather than a mud-puppy. Even when two slaves peeled the filthy cloth from her body, Aylah did not utter a sound.

She endured the series of baths, moving and turning as ordered. After three soakings and soapings, Aylah emerged clean at last . . .

"But her hands and feet might be made of horn! She must have run about barefoot on stones to create such hardened skin." Hattah pushed

Aylah onto one of the benches and summoned maidservants to rub
scented oil into the rough skin of her hands and feet. As the maidservants labored over the marks of Aylah's past, Hattah set her hands to
the matted mass of Aylah's hair.

Hattah tried to untangle the knots with her skillful fingers, without
success. At last she shook her head. "I think we must cut all this off and
let her hair begin again." The Mistress of the Baths reached for the
ivory handle of the knife that lay among the tools with which she created beauty. The bronze blade curved like a sickle, and its edge was
new-honed each morning. The blade could slice through any barrier of
flesh or bone. To sever hair from a girl's head would be an easy task for
the gleaming bronze.

"No!" The word burst from my lips; the maidservants all paused in
their work, staring, and Hattah turned her eyes from Aylah's tangled hair
to me. I straightened my back and pretended my face had not flushed hot.

After a long moment, Hattah spoke. "Why not, little moon? Have
you seen that ill will befall if I cut away the knots and tangles? Has Our
Lady spoken to you, sent you a Sign?"

I shook my head. "No—at least, no Sign I recognize as such. But you
must not cut it—surely we can oil her hair, and comb out the knots? I
will do it myself."

Hattah looked from me to Aylah and back again to me. "Very well."
She set the ivory-hilted knife aside and took up a sandalwood comb
instead. "Comb out her hair, Delilah, if you can."

Hattah handed the sandalwood comb to me. The comb had been
well-made, its teeth polished smooth so they would not snare hair;
across the wide handle serpents twined, their carven bodies weaving the
emblem of eternity. It weighed oddly heavy in my hand.

The Mistress of the Baths stepped back, away from the still figure of
Aylah. Now I must do as I had so rashly sworn to do. I prayed in silent
haste. *Please, Bright Lady, let me comb out Aylah's hair and I will—*

I would what? I had nothing to offer up in exchange for the Lady's
favor. Nothing save my love for Her. *O Lady Atargatis, let my hands be skillful*

and my touch gentle. Grant me this, and I shall do whatever you ask of me. And let Aylah speak, if she can, I added.

I waited, but there was no Sign to indicate that the goddess had heard. Still, I must act as if She had agreed to the bargain.

I studied the tangled thicket that was Aylah's hair. Only her hunched shoulders revealed that she had heard my plea, and Hattah's acquiescence. I lifted the sandalwood comb, glancing from its shining wood to Aylah's dull hair. The comb alone would be useless. I took a deep breath and turned to Hattah.

"I must have a bowl of oil. Warm olive oil would be best. Will you have it brought here?" It was the first time I had given an order to one of the chief handmaidens, and that Hattah asked no questions, but merely sent a maidservant off to obtain what I had asked for, surprised and pleased me.

Even after soaking Aylah's hair in warm olive oil, combing the knots to smoothness took all the afternoon, and I was tired and cross by the time my task ended. But my hard work was rewarded, for my new sister's hair lay smoothly down her back. The oil darkened its color, but that was easily remedied. Once again the bath maids scrubbed Aylah's skin, and this time they washed her hair, too. As her hair dried, the maids stroked it with silk to make it shine.

At last Hattah nodded, and motioned to Aylah to stand before us. Only then, as twilight darkened the sky and the servants lit the oil lamps, long hours after I had led her into the bathing rooms, did we see Aylah's true appearance.

Skin white as new ivory pulled tight over sharp bones. Hair pale as morning sunlight fell straight as a bowstring to her waist. Only her mouth had not altered; she kept her lips pressed together as if she feared words might utter themselves did she not guard against their escape.

Too thin, too pale, too silent—but somehow all these faults did not matter. Despite her flaws, Aylah was beauty itself, fair as the jeweled image of Our Lady Atargatis that stood behind the great altar in Ascalon's Temple. I heard some of the maidservants sigh, envious.

"Once there's some meat covering those bones, you'll be passable enough, Aylah." With Hattah's prosaic statement, the odd sense of awe vanished. Aylah became once more just another girl new-come to the Temple. Of course, Hattah rarely spoke well of any of us, saying all girls were vain enough without her adding to our high opinion of ourselves. For her to call Aylah "passable" was high praise indeed.

Now Hattah turned to me. "You—Night-Hair—take her to the Mistress of Clothing and have her dressed properly. And it's time and past for the evening meal, so get her something to eat before her bones slice through her skin. And yourself, too. I don't want to see you both looking like your own ghosts. Now run along, the pair of you."

"Come, little sister," I said, and grasped Aylah's hand; she resisted, and I tugged her hand, glancing back to see why she did not follow. When our eyes met, Aylah shook her head; her cheeks burned red. Aylah gestured, a flowing wave of her hand indicating her unclad body. I understood and smiled, hoping to ease her worry.

"That does not matter. Only the priestesses and the women servants come here. You will have clothing soon enough."

Aylah ducked her head; honey-soft hair veiled her face. Her hair alone adorned her better than a queen's robe. I told her so, but all my flattery gained was a shake of her head. I hesitated, thinking that I could ask for a drying cloth to wrap about her. But I changed my mind and released her hand that I might untie the knots that held my spangled skirt close about my waist. Clad only in my plain underskirt, I offered my outer skirt to Aylah; she stared at me as I slid the silver-sewn garment about her and tied its strings around her waist.

"There," I said, and as I straightened, I saw the Mistress of the Baths smile at me, and nod. Hattah's rare approval warmed me—I had earned it twice within a short span of hours—and I clasped Aylah's hand again and hurried her away before Hattah found anything to criticize in my looks or behavior.

Derceto

"The land of Canaan was a land of gods, a land of goddesses. Men built great temples to these gods, these goddesses." When he sang these verses, Orev fitted their words with great care to the ears of those who listened. Sometimes the gods were evil and cruel, enemies of Yahweh. Other times, to other listeners, Orev sang of goddesses more loving than any mother. False gods or true did not matter to the song's own truth. *"And the men and women of Canaan gave all they possessed to these gods, served them as if they were living kings and queens, never seeing their own folly . . ."*

She was High Priestess of Our Lady's Great House in Ascalon; she acted, when the occasion demanded it, as Goddess-on-Earth. *What more could any woman desire?*

Bitter amusement curved her scarlet-painted lips. *What more indeed? O Bright Lady, were You as foolish as I was as a child, when You were young?*

Briefly, Derceto wondered if the gods ever had been young. She supposed it did not matter. The grinding-stone of Time wore away youth and youth's wild bright ambitions, until at last all that remained was smooth discontent, and the knowledge that no matter what the gods granted, never would it be enough. Not for her.

Once she had loved Atargatis with all her heart. That had been long years ago, when she had been only Derceto, New Moon in Our Lady's service. Like every girl who set her feet upon the Moonlight Path, she had yearned to become High Priestess one day—to be the Goddess's vessel on Earth, to rule as Lady of the Great Temple, a rank as high as that of a queen.

I wonder why I bothered. Did I think it would make me happy? Derceto supposed she must have believed that, long years ago. Before she had been chosen and the Crown of Atargatis had been set about her brow.

I saw only the glitter, the gold, the beautiful men. The power. She had thought Atargatis's Crown would raise her high, set her above all others. And so it had. She need only lift her hand or utter one word to have her lightest whim obeyed as absolute law. She wore garments and gems fit for Atargatis Herself. She commanded as Our Lady's lover any man for whom she felt even fleeting desire.

She was Derceto, High Priestess of Atargatis, trapped beyond any escape. She had held out eager hands for her own shackles. Now, far too late, she understood the smile with which High Priestess Zimmarli had greeted death. As she watched Zimmarli slip away from them, Derceto had heard the soft whispers of other mourners. "She smiles—Our Lady must reach out to her." "See how she smiles, as if a lover awaits her in the Land Beyond."

See how Zimmarli smiles, to leave all this work behind her, to lay her burden in my hands. Derceto rubbed the mark Atargatis's Crown had pressed into her forehead. *Now I know, Zimmarli. You smiled only because you no longer had breath to laugh. You knew how much I desired to stand as High Priestess before Our Lady's altar. And so you granted my wish. What better punishment for one you always thought too proud and willful?*

For what Derceto had not seen was the labor behind the glory. The High Priestess not only stood in dazzling brightness as Goddess Incarnate, she ruled the Temple and all it possessed. Derceto stared down at the rolls of papyrus stacked neatly upon the table. A dozen at least, each a report that she must read, and consider, and answer.

Farms and orchards, herds and flocks, grain fields and grapevines. For a moment

Derceto longed to sweep the entire lot of meticulously scribed reports into the nearest fire pit. *Here I sit, studying the grape harvest and wondering what we must do if the rains are late again—and all I hear from the Prince of the City is how sweet and pleasant my life must be compared to his!*

In the eyes of gods and men, the Prince of the City and the High Priestess of the Great House loved each other as meat loved salt. They stood beside each other during feasts and festivals, performed flawlessly the rituals that shaped night and day, spoke honey-sweet words. In the eyes of those who dwelt in Ascalon the Beautiful, Derceto and Sandarin, Temple and City, served in devoted partnership.

I always thought most men and women blind. Derceto shook her head; heavy curls swept across her back. Absently, she drew one long ringlet over her shoulder, stroked the dark hair over the curve of her breast. Well-tended, her body still woke desire—Sandarin could not truthfully complain his duty as Our Lady's Consort was displeasing. But Temple and City battled endlessly, and Derceto refused to surrender even a finger's-length of what belonged to her.

Not farmland, not sheep, not gold, not slaves. Most certainly not the right of first choice of any girls and young boys brought into the market from faraway lands. Derceto smiled as she remembered that struggle. Sandarin had lost, and was not likely to forget that humiliation soon. *But I will never let power slip out of my hands. I rule a domain as great as his.* Truly, in other lands she would have been called "queen"—many rulers governed less than she did as High Priestess.

For a Great Temple was a city within a city. Its denizens must be fed and clothed and bathed, its rituals supplied with incense and oils. Within the walls of the House of Atargatis dwelt not only fully initiated priestesses who tended the needs of their goddess, but dozens upon dozens of women and girls—for bread did not bake itself, nor did skirts sew their seven tiers together without the aid of human hands.

As in any great queen's palace, the House of Atargatis required artists and clothiers, gem-carvers and idol-makers, bakers and cooks and sweet-makers; hairdressers, perfumers, and jewelers; seal-makers and scribes. Each task required someone to fulfill its demands: honey for the sweet-maker meant beekeepers to tend hives. Offerings to the Temple required scribes to set down what had been given, and by whom—which meant clerks must cut reeds into pens, ensure that precious papyrus was not wasted, and that still others must prepare small clay tablets upon which yet another clerk would impress the name of the gift and the giver, and the Temple seal. Then the kiln-workers would dry the tablets, and finally a messenger would deliver this enduring record to the one who had given the offering. Two generations ago, she who had then been High Priestess had decreed that each offering, no matter how small, must be acknowledged. Now the scribes and messengers and clay-workers occupied an entire building that had been erected outside the Temple to house them; the Temple wall had been opened and extended to enclose the new building.

That had happened long before Derceto had been given to the Temple—*And I am no longer young*—but the Court of Scribes was still called "the new court."

And all the skills that the priestesses were taught required those who could teach them. Dancing and singing were only two of the talents a priestess needed. The womanly arts any girl must know, such as spinning, weaving, and sewing, must be learned as well. So there must be those who could teach such tasks.

As a priestess passed through the gates from one court to the next, she gained not only knowledge but tangible marks of Our Lady's favor. A fully initiated priestess wore her hair knotted up with scarlet ribbons; from the sacred knot, symbol of the Bright Goddess, long curls fell down her back. The sea's blue and green glittered upon her eyelids; the crimson of blood gleamed upon her lips and cheeks. A wide belt of red leather girdled her waist above a seven-tiered skirt whose colors proclaimed her precise rank and function. Golden doves rested upon her breasts, and golden bees hung from her ears; golden snakes circled her arms. The tips of her breasts, too, glittered gold.

The work of a dozen men and women produced the image worshippers saw when they gazed upon a Full Moon of Atargatis.

Such a priestess wore gold and gems, but her most precious adornment was the tattooed serpents that coiled from her elbows to her wrists, slid in blue midnight shadows under her skin. The bracelets of gold might be set aside. The serpents that dwelt beneath her skin remained with her forever.

So in addition to all else, the Temple required artists who could incise images into the skin, as well as apprentices to grind paints and hone needles to the sharpness of a bee's sting.

And within the innermost court lay the sacred pool in which seven fish-oracles swam in lazy, well-fed circles, awaiting petitioners who would see the future. Their names were Utu, Nanna, Enki, Inanna, Gugalanna, Enlil, and Ninurtu. Temple tales claimed the names, and the fish, had been brought from a land far to the east. The fish gleamed bright as gems; Utu, whose scales glowed like polished gold, was the largest and the most important. Each fish had its own servant, who fed it and who cleaned the turquoise tiles that lined the pool.

In the Temple kitchens, there was a cook whose only task was to grind and mix the special food that the seven servants scattered over the placid, clear water of the sacred pool so that the Seven Fish might eat of it, if they chose.

Sometimes I wish I were one of those fish. To have nothing to do but eat and sleep, to swim endlessly in pretty circles—

"My lady Derceto?"

The Master of the Temple's eunuchs had come in soft-footed as a cat; he knelt before her and lifted the fringed hem of her skirt to his lips. High Priestess Derceto gazed down at the Master of Eunuchs, seeing only his bowed head as he awaited her permission to rise. He would kneel there for hours if she chose to remain silent.

She made him wait just long enough to trouble his mind, set him searching his memory for anything within his purview that might have offended her, before she bade him stand. *Power still tastes sweet.* She smiled, and saw the Master's face smooth, his mind eased by the mere curve of her lips. And as she listened to the Master of Eunuchs, Derceto forgot her fleeting wish that Bright Atargatis transform her into a fish.

A girl had been purchased in the slave-market, the Master of Eunuchs told Derceto—she could not imagine why this should interest her, until she learned that one of the Prince of the City's servants had been staring at the creature, as if tempted to purchase her. That interest had been sign enough for the High Priestess's servant instantly to bargain for the dirty child. He'd paid far too much, simply to keep the Prince's servant from gaining even the smallest of victories over the Temple.

He'd been appalled, too, at the child's condition. The seller was a fool, and how much a fool had become apparent only after the girl had been cleaned and combed and fed. The grime had sluiced away, unveiling a golden pearl—a pearl his action had gained for the Temple.

Derceto gazed unblinking upon her Master of Eunuchs. *Yet another tangle. Did it not occur to my most loyal and most foolish servant that Sandarin might have set this strange girl in his path as a snare?*

At last Derceto sighed, and said, "Bring the girl to me. I wish to look upon her." And then, "No. I shall go to the Court of the New Moons and see her there."

Derceto knew one simple way to end any uneasiness over the girl's true origin. As the Temple had bought her, so too could the Temple sell her—possibly even to the Prince of the City himself. That would be amusing, especially if Sandarin had intended the girl to act as a spy within the Temple.

But her visit only added to Derceto's endless worries. After the next morning's ritual, she had gone in all her finery to the Court of the New Moons, and there endured wide-eyed stares from twice a dozen small girls, and wails from two of the youngest, who were startled by the sight of her elaborate headdress.

And when she looked upon the new girl—a girl who glowed like a sea-pearl—Derceto knew she had come too late. For the golden stranger stood with her fingers entwined with those of one of the Temple's true treasures, the girl called Night-Hair.

Already it was clear that Delilah—a girl whose family had paid handsomely to gain her a place as one of Atargatis's Daughters, and for whom the Mistress of the Dance had great hopes—loved the new girl, Aylah, dearly. Selling Aylah would distress Delilah, and it would be foolish for the Temple to give Delilah any cause for grief. Those who taught and tended the New Moons swore Delilah would one day earn great wealth for the Temple.

More important, the Seven Fish foretold that Delilah would become the greatest priestess the Temple would ever know. *"A fire undying."*

Still, oracles could be overturned, by a greater fate or by a more powerful passion. Therefore Delilah's love for the Temple must not be allowed to lessen, to falter.

So Derceto had merely smiled upon the awed children and gone away again, knowing she would lose too much sleep as she tried to decide whether the man who sold Aylah had been a mere fool or Sandarin's clever agent. Could any man be so stupid that he sold a child such as Aylah in so neglected a state she brought little profit? Had Sandarin deliberately placed Aylah in the way of Derceto's servant, knowing he would bid against the Prince's man? Was Aylah simply a silent, docile girl, or a well-tutored tool of the Prince of the City?

Another night I shall not sleep unless I drink poppy syrup. Derceto rubbed her temples with the henna-red tips of her fingers. Poppy syrup and valerian, to grant her sleep without true rest. *I wish the Prince of the City may sleep as well as I do this night!*

Sandarin

Mortal consort of an undying goddess. Lord to Our Lady. As a beloved
to his beloved—so was the Prince of the City to the High Priestess of
the Great House of Atargatis.

Sandarin listened as the Chief of the palace eunuchs oozed flattery,
waiting for the bitter news hidden within all this sickly sweetness. For
no one knew better than those who served in the City Palace how ill-
suited were the Lord and Lady who ruled over Ascalon the Beautiful. *In
the City's name, why can no one ever speak plainly, and to the point?*

Save for his brother Aulykaran, who never flattered, Sandarin knew
himself hemmed in by sycophants. *Those who supposedly serve me would tell me
black was white and snow, fire if they thought such nonsense would please me. How am
I to choose aright, to decide what is best, if I cannot trust my advisers to give me truth?*

"O Beloved of Lady Ascalon the Beautiful, Lord of the City Walls,
Keeper of—"

Sandarin lifted his hand; rings heavy-set with emeralds, the gem best
loved by Atargatis, flashed green fire. "Jaleel, there is no need to drone
through each of my titles. We both know them. Now tell me plainly
what brought you here—without veiling the matter in endless layers of
useless words."

"O Lord of the City, I but thought to ease what you must hear."

"O Lord of the Palace Eunuchs, I think perhaps another, who reveals what I must hear, should replace a servant so fearful."

Sandarin threatened this at least once each moon—but this time Jaleel did not retaliate with his usual complaint that he was an old, old man, and that if his hard work no longer pleased the Prince of the City, perhaps Jaleel should leave Palace service. Instead, Jaleel hesitated, and never before had Sandarin seen the Chief Eunuch fumbling for words.

At last Jaleel said, "O Prince, I have failed you."

Sandarin sighed. "How have you failed me, O best of servants?"

Jaleel bowed his head. "The man I sent to the market to purchase new slaves acted unwisely. When he returned, he told me there was a child offered up in the marketplace—a girl. The seller seemed a fool—the girl had been brought from a faraway land, and had she been cleaned and well-tended, would have commanded as much as a necklace of matched sea-pearls. But she was nothing but dirt and bruises."

Why are you telling me this? Sandarin did not voice this thought; he nodded, indicating Jaleel should continue.

"The City's servant would have passed her by, save for the fact that the Master Eunuch who dwells in the Great House of Atargatis seemed intrigued by her. Lest the Temple gain her, your servant offered a high price for the girl—only to have the Temple bid higher. At last your servant saw it was useless, for clearly the Temple meant to possess the girl no matter her price, so he hastened back to tell me what had occurred. And now I lay this knowledge in your hands, my prince." Jaleel bowed and drew back, to stand with folded hands, waiting.

You mean well, but why, Blessed Atargatis, must I be served by well-meaning fools? Sandarin forced himself to smile. "My thanks for your news, Chief Eunuch. I trust you to convey my gratitude to the servant who acted so on behalf of the City Palace, and reward him as you deem fit."

There; a safe enough command, one that would ensure Sandarin need not face the man who had nearly purchased disaster.

Does it occur to no one but me that the Temple may have placed that girl in the path of my servants? That she may have been a lure, a spy to dwell beneath my roof, to lie with me in my bed? Well, you have failed this time, Derceto. Sandarin thought of the High Priestess's fury when she discovered that the Temple had paid overwell for the privilege of acquiring its own trap. *I wish I had been there to look upon her face at that moment. I wonder what she will do with the girl now?*

Aylah

Never in all her life had she been so clean—not even before raiders had stolen her from her tribe and she had started upon the long road that had led her here. It had taken long hours for those who now owned her to free her from the filth that shielded her, hid her true coloring. She had hoped, at first, that the stern-faced woman who commanded those who bathed her would cut off the long tangles of her dirt-dull hair. With her hair shorn, her worth diminished.

But the night-dark girl into whose charge she had been given refused to be defeated by knots and grime. The dark girl had labored long, and with great care, until at last she had triumphed. And then she had stared, as Aylah had known she would, as all stared when they saw Aylah's hair gleaming smooth and bright as gold.

Those who had tended her fell silent; one of the maidservants reached out as if to touch that shining fall of hair. Aylah wished, now, that she had fought these women, scratched and bitten them until they abandoned their efforts, as those who had sold her to them had. But she was tired of that endless struggle—and she had been oddly unwilling to scratch and bite the dark girl, who tried so hard to be kind.

I will wait. I will eat, and gain strength, and then I will escape from this strange place.

Aylah instinctively recognized a cage, however opulent and comfortable it might be. And this was a lavish cage indeed.

That night Aylah lay beside her new sister in a clean soft bed that only the two of them shared. Delilah slept easily, her breath gentle sighs upon the soft air. Aylah remained awake, savoring the odd sensation of comfort. *I am not hungry. I am not cold. I am not tired.*

She slid her fingers through her silk-smooth hair. *I am not dirty. My skin does not itch.*

Sleeping, Delilah flung out her hand; her fingers touched Aylah's, as if they wove a pattern through Aylah's pale hair. *And Delilah likes me.* Already Aylah knew that Delilah's fondness for her ensured safety, at least for a time. Aylah had learned to read men's and women's thoughts from the lightest shadow upon their lips, the smallest flicker of their eyes.

The High Priestess does not like me. She would have sold me again, had I not been with Delilah. Aylah smiled in the darkness, and curled her fingers around Delilah's. *I did not choose this temple, but here they will feed me and clothe me. So I will not run away from this place. Not yet. I will wait. And I will make Delilah love me, and she will make the others treat me kindly and well.*

Content with this decision, Aylah closed her eyes. Still holding Delilah's hand, she allowed herself to sleep at last.

Delilah

I was pleased that the High Priestess came herself to gaze upon my new sister, and nod that, yes, Aylah was favored by Our Lady and would bring honor and riches to the Temple. When I told this to Aylah, when High Priestess Derceto had gone away again, I learned that Aylah was not mute, as I had half-feared.

"She does not like me."

Those were the first words I heard Aylah speak, and they shocked me. "Of course she does. The High Priestess loves us all." So I had always been taught, and I had no reason to doubt this truth.

Aylah stared at me, silent again. "No," she said at last, and then, as I tried to think what to say, she twined her fingers through mine. "You are good and kind, Delilah. May I have more to eat now?"

I smiled, and squeezed her hand. "Of course. There is always bread and cheese in the kitchen, and sometimes honey-cakes. Come, I will show you the short way."

So began my life with Aylah, who became a sister dear to me as though we had been of one birth. Good food soon softened the sharp angles of bone beneath her skin; careful lessons soon taught her how to behave in the House of Atargatis. Unlike me, she did not utter the first thoughts that came into her head, but kept her words locked behind closed lips until she knew what words would be wise to speak, and when.

She was always wiser than I.

But it was long years before I learned that, wisdom hard-won. While we both dwelt within Our Lady's House, I thought us equal in all things—save those in which I thought Aylah surpassed me. Was Aylah not the sister of my heart, a gift bestowed upon me by Atargatis Herself?

When we told Chayyat we wished to become true heart-sisters, we were let to choose whatever charm we wished from the jewelry-makers' workshop, that we might exchange sister-tokens to seal our bond. I chose a coral amulet of a fish for Aylah, and she, after much slow deliberation, gave me a lion's claw bound with copper wire. Once accepted, such tokens were worn always, knotted into a strand of hair.

A sister like me and yet unlike—she spoke words I had never even dreamed of uttering. She came to us a stranger from a far land; even she did not know where her first home lay.

"Strange men came to our land and took what they wanted. Horses, furs, women. They wanted me, and so they took me as well. It was because of my hair; it is an unlucky color."

"It is a beautiful color," I said. Her hair shone pale as dawnlight when the sun stroked its length.

Aylah shrugged. "Gold summons greed. No one sees me. They see only my yellow hair."

"That is not true, Aylah. Everyone here loves you."

She looked at me with an expression I could not understand, fond and rueful, as if I were a small and foolish child and she already wise as the Goddess-on-Earth. "They value me. That is not love. My hair and my eyes—that is why Derceto's servant Summati bought me for this Temple. That, and—"

"And what?" I asked as she stopped, and she only shrugged.

"Is that not enough, Delilah? I am here now." Her words seemed to drop from her lips like cold stones.

I stared at her, trying to understand. Surely she could not be unhappy in the House of Atargatis? "But—" Oddly, I found myself seeking words, I who too often spoke too freely. "Don't you wish to live here, to serve Our Lady Atargatis? To be a priestess? You could be High Priestess of the Temple one day. You could be Goddess-on-Earth."

"No," she said, and that was all she said that day. And for once, I did not tease her to tell me more. I think, now, that I was afraid of what I might hear, if I forced her to speak.

But that day, I thought only that I was right, and Aylah too modest. There must have been a reason she had been brought into the Temple; I decided that Lady Atargatis had desired Aylah for Her daughter, and guided Summati the day he had gone to the bazaar to buy spices and had returned instead with a silent child from beyond the lands we knew. I knew the reason in my bones—my heart-sister would someday reign as High Priestess of the House of Atargatis.

I could not even hate Aylah for this; were I the goddess, I, too, would choose Aylah over myself. I consoled myself with the knowledge that I, as Aylah's heart-sister, would stand above the others of Our Lady's priestesses.

But any status we might earn was still long years away; now we were both merely New Moons in the Lady's House in Ascalon. We had much to learn before we would be permitted to act as the goddess even in small rituals.

Samson

"Now there was a village called Zorah, and in that village lived a good man named Manoah, a man whose good wife had no child. No child, and they both growing old . . ."

The trouble that followed Samson through life like an overfaithful servant began even before he was born. Orev sometimes wondered if any of what followed would have happened if Samson's parents had owned even a handful's more wisdom between them. But that question Orev never asked aloud; he had learned very young that silence repaid threefold rewards.

Later, when all the passion and pain lay long years in the past, Orev often began his songs of Samson by saying, "Samson was a great hero and a simple man, and his tale begins simply . . . Now listen, it happened in this way . . ."

And, in a sense, all had happened as Orev sang it now. Truth wove through songs as a thin thread of gold through an embroidered robe. Sometimes the gold gleamed bright; sometimes the gaudy colors of the other threads hid it utterly.

"Listen, it happened in this way . . ."

. . .

Men never think children overhear what is said. Women know children
listen, but like to think they do not understand. Orev learned a great
deal simply by keeping his own mouth closed as his elders talked. Silence was nearly as good as being invisible. What interest could a boy
playing silently with a bit of string or a wooden peg have in the chatter
of his elders?

A great deal, of course. Staring intently at the cat's cradle tangling
his fingers, or moving a wooden peg about as if it were a shepherd and
pebbles its sheep, Orev heard almost everything that passed in Zorah.

Not that overmuch of import happened in the village. Zorah lay on
the border of the lands claimed by the tribe of Dan; the lands of the
tribe of Judah began only a valley and a hill to the south. A small village on the edge of the smallest tribe; until Samson's arrival in the
world, the only thing of interest that had happened in Zorah was Orev's
birth. And that, Orev knew, was of interest only to him.

Samson's birth, on the other hand, embroiled all Zorah in violent
argument and in whisperings behind veils. And all, Orev knew, because
Manoah and Tsipporah were neither dull enough nor clever enough to
hold their tongues.

Manoah had married late, as men must who are not rich in land and
flocks. His wife, Tsipporah, was half his age, neither pretty nor plain,
and came to him with a dowry consisting only of a chest of linen and
herself. A good enough bargain for both. Zorah's folk happily celebrated the marriage and awaited news that Manoah's wife had conceived. Why else did a man marry, after all, but to get sons?

Orev himself had been born just before that wedding and sometimes
thought he remembered it—although he knew he remembered only
hearing of it many, many times. Not because the wedding itself had
been anything out of the ordinary, but because of what came later.

By the time Orev was fourteen, it was clear to everyone that Manoah
had chosen his wife unwisely. "Fourteen years wed, and no child." "Well,

what did he expect? He should have married a widow, one who had borne children." "She should pray harder to Yahweh." "Perhaps it is not her fault, but—"

But that the blame might lie with the man, and not with the woman, was hinted at only in whispers, and by the older women. Orev knew he heard such words only because he sat silent, and never reminded the women he had keen ears. And because he had been born with a clubbed foot and so must, in the minds of many, be dull-witted as well as lame, they often spoke freely even when they knew he sat within earshot.

"But Yahweh watches over His people like a loving father. And lo, one day Manoah's wife went into the fields, and there she met an angel, Yahweh's messenger. And the angel told her she would bear a son . . ."

An aging husband, a barren wife—a common enough misfortune. Had he been a wealthier man, Manoah might have taken a second wife, or a concubine, or bought a handmaiden to serve Tsipporah—any one of the three would have been good enough to get sons upon. But like most men, Manoah could not afford a second wife, or a concubine, or a handmaiden to serve his wife.

Then, when any sensible man would have long since lost hope, Manoah proudly announced that he had been greatly blessed by Yahweh. His wife was at last with child.

And then, when any sensible man would have closed his lips and smiled, Manoah spoke half a dozen words too many.

Although that hardly mattered, as by the time Manoah spoke to the men of Zorah, every woman in the village already knew that Tsipporah claimed to have met an angel in the fields. Orev himself had heard her, and could think only that if Yahweh were truly merciful, He would strike Tsipporah dumb before she could utter another word. Why say anything at all, save that she was at last with child? Why answer questions no one had asked?

. . .

"A son who would be strong and great, a hero who would deliver our people from the yoke placed upon their necks by the Philistines..." Or, if Orev sang the Song of Samson to those who were not Hebrews, *"A son who would be strong and brave, a hero who would do great deeds..."*

A dozen generations ago, Samson's forefathers had come into this land as conquerors. The great and ancient city of Jericho had fallen before them. But to the surprise of the surrounding kingdoms, the Hebrews had not claimed Jericho as their own. The Hebrews, who might have ruled Jericho and its land, had instead destroyed the city and its mighty walls, not a stone left upon another. The ruins of Jericho remained their greatest battle prize. Only owls and jackals inhabited the shattered city now.

Once Jericho had been swept away, the Hebrews seemed to lose interest in conquest. But the lesson of Jericho remained, and for half a dozen generations the Hebrews had gone where they pleased, driving their flocks from plains to hills as the seasons demanded. No one dared hinder them, and they did not demand much of the lands they ranged over.

But that time, too, had passed. The Sea People had swept into Canaan from the west, gradually claiming the land for their own. Now the Hebrews dwelt in the hills, existing peaceably, but on Philistine sufferance. Somehow, in the lifetimes that lay between Joshua's triumph and Samson's birth, the Hebrews had surrendered power to the rulers of the seacoast and the fertile plains. The Five Cities ruled Canaan now.

How that had come to pass, no one living could quite explain.

"It is because the Five Cities are ruled by a single lord each. No one argues with him when he passes a law or claims a tax." This was Manoah's opinion, oft repeated. Several of the men who sat with him under the olive tree by the village gate nodded agreement. Others shook their heads, and Hamor drew in his breath and began the same counterargument he raised each time the topic was discussed.

"That is folly, Manoah. You might as well say it is because they have a city wall. It is clear that the true reason is the gods of the Five Cities—"

"Do not say again that many gods are stronger than our One. What have the gods of the Philistines ever done half so wondrous as—"

The deeds Yahweh has performed? Orev finished silently, and began moving away from the arguing men. If he moved slowly and with care, he could walk almost as well as any other young man. The clubbed foot that marred him, marked him forever as lesser, inferior; he could not change. But he could pretend, at least to those who watched, that the painful weight of his malformed foot did not matter.

It did, of course. Orev never deceived himself; he knew he could not afford that luxury.

"—why, my own wife, barren these many years, now bears fruit, thanks to Yahweh's greatness. Now tell me, Hamor, can the idols of Philistia do as much?"

Yes, high time to go elsewhere. The conversation was about to turn heated, and Orev knew precisely who would say what.

Having left the circle of men, Orev headed down the hill from the gate to the well, where the women stood gossiping. Tsipporah, Manoah's wife, smiled at Orev as he approached. "Have you come to carry my water jar for me, Orev?"

Without awaiting his answer, she continued talking. "You have had six children, Serach—tell me, did you crave strange foods when you were carrying a child?" Tsipporah didn't give Serach a chance to speak, quickly adding, "I crave all manner of things forbidden to me now. Wine, and meat, and—"

Orev watched the two oldest women in the village whisper to each other behind their hands. He liked Tsipporah, who treated him kindly, when she noticed him. Unfortunately, like her husband, she also didn't know when to stop talking.

"Let me carry your water jar, Wife of Manoah," Orev said hastily, and more loudly than he usually spoke. He reached for the heavy jar, lost his balance, tipped cool well-water over Tsipporah's feet.

"Have you *no* wits at all, Tsipporah? Orev can't carry a full water jar, and neither should you, in your condition." Basemath, wife of Asher, the wealthiest man in the village, began issuing orders. "Orev, go to my house and tell my handmaid Ellah to come carry water to Manoah's house. And you, Tsipporah, walk with me. You remember that I promised you my recipe for spice-cake."

As simply as that, the immediate danger vanished. Tsipporah walked off up the hill with Basemath, and Orev headed towards Asher's house, as its mistress had bidden him.

You are a kind woman, Tsipporah, but neither you nor your husband has the sense Yahweh granted goats. Even at fourteen, Orev knew how to judge men and women—another skill he had needed to learn young.

After giving Basemath's message to Ellah, Orev continued on past the house and its garden, into the small orchard on the hillside behind the village. There he lowered himself carefully to the ground beneath the oldest olive tree in Zorah and stared back down at the clustered houses.

The sun stood at zenith; light poured down over the mud-brick buildings like molten gold until the village seemed formed of the precious metal. At midday, no shadows lurked between the houses or along the low stone walls.

Manoah's house lay at the northern edge of Zorah, farthest from the village gate and the path down to the well, and had been built against the village wall, which formed the back wall of the house itself. Orev studied the house: small, old, and rather shabby-looking, Manoah's dwelling possessed a singular advantage. A woman who did not wish to be seen leaving Zorah could easily slip out through the midden gate. Manoah's house itself would hide her from inquisitive eyes.

And then, if she chose, she could walk swiftly away. Once over the rise of the hill, a two hours' walk southward would take her to the Lady's Grove at Timnath . . .

Was that what Tsipporah had done? If she had dared enter Timnath's Grove on one of the nights of the full moon, she could have found half a dozen men hot to lie with her before she had taken as many steps. If she had done so, who could blame her? Without a son to care for them in their old age, how would Manoah and his wife survive? No, Orev couldn't blame either Tsipporah for daring so greatly or Manoah for proclaiming himself blessed by Yahweh.

And if Manoah and his wife had merely announced that she had at last conceived, the villagers would have congratulated them, and that would have been an end to the matter.

Why did they have to proclaim themselves visited by an angel of the Lord? Manoah should just have said "My wife has been blessed," and no one would have thought any evil. Now—

Now there was gossip, and harsh whispers, and for all the coming child's life, unkind people would be able to doubt. There would be trouble.

Orev realized later that he'd made the same mistake he often silently chastised others for: underestimated another's power to bend events to his or her own will. For Basemath had used her unassailable position as the well-dowered wife of the richest—and therefore the most important—man in Zorah to force public compliance, if not private silence, with her implacable acceptance of Tsipporah's story. Orev also listened outside the wall as Basemath ordered Tsipporah never again to mention angels, and told her that Manoah must seal his mouth as well.

It was the first time he'd witnessed small power used for great good. What, after all, was Basemath but a woman speaking to another woman? Yet the silencing of Tsipporah meant that the harsh gossip faltered and faded. By the time Tsipporah's son was born, not only did no one bring up the child's questionable paternity but several of the women admiring the sturdy infant swore they remembered Manoah's father, or possibly his grandfather, had also had just such golden hair.

And as if to prove they had nothing to conceal, Manoah and Tsipporah bestowed upon their son a name honoring his sun-bright hair.

Samson. The Son of the Sun.

. . .

As if Samson's very birth blessed all within his village, soon after Orev found himself granted something he had not dared dream of: a way to earn his place in the world—more, an honored place. For a harper traveling south from Shunem lost his way, and wandered into Zorah tired and hungry and offering to sing a tale of great deeds in exchange for his food and lodging. Later, Orev realized that Balim had been, at best, a poor harper and worse singer—but the man could weave a song out of any story, turning dull acts into grand deeds. With the rest of the villagers, Orev listened as the harper Balim sang of how the warrior Joshua had slain forty times forty men. And then, to please the women, Balim sang of a pretty widow who followed her husband's mother to a new life with a rich new husband.

Balim swore the tales all true, which Orev doubted. But the telling of them drew Orev; out of nothing, the harper created life. More, it was a task Orev thought he could emulate. A lame man was useless, a burden. A lame harper gleaned praise and payment.

Before Balim left Zorah, Orev had vowed he, too, would become a harper—and a better one than Balim. All he needed was a tale to tell, and a harp.

"Songs are everywhere," Balim told him. "That one of the widow— I heard it as gossip by half a dozen wells down near Bethlehem. And most men and women will listen to anything that lets them rest and laugh and weep for others."

"I need a harp, too," Orev said, and Balim smiled and untied the cloth he carried his belongings in. He pulled out a harp that even Orev could tell was old, its wood dry and its strings fraying.

"Take this one," Balim said.

Orev accepted the harp, thinking already how he would oil the wood to make it shine again. "Why?" he asked, and Balim shrugged, as if handing a harp to a boy he barely knew was of no import, rather than a great gift.

"Because all harpers are brothers, I suppose. And because you are the one who truly listened to my tales—I could see you thinking how you would sing them better, you know. And because I'm tired of carrying my old harp as well as my new one. But don't go telling people I taught you, because I have my reputation to think of, boy."

Orev had thanked him, and promised he would say nothing, if Balim would only show him once how to coax music from harp-strings. The bargain struck, Balim remained another day, taught Orev enough to begin. Creating songs proved simpler than Orev had feared; unexpectedly, he had found his true gift from Yahweh.

He was no longer Orev, the crippled orphan. He was Orev, Zorah's harper.

As if in gratitude, the village of Zorah provided Orev with the substance that formed his greatest song.

Samson.

Samson grew swiftly from an infant waving his hands at everything he saw, as if trying to grasp the world, to a boy asking endless questions that no one quite knew how to answer. Oddly enough, it was Orev who became the boy's closest friend. Life opened few gates for a lame man; luck and determination had led Orev to one that opened a path to honor and praise. A harper needed tales to tell, and a boy whose birth was foretold by an angel provided food for at least one song. Orev did not realize, at first, that Samson's life would become the heart of his own, be the spark that kindled an undying flame in his songs. Orev was already nearly grown when Samson was born, and what interest did a babe hold for a boy of fourteen? But as Orev grew into manhood and Samson became a boy—a sun-haired boy taller and stronger than any other boy in Zorah—Orev found that Samson owned something worth more than the size and strength bestowed upon him by their god.

Samson also possessed a kind heart.

By the time he was seven, it was simply a fact of life in the village of Zorah that Samson would willingly shake rattles to amuse infants as their mothers baked or spun, happily pick stones out of the fields to clear them for planting, carry water jugs up the hill from the well, sit patiently as the eldest woman in the village droned endless complaints.

So of course it was Samson who befriended Orev, the lame harper. At first Samson's cheerful interest had angered Orev. *Too good to be true* had been Orev's thought when Samson asked, most politely, to sit and listen as Orev labored to master the skills he hoped would be his livelihood. And then, *Must I suffer watching Samson flaunt his perfection? Do I not endure enough without being forced to admire the angel's son?*

But before he could summon the words to send the boy away, Samson asked, with the shattering frankness of the very young, "Why does your face look like that?"

Odd words, to change a life forever, but they made Orev look again at the boy standing before him. Samson regarded Orev with eyes clear and blue as the summer sky, waiting.

"Because I was thinking unkind thoughts," Orev said. "Do you truly wish to listen as I work?"

"I like songs." Samson apparently took Orev's question as permission, and sat down cross-legged at Orev's feet.

"You may not like mine. I am not going to be singing whole tales but practicing, testing to learn which words sound best together, and how many times I must repeat them—or if I must sing them only once."

"Like Abner with his spears, only with words? All right. Test them."

Orev looked down at Samson and fought the urge to laugh. *No, you have no pride, Samson, but you have something that may prove even more dangerous— you are as stubborn as a badger.* Most would let Orev alone, unless they needed something from him. Samson insisted that Orev open himself to another's interest.

Ah well, he's only a boy, no matter how highly he's regarded. It can't hurt me to befriend the darling of all the village. "Very well, Samson, I will test my songs, and you will listen and tell me if they sound well or ill."

"Will they be true songs?"

"Are not all songs true tales?" Orev suddenly wished he had spoken less freely; there were tales it was not wise to examine too closely.

"My mother says," Samson began, and Orev held up his hand before Samson could mention angels.

"And a boy should listen to his mother, and obey her, of course. But is your mother a harper? No, of course she is not—"

"Why aren't women harpers?" Samson asked, and Orev grasped this distraction, discussed the matter as if it were of serious import. Orev neither knew nor cared why women were not harpers—but he did know it was better to argue whether a girl might sing for her living as well as a boy than to answer awkward questions about a mother's bed-time tales.

Pious truth or blasphemous lie, Tsipporah? Neither is good for your son to hear. Did you and Manoah never think what a burden you laid upon the boy's shoulders? Samson— Son of the Sun—could you not at least have named him something less potent?

Orev gradually turned their talk back to how songs were made. "Like a pearl, each contains a grain of hard truth. But they are coated with pretty words and polished with dreams. That is how men create songs—much as women weave thread into cloth, and then embroider upon that cloth until it becomes bright with—let us say with scarlet poppies.

"Now, if I weave dreams and truth together well in my songs, men will think them the same. That is the truth of songs."

Proud of this explanation, Orev reminded himself to memorize those fine words to use again. He smiled at Samson, who regarded him with grave eyes and said, "But isn't that the same as lying?"

Oddly, Orev felt the urge to laugh. He set his harp aside and laid his hand on Samson's bright hair. "Yes, in a way. And no, in another." Orev reached for the harp again, and set his fingers upon its strings.

"Now listen. 'Once there dwelt a man who longed for a good wife. A fair maiden pleased his heart, and it pleased him to work many years to win her. Many years he labored, and was repaid, repaid at last by two good wives instead of only one.' Do you recognize the tale?"

Samson shook his head. "Is it new?"

"No, it is very old. Tell me, if I sing it thus—'Many years he labored,

and was repaid, repaid with the fair maiden's sister, a woman he did not
desire'—now do you know the tale?"

Samson stared at him, reproachful. "That isn't fair. You didn't sing
it the right way the first time."

"It is still Jacob's story, and Rachel's, and Leah's, is it not? There is
no right way to sing a tale, Samson."

"Is there a wrong way?"

Orev smiled. *Those who think this boy dull-witted merely because he is strong and
sweet-natured are fools.*

"A good question, Samson. Yes, perhaps there is a wrong way—but
I like to think that all ways to sing a tale are right."

Samson nodded, grave. "Let's walk back now. Mother's baked honey-
cakes today." He picked up Orev's harp and started off up the hill.

Orev looked up the hill after the boy. The setting sun's rays turned
Samson's hair into a halo of fire, as if he were a beacon of light. *I don't
know whether you're not ready for the world, Samson, or the world's not ready for you.
What I do know is that your life is never going to be simple, or ordinary.*

Perhaps his father was an angel, after all.

That Orev had watched and worked and formed himself into a
harper eased his way in the world. A lame boy could be treated as a village pet—especially when he ensured his good treatment by being a
village servant. But a lame man needed a safe place in the world; a
harper received respect and, if he were good enough, glory. More important to Orev, at least when he began his career as harper, those who
entertained with tales in song were fed and lodged. Orev sang out a
modest living in his own village, and in a dozen others within a three-
day walk.

Until the day young Samson questioned him, Orev had never truly
thought about the tales he sang, and why they were sung as they were.
To answer Samson, Orev had reached beyond his prosaic decision to
learn to sing for his keep, seeking a better reply than "people will pay
for harpers' tales." And in so doing, Orev had for the first time understood the wonder of what he could do, how a tale could be molded to

change what men and women believed. As if he had reached for a plain clay cup and found that true gold lay beneath, Orev thought.

Or as if he had finally let the songs touch his own heart, as well as the hearts of others.

For that, he would always be grateful to Samson.

Delilah

"Now in those days women did as pleased them, with no man to say them nay. It pleased priestesses to dance before the image of their goddess. It pleased men to offer silver and gold and jewels to see such women dance."

All New Moons were taught every task the Temple required; our talents were weighed and judged, and our paths carefully decided. I knew how I wished to serve, and prayed that I would be chosen to dance before Our Lady.

I danced well, but so did a dozen other girls. I slipped out of my bed at night and practiced long hours in the garden, seeking to gain advantage over the others. But although I knew that the goddess's love danced through my blood like hot wine, I could not be certain that I would be chosen merely for my own talent. Still, I possessed an advantage in the Dance that other girls did not.

Aylah.

For Aylah was more than my heart-sister; she became my mirror.

She was sun to my shadow, sweet as new honey where I was tart as unripe apples. Even our bodies mirrored each other as we grew, for Aylah ripened into a gold and ivory goddess, her breasts and hips full and shapely. I grew as tall as she, but my body remained slender, my curves subtle. When we practiced—for I loved to move to music, and Aylah seemed to find pleasure in that too—it seemed to me Day and Night danced together.

And that, I hoped, would be something only Aylah and I could offer to Our Lady's service. The Temple's dancers danced not only to honor and praise Bright Atargatis but to draw gifts to the Temple. Dancers performed in wealthy households, at great feasts and festivals; such service must be richly rewarded. The more acclaimed the dancer, the greater the offering made to gain her talents for an evening, or for a night.

Aylah and I practiced together so often that when we stood with the other New Moons of our age, and were told we would all learn the first dance in Our Lady's honor, I felt no fear at all as we paced the undemanding steps. I knew Aylah and I would impress Annemil, the Dance Mistress, with our skill and grace. And when I slanted my eyes to see her face, I saw Annemil smile as Aylah stepped and turned in the simple pattern.

Our Lady's dances were of such importance to Her worship and Her Temple that all New Moons trained before the Dance Mistress for half a year. She watched, and judged, and decided who should continue training, readying them for the Dance. As I had hoped and prayed, the Mistress of the Dance chose Aylah and me to keep on as students.

"The two of you may be called to dance," Annemil said, "but remember, I promise nothing, save that I will teach you the dances. Only the Seven know what you will become, or how you will serve Our Lady."

Overjoyed to be chosen to continue dance training, I barely heard the warning. I stammered my thanks and swore I would work harder than any New Moon yet had to become perfect in the Dance. Aylah said nothing, not even a murmur of thanks. Later, I asked what troubled her that she had not spoken, and she said only "There was nothing I needed to say, Delilah. We all know it is a great honor to be chosen for this." Then she smiled, and since it was simplest to believe she jested, I laughed.

"Yes, and we will be the best dancers the Temple has ever seen since its first stones were laid down! I will dress as Night and you as Day, and we will wear jewels beyond price. And we will glean great offerings for Our Lady and Her House, and everyone will ask for us—" Suddenly I feared I risked my good fortune by prideful boasting. Hastily, I added, "If we are called to dance when we become Rising Moons, of course."

Aylah smiled again. "I do not think you need worry over that. You will be chosen."

She sounded so calmly assured that I took comfort in her certainty. Of course I wished to believe her, which made it simple for her to convince me that what I most desired would indeed come to pass—and also to evade questions about her own wishes.

Aylah always seemed happy to dance along with me; I believed she too loved the things I loved. Later, when I had painfully gained wisdom, I looked back and wondered if Aylah copied me out of habit, because she did not care what she did—and so my passions gave her a path to follow.

When we turned fourteen, our training as priestesses began in earnest; until then, I had not realized how softly the New Moons were treated. Rising Moons labored harder than any slave in the Temple's fields.

Fourteen was the age at which New Moons were taken to stand before the Lady's Mirror—the sacred pool, into which we would look, so that the sacred fish might reveal our future.

"As if the Temple did not have our future laid out like the tiles on the dancing-floor," Aylah said, the day Nikkal summoned those of us who were to look into the Mirror and told us to prepare ourselves for the ritual. Aylah's voice held nothing, neither pleasure nor resentment, as indifferent as if she said, "The Hunter's Star rises as Seven Maidens set." She stated a simple fact. No more, no less.

"Aylah, don't you—"

"Believe? Delilah, for four years the Temple has trained us to dance before Atargatis, and before any who offer enough to hire us to play goddess for their own pleasure. Do you think that the Temple will set

all that work aside and put us to other service? That we will be allowed
to see anything in the Lady's Mirror that the Temple does not wish
us to see? Or that the fish will say anything the Temple does not wish us
to hear?"

For an instant my body ached, as if someone had struck a blow to
my heart. *How can she speak so? As if—* As if she did not trust Our Lady
Atargatis. The thought so pained me I shoved it away. Aylah jested, I
told myself; she often did so. This was but one more jest. So I laughed
and said that the Mirror's fish would show Truth, as they always did.

"Yes, just as they always do."

That, too, I laughed at, as another jest.

But I felt uneasy in my bones; such jests held danger. I forgot it soon
enough, for I was wild to look upon the fish-oracles, to hear what they
had to reveal of my future.

The gate that led to the Court of Peace had been hung upon its bronze
hinges so long ago that the ivory panels set within the cedarwood had
darkened until they now glowed like honey. Images of Atargatis had
been graven into the ivory: as queen gazing serenely from a window; as
mother offering nourishment, her hands cupped beneath her round
breasts; as dancer with the moon beneath her feet and stars in her hands.
And above all these, in a single round plaque of ivory so old it was darker
than amber, Atargatis as Lady of the Sea, half woman and half fish.
That image was older than either Temple or City; had been carried here
by those who fled the destruction of the Bull Court of King Minos.

I had also been told that the Atargatis portrayed in that ancient
ivory held up a mirror, so that Her worshippers might gaze upon themselves and judge whether they were worthy of entering Her presence.
But as I stood waiting with my sister priestesses for the gate to open, I
could barely discern the half-fish form of the goddess. Time had blurred
the outlines of the image. I could not see the mirror.

I longed to ask if Aylah saw a mirror in the goddess's hand, but did
not dare. This was one of the most important rituals we would ever

undergo; it must be done perfectly, lest our bright future vanish. There had been New Moons who had entered the Court of Peace by the ancient Ivory Gate and left again not as Rising Moons but as mere maidservants, or disappeared through some secret gate into the world outside, banished from Her service.

Or so whispered tales claimed. When I had warned Aylah of this, she merely said, in her calm way, "I have heard these stories too, Delilah. And never can the teller put a name to the girl who fell from New Moon to kitchen slave, or who was sent away, never again to enter Our Lady's presence."

Her words had soothed me—but that had been before I stood beside Aylah and waited until my name was called to enter through the Ivory Gate.

A dozen of us awaited the judgment of the fish that day, and I was the last summoned into the Court of Peace. It was hard to stand quiet for so long; harder because those girls who entered through the Ivory Gate did not return by that path. There was no chance even to guess what had transpired within the court, what had been revealed about another's future.

One by one, the New Moons heard their names called by Priestess Sigorni, Keeper of the Ivory Gate. Each New Moon walked forward when summoned and passed through the opened gateway. After each girl had passed through, the gate was closed again, leaving the rest of us to stand and wait.

Aylah stood beside me, of course. Inarrah and her heart-sisters, Hehsedo and Tomyrit, held hands, clearly as anxious as I. Inarrah owned the gift of Seeing, and her heart-sisters did not. No matter what path Our Lady planned for us, each of us hoped to serve with our dearest friends. My seeking eyes met Inarrah's; I tried to smile, and she to smile back. All we could do now was hope, and pray.

One by one, Sigorni the Gatekeeper called each girl's name, summoned her forward to pass through the Ivory Gate. Cabira. Ohlibah. Firdausi. Her twin sister Fajurnin. Donatiya.

Hehsedo and Tomyrit were called in their turns, leaving Inarrah clenching her hands at her sides. Her knuckles paled as her muscles tensed.

"Inarrah."

That left only two more New Moons: Aylah, and me. Time stretched, endless, and I began to fear we had been forgotten. Worse, we would be rejected—

And then Gatekeeper Sigorni called Aylah's name. Aylah reached out, fox-swift, and squeezed my hand; I had not realized my skin had grown so cold until I felt her warm fingers.

Then I waited alone, the last of all the New Moons to be judged by the Seven Fish, my empty stomach as painful as if a rat gnawed within it. Aylah must be given to the Dance, she *must*—I called back my uncautious prayer, realizing my error.

No, we must be together. Please, please let Aylah and me follow the same path through life. That is all I ask—

"Delilah." Priestess Sigorni's quiet utterance of my name cut my desperate plea short. I took a deep breath and stepped forward to walk through the Ivory Gate and learn whether my prayer had been answered.

No one had ever warned me that a god's answer might hold more peril than any demon's curse.

Or that the granting of all I desired might destroy all I held dear.

The gate closed behind me; I heard the bar dropped across it. *It is too late to turn back.* The unruly thought came unbidden. I had spent my impatient days awaiting this summons. Now, at last, I looked upon the Temple's heart, the oldest and most sacred place within Our Lady's House.

A round courtyard, its walls painted in spirals of red and black and white and its floor of stone glowing pale as pearl. A dozen steps would take one across the space. I was surprised to see the Court of Peace was so small.

At the center of the court, like a gem within a golden casket, lay the mirror in which my future would be revealed.

The Lady's Mirror was not truly a mirror, of course. No disk of polished bronze or even of silver, but a pool set within the courtyard floor, a pool that held seven fish. The fish were said to be immortal, Atargatis's own children that she had bestowed upon Her Temple long lifetimes ago. Children who possessed the gift of unveiling the future to the Seer-Priestess who oversaw their welfare.

"Welcome, Delilah. Come forward." High Priestess Derceto herself stood next to Seer-Priestess Uliliu beside the tranquil water of the pool, witness and judge.

I drew in a deep breath and bowed, then walked forward over stones smooth-polished by the tread of bare feet over the uncounted years since the floor had been laid down. When I stood before the High Priestess, I stopped and bowed again, taking care to make each movement graceful, perfect.

I straightened, bowed to Uliliu. Seer-Priestess and High Priestess stepped back, and I took the last step and stood upon the brink of the pool. I bowed one last time, to honor Our Lady's Children; knelt at pool's edge. Seeing me there, the Seven Fish eagerly swam towards me, swift swirls of gold and bronze and silver.

Beside me, Uliliu tossed a handful of seeds into the pool. The fish swarmed about the food; Uliliu gazed intently at them as the fish gulped down the offering.

For a time the only sounds came from the light splashes of water as the fish struggled over the food. I remained on my knees beside the water, my head meekly bowed. I tried to bind my curiosity, but could not resist slanting a glance at the feeding fish. What the Seer-Priestess saw here determined what I would become.

Uliliu stood as if in prayer, her head bent and her hands outstretched. Three of the fish abandoned the quarrel over the food she had tossed to them and swam up to circle below her feet. She sowed the pool with another pinch of grain; the golden fish Utu flashed after the prize and devoured most of it before the other fish could interfere.

It seemed to me that I knelt there beside the sacred pool for half the day, but it cannot truly have been more than a handful of minutes. It was, though, long enough for me to silently remember all my faults. By the time Uliliu spoke, I had nearly persuaded even myself that I had somehow offended Lady Atargatis, and the fish had unveiled this knowledge to the Seer-Priestess. I would never become a Rising Moon, let alone a Full Moon, never sit beside High Priestess Aylah as her dearest friend and counselor.

Uliliu is trying to decide how best to tell me that Atargatis rejects me. That I am not worthy to rise higher in the Temple. That—

A pinch upon my ear, sharp and hard, recalled me to my duty here.

"Listen, Delilah, and heed what Our Lady's Children say." Seer-Priestess Uliliu regarded me sternly; I forced myself to keep my hands still and not reach up to rub my ear. Uliliu had strong fingers and keen-honed nails.

"I listen," I said, relieved I remembered the proper response.

Uliliu raised her hands over the Lady's Mirror. "Grace and gold; the sun consumes life as the dance the dancer."

I tried desperately to unravel these words, but even as I sought meaning in what she had said, Uliliu lowered her hands and turned to High Priestess Derceto.

"The omens are strong and clear. Delilah's path is the Dance."

After that, I was too excited to heed anything but the fact that I had been given my heart's desire: I was to dance for Our Lady. That joy consumed me utterly—and for that one shining moment, I forgot even to wonder if Aylah, too, had been chosen for the Dance.

Of course I remembered to worry about Aylah the moment I left the Court of Peace. I walked out through the small gate behind the lemon tree that shadowed this private exit, to find myself awaited by two Rising

Moon priestesses. They smiled, and welcomed me, and led me to my new home: the Court of the Rising Moons.

I had forgotten, as I had waited anxiously to hear my future, that becoming a Rising Moon meant leaving the Court of the New Moons, in which I had lived all the years I could remember. For one terrible heartbeat, I feared I had lost all my happiness; that I would never again see Aylah, never again feel at home in this strange new world I had entered. To my surprise and mortification, tears burned my eyes.

But the two Rising Moons who escorted me saw my distress and stopped. One—I thought her name was Lezaht—put her arms around me and said, "Don't be afraid to weep, little sister. You have undergone a great change today, and now all seems strange to you. But soon you will smile. Come and see where you now shall live, Rising Moon Delilah."

I nodded, and blinked back my tears. I almost asked whether Aylah awaited me, but feared to hear the answer. So I walked soft and quiet, as I had been taught, until we reached the Court of the Rising Moons.

And when I entered my new room, I learned that Lezaht was right. I smiled. For Aylah stood by the window that overlooked the Rising Moon courtyard. All my fears fled, and I ran across the room and flung my arms around Aylah.

She hugged me close, and there was laughter in her voice as she said, "You see, Delilah? I told you the future as well as Our Lady's Fish could."

"Oh, Aylah—I am a Rising Moon now. And I am to be a dancer! To dance for Our Lady's joy and glory!" I whirled away from my heart-sister and spun across the room, already feeling the weight of dancer's bells about my ankles.

"Did you doubt it?" Aylah asked.

"I don't now." I stopped spinning and waited for Aylah to speak of her own oracle. "And you?"

"I am to be thrown out into the streets of Ascalon with no more than I came in, of course." Aylah regarded me slantwise, and I laughed.

"You, too, are to dance! Oh, Aylah!" I twirled over and hugged her hard, and said, "We will be—"

"The best dancers the Temple has ever seen," Aylah finished, but this time she smiled and her voice teased. "Yes, Delilah, I know."

"Well, we shall be." I had no doubts, not now. I looked about the chamber that now was ours. The room was larger than the one we had occupied as New Moons, and its walls adorned with spiral patterns, intricate knots painted in blue and yellow that reminded me of the turns and whirls of Our Lady's Dance. I traced my fingers along the serpentine lines and heard Aylah laugh softly.

"You see, Delilah? Even this room was prepared for dancers—as if our fate were known before the Oracle revealed it."

I stopped and stared at her. Something cautioned me not to question her, but I ignored the warning. "What do you mean? How could the room—"

Aylah laughed again, her laughter sounding oddly bitter. "You are the perfect priestess, Delilah; you doubt nothing. Do you not see that this room has been new-painted with Dance sigils? That our possessions awaited us here? All was foretold, all readied for us, before we stood by Our Lady's Mirror and Uliliu stared at the fish. I told you the Temple would not squander such a treasure as you."

On such a perfect day, I refused to heed her cynical words. "Or such a treasure as you, Aylah."

She turned and set her hand upon the painted wall, traced the dancer's knot with her fingertips, just as I had done. "Yes, I suppose the Temple knows my value as well as it knows yours. Come, let us arrange this room as we would have it. Your chest is over there; you had best make sure nothing was left behind."

As she so often did, with a few words Aylah lured my mind into a different path, one simpler and easier to follow. I loved Aylah, but I did not understand her—not then, and not for long years after. I knew only that she was beautiful and clever, and that when I looked upon her, I saw what I wished to be.

I did not understand, then, that when she looked upon herself, she saw both less than I saw and more. Even new-come to Our Lady's House, Aylah understood that fine words and solemn vows could not protect her from the fate that awaited her. She told me this at last, that first night after we had listened to our futures foretold by the Seven Fish, our first night as Rising Moons.

A calm night, peaceful; we lay together in bed, watching the shadows cast by the full moon's light. Dark flames danced upon the wall— shades of leaves of a pomegranate tree in the garden beyond our window. But when I told Aylah that, she shook her head; her hair slid over my arm like an uneasy serpent.

"It is fire," she said. "Black fire. Even here, I cannot escape the flames."

Her skin pressed chill against mine; I put my arms about her. "They are moon-shadows, nothing more. Don't be afraid, for nothing can harm you here. Our Mother Atargatis protects us."

"Our Mother Atargatis will do what She must." For a moment Aylah lay silent, then said, "Do you know why I am here, sister?"

"To serve Atargatis," I said.

"Yes. To serve Atargatis." Again she hesitated before she spoke again. "Fate sent me here. Long ago, a seer in my own land foretold that I would save the Moon if given to the Sun. That is how I am to serve Our Lady—I will be sacrificed to the Sun. I will burn, Delilah."

"No, you will not. Our Lady does not ask for such tribute." Other gods might, but not the Lady we served. I stroked Aylah's shoulder. "That seer was wrong—or read the future badly. You are safe here."

As if she had not heard me, she said, "I wish I knew when. That is all." Her voice was flat, revealing neither fear nor grief.

I flung back the blanket that covered us, rose to my feet, and walked over to the window. For half a dozen heartbeats, I looked out upon the moonlit garden, at the branches troubled by the night breeze. Then I reached for the shutter and pulled it over the window.

"There," I said into the sudden darkness. "Now there are no more shadows."

I tied the shutter closed and padded back to bed, feeling my way cautiously. When I lay once more beside Aylah, I said, "No one will harm you, sister of my heart. We will find another seer who will summon a better future than the last."

She sighed, and pressed her cheek against mine. "No good comes of trying to cheat the gods, Delilah."

"I would never try to cheat Atargatis." I spoke the words solemnly, as a vow. "And you are Her daughter. She will protect you." I was always less wise and more trusting than Aylah.

"Atargatis may love me as Her daughter, but the Temple does not."

I hugged Aylah hard. "Everyone in the Temple loves you, Aylah. They do."

For a moment she said nothing, then she kissed my cheek. "You are a true sister to me, Delilah. Now promise you will tell no one what I have told you. Leave my fate in the hands of the goddess."

Glad to hear that Aylah trusted in Atargatis, I promised to keep her secret. That vow I kept, although I forgot the first.

Derceto

"Now the children of Israel had done evil in the eyes of their god Yahweh, had forsaken the old ways that had brought them safe through all peril." Safe enough words for listeners; not even Hebrews could object to Orev singing what the great prophet Samuel himself had railed against. *"The children of Israel forsook the old laws, until every man did what was right in his own eyes. And so in those days, the Philistines ruled over all the land, and no man could stand against them."*

Another raid upon the outlying farms—and what am I to do about it? Will Sandarin send armed men at my bidding? No, if I ask for City soldiers to protect Temple lands, he will smile and say that so rich a Great House must surely be able to provide for itself. As if Our Lady deals in swords and spears!

Sometimes Derceto longed for the days when she had been only one of the Temple's most favored Full Moons. On truly bad days, she wished she were a little New Moon again, a child to whom nothing mattered beyond Our Lady's Gate. But she was High Priestess, and must confront the world beyond the Temple—an uncertain, changing world that even Temple walls could not deny forever.

The Five Cities had ruled the Sea-Lands of Canaan time out of mind. But the Five Cities no longer reigned unchallenged. A dozen life-times ago, a new people had fled bondage in Egypt and sought sanctuary in the sweet land of Canaan. At first the new tribes had dwelt peacefully enough at the borders of Canaan, in the hills and far valleys. But two peoples cannot share a land both covet. The Hebrews began to raid the lands of the Five Cities, claiming they belonged to them, a gift from their god. People already dwelling in Canaan meant nothing to these fierce men, who scorned all gods other than their own.

But in truth, it did not matter that the Hebrews scorned all gods other than their own. Perhaps the gods and goddesses had quarreled with the Hebrews' god; if so, prudence dictated that mere mortal men and women remain aloof from heaven's battles. As proof, historians offered up the examples of the Swan Court and the Horse Court.

Their kings and queens meddled in the affairs of the gods—and what remains now of gold-proud Mykenae and of windswept Troy? Naught but ruins. So the Temple records told.

The Bull Court had suffered the same fate; its king chose to deny its queen-goddess her desire, and her anger had moved Earth Herself. The Bull Court now lay buried in rock and ash; only those who had fled before the final cataclysm had survived. The Five Cities held all that remained of Knossos, Queen of the Seas. The Five Cities, the Bull Court's children, wore new crowns of empire, unchallenged until the Hebrews took up arms against them. The Hebrews regarded Canaan as theirs, and would brook no opposition.

For all the long years that the Hebrews had harried Canaan, the warriors of the Five Cities had restrained the worst excesses of these foreigners. And the Lords and Ladies of the Five Cities had chosen to turn veiled eyes to Hebrew settlers in Canaan, so long as the newcomers remained peaceful.

Nor did the Five Cities care that the Hebrews had conquered cities beyond the high hills between the plains of Canaan and the lands to the east. The Five Cities looked to the sea, not to the land, for their wealth.

We of the Five Cities should have looked to our mines, our metalworkers and swordsmiths. Derceto wondered if it were too late for the Temple to claim the same right to smelt iron and manufacture weapons that the City owned. Armed clashes between the Hebrews' fighting men and the Five Cities' warriors had suddenly become commonplace. The warriors of the Five Cities won, for the most part. The Hebrews still worked only in bronze, while the Five Cities owned the art of creating weapons from a new metal.

Iron.

Bronze blades and spearheads had taken men down the Dark Road to judgment for a thousand years. But bronze could not stand against cold iron.

The gods had bestowed the secret of forging iron to the Five Cities, and that secret was cherished. Only the people of the Five Cities might possess or work iron. Once the rulers of the Five Cities and the Great Houses of the Gods had believed that holding the knowledge of this new, deadly metal for themselves alone would keep the world as it had been before the Hebrews came to Canaan. The Five Cities armed their warriors with iron-bladed swords and iron-tipped spears, and forbade any other people to work the dark hard metal. The only smiths who possessed the knowledge of forging iron were subjects of the Five Cities.

But now there are more of these Hebrews, always more. I wonder if I dare claim that Our Lady's House needs warriors of its own? Warriors loyal to the Temple, not to the City . . .

Derceto considered the matter, thought of the outcry if Atargatis, the Lady of Love and Light, suddenly demanded armed men to serve Her. Even for the High Priestess of Atargatis's Great House in Ascalon, there were limits beyond which she must not venture—not if she were wise.

Derceto considered herself wise. *Temple guards? No. Not yet. But I will ask Sandarin for aid—before witnesses, so he cannot deny me without risking accusations of impiety.* Yes, that might work. Derceto frowned, and then rubbed her forehead. Once it would have been to smooth away the lines left by discontent. Now it was to soothe her aching head.

She leaned her head against her hand, then called softly for her wait-ing handmaiden. Mottara understood without need of words; she went silently away, soon returning with a linen bandage wet with cool water and a small clay bowl. Silently, Derceto reached for the bowl as Mottara held it out to her. From the liquid filling the bowl rose the sharp scent of willow, familiar and comforting.

At least, Derceto thought bitterly, *I can still have willow-bark tea.* Warriors for the Temple would have to wait.

Delilah

"And men gave great treasures to see the dark priestess dance, the priestess named Delilah. To gaze upon her as she danced before all men's eyes, wild and free as hot summer wind . . ."

Our days were kept too full for introspection, and so I soon folded Aylah's keen-edged words of seers and fires away in my mind, as if they were garments not needed for a season. To learn all we must know occupied our days—for we were Rising Moons now, and much was expected of us by our elders. Newly consecrated to Atargatis, we set our feet upon the long path all those called to serve Our Lady must walk. Now began our true transformation from girl to priestess.

Lessons claimed all the hours of our days. Dance, of course, for me and for Aylah, long hours of careful practice, until each step, each supple movement, became perfect. And now that we were Rising Moons, we had to learn custom and law, trade routes and Temple history. The lore of the Five Cities must be mastered, as well as all the rituals and prayers due Our Lady.

But history and trade seemed pallid things compared to the Lady's Wisdom; knowledge we both longed and feared to learn. One day we would be Full Moons, our bodies vessels for Our Lady. When we sat dutifully listening to dull matters of roads and taxes, our minds wandered—at least mine did—to the more enticing lessons: how to touch, to kiss, to summon the goddess for Her worshippers.

The Lady's Dance already burned in my blood; I found it hard to sit and listen to Master Indiones drone on about the lore of metal-craft and the difficulties of controlling the secrets of ironworking when I could think of what the Mistress of the Lady's Arts had told us that morning. *"There are seven kinds of kisses, and you will learn all of them . . ."*

"Now, the Five Cities have laws that are fair and just, and ask only that all who dwell in the land of Canaan abide by those laws. But this new people, these Hebrews, do not abide by any law, but do as pleases them. And at first the Five Cities had looked upon the Hebrews as a mere nuisance, as easy to destroy as a buzzing fly—"

"Has Wise Indiones ever tried to destroy a buzzing fly?" Aylah whispered in my ear as Indiones droned on. I thought of how hard flies were to catch or kill; swatting the vexing insects merely seemed to encourage their attacks. I pressed my lips tight so that I would not laugh aloud and earn extra lessons as punishment. Temple Eunuch Indiones had instructed the Temple's children so long no one remembered who had preceded him. There was very little Indiones did not know about the history of gods and men—but his nature was solemn and his reprimands severe.

"But although the Five Cities had offered fair bargains for the land the Hebrews coveted, the trade was refused. Now, as you all know—or should know, as I have repeated it often enough—no other people dwelling in Canaan may have a smith of their own. Any man who wishes to sharpen a blade must come to a Philistine smith. Who rules iron rules all. Write that down. Now, the Hebrews have a strange god . . ."

Dutifully, we scratched the words into the wax of our tablets. I could not imagine why we needed to know anything about iron, or Hebrews, or any gods other than our own. My mind drifted back to the Lady's Arts. *"Your body is a living temple. Men will worship it . . ."*

"A hard law, fit for a hard metal," Aylah said as we left the classroom and our lesson in the customs and judgments of the Five Cities.

"What law?" I asked, and Aylah sighed, as if she despaired of me as much as Indiones did.

"Didn't you listen at all, Delilah? Remember, we are to concentrate our minds on the lesson before us at the time." Aylah made her voice prim, and I laughed as she went on. "The law that no one save a man of the Five Cities may work in iron."

"Oh, that. Well, why should those who are our enemies forge blades the equal of ours? Should not our own soldiers possess the best weapons?"

Aylah slanted a glance at me, her eyes gray and hard as iron itself. "The world changes, Delilah. Do you think only weapons are made of a metal harder than bronze? Does a man with an iron plow wish to carry it from his fields to a Philistine forge to have it sharpened? Do you think the way to win men's hearts is by making their lives harder than they must be?"

I shook my head, although in truth, I did not understand why Aylah cared about such matters. "But do you think it right to set a sword that may slay one of our own people into the hand of an enemy?"

"Your people," Aylah said. "Not mine."

There was no bitterness in her voice; she merely told truth, as she saw it. I caught her hand in mine. "My people are your people, heart-sister. Does not everyone here love you?"

I knew that the Temple cherished Aylah, that the Dark Moons, the eldest priestesses who waited to join Our Lady in the Land Beyond, hoped for great things from my heart-sister. With Aylah's beauty and her quick wit, her graceful dancing, she could rise high. I knew in my heart that Aylah was being groomed to one day take her place as High Priestess. I never said so, fearing that voicing the words would be tempting Fate to set snares across her smooth path.

But what I dared not say, Aylah spoke freely, careless of even a teacher or a priestess overhearing, let alone one of the gods who joy in meddling in the affairs of men and women.

"Yes, everyone here is kind to me. Perhaps they think to see me wear the crown of Goddess-on-Earth one day, and wish me to look upon them with favor." Aylah smiled, a movement of the lips only. Her eyes remained cool and keen as iron blades.

So sure was I that Aylah's destiny was to become High Priestess it never occurred to me that she might be jesting—or that she might not wish to wear that crown. All I could think of to say was "Hattah does not seek your favor."

"Hattah," said Aylah, "is a clever woman, and wise, too. Why else do you think she is Mistress of the Baths?" As I stared, Aylah looked at me and laughed, softly, as we had been taught. "Close your mouth before something flies into it and steals your words," she said. "Come—it is past time we must go and let my lady Tannyair instruct us in the proper way to adjust our veils on all occasions, and you know what she is like. If we are late, she will moan and wail about how the Temple ran more smoothly when she came to it, and how in *her* day no girl dared act carelessly or lack respect."

"And how Rising Moons scrubbed the Temple steps on their knees—"

"With their own hair—"

"And never spoke unless Atargatis Herself granted permission!" I finished. For a moment, guilt lay in my stomach like a cold, heavy stone; how could I speak so lightly of Our Lady and those who served her?

Aylah laughed at my impious words. "Yes, if Holy Atargatis is angered, Her priestesses make Her displeasure known."

Aylah's reckless words made me uneasy, but at least she was again happy—so I decided that Atargatis had not been angered after all. I did not tell these thoughts to Aylah, for I could hear her words echo in my ears as clearly as if I had: *"Perhaps Our Lady Atargatis was not angered, but if any of Her priestesses overheard us, they would be angry enough for both themselves and the goddess."*

No, I decided, it would be far wiser to accept Our Lady's gift of laughter—and hasten on to Priestess Tannyair's class.

. . .

The most visible sign of our new status as Rising Moons was the out-line of serpents entwining our arms. I had longed to wear those ser-pents beneath my skin since I had first set eyes upon one of Lady Atargatis's favored priestesses. And I was willing to pay the price un-flinching.

So when I sat before the Painter of Skins who would create the sym-bols upon my flesh, I vowed silently that I would not utter a sound, no matter how great the pain. I remembered my lessons in creating peace within myself and called upon that skill now, as the artist took a thin piece of kohl and traced the pattern upon my skin.

Once the image seemed good to her, she took up a bone needle and dipped it into a little pot of ink. After warning me not to move, lest the pattern be ruined, she set the point of the needle against my skin and began tapping the dark ink into the outline she had drawn.

The constant prick-prick-prick of the needle hurt, but I kept my face smooth and my lips closed over words of complaint. Some of the other girls squeaked like trapped bats as the Painter of Skins traced serpents upon their smooth flesh and tapped ink through their soft skin.

When at last the patterns had been finished—a process that began at the dark of one moon and ended at the dark of another—serpents coiled from my wrists to my elbows, outlined in midnight ink. Some-day, if I were fortunate, that outline would be filled in with deep ebon-blue, later still be shadowed scarlet, and perhaps even gilded, did I rise high enough in rank.

That goal drove me to work hard at the new lessons assigned to us. Each Rising Moon embarked upon her course of study—some learned the virtues of herbs and plants to heal or harm; others the mysteries of the stars and sky, to gauge the weather from the scent of the air or pat-terns of the clouds. For Aylah and me, half the day now was given to studying the dances we must know to please our goddess . . .

And Her patrons. For men and women of wealth and power needed the Temple's sacred dancers to perform at banquets and at festive occasions. Patrons paid much to hire Our Lady's dancers, whose art might gain the goddess's favor upon a wedding or a naming.

So it was twice important that those of us chosen for the Lady's Dance learn its steps well.

Even before we set our feet upon the dancing-floor, the half a dozen Rising Moons who had been chosen to dance learned that all they had already been taught meant nothing now. We all gathered in the Dancing Court—one of the oldest courtyards in the Great House of Atargatis—eager to begin. The dancing-floor was smooth-polished stone dark as deep night, the labyrinth pattern of the Dance formed of yellow tiles inlaid into that shining black stone. So many feet had danced that intricate pathway in the long years since it had been laid down that the tiles glowed pale as lamplight.

Flute-players and drummers waited for us, as did Dark Moon Priestess Sharissit. Once she had been Lady of the Dance, the most sought-after of the Temple's dancers; now she served as Priestess of the Dance and taught those chosen to follow the same path she had done.

"So you are my new students." Sharissit regarded us intently, as if she would look into our hearts. "And like all the others I have taught, I suppose you think you already know how to dance?"

Silence; no one dared answer. I looked into the Dance Priestess's eyes, and heard myself saying, "If we already knew how to dance, my lady Sharissit, we would not have been given into your care, that you might instruct us."

The Dance Priestess studied me a moment. "A good answer—and as you are so bold, I am certain you will be pleased to be chosen first to show me what you can do when the music calls."

Aylah's fingers brushed my hand, and I sensed her rueful amusement. Now that it was too late, I wished I had remained silent rather than trying to be clever; I only hoped I had not angered the Dance Priestess.

Sharissit lifted her hand, and the musicians began to play. Without saying a word, our teacher walked to the beginning of the dancing path; she stood there a moment, then gracefully, unhurriedly, began to dance. I watched her closely, knowing this was the first lesson. I memorized the steps, the turns, even as I admired Sharissit's skill. A Dark Moon she might be—past her fruitful years—but she still became the Dance itself when the music called.

When the music ended, Sharissit stopped, then turned and pointed at me. "Go to the beginning of the labyrinth and dance. Let us see whether you have the same talent for dancing as you have for clever answers. And the rest of you may stop smiling and giggling behind your hands. Your turns will come next. Before I can teach any of you, I must see what you must unlearn first."

The other girls quickly looked at their feet, or smoothed their expressions until they were appropriately grave. Priestess of the Dance Sharissit beckoned me forward.

"Begin, Delilah," she said, and I stepped onto the yellow path.

The moment my bare feet touched the smooth tiles of the labyrinth, I knew this was why I had been born, why I had been claimed by Lady Atargatis as Her own. My body swayed to the Lady's music as if I been summoned by that tune since the day my mother had conceived me in the Grove.

Almost unheeding the music, I danced the spiral path set in time-worn yellow tiles upon the ancient stone floor, stopping only when the musicians stopped. Silence seemed to echo against the walls. The magic drained from my body, and I looked back to see everyone—the Dance Priestess, the flute-players and the drummers, the other Rising Moons who also would learn to dance—staring at me.

I did not know what to say, and so I stood silent too, waiting.

At last, the Dance Priestess spoke. "I see you will learn nothing from me." Sharissit had taught Temple girls to dance since before I was conceived; to hear myself so easily dismissed hurt as if her words were stones against my flesh.

I stared down at the yellow tiles beneath my feet, vowing I would not weep. Tears would leave dark tracings of kohl down my cheeks, reveal my pain and shame to all who watched. As I fought to keep my face smooth, I heard Sharissit say, "Come and stand before me, Delilah."

As I walked towards her, the priestess ordered the flute-players and the drummers to begin again. I tried to ignore the sound, but my body could not resist the seductive patterns their music wove. My body swayed, my feet matched the music's rhythm.

I stopped before Sharissit. She made me stand as she walked slowly around me, studying me as if she were judging the worth of a slave at the market—or as if I were a rare gem she had not thought to lay her eyes upon.

When Sharissit stood facing me once more, she smiled. "Sweet Atargatis has granted you a rare gift, Delilah. Have you always danced so?"

"I have danced only to amuse myself, and my sister-moons," I said. As New Moons, we had been encouraged to attempt any skill we wished. I had loved to let my body flow with music, let my feet choose their own path in time to timbrel or drum. But I knew better than to claim great skill.

"Now you will dance to amuse the goddess, and to honor Her and reveal Her grace to Her worshippers," Sharissit said. "You will be a jewel in Her crown, Delilah—if you will be taught. Now you dance as Our Lady Atargatis wills it, but you must also learn to dance when only you will it. The goddess's grace is given at her pleasure. What happens if you must dance and She does not choose to share Her blessing with you that day?"

I did not know, so I merely shook my head.

"I will tell you a secret, Delilah. Long-practiced skills will serve you well during those times you call upon the goddess and She does not choose to answer. Will you learn?"

I lifted my head and looked into Sharissit's eyes. "I will learn, Priestess of the Dance. But you said you could not teach me."

She smiled. "I cannot teach you what you possess already—to entwine your body with the music, to give yourself utterly to the Dance. But the proper steps, the correct forms, those I can convey to you. And there are others, finer dancers and teachers than I, who also will instruct you when you have learned all I can teach."

After that, she sent me back to the beginning of the spiral path, and had me dance its curves and turns again. This time I was so nervous I fell over my own feet; Sharissit laughed and waved me aside, and pointed at the next girl, ordering her to try.

Breathing hard, my hands shaking, I went to stand beside Aylah. "I do not know why I could not do it the second time," I whispered. "I tried, I did."

"You tried too hard." Aylah laced her warm fingers through my trembling ones. "You are not a dancer, Delilah, you are the Dance. When Sharissit sent you back to dance a second time, she knew you could not do it. Not from here."

Aylah touched my forehead with her fingers. "Here is where you keep steps you have learned, practiced. Here"—she lifted our entwined hands and pressed them against my heart—"here is where you keep Dance itself. When you can join the two, you will become the greatest dancer the Temple has ever possessed—just as you have always said you would. And the most costly."

"Do you really think so?" I asked, and Aylah nodded solemnly.

"Yes. And—"

"If you cannot stand quiet for even one turn of the sands, perhaps you need more work to do." Sharissit spoke quietly, but her trained voice carried clear and strong across the dancing-floor. Silence, sudden and almost tangible, filled the courtyard. Aylah and I were not the only girls who had whispered or giggled as they waited for the Dance Priestess to take notice of them.

"You, Aylah—stop whispering to Delilah when you two think I do not notice and go stand over there." Sharissit pointed at the time-smoothed yellow tiles that formed a seven-pointed star at the beginning of the spiral path.

I let Aylah's hand slip from mine, and she walked meek enough to the edge of the dancing-floor—but not before she glanced at me. A swift slant of her pale eyes, a lift of her brow, and Aylah conveyed the message *You see, Delilah? You were chosen and so shall I be. I told you so before we started.* I bit my lip to keep from laughing. For all her solemn ways, sometimes it seemed to me that only Aylah could draw true laughter from me.

Once again the flutes and drums began. Upon Sharissit's signal, Aylah began the dance, and before she had turned even once to the changing music, unease slid beneath my skin, chilled my joy.

For Aylah danced exactly as Sharissit had shown us. And that was all.

When Aylah reached the end of the pattern, she stopped, and bowed to the Priestess of the Dance. My heart seemed to knot painfully in my chest as Sharissit looked upon Aylah. If the priestess rejected my heart-sister, I must dance alone . . .

But all the Priestess of the Dance said was "Very good, Aylah."

And later, when I told Aylah how I had feared I would be forced to choose between her and the Dance, how cold my skin had turned, and how fast my heart had beat with fear, she smiled and put her arms around me. "Poor Delilah," she said, and laid her cheek against mine. "You worry too much. I told you the Temple knows how to value us."

I do not know if Dance Priestess Sharissit truly wished to teach Aylah; I do know that she treated all her students fairly. Aylah claimed that the Priestess of the Dance had been commanded to accept her as one of the Temple's dancers, and only shook her head ruefully when I swore she danced as well as I. We both knew better. I always surrendered myself to the passion of the Lady's Dance, while Aylah merely knew the steps perfectly. To watch her dance was to see precisely how each movement should be done—yet although she danced flawlessly, she danced without joy.

But that did not matter, for when the two of us danced together, only the most critical noticed anything amiss.

The Temple wasted nothing, and twice never wasted such an asset as Aylah and I together created. As we studied, we were watched, and judged, and molded into a prize that would garner much profit for the Great House of Atargatis. My darkness and Aylah's dawn-pale looks, our ability to dance beautifully together, my passion enhanced by Aylah's precision, were praised, and we were given extra attention by the Priestess of the Dance.

New dances were created to take advantage of our talents. Special garb was fashioned for us to wear when we danced before Atargatis, or at a feast or festival. I was clad in black and silver, Aylah in crimson and gold; I Night to Aylah's Day.

The first time we wore full dancer's garb, its burden surprised us. The spangle-sewn tiered skirts and the wide bands of bells about our ankles weighed heavier than we had expected.

"Night and Day," Sharissit said, when we stood before her adorned and laden with the new clothing we would wear when we danced. "Well, Little Sun and Little Moon—now you shall begin again."

And we did, for dancing in full ritual costume required of us more strength and care, that we might perform the steps with grace and reverence. I worked hard to perfect the turns, to move lightly, to ring the silver bells about my ankles to the rhythm of the dance. I encouraged Aylah to work as hard as I, for I knew, from the attention we received, that the Temple had the highest hopes for us.

"Both of us," I told Aylah, as we sat upon stools in the baths after one of the grueling lessons. It was pleasant, after such hard work, to do nothing, to let others pour rose-scented water over us to wash away our effort, and to knead soothing oils into our sore muscles.

Aylah slanted a glance at me. "High hopes. Yes, I suppose they do. They believe we shall earn great offerings for the Temple."

"Of course we will." Confidence filled me now; I would have to be a fool not to see how highly Sharissit valued my skill—and I had heard the Temple servants gossip when they did not know I overheard them.

"Yes, the Temple will use us as they wish, and we can do nothing save bow and act as the High Priestess commands." Aylah's words seemed to hang flat and heavy in the bath's moist, heated air.

I stared at her as the bath slave unpinned my hair and started to comb sandalwood oil through its heavy length. "Aylah," I began, and she shook her head.

"There is no need to speak now," she said, and I closed my lips over the words I had wished to say.

But I was troubled in my heart, for it seemed to me that sadness burdened Aylah's days. I remembered the prophecy she had told me, all those years ago, when we still were only New Moons: *"I will be sacrificed to the Sun. I will burn, Delilah."*

Now I thought I knew what those fearful words really meant. Later, when we lay under the pomegranate tree in the garden belonging to the Court of the Rising Moons, I told Aylah, thinking to reassure her, to make her happy. "You remember the words you said to me long ago, that you were to be given to the Sun? Well, now you have been—you dance as the Sun, Aylah. That is what the Seer's words meant." I smiled, and squeezed her hand.

She regarded me intently for the space of a long indrawn breath. Then she smiled. "Perhaps it is, heart-sister. Perhaps it is."

That was all she would say, but she seemed more content, and I prided myself upon easing the burden she had carried. Aylah laughed more, after that day, and I believed she had forgotten the Seer's prophecy. Soon I, too, forgot again. Between the hours we spent under Priestess Sharissit's instruction and those spent learning to perform the many Temple rituals, there was little time to brood upon possible futures.

The House of Atargatis was all our world, a world in which nothing changed. But beyond the Temple walls, beyond the high walls of Ascalon, time-honored ways of life had begun to shatter. Rather than ruling the heavens and the earth as equals, the Lady was in many places being relegated to tending hearth and home, childbirth and marriage.

The Temples of the Five Cities refused to pay heed to this shift, refused to permit such a change within their walls. The upper priests and priestesses sought to keep the knowledge of these impious new ways from both worshippers and the lower-ranked servants of the Lords and Ladies of the Five Cities.

Without success; nothing spreads faster than forbidden tales.

The Hebrews were blamed for much of the conflict between the elegant, time-burnished old ways and the brash, arrogant new. Having settled in the hills, the Hebrews now sought to move down into the fertile plains ruled by the Five Cities. A few battles had been fought, and thus far the Hebrews had been held at bay—they and their strange invisible god who dwelt in a holy, deadly box.

"Their magic box is called 'Ark,' Lady Delilah." The maidservants who tended us priestesses knew all the bazaar tattle; we always listened, although propriety demanded we order such loose tongues to be silent. As she wove the silver ribbon through my hair, Mala went on, "It is formed all of gold, with two winged demons crouched upon it, and these demons slay any who dares touch the box they guard. The Hebrews' god is imprisoned within this Ark, and they say whoever releases him will become king of all the world."

"Who says so?" I asked, and Mala said, "Why, everyone! And the Hebrews plan to conquer the Five Cities and raze the Temples and sow the ground upon which they stood with salt."

That I did not believe; who would be foolish enough to slay the earth itself?

Samson

"Now Samson grew strong, stronger than any other man who ever lived. And he grew to be the best of sons, the best of men. Always he used his great strength for good, to help those in need . . ."

Long before Samson was old enough to be considered a man grown, it was clear to any with eyes and wits that whoever had fathered him upon Tsipporah had not been her husband, Manoah. But since young Samson had always been strong enough to knock sense into boys twice his age, it rapidly became ill-judged to say anything against either his mother or the man Samson honored as his father.

And what is never said is forgotten.

By the time Samson was sixteen, the people of Zorah had managed to fold away any knowledge of his birth save that it had been a late blessing to his parents. That Manoah and Tsipporah were short and dark, while their golden son stood a head taller than any other man in the village and could lift a half-grown calf and carry it as a woman carries her infant—why, that meant only that Samson's parents were indeed favored by Yahweh.

Just as his mother had always claimed.

· · ·

Samson grew into a young man who looked very little like anyone else
in any village Orev knew, and he remained Orev's friend. Orev truly
appreciated that, for to be Samson's companion only added to Orev's
importance. Being Zorah's harper had gained Orev a certain standing
in the village; its people took pride, now, in having their own singer of
songs and tales.

But Orev knew that being a harper and Samson's friend granted
even greater status.

For Samson, in addition to being taller and stronger than any
other young man in Dan, also possessed an odd ability to draw others
to him. Perhaps that was an inevitable result of his exceptional strength
and his handsome face. Tall, strong, handsome; if Yahweh had bestowed these attributes upon Samson, surely Samson must also have
been blessed with wisdom and good judgment. So men admired him,
women desired him—and Samson remained oblivious to his own worth
in the minds of others. And as the Five Cities pushed harder against
Hebrew attempts to move west, towards the fertile plains, an increasing
number of Hebrew young men grew impatient with caution. They demanded action, longing to take the land by force from the Philistines.
Now Samson's unconscious lure, his very appearance an implicit promise of greatness, turned into an unexpected problem.

For years, Orev had heard the men of the village complain, bitterly,
that the Five Cities ruled too harshly. But now the precarious balance
of opposing peoples and gods that had been known as peace in the
land of Canaan seemed to have tipped too far. The new generation of
Hebrews intended to do more than complain. They intended to strike,
and to conquer. Just as the Hebrews had conquered long ago, when the
war-leader Joshua destroyed the city of Jericho. The restless young
men saw no reason that heady victory should not be repeated in their
lifetimes. They lacked only two things to set Canaan ablaze, or so they
thought.

Weapons—weapons stronger than the deadly iron of the Five Cities.

But even stones could kill, and bronze blades had slain men for twice a thousand years before iron had been dreamed of. Orev had heard enough careless talk to know that lack of iron weapons would not deter those who hated the Five Cities, if only they possessed the one thing they fiercely clamored for, the one thing they must have in the inevitable conflict.

A leader.

A war-leader was more precious, and harder to find, than iron swords. So Orev didn't worry overmuch about rumors of rash men training for war and laying up stores of stones for slings and straight wood for spears—until the day he journeyed to Eshtaol, to sing at a wedding feast, and four men took him aside and asked if he was the harper who was Samson's friend.

Unease pricked Orev's skin, but there was no point in lying. "If you mean Samson who dwells in the village of Zorah, the son of Manoah, then yes, I know him."

The four exchanged glances, and smiled. Their spokesman said, "I am Jehu, and these are Netan, Achbor, and Eli. We wish you to take a message to Samson for us."

"Why not walk over to Zorah and speak to him yourself?" Orev asked.

Again they looked from one to another, this time apparently silently consulting. Jehu shook his head. "No. It will be safer if you carry our words to him."

"Why? I know Samson well; his nature is sweet as honey and he does not anger easily. You may speak to him without danger."

"The danger would be to him," Jehu said. "Until all is prepared, it must not be known."

What must not be known, you fool? You've already told me all your names. It would be the work of a few words with the nearest Eshtaol housewife to learn more about the four than they knew about themselves. But since Jehu, Netan, Achbor, and Eli doubtless were not as sweet-natured as Samson, Orev did not wish to anger them.

"Very well. Tell me what you wish me to say to Samson, and I will tell it to him."

Jehu drew in his breath, and then spoke low and swiftly. "Tell him we will follow him. Tell him we are not the only ones who but await his signal. Tell him there is a meeting place prepared in the hills, where the three streams meet. Tell him someone waits there each new moon."

Is that all? Orev let no sign of his irritated amusement touch his face. "When I see Samson, I will tell him."

"You will remember all I said?" Jehu asked urgently, and Orev allowed himself to laugh.

"Brave Jehu, I am a harper. I remember hundreds of words and have them ready to tell perfectly at any time. I can remember forty words easily enough."

Orev set the incident aside until the wedding feast was over and he returned to Zorah. But once home, he set out in search of Samson without wasting any time in rest. It was never very hard to track Samson down—he was always helping someone build something, helping someone carry something, or lying under the ancient oak on the hillside above Zorah.

This time he was under the oak. When he saw his friend, Samson lifted his hand. "What troubles you, Orev? Why have you hastened up here when you've just returned from Eshtaol? Sit down."

"What makes you think I've hastened?"

"I watched you walk up the road, and then go to your house, and come straight here. And you look troubled. What's wrong?"

What's wrong is men assuming your common sense means you're a great warrior. Orev sat beside Samson. "Samson, do you know four young men named Jehu, Netan, Achbor, and Eli?"

Samson shook his head. "Why? Should I know them?"

"Probably not, if you are wise," Orev said, and then repeated, perfectly, the message Jehu had sent.

When Orev fell silent, Samson frowned. "I wish they'd stop sending me messages. Orev, do I look like the leader of warriors to you?"

Orev considered the matter carefully; his friend deserved an honest answer. "Samson, many now seek a man to follow, to lead them to war with the Five Cities. And you look like no other man in all of Israel and Judah. You are taller, and stronger, and very fair to look upon."

"That's not a very good reason to think I can lead them to war."

"Sometimes, Samson, it is all the reason men need."

If he could have had only one prayer granted, Orev would have begged for the ability to strike men mute. As far as he could tell, most of the world's troubles began because someone couldn't keep his mouth shut. *And see what harm befalls? No matter what Samson does, he will be at fault.*

The trouble began when someone boasted of Samson's prowess—something Samson himself never did. Orev had traveled to Beltorath, knowing harpers were much prized there, and Samson had chosen to accompany him. Fate turns on trifles; Orev never did have an opportunity to claim a space in the marketplace and offer songs for sale that day. And Samson's life was forever changed.

Beltorath lay just to the east of the Way of the Sea, in a pleasant valley that permitted easy access to the town from the trade routes; a position that granted it an importance greater than its size alone justified. As a result, Beltorath had become home to an endless market, where merchants offered the treasures of the wide world to any who passed by.

The market lured others to Beltorath as well. Men seeking amusement gathered there, as did those who plotted mischief. What better place to meet than an open marketplace? Who would think that men talking where any might see them plotted secrets? Or, if they were foolish enough to do so openly, that those secrets could be of any great import?

Samson and Orev had wandered idly through Beltorath's bazaar, Samson staring in amazement at the vast array of merchandise spread out so that men's and women's eyes might gaze upon it, and desire it, luring them to purchase what they saw. Everything the world produced seemed available here: useful tools and pottery, beautiful fabrics and exotic gems, extravagant spices and rare woods, rich gold and silver jewelry, and useless trinkets proclaiming that their purchaser had once visited Beltorath's famed marketplace.

Past the marketplace and its booths lay the sheepfolds and the pens for goats and for bullocks, the lines where fine horses were tethered until a potential buyer wished to examine them. Orev subtly guided Samson's steps in that direction, rather than to the street where slave traders offered their living wares. Samson could neither buy nor free them, and Orev thought it better to avoid the area than to embark on an endless and pointless argument.

For if I hear one more time that among our own people slaves have rights and are granted freedom after seven years, I shall run as mad as they say most harpers are by nature.

Afterward, he wished he had led Samson to the slave-market. It would have been easier to smooth over any trouble there than to mend what happened when they passed through the beast-market.

As Samson admired the horses, and began a long discussion with one of the traders about whether a horse or an ass was of greater use, Orev glanced back the way they had come.

I was right; we are being stalked. The harper recognized the angry longing on half a dozen faces; young hotheads who hungered to strike out against the Five Cities. Orev had a keen memory; he remembered Jehu's face, and Achbor's. If those two were there, the others slowly approaching must also be eager to rise up in violence. Orev touched Samson's arm. "Since you are not buying a horse, let us go on. Others will wish to see this fine animal."

Ignoring the protests of the trader that merely discussing the beast with so knowledgeable a man as Samson brought pleasure, Orev drew him away from the horse lines. Trying to avoid encountering Jehu and his friends, Orev led Samson around the animal pens, heading back into the maze of the marketplace, only to find their way blocked by a broad circle of sand surrounded by men yelling encouragement to two wrestlers.

As Orev and Samson paused, the match ended—apparently in a draw—and both men bowed to each other, and all those who watched stopped yelling and either fell silent or muttered sullen curses. A draw meant no one who had gambled won—except the man who guarded the pledges.

As the two men walked out of the circle, another strode onto the sand of the wrestling ground. Silence honored him; he stood taller even than Samson, broad with hard muscle and so clearly a certain victor that no one would wager against him.

"What is he?" Samson asked, and Orev said, "A Rephaim, I think. A tribe of giants. I did not know any still lived."

The moment's pause proved disastrous; before Orev and his companion moved on, those who had tracked Samson through the market gathered around him. Before any of Samson's would-be followers spoke, the giant standing in the center of the sand circle shouted out,

"I am Kimmer, Champion of Gath, and no man has yet beaten me on the sand. Who dares challenge me? Never have I been thrown, so any man who throws me even once shall be given a silver bracelet. Any man who defeats me shall have the gold band I wear about my throat and be proclaimed Champion in my stead."

The giant's voice rumbled, thunderous; only silence answered him.

Samson touched Orev's arm and began to turn away from the circle of sand. But Jehu moved faster, stepping sideways to bar Samson's retreat. "Well met, Samson, and at a fair hour. I am Jehu, whose name you have been told by your harper."

I am not "Samson's harper." For some reason, the words stung, but Orev refused to yield to unreasoned anger. And he could tell by Jehu's face that the man's nerves were strung bowstring tight. Such a man was a danger to himself and others, so Orev held his tongue as Jehu swiftly continued.

"Samson, you challenge the Philistine champion, of course? Trust us, he is no match for you—your victory will show the Five Cities they do not rule the world."

"I challenge no one." Samson's calm refusal only spurred those who had followed him to anger.

"You must. Honor demands it." This set off the pack of them; cries of "Samson challenges!" and "Yahweh commands it!" caught Kimmer of Gath's attention.

The giant slowly turned and stared over the heads of those standing outside the circle of sand. His eyes met Samson's. "So you challenge? Good. You—little men—make a path for Samson the brave."

As the Hebrews cheered, the rest of the men surrounding the wrestling ground silently obeyed Kimmer's command. The nearest backed up, jostling into those behind them, to open a pathway onto the sand for Samson.

Samson looked at Orev. "I see I must fight, whether I will or no. Have you any words of wisdom for me, Harper Orev?"

"Let him throw you swiftly and accept defeat gracefully," Orev said, and heard a hiss of "Coward!" He did not recognize the voice.

Samson stared at Kimmer of Gath, who waited patiently. "Wise counsel, Orev. But I think the Champion of Gath will not be fooled by so easy a victory."

"Then fight fairly, but be careful" was all Orev could think of to say. He tried not to imagine what he could possibly tell Manoah and Tsipporah if Kimmer of Gath harmed Samson.

Samson walked through the gap in the waiting men, onto the hot pale sand. He bowed to the giant; Kimmer bowed in return.

At first the match moved slowly, as both Samson and the giant from Gath tested each other, judging speed and strength. Then they closed, entering upon a long struggle that ended with Kimmer of Gath lifting Samson and tossing him to the sand. Samson rolled out of the fall and up again in one fluid motion, spun to face Kimmer again.

"Well done!" Kimmer called out, and Samson smiled, accepting the praise.

The watching men cheered both wrestlers; the sound made it impossible for Orev to call out advice to his friend. He could only hope

Samson would not make it necessary for Kimmer to win by injuring him. For all his height and strength and his uncommon good sense, Samson was young, and Orev knew precisely how cautious and sensible young men were—especially when roars of exultant approval urged them on.

Be wise, Samson. On the next fall, stay down; yield. Admit defeat and we can leave before anything worse occurs—

Even as Orev formed the thought, it was too late. Kimmer charged Samson, reaching out, and Samson grabbed the giant's arm and fell backwards, using Kimmer's massive bulk to send him flying across the sand. The Champion of Gath, who had never been thrown, did not know how to save himself. His head slammed into the sand with all the power of the throw and the weight of his body behind it. The crack of bones breaking echoed in the sudden silence. Kimmer, Champion of Gath, lay where he had fallen, his body limp and his head bent beneath his chest.

Samson ran over and knelt beside the mass of flesh that only moments before had been a living man. "No," he said, and rolled the body onto its back; Kimmer's head fell sideways, the bones of his neck smashed by his own weight. The giant's body seemed to shrink as the soul departed; that, more than any other sign, proclaimed death.

The silence lasted only a few heartbeats. Then Orev heard men's voices raised, shouting, a chant that chilled his blood.

"Samson! Samson! Samson!" The young men who had urged Samson to wrestle pushed forward, reaching for him, eager to lift him up, to praise him.

Samson did not move; he remained kneeling beside the man he had killed. "Be silent. Can you not see this man is dead, and at my hand?"

"So should all Philistines be." The man who spoke glared hot-eyed at the dead wrestler. "I am Enoch, Samson. Only speak one word and I will follow you until Canaan is ours and we can walk as free men."

Samson looked up at Enoch. "I need no followers. And I walk a free man now."

Enoch spat at the dead man lying at his feet. "You won't if this dog's fellows call up the Philistine guards against you." Enoch turned to face the rest of those who had shouted Samson's name in triumph. "Are we going to let Philistines take Samson, the first man to strike a blow against the Five Cities?"

Shouts of *"No!"* rose loud and fast; Enoch smiled, a predator's flash of teeth. "Come then—let us drive off the guards. Stones will set them running. For Samson!"

Behind Enoch, Samson set his hand on the dead man's face, gently closed the sightless eyes. Then he stood and touched Enoch's shoulder. When Enoch turned, Samson said, "Leave the guards alone. Leave the marketplace alone. Leave this town in peace, Enoch."

For a moment Orev thought Samson's quiet words might prevail. Enoch's gaze slid away; he could not meet Samson's calm eyes. Then, between one breath and the next, Enoch spun around and raised his arms. "Come, friends! Let us hunt down the guards, purify this marketplace with the blood of those whose deeds corrupt it!"

"For Samson! Samson!" Chanting this battle-cry, the crowd wheeled around, started off towards the market-stalls. Some paused to catch up small rocks, others waved staves.

A cry of alarm cut the air; someone had seen the mob and fled. The hunters began to run, chasing the fleeing man.

"You damned ignorant fools," Orev whispered.

"I have to stop them," Samson said, and Orev shook his head.

"You can't stop them. No one can stop them, Samson. They lust after blood, and if you don't lead them in the chase, they'll turn upon you and claim yours. And if you stay here, the Philistines will seize you for slaying their Champion of Gath in the wrestling ring."

"He didn't deserve to die," Samson said, and Orev grabbed his friend's arm.

"Well, I don't deserve to die either, and I cannot escape on my own." For the first time in years, Orev called upon his lameness as an excuse. Nothing but the need to save another would move Samson from doing what he thought was right—and Orev had no intention of allowing his friend to surrender himself to the Philistines in a vain attempt to cloak the folly of others. The only thing that mattered now was taking himself and Samson far away from the circle of sand outside the market of Beltorath.

They walked, heading east to the hills, and did not look back.

The day had seemed longer, the road dustier, and the stones in the road harder than Orev had thought possible. At last he grew weary of either trying to keep pace with Samson or watching Samson try to shorten his strides to stay by him. He stopped, and almost wished he hadn't; pain that movement had nearly numbed flared up his lame leg, keen as a heated blade. "We should rest soon—as soon as we can find some shade," he said.

Samson glanced at him, and then concurred. "Yes, it's time to stop. You look—"

"I'm not tired," Orev snapped, only to hear Samson finish, "Too red. The sun burns hotter here."

Glad of the excuse, and gladder still that the sun's fire hid the rush of blood to his face, Orev nodded. *I should have known better than to think he would fling my lameness at me.*

"Where can we find shelter in this deserted land? No trees, no springs—nothing."

"Remind me again why you decided we should travel this road," Samson said, and then, "Look. Lion."

Orev looked and saw nothing, save bare earth and barer rock. Samson laughed. "Not stalking among the rocks. Look at the stones themselves."

Orev looked again, and saw that what he had taken for an odd gap in the massive stones was instead a gateway—or the remains of one. Two upright stones, crowned by lions carved into ancient rock, were all that remained of what once had been a gateway into a fortress. Time had smoothed the lions to sleek ruddy images facing one another above the narrow opening. One of the stone beasts had been carved with a heavy mane spreading over its neck and shoulders. The other lacked that embellishment; a lioness.

"A mated pair, guardians of the gate until time ends." Orev moved to lay his hand upon the lioness's stone flank. The sun's heat had soaked the rock; the carved muscles felt warm as life. "I have heard a man sing of such a gate. The Song of Helen—a woman for whom a thousand ships sailed to far-off war—"

"Why?"

"Because she was so beautiful all men desired her, and one prince stole her from another. When will you stop asking why?"

"When I know everything, and so never will I cease asking."

"A wise answer." Orev traced the outline of a huge stone paw. "A lion gate guarded one of the cities in that song."

"This city-that-was?" Samson spread his arms, indicating the barren heaps of stone beyond the lion gate.

"No, a city far away, across the sea to the west."

"What was it called, that city?" Samson asked, and Orev smiled.

"At least you now ask what, and not why. Mykenae was its name, and through its Lion Gate the High King drove in his chariot, down to the black ships that waited—" Orev stopped, shook his head. "No. I will not be tricked into singing the whole Song of Helen when we should find shade, and drink and rest." He looked at Samson and added, "Very well, one question only. Then we rest."

"What happened to the High King?"

"He went to war, and when he returned long years later, his queen slew him." Orev added, before Samson could ask, "Because the king had sacrificed the queen's daughter to a goddess so that the black ships might sail, that's why. Now we rest."

Orev unfolded his cloak and spread it in the shade cast by the stones of the ancient gate. He opened his goatskin pouch and drew out hard bread and a lump of harder cheese. "We must earn more food soon. This is all we have."

Samson didn't answer; his eyes seemed to look into the past, see the city as it once had been.

"The city is gone, yet the gate remains, guarding . . . what?" Samson stared at tumbled stones and rock-bound weeds, at wild poppies scattered like splashes of fresh blood among the ruins. "Perhaps those bees?"

Orev's gaze followed Samson's pointing hand. It was true; bees flew towards the lion's head, disappeared in shadow behind it.

"Bees mean honey," Samson said, and despite the lure of honey for the stale bread, Orev shook his head.

"Bees mean stings." Orev felt obliged to point this out, although he knew that if Samson had decided to gain the honey, he had little chance of dissuading him.

"They won't sting me." Samson's serene conviction might be true, but Orev still pushed himself to his feet and moved away from the lion gate. Even if bees wouldn't sting Samson, they would feel no such reluctance to attack Orev.

As he watched Samson reach into the crevice behind the lion's head, Orev noted his friend's slow, careful movements; unangered by this human intruder, the bees swirled around Samson, landed upon his skin and hair, paying him as little attention as they did the stone lions guarding their hive.

"Come on. The bees won't harm us." As bees crawled over his face, Samson whispered something Orev couldn't hear, then pulled out a handful of honeycomb, its rich sweet liquid clinging to his fingers, slipping down his wrist. "Have some honey. It's good."

"Come away from the hive before the bees sting your eyes out." Orev's fear transmuted to anger. "Are you *trying* to get yourself killed?"

Samson only laughed, and licked honey from his wrist. "Bees like me. They'll not wound me."

"Someday, Samson, you'll encounter a creature that doesn't like you—then what will you do?"

"I don't know," Samson said, and brought the honeycomb over to

Orev. "Make the creature like me, I suppose. Here, eat this. There's plenty for us both."

Orev took the honeycomb and had to agree that it made their humble meal infinitely more palatable. The two of them remained still, eating quietly, as the bees hummed their endless song, intent upon their eternal labor. A peaceful sound; Orev closed his eyes to listen and wonder how he could re-create such bee-song with voice and harp. Surely it could be done . . .

The steady hum changed, turned harsh and angry. Orev looked up at bees that seemed to boil in and out of the hive behind the stone lion's head. "Time to leave this place to the bees," he said, and Samson put a hand on Orev's shoulder.

"Be still. Something troubles them; don't add to their worries." Samson seemed to listen, as if he could understand the frantic buzzing. After a moment, he rose to his feet and, moving with slow care, walked through the standing stones of the lion gate.

Curious, Orev waited as the bees seemed to settle once more into a calm industry. Ignored by the diligent insects, Samson walked back through the gateway. In his arms, he cradled a golden-brown beast. He set his burden down beside Orev, who found himself gazing at a lion cub. The cub stared back and hissed.

"Samson, are you mad? Its mother will rend us both like butchered goats!"

Samson shook his head. "Its mother lies dead in the rocks beyond the gate. Half a dozen arrows are buried in her flesh, but she dragged herself back here for her cub. Hunters should finish off their prey, not leave a wounded beast to die slowly." Samson frowned and ran his fingers down the cub's back; it arched like a kitten against the caress. "I think it's hungry," Samson added. "Give it some of the cheese."

Sighing, Orev cut off some of the dry cheese and dropped it in front of the animal. As the lion cub pawed and licked at the unfamiliar food, Orev said, "I suppose it's no good saying you should cut this little beast's throat now. It would be kinder than letting it starve."

"It's past needing its mother's milk," Samson pointed out. The cub's coat had lost its infant spots, was losing its soft fuzzy texture, smoothing into what would become a sleek tawny pelt; clearly it had been weaned already. "And it's old enough to run along with us, if it chooses. We'll need to find it some meat soon."

Orev didn't bother to enumerate the myriad ways in which adopting an orphaned lion was a bad idea. "Well, in that case, we'd better move on. There's nothing here but honey and lion meat, and only jackals and vultures will eat that."

Samson agreed and, before Orev could object, reached down and lifted him easily to his feet. They gathered up their few belongings and started off down the hill to the strip of hard-packed earth that passed for a road.

The lion cub skittered after them until it reached the edge of the road. There it sat and mewled, piteous as a starving babe. Samson turned back and scooped the cub up, settled it into a fold of his cloak.

"Samson—" Orev began, and stopped as his friend looked at him with eyes as round and innocent as those of the lion cub nestled in his arms.

"He must be weary from hunger, if he wishes to be carried." Samson scratched the cub under its chin; it leaned into his hand. "What were you going to say, Orev?"

"Nothing important," Orev said. "And since no one's going to carry *us*, I suggest we start walking."

So the two of them—three, if one counted the lion cub—continued their random journey. Despite the hard road and hot sun, Orev enjoyed the serenity the wilderness offered. He refused to think of what lay behind them, or ahead. He knew it was already too late to hope for peace when they reached the lands of men once more.

Delilah

When I am weary or foolish enough to look back upon that long-ago time, it seems to me that all changed between one day and the next; that suddenly the only gossip I overheard concerned the newly risen Hebrews and their faceless god. I know it cannot truly have been so; it seems so only because that god and I warred over those I loved, and so I think too often on what might have been.

It was true that the Hebrews had moved against the Five Cities, and that these wanderers were fierce fighters. They coveted the land ruled by the Five Cities, its fertility, its access to the sea. The Lords and Ladies of the Five Cities sought to control this threat, and for a time, the Hebrews were beaten back to their hills.

But the peace that had been our greatest blessing from the gods had been shattered. The borders were no longer firm as stone walls, nor the roads safe. The first raid upon a merchant caravan by bandits from the hills caused an uproar that must have woken the sleeping stars. The Lords and Ladies of the Five Cities met and sent half their armies to capture those who had committed this outrage.

By the time a dozen full moons had risen, wise merchants hired their own guards when they traveled. Soldiers patrolled the border between the Hebrews' lands and our own. Things had changed so that no one thought a skirmish worth more than a passing word, unless one of the men who died in it belonged to the speaker's family. A troubled time; an uneasy, precarious compromise between true peace and outright war.

In Ascalon, in the Great House of Atargatis, we seemed untouched by the strife in the world beyond our walls. Illusion again, for the Temple's farms lay at risk, as did the Temple servants who tilled the soil and gathered in the harvest.

"At least the Groves are untouched." Priestess Iliat, a Full Moon, said to her friend Gildori as they walked across the Garden Court, and Gildori answered, "Untouched this moon. But next moon, and the next?"

Iliat frowned. "Surely no man would dare—" Then she saw me and stopped; clearly what she had been about to say was not for a mere Rising Moon to hear. I was just far enough away that I could feign indifference, as if I had not heard.

But I had, and the words sang a harsh song that I could not banish from my mind. I repeated them to Aylah, who put her arms around me and pressed her cheek to mine in comfort. Then she said, "If these Hebrews are wise, they will leave the Groves in peace."

"They are men. Wisdom is for women." I repeated what I had often heard Nikkal say. I had no reason to doubt its truth. "Shall we pray to Our Lady?"

"For what?" Aylah asked.

"Why, for all to stay as it is," I said.

Aylah pulled away and regarded me, her eyes steady and a little sad, as if she were far older than I. "Even gods change, Delilah. But if you wish it, we will pray to Atargatis. Perhaps She will listen."

Heartened, I opened the curtains veiling the small image of the goddess that stood in a niche in our bedchamber wall. There, standing beside my heart-sister, surrounded by the familiar scents and sounds of the Temple, I lifted my hands and prayed. I prayed for our future to be as serene as I believed our past to have been. Aylah prayed silently, as

she often did, and I believed she petitioned Atargatis for the same boon
I did.

What else was more worth asking of the goddess than peace and
prosperity, after all?

But of course the Hebrews prayed too, to their own harsh god, and He
granted them what they asked of Him: a hero.

I first heard of him one hot day as the Temple maidservants gossiped
while they spread new-washed linen to dry in the sun. I had been given
the responsibility of overseeing this task—learning how to command
others was part of a priestess's training.

It was there, sitting silent and merely watching, that I learned two
things of great importance. The first was that, after a time, the maidservants seemed to forget I was even in the garden. They laughed easily and spoke freely—and loudly. I could hear most of their chatter
clearly.

The second was that the quarrelsome Hebrews claimed a new hero
had risen, a man who would gain them victory over us and our gods.

A man named Samson.

Long moons later, when we lay in each other's arms, I told Samson
how I had first heard his name, his exploits, expecting him to laugh.
But he looked at me gravely and said, "To listen in secret is ill done,
Delilah."

I had never before heard such folly; to listen in secret was to obtain
knowledge. There was much no one would say before the New Moons
and the Rising Moons; we were supposedly kept in sweet ignorance of
the schemes, the alliances and feuds, that lay behind the serene façade
of the Temple's rituals.

But it is hard to keep secrets in a large household, or to keep its children ignorant of truth—and the Temple was a larger household than
most palaces. I was not the only girl who learned to remain still and
gain knowledge in secret.

So I sat quiet and listened as the maidservants giggled and chattered. Some may think that servants and slaves pay no heed to battles and to politics, but they are wrong. A battle lost or won, a law passed or revoked, can change a slave's life as greatly as that of a prince. Troubled borders engender troubled minds.

"They say he is taller and stronger than any mortal man should be. Did he not slay Kimmer, the giant of Gath?" "Perhaps he is not mortal." "I heard from my sister, who had it from her cousin, that his mother lay with a god to beget him." "A Hebrew god?" "The Hebrews have only one god. They're too poor to have another." "No, they boast of it. As if one god were enough . . ."

I had to listen hard to hear all this, but then the maids began arguing over whether any people could survive with only one god to aid them. After that, I could hear easily enough.

"Well, one god or forty, I heard that this Samson is their new leader." "And I heard even the Hebrews think him half-mad. Who ever heard of someone driving thieves away from a caravan and not asking one silver piece in payment?" "He is strong, this Samson; the Hebrews will follow him against us." "When have the Hebrews followed any man for long? Samson will be no different—king for a moon, then gone."

I thought the woman who said that last spoke too fiercely, as if by saying no one would raise Samson up against us, she could make it truth.

Samson. Son of the Sun. An odd name for a Hebrew. I did not know, then, that Samson was unlike most other Hebrews—unlike most other men.

"They say that Samson calls down fire from heaven to slay his enemies, and that he takes any woman he wishes as his prize. They say—"

I must have made some motion, because Nurshali, eldest of the maidservants, snapped out, "And I say I hear too much chatter and do not see enough work! Do you want the priestess to say you cannot even lay out the washing without taking all the day about it?"

As easily as that, Nurshali reminded the maidservants of my presence.

The careless talk ceased, but I had heard enough to intrigue me. I did not think I would hear any more truths from the maidservants—but there were others I could ask.

But before I found my quarry—Lolarsa, a handmaiden who always knew all the gossip between the Salt Sea and the Cilician Hills—a wide-eyed New Moon stopped me on the path between one court and the next and blurted out that Dance Priestess Sharissit wished to see me at once. That summons promptly drove all else from my mind; I forgot Samson and his powers and his strange jealous god. I asked the New Moon—she could not have been older than eight or nine, and seemed very young to me—why I had been summoned, and the little girl ducked her head and said that she did not know.

"I know only that Dance Priestess Sharissit said I was to find you at once and you were to come to her at once. You *will* go at once, won't you?" She stared at me, anxious, and I smiled.

"Of course I will. And I will tell her how dutifully you carried out her orders. What is your name, little goddess?" I tried to act as I thought Nikkal would in such a case. Nikkal would smile upon the nervous child, would ease her worries, would praise her—

"My name is Ruaz, Priestess Delilah," the child said, and I smiled again, and bent and hugged her, and kissed her upon her soft cheek.

"Thank you, sister. Would you like to lead me to Dance Priestess Sharissit, that I may swiftly obey her summons?"

New Moon Ruaz nodded, and I took her hand and let her guide me to the Dancing Court. Dance Priestess Sharissit awaited me there; she sat upon an alabaster bench, and Aylah sat quietly upon the ground before her. "I am here," I said, and as the Dance Priestess glanced at my guide, I added, "New Moon Ruaz is quick as a cat and clever as a fox. She did your bidding swiftly and well."

"I expected no less of her." Dance Priestess Sharissit smiled at Ruaz. "Thank you, child. You may return to your friends now."

New Moon Ruaz bowed and backed away, as protocol demanded.

Then, as she turned, the careful dignity vanished; she fled down the path and disappeared into the cool shadows beyond the gate. Her silver anklets chimed swift and hard, echoed in the heavy air and then faded. Only then did Sharissit laugh.

"I suppose I grow older than I like to think, for the New Moons now seem little more than babes to my eyes. No, do not draw breath to contradict me; I did not summon you both here to talk of the New Moons, or of my faded glory." Sharissit pointed at the ground beside Aylah. "Sit, Night-Hair, and listen."

Taking care to move with grace, I lowered myself to sit beside Aylah. I slanted a glance towards her; Aylah moved her shoulders in the slightest of shrugs. My heart-sister did not know why we had been ordered to wait upon the Dance Priestess's pleasure. I suppose she thought I looked worried, for she reached out and took my hand, twined her warm fingers through my cool ones.

Sharissit smiled down at us. "I have glad news for you, my Sun and my Moon. You have been asked for, and will dance at a feast Lord Aulykaran gives to celebrate."

"To celebrate what?" Aylah asked, as I stared wide-eyed at the Dance Priestess.

Sharissit laughed. "Why, to celebrate the fact that it is the second day of the month, or that the moon is not yet full, or that he has a new tunic. It does not matter. What matters is that you will dance before him and his guests."

I could not believe it; surely Aylah and I were not ready! Most dancers trained three years before being trusted to dance for the Temple. Aylah and I had studied with Sharissit for barely half a year. As I stared, Aylah asked, "When are we to perform for Lord Aulykaran, Dance Priestess?" Aylah's voice held nothing but serene questioning. I was glad she had spoken, for my skin seemed to burn even as my blood beat cold as melted snow. For once I could not summon my voice—nor did Sharissit fail to note this.

"Seven days from now, so we will have much work to do to make you ready." The Dance Priestess turned her calm gaze upon me. "You have no words you wish to say, Delilah?" She smiled, to show me she half-jested. "Nothing at all?"

I tried to answer, and realized I had been holding my breath. "I— But how can we be ready? For such an honor, for such an occasion, for such an audience—"

"You will be ready because I say you will be ready. Now breathe easy, as you have been taught. And do not mouth falsely modest objections, Delilah. You know very well that you are the finest dancer the Temple has trained in two lifetimes. Unless you fall flat at Lord Aulykaran's feet, your dancing cannot fail to please." Dance Priestess Sharissit said all this with such calm assurance my blood ceased its fierce beat, slowed and gentled.

Aylah slid her arm around my waist. "And from all I have heard, if you do fall upon your back at Lord Aulykaran's feet, that too will please him well."

Dance Priestess Sharissit laughed softly, and I put my hand over Aylah's and stroked it in silent thanks. Aylah, who seldom jested, had done so to ease my needless panic—for the Dance Priestess would never consent to send us to perform if she did not think us ready to bring honor to the Temple.

"Seven days?" I said, and Sharissit understood all I did not say. She reached out and touched my cheek, and then Aylah's. "Seven days," she answered. "You will be ready, never fear. And until the day of Lord Aulykaran's feast, your time belongs to me alone. Now I command you both to rest today, and amuse yourselves as you wish. Tomorrow we begin."

For seven days, Aylah and I practiced—danced until even I fell asleep exhausted each night. We were excused from all other duties, including prayers; our time belonged only to Sharissit, as she had told us. It was she who chose the dance we would perform—an old-fashioned but intricate pattern called *Night and Day*. The ancient dance might have been designed for us, the Temple's Moon and Sun.

By the time we stood waiting behind the sky-blue curtain that veiled us from the open courtyard in which Lord Aulykaran had chosen to hold his feast, Aylah and I could dance *Night and Day* blindfolded—we had done so half a dozen times in those seven days before the feast.

I thought only of the coming dance, and how I must perform to please Our Lady, and Her Temple, and Lord Aulykaran, who had given a rich offering to the Temple to gain our presence here. The more I thought upon what I must do, the more nervous I became. To my horror, I began to tremble; the tiny bells sewn upon my skirt chimed faintly, betraying my fear.

Aylah caught my hands. "Stop thinking, Delilah," she said. "You are Dance itself, and will forget all else when the music calls you."

"I can't." I could not imagine what had made me believe myself a dancer. My body seemed a burden, as if it had been turned to stone.

"You can, and you will. Aylah is right, Delilah." Sharissit nodded approvingly at Aylah and then said, "For all dancers there is a first dance, and this is yours. I will not force you to endure a long lecture on what I expect of you, and how you must behave. If you do not know these things by now, you are beyond help. Now stand properly; it is time."

Then, as I tried to explain that I could not, that I had forgotten all I thought I knew, I realized it was too late. The rise and fall of voices beyond the curtain ceased, and the music began, a slow, steady drumbeat. Servants drew aside the blue curtain, revealing us to the waiting audience. Aylah and I paced a careful path out into the center of the courtyard, bowed before the high table at which Lord Aulykaran and his most important guests were placed. Both the High Priestess and the Prince of the City sat there, watched us with cool judging eyes, and I knew this dance would determine my future.

I forced myself to forget the flaring lamplight and the heavy scent of roses and that the smooth inlaid stone floor was unfamiliar to my feet. I must forget that many strangers watched, eager to see the Temple's newest dancers, must forget everything except the pattern of the dance.

The even drumbeat ceased, and the true music began. And Aylah was right.

I opened myself to the music, and I danced.

Aylah and I wove the pattern of *Night and Day* across the cool jeweled floor; the only sound was that of the music, and the sweet ringing of the tiny bells upon our skirts and about our ankles. When the music stopped, and the dance ended, Aylah and I stood once more before the high table. In the silence, we bowed; I glanced up through my lashes and saw that even the High Priestess and the Prince of the City stared at us as if amazed.

Lord Aulykaran smiled. "Most beautifully done. You must be very proud of them, my lady Derceto. The Temple's dancers are marvels, are they not, Brother?" He did not wait for either to answer, but beckoned Aylah and me to come forward. When we stood before him, Aulykaran lifted a necklace of Persian turquoise and creamy sea-pearls from his neck. "This is scarcely enough reward for such devout priestesses as your new dancers, Lady Derceto. Yet mere gems are all I have to offer."

His gesture pleased me because it told me Aylah and I had succeeded, not because I expected ever to wear the lavish ornament about my throat. Any such reward belonged to the Temple, just as did the offering he had made to have us dance at his feast. Aulykaran knew this, of course; he let the strand of precious stones slide from his hand to coil on the table before Derceto. The High Priestess smiled, accepting the beautiful necklace on behalf of Bright Atargatis.

The Prince of the City glared at his brother and then unclasped a heavy gold bracelet from his wrist. "Very well danced, as if they were the Goddess Herself." Sandarin shoved the wide band of lapis-inlaid gold over to Derceto.

Although I should have kept my face smooth, a painted mask, I smiled—I could not help it. Aylah and I had danced well; so well we had gained rich gifts for Our Lady. I do not think either the High Priestess or the Prince of the City noticed my lapse; they seemed intent only on each other. Lord Aulykaran smiled back, and winked at me.

Now the other feasters called out praise, and many promised fine gifts to the Temple. I hardly noticed, for Aylah gently pinched my hand, and I remembered to bow again before retracing the path across the courtyard to the room where the Dance Priestess awaited us.

"Well," Sharissit said when Aylah and I stood before her, awaiting her judgment on our performance, "I see you did not trip on your skirts after all, Night-Hair." Then she smiled. "Your dancing honored Our Lady. You did well. Now it is time for you to come home and bathe and rest."

I had hoped to remain to savor both the feast and the praise, but even as Sharissit spoke, weariness swept through me like a wave. I could barely stand, and fell asleep in the litter as we were carried home to the Temple.

Sandarin

"Are you mad, Brother? Do you think our family's made of gems?" Sandarin glared at Aulykaran, who merely smiled and shrugged.

"The little priestesses danced very well—so well they caused even drunken men to be silent. Surely they deserved their reward?"

Clearly Aulykaran intended to act even more obtuse than usual. Sandarin sighed and pressed his fingers to the pain throbbing between his eyes. "I suppose you thought your gesture a grand jest—"

"I thought to persuade you to make your peace with Our Lady," Aulykaran said and yawned. "By Her bright eyes, I'm weary. Almost dawn, Brother; past time to be in bed."

"I am perfectly at peace with Our Lady." Sandarin struggled to keep from losing his temper completely; shouting would do no good, and Aulykaran would merely laugh at him. "It's Her High Priestess who causes discord. And if you think giving Derceto gems for the Temple will sweeten her, you aren't nearly as clever as you fancy yourself."

Aulykaran's bestowal of the pearl-and-turquoise necklace had forced Sandarin to display equal generosity. The Prince of the City could not be seen to slight the Temple—especially when his brother had just presented so extravagant a gift. From the glint in Derceto's eyes, she had known exactly how to value Sandarin's offering.

Aulykaran yawned again. "Brother, both you and the High Priestess waste far too much time in fighting that could be put to far pleasanter use. I don't even want to contemplate what your nights as Consort with Atargatis-on-Earth are like."

"I do my duty as Prince of the City," Sandarin said, "and Derceto does hers as High Priestess."

His brother sighed. "Duty, always duty. Oh, and deception too, of course. Never mind, Sandarin; I'm certain you and Derceto will some- how resolve your differences. Or perhaps the next High Priestess will be less—"

"Ambitious?" Sandarin suggested, as for once his brother seemed at a loss for the perfect word.

"An unambitious High Priestess? And I thought you didn't know what a jest was!" Aulykaran stretched, supple as a panther.

And about as much use as a panther, too. Sandarin contemplated explaining how difficult it was dealing with High Priestess Derceto, who lived for power. That Ascalon the Beautiful might have needs other than those of the Temple never seemed to occur to her—or if it did, she didn't care. Sometimes Sandarin wished he'd never become Prince of the City. High rank and great power were his, but as the years wore on, he en- joyed those favors less and less.

"Go to bed, Brother," Aulykaran advised. "Go to bed, and dream of dancers bright and dark. That's what I intend to do. And I think I shall hold another feast soon—or perhaps you should. Yes, I think you should hold a great feast and offer the Temple whatever it asks to have the Sun and Moon dance before you."

Since there seemed nothing else to say, Sandarin decided to take his brother's advice, and go home to bed. In sleep, he could forget about Derceto's schemes, and about the bandits in the hills and the robbers on the highways. Let his brother dream of pretty dancers; Sandarin prayed only that he would indeed sleep—and not dream of anything at all.

Samson

"Now Samson grew strong and bold, and he went forth into the world, went to try his strength against his enemies." So Orev sang, for those were the words his listeners wished to hear. What great man lacked enemies, after all? Orev chose his words carefully, that each man or woman who listened might believe his or her enemies had been Samson's.

And it was true that Samson had enemies, although he himself had been no man's foe—not willingly. Always Samson had been softhearted and kind. Too kind.

Until the day Samson first lost his temper, Orev hadn't believed anger to be a part of his friend's sunlight nature. In all the years Orev had known Samson—as infant, as child, as boy, as young man—never had he been ruled by strong passions. Witnessing Samson angered was as startling as watching a jar of honey kindle into a pillar of fire.

And just as unexpected.

The day dawned cool and fair, with a sweet sea-wind blowing from the west. Needing no words, Samson and Orev bundled their few possessions into the carry-basket and set off down the long road that wound through the hills separating the highlands from the sea-plain. They did not hurry, permitting chance or luck or their god's will to set their path for them. The lion cub—which Samson had named Ari—followed, happily pouncing upon shadows until he tired and Samson scooped the cub up and carried him.

Yes, a fair day. Even Orev's lame foot pained him less than it usually did, as if in some way the softness of the air and the warmth rising from the hard-packed dirt of the road acted as balm; he barely needed his walking-stick. And had he and Samson remained upon the main road, perhaps that day would have ended as softly as it had begun.

Or perhaps not. Perhaps the path Samson must walk had been set before he was born, and nothing would have changed a step of it.

All Orev knew was that had they continued on the main road, rather than turning aside because Samson's keen ears detected a noise, the events of that day, at least, would have flowed more smoothly than they did. He knew also that, in a sense, it did not matter, as soon or late Samson would have learned about the Foxes. For one thing, not one of the Foxes owned an ounce of common sense or caution.

But Samson's anger might not have burned so fiercely if he had not first met them over the bodies of men struck down in his name.

It was the yipping of foxes that first drew their interest and made them pause upon the road. The noise came from beyond the ancient, twisted oaks that sheltered the rough road from the westering sun. Samson stopped, listened, and frowned.

"Foxes?" Orev said, taking advantage of the moment's rest to set down his harp and stretch his arms.

"At this hour, and in such numbers?" Samson shook his head. "Not unless all the foxes in Canaan have run mad. We'd better go look."

Orev walked behind Samson through the shrub oaks and down into the streambed that paralleled the road. At this season, the streambed was dry, an apparently safe pathway of water-smoothed pebbles, with only a few puddles easily covered by a man's hand to show that water flowed here during the winter rains.

Glad to see the stream's pathway, an easier route for a lame man than the surrounding rocky land, Orev caught up to Samson and laid a hand on his friend's arm. "Slowly, Samson. From the sounds of revelry, we need not hasten."

For the vulpine yips had continued, rising to exultant triumph, as he and Samson pressed through the bushes and down to the streambed. Whatever rejoiced beyond the outcrop of rock had no intention of fleeing.

"No, we need not hasten now." Samson's words fell heavy into the hot summer air. "I fear we are too late, Orev."

Orev glanced at Samson's face as the noise that had begun as the quick sharp yelps of foxes changed. Still a predator's clamor proclaiming conquest, the noises now also clearly told that the predators walked upon two legs, rather than running upon four.

Not foxes. Men.

Half a dozen donkeys lay dead, dark blood from their slashed throats dyeing the white pebbles of the streambed crimson. Two men had been flung down like broken dolls beside the dead animals. Blood covered the men as well; whether it was their own blood or that of the slain beasts, Orev could not tell.

Standing in a circle about the bodies were almost a dozen men—young and filled with the exultation killing roused. Not Philistine, not Bedu, not Moabite; Hebrews, perhaps, although Orev had never seen Hebrews so strangely garbed before. Each man wore a rough reddish brown tunic and a fox-skin, the head over the man's left shoulder. From a braided rope belt hung fur plumes tipped with white. After a moment, Orev realized that the men had tied fox tails to their belts.

He stopped beside Samson, who said nothing. But Samson's silence seemed to reach out, flow from Samson to the circle of rejoicing men. Slowly, the men fell silent and turned to gaze upon Samson as he stood, waiting. At last, when the only sound in the streambed was the buzzing of flies drawn by the spilled blood, Samson spoke.

"Who killed these men and their beasts?" he asked, and the men shook off the silence. Smiling, the one wearing the most fox tails in his belt came forward.

"We did, Samson. A great victory!"

"A great victory? A band of strong men against two merchants and six donkeys? Are you madmen?"

"No, we are the Foxes—Samson's Foxes! We shall make the high roads safe—"

"From what? From yourselves?" Samson walked forward until he stood beside one of the dead merchants. "This was an old man." He stooped and straightened the slight body, drew the dead man's cloak over his face. Then he did the same for the other, saying as he rose, "And this was an unbearded boy. What harm did they do you, that you should murder them?"

"They were Philistines! That is harm enough. It is time we claimed the land Yahweh bestowed upon us. It is time we followed a leader to victory." The man straightened his shoulders, regarded Samson intently. "You are that leader, Samson. You have done great deeds. You are favored by Yahweh, and we will follow you against armies. You have but to command and we will obey."

"And the six donkeys? Were they oppressors too?" Samson spoke slowly, his voice oddly flat.

As the Foxes stared at Samson, clearly unable to comprehend that their chosen leader had no interest in commanding them, Orev tried to neither laugh nor weep. No one who knew Samson would even dream that he would lead anything but a horse to water—and even then, he'd be more likely to carry water to the horse.

"One can't create a fire without burning sticks," one of the men offered, and Samson turned to stare at him. Under Samson's steady gaze, the man stepped back a pace.

"Not only are you murderers, you are fools as well. Alive, the donkeys might have some use. Dead, they are nothing but a feast for crows. Now help me carry these men to the nearest village. They must be mourned and buried." All this spoken in the same flat, unyielding tone, so unlike Samson's true voice that only now did Orev realize what he heard: Samson angered.

The Foxes stared at Samson, plainly baffled—and displeased. At last one stepped forward, slender and edgy as a gazehound. "Enoch said we should leave the bodies as a warning to others."

"So Enoch leads you," Samson said. "Then why ask me what I wish you to do? Tell me, what names do you call yourselves? And does your mother know you roam the roads slaying travelers, maiden?"

The slender one flushed scarlet. "I am Beriah, and I go where I please. Not only men are warriors. Deborah led an army."

Now that Samson had rent the veil of illusion, Orev could not imagine how he had taken Beriah for a boy. Even shorn hair and fox pelts could not hide a slender throat or deepen a voice. As only Beriah spoke her name, Orev said, "So there is a vixen among the Foxes, and I know her name, that I may weave it into a song someday. But you others"—Orev swept his hand through the air, indicating the rest sullenly waiting—"you have no names as yet. So. Enoch, and Beriah. And there was a man named Jehu, and his friends Netan, Achbor, and Eli—"

"Jehu is dead, slain by Philistines. As are Netan and Eli." A pallid young man whose face already bore lines of worry etched beside his mouth stepped forward. "I am Achbor, and I fight for Samson and for Yahweh, and for the rights of our people to live where and how they please, to travel where they wish and to be free of false gods."

Anything else? Orev wondered just how Achbor thought the slaying of donkeys would achieve these goals. He glanced at Samson, still as stone beside the slain men.

"I need no one to fight for me, Achbor. And surely Yahweh comes before any man?" Samson gazed steadily at Achbor, whose face turned a dull crimson.

"Of course. I misspoke, that is all." Achbor looked as if he longed to continue speaking, but another of the Foxes caught him by the arm.

"Be silent, Achbor; you know nothing of warriors' ways." This Fox

looked what the others clearly wished to be: a warrior. Orev wondered
where he had learned his war-craft. "I am Ichavod, and in Enoch's ab-
sence, I lead this pack."

Swiftly, Ichavod counted off the names: Terach, Irad, Jobab, Hirah,
Dawi, and Golyat. All bore an odd, elusive resemblance, as if they were
all sons of one father. Even Dawi and Golyat, clearly twins, seemed
brothers to the rest as well. "Achbor, Beriah, and I, of course. And you
know Enoch." Ichavod's eyes seemed to glow hot, like dark coals.

"Yes." Samson's hands had closed into fists. "I know of Enoch."

"Then you know he is truly dedicated to our cause—as are we all."
Ichavod might have said more, but Terach blurted out, "I can tell you
all our stories, how it is we came to become Samson's Foxes, to fight in
his cause." He gazed longingly at Orev—or rather, thought Orev, at the
harp slung over his shoulder. "I cannot carry a harp with me, but I can
sing our tales well enough. Listen and I will tell of how Samson slew
the evil giant of Gath, the first of Samson's great feats—"

*That is all this mad tale lacks—a boy who wishes to be a harper and exalt murder
in song. Next he will be asking for the loan of my harp, that he may immortalize this
great triumph of theirs against two merchants and half a dozen asses.*

Samson stared at Terach, who faltered and fell silent. "I never willingly killed any man. And what are these great deeds I am supposed to
have done?"

Now it was Terach's turn to stare, wide-eyed. "Many! Everyone
knows that Yahweh granted you the strength of ten men—that a score
of Philistines fled when they only heard your voice. That you carried off
a cart laden with iron blades—"

That every hero and outlaw has been renamed Samson in every song. Orev sensed
Samson had already lost his first and most important battle. *Easier to
defeat a hundred good men than to silence one good song.*

Samson turned his gaze back to Ichavod. "If you will not do as I
ask, and help me carry these men you have murdered to be buried with
the proper rites, then there is nothing more to say."

Ichavod met Samson's gaze unflinching. "They deserve no more than any other dead beast. Farewell, Samson. You will see us again, when you need us."

The Foxes had remained silent, some staring at the ground and others gazing in awe or bemusement at Samson. Now, at a sign from Ichavod, they retreated, moving with more silence and skill than Orev had expected. A few breaths, and they had vanished into the rocks and brush beyond the dry streambed.

A moment later, Orev heard the *yip-yip* of a fox, the sound faint and far-off. *But not, I am afraid, far enough. At least they are gone now.* He sighed and set down his harp. "Samson, my friend, I agree these men must be decently buried. Shall we go to the nearest village and seek aid there?"

Samson did not answer; for a heartbeat he did not move. Then he bent and grasped a stone the size of a man's head, hurled it to smash against the outcropping of rock. As Orev stared, Samson reached out to the overhanging branch of a young oak and ripped it from the tree. Orev did not wait to see what else Samson would break with the makeshift club.

"Samson." Orev spoke softly, as if to a wounded beast. "Samson, the Foxes are gone. You should have shown this anger to them."

Samson stared at the branch in his hands, unclenched his fingers, and let the weapon fall to the dry streambed. He drew a deep breath, and slowly the lines of his face eased, the flat brightness vanished from his eyes. "No. If I touched one of them, I would have killed him. I will not wield anger as a weapon, Orev. I will not."

If you had killed one of them, perhaps the rest would have feared you too greatly to defy you. Or perhaps not; the Foxes seemed to love the scent of blood more than they honored Samson. Samson already carried the guilt of one man's death— *And that death was sheer mischance, not a thing done in rage. Samson fears his own anger as other men fear fire.*

Orev spoke calmly, as if Samson had said nothing. "These men must be buried, Samson. We cannot leave them for the vultures and jackals."

"Their deaths lie at my feet; it is only right that I bury them. I will gather stones, Orev. You see if either carries a seal or a letter. They must have kin who will grieve for them. At least we can tell them that they were buried, and where they lie."

That was their first encounter with Samson's Foxes, but it was not the last. Having tasted blood, the Foxes grew bold, hunting the roads for easy prey. Orev had long wondered what it would take to anger Samson; now he knew.

Injustice.

The Foxes—Samson's Foxes—hunted and killed, and Samson's name, already ill-hearing for the Philistines, became a fearsome thing. That Samson loathed the Foxes and refused to command them—save to order them to cease their banditry, a command the Foxes ignored—was unknown to the Philistines. Orev doubted the Philistines would have believed it, even if told.

No one could truthfully claim Samson did not try to stop the Foxes. With a self-control hard as Philistine iron, Samson chained his anger, then sought out Enoch and begged him to disband the group. Enoch merely said, "You do not understand yet, Samson, but in time you will embrace your destiny. The Philistines must be driven from our land, killed if they will not flee before the power of Yahweh's people. Your Foxes know this."

"What can *your* Foxes do against the might of the Five Cities?" Samson asked, and Enoch laughed.

"We can bring them fear. And there are many Foxes now, Samson, and more come to join us with each moon that passes."

When Samson returned after that meeting, Orev almost hesitated to ask what Enoch had said, for his friend looked weary and sad. But when Orev asked, Samson told all that had passed between him and Enoch.

"He would not listen," Samson finished. "It was as if I spoke to a—a talking statue who could recite only one speech. And do you know what he said, as I left him? *'You are our hero, Samson. In time, you will lead us to glory.'*"

As Samson recited those words, fear coiled about Orev's heart like a cold serpent. *I was right; no one cares what Samson is, only what they wish him to be in their eyes.* But he kept his words light; Samson needed nothing more to trouble him.

"Glory? Not riches?" Orev, practiced in seeming to be what he was not, shook his head and sighed ruefully. "If only you were to lead us to riches, Samson, you might be of some use yet."

Orev gained his reward; Samson smiled, if only for a moment. But the trouble had not passed, and they both knew it.

For the Foxes only grew bolder—and less merciful. During the Time of Ripening, when grain shone like heavy gold in the fields, the Foxes set upon and slew a dozen women traveling to the ancient shrines in the hills west of the Salt Sea, and left the bodies for the jackals and the ravens. Orev feared what Samson might do when he heard of that massacre; feared that Samson must burn hot with anger at such news, and rage and murder in his turn.

But Samson listened, silent, his face smooth as a funeral mask. After, he sat quiet for long hours. *"I will not wield anger as a weapon, Orev. I will not."* Samson's vow seemed to echo in the still air as Orev waited, patient; watched the fire and added twigs as the sun set and the stars rose.

At last, when the Huntress had risen above the eastern horizon, Samson said, "Orev?"

"Yes, Samson?"

"I cannot permit these Foxes to slay travelers—"

"And to claim the crime yours," Orev reminded him.

"No. But how am I to stop them? I cannot tend all roads between Dan and Beersheba."

"No, that is beyond even you. But there must be something you can do. Let me think upon it."

Samson waited patiently; at last Orev said, "Could you tend one road, Samson?"

Samson frowned. "One road? Which?"

"Whichever you choose. But on that road, travelers of the Five

Cities—any travelers—must know themselves safe. And they must know that safety comes from your care of them. So I ask again, can you tend one road?"

Silence, and sparks flying from the fire up into the hungry night sky. It was Orev's turn to wait, patient, for an answer.

"Yes," Samson said, "I can tend one road. And I can keep it clear of Foxes, too."

"That is as much as men can ask."

Samson laughed, the sound oddly bitter. "They can ask more than that, Orev—much more. Still, that is all I can do. It is not enough, but it must suffice."

Even the gift of a safe road, the highway Samson had chosen, after much discussion with Orev, as the best to place under his protection, might not be enough to protect Samson himself from the anger of the Five Cities. As Samson said, he could guard only one road. And Orev helped ensure that those who traveled that road knew whom to thank for a safe journey.

The Lion's Path, Orev called that high road, knowing the name would catch men's fancy. The evil done by the Foxes and those who emulated them weighed heavy against Samson. Orev hoped the Lion's Path would tilt the balance in Samson's favor.

"Samson strode the high road like a lion, master of beasts of and men. Stronger than a lion, swifter than a leopard, Samson emerged always victorious. And all men feared to face him in battle or to stand before him for judgment . . ."

The day had dawned fair and hot; the rains had ended two moons ago, and the road lay dry and smooth beneath the summer sun. Samson sat upon the crest of a low hill overlooking the road from Shawafir to Gath, watching to see that all was well and tossing small stones for Ari to chase. Just as Orev dared hope the day would remain as serene as the silver dawn had promised, the half-grown lion froze in midpounce. Ari stared down the hill and growled. As if the growl were a signal, Samson rose slowly to his feet.

"Trouble?" Orev set aside his harp, awaiting Samson's word.

"A trader's caravan on the road." Samson bent and put his hand on Ari's tawny head. "And beasts of prey lurking beyond the rise—see there, the dark shadows?"

Orev stared, but saw nothing, save some rocks. "I must trust to your senses, and the lion's. What now, Samson?"

His friend smiled. "Now I rid this road of vermin. Of your goodness, go down and warn the merchant to halt and wait. Take Ari; I do not wish him hurt."

"Or me either, I trust. Put the tether on your lion, or he will not stay with me."

Samson looped a length of leather about Ari's neck, handed the end of the lead to Orev. "Come along," Orev told the reluctant lion. "Your master needs no help from a lame harper and a lion too lazy to hunt his own meat."

Orev made his way to the road and walked down the rise to the merchant's caravan. He held up his arm, a silent order to halt, only to realize the train of donkeys had already stopped.

The man who led the caravan stared. "Come no closer," he said, and Orev paused, pulling Ari to his side.

"I come to warn you," Orev said. "I am Orev, a harper, and I walk with Samson, who guards this road. He tells you to await him here, for thieves have set a trap for you where the road passes by those rocks." Orev gestured, and the merchant stared at the rockfall where the road curved.

"Why should I believe this tale?" the man demanded, and Orev shrugged.

"I could say 'because it is truth,' but that, too, could be a lie. You can forge onward and chance meeting thieves, or wait and move on again when it is safe to do so."

The merchant hesitated, glanced from Orev to Ari. Orev said nothing, merely scratched Ari behind the ears. At last the merchant said, "I will wait. But do not come any closer."

"The odor of asses is no joy to me," Orev said. "I will wait here, with Samson's lion."

They all waited, tense, stretching their ears for the sound of battle ahead. Only silence for long minutes, then a faint clattering, the sound muted by the rocks between them and danger. The merchant's men stood tense, daggers drawn.

"Look, someone comes!" The warning rose shrill into the bright air; Orev turned and looked, and smiled.

He unbound the leather leash, freeing Ari. "Go to your master," Orev said, and the lion padded off to Samson.

Samson greeted Ari, stroking the beast's broad forehead, then strode up to Orev and the staring merchant. "I greet you, men of the Five Cities. The road ahead is safe now."

The merchant regarded Samson skeptically. "So you say. I saw no thieves, and doubt I shall see any now."

"If you doubt, come past the bend, to the rocks, and you will see those who awaited you lying dead."

To Orev's surprise, the merchant agreed—although he ordered the caravan he commanded to turn back if he did not return within a quarter hour.

Past the curve around the outcrop of rock lay a small hollow; that the thieves had waited there was clear from the swords upon the ground, and the three men lying dead among the rocks.

As the merchant stared, Orev asked, soft-voiced, "Three men, Samson? How?" Samson smiled grimly and said, "I hurled rocks down upon them, crushed their skulls. That one, wearing the fox pelt, was the leader. With him dead, the others panicked and fled."

"They carried swords, and still you triumphed over them?" The merchant looked upon the dead men, made his decision. "I thank you, Samson, and will offer dogs to Dagon in your name. What do you ask,

Samson, slayer of the Champion of Gath, for keeping my men and beasts and trade goods safe?"

"I need no dogs slain on my behalf, and I ask no payment for doing what any man should do," Samson said, and the merchant stared as if doubting the evidence of his own senses.

Then he rallied, and bowed to Samson. "Perhaps you need no payment, but I would anger my gods did I not honor your service to me. Choose whatsoever you wish that is in my power to grant you, and it is yours."

Samson glanced over at Orev, who nodded. The favor Samson had given must be balanced by a favor taken; Orev only hoped Samson would choose wisely among the merchant's wares.

But Samson did not ask to go and look upon the goods the merchant carried. Instead, he walked over to the sword the leader of the bandits had carried. The weapon lay where it had fallen when stealth had proven more powerful than armed men, and stone stronger than bone. Samson caught up the weapon, gazed upon the dark glint of the iron blade, the flash of wild asses' teeth set into the hilt.

"I claim this," he said, and Orev smiled as the merchant tried to hide his relief that Samson's choice cost him nothing.

But, as a clearly honorable man, the merchant asked, "Is that all? You may claim anything that is mine to give."

"This suffices." Samson swung the sword, testing its weight and balance. "A worthy gift, and one that will aid in keeping the road safe for men of goodwill."

The merchant stared, then bowed. "If that is all you ask, then take it with my goodwill and my thanks."

"It is all I ask."

Orev sighed inwardly, but said nothing. Standing beside Samson, he watched as the merchant and his servants and pack animals took to the road again. They moved hastily, with many looks back over their shoulders. Clearly they could not believe their good fortune. When the small caravan passed from sight around the next hill, Orev turned to Samson.

"'Choose whatsoever you wish,'" Orev mimicked the merchant's fervent offer. "Samson, you might at least have asked for a skin of wine and some bread and cheese as well as that sword—which was not even the merchant's to give. Since you slew its owner, it was yours by right."

Samson smoothed his hand down the iron blade, frowned. "He didn't care for it well. The blade needs polishing and the edge whetting."

"You could have asked for a whetstone, too. Samson, you're a fool sometimes."

"All men are fools sometimes."

"Well, you are more of a fool than most."

"Perhaps I am." Samson ran his thumb along the edge of the sword. "But not such a fool as to ask for what will not be freely given."

Orev had to agree. Easy enough for a merchant to offer all he had as a reward, an offer the man undoubtedly meant at that grateful moment. Later, however, when the threat and fear faded, a too-greedy request might be resented. The bandit's sword had cost the merchant nothing. "That's all very well—but remember we can't live on stones and air."

"I won't ask payment for guarding the road against those who use my name as their war-cry when they attack peaceful travelers." Samson looked as stubborn as he had when he was five years old and had refused to let the older boys throw rocks at an injured dog.

Orev knew arguing with his friend in this mood was pointless. Time now for persuasion. "Admirable, Samson. But you should consider the feelings of those you protect. If you will take nothing, you leave them forever in debt. That is not kind."

Samson considered the matter as he wrapped the sword in the cloak of its previous owner. At last he said, "I would have no one indebted to me. If a man wishes to reward me, he can tell us a new tale. Then you will have fresh fodder for your songs."

Samson seemed so pleased at this decision that Orev lacked the will to point out that they could not live on songs, any more than they could on stones or air. *At least not while we roam the high roads. Still, new tales will be of value when we find a place where I may sing for our suppers.* So Orev simply nodded and said, "A wise decision, Samson."

Let Samson ask only a story told as his reward. There was nothing to stop Orev from requesting a more tangible expression of thanks, after all.

Soon word began to spread that if a man would send precious trade goods, the safest road by which to send them was called the Lion's Path. Samson could not enforce his will everywhere, but that road lay under the protection of his sword. He guarded all who traveled peacefully upon that highway. And he asked for nothing, save new tales from those who passed by.

Orev, less high-minded and more concerned than Samson with where their next meal might await them, graciously accepted gifts on Samson's behalf. He was careful to confine the offerings to food: a few loaves of travel-bread, a basket of figs, half a dozen dried salt fish. He knew Samson must know—but so long as neither of them mentioned the matter, no harm was done and they ate as well as many and better than some. For Samson, that was enough. Orev hoped, eventually, for better things.

But matters grew worse, not better. To Samson's anger and Orev's dismay, the group that called itself Samson's Foxes began to travel farther and farther seeking prey. No traveler, however humble, felt safe upon the roads, and the caravans of the wealthy doubled their guards, at great cost not only to themselves but to those who bought their goods.

Worse yet was the sudden increase in the number of groups claiming to be "Samson's Foxes." Sometimes it seemed to Orev that every brigand in Canaan boasted of pillaging in Samson's name.

Worst of all, groups of warriors from the Five Cities began to harass travelers in the guise of Samson's Foxes. What better way to vilify the Hebrew hero Samson than to claim robbery and rape were done on his order?

· · ·

In the long years that followed his time with Samson, Orev would think back to those now-famous days and see how each small word spoken by each chance-met man led inexorably to the hero's end. Only when all events had befallen could the pattern be seen.

Who would think that a brief encounter with a master of stone would hold any import to Samson's life? If only Samson had not spoken with the man . . .

But Samson would happily talk with any man or woman he met. "I like to learn new things," he told Orev often. And to walk and talk with a master builder, one who created city walls and temples, had been a great joy to Samson.

The mason had been traveling north, leaving Canaan and the rule of the Five Cities. Like any sensible man, he chose the Lion's Path for his journey, and was pleased to have the company of Samson himself on the road. "It is better that I work elsewhere for a time," he'd told Samson and, when asked why, had simply said, "Because I told those who rule Gaza the truth."

Samson had thought that over. "Men do not seem to like hearing truth, from anyone."

"No, they do not—and twice not when they have set their minds on building quickly and cheaply. You would think men would not wish to offend their god by offering up a shoddily built temple!" The man had brooded on this for a few strides. "And so I told them, after I had explained that to build a great temple in such a style was folly. Stone too soft, and pillars that will give way the moment the Earthshaker clenches His fist—"

And then, encouraged by Samson's sympathetic interest, the man had spent an hour sitting beside the road, drawing lines in the earth, showing Samson precisely how and why the Great Temple of Dagon that Gaza now erected must fall.

"Unless, of course, their god protects them." The master builder's tone left little doubt that were he Dagon, he would not bother to exert himself for such worshippers. "If not, then—see, Samson, here and here—weakness."

Samson had observed this with grave attention, while setting small flat stones one atop the other. A push of his fingers and the mock temple fell, became only a heap of pebbles. "Perhaps the earth will not tremble beneath Gaza."

"Perhaps not. Who can say what the gods will do?" The master builder wiped his hands on his tunic and rose to his feet. "I only know I would not let my wife or my daughter worship in that temple, and not simply because Dagon is no god of mine."

"Now Samson was as wise as he was strong, and as strong as he was wise. And men came from the ends of the land—yes, even from Dan to Beersheba, to ask him to judge among them . . ."

But the Lion's Path, too, proved a kind of trap. As time passed, those who traveled the protected road began not only to press more offerings upon Samson, but to ask him to settle new arguments and long-standing quarrels.

A merchant had overloaded the pack donkeys he had borrowed, and one of the donkeys had pulled a tendon—see, here was the donkey, limping. What did Samson think the owner of the donkey should do?

A man who had traveled down to Ashdod to sell his daughter as a house slave came to Samson complaining bitterly that the ungrateful girl had bitten his hand—see, there were the marks of her teeth—and run away. Would Samson hunt her down and bring her back?

The Lion's Path was too far for those from the eastern hills to travel upon it—did he expect old men to journey forty leagues out of their way? Why did Samson not protect the hill roads as well?

Sometimes Orev thought that being companion to a man who wished to see only good in life was a tricky and thankless task. Orev considered what words would best serve to persuade Samson to do the sensible thing and leave this high road he had claimed for his own.

Fortunately, the travelers themselves provided the excuse.

Reluctantly, Samson had striven to answer the pleas and complaints, to judge what was best when problems were laid before him. When the quarrels were petty and the questions simple, Samson's answers usually satisfied everyone. But as if Samson summoned trouble by merely living quietly, the peace of the road he guarded ended abruptly when two rich merchants decided that their quarrel could be settled only by Samson, Lord of the Lion's Path.

To find him, the merchants ordered their slaves to shout out his name every dozen strides. Samson, off hunting with Ari, did not hear them. Orev, sitting upon a rock by the roadside as he tuned his harp, both heard and saw them.

"You there—with the harp. Come down here," the fatter merchant demanded.

Orev looked into the merchant's round, greedy face, then turned his eyes upon the second merchant, a man thin as a gazehound and clutched by the same hunger that lurked in the fat man's eyes.

"No," said Orev. "I'm quite comfortable as I am."

The fat man stared at him. "Do you know who I am?" he demanded.

"No," Orev repeated. "I know nothing of you, save that you are rude to harpers by the roadside. Why should I come down?"

"Be silent," the thin man ordered the other merchant. "I will handle this." He then smiled at Orev—unconvincingly. He seemed out of practice; Orev decided the thin man didn't smile much.

"No, *I* will handle this." Orev's voice rang strong and clear. "Tell me why two merchants with a dozen armed men at their backs have been yelling for Samson this hour past."

Given free rein to air their grievances, the two merchants began a tale of woe and cheating that Orev thought could not be bettered by even village storytellers. He rubbed his hand over his brow, then sat, chin upon one hand, and regarded the two merchants intently, as if memorizing every twist and turn of their convoluted tale.

"And not only that, but the goat died!" The fat man practically wept.

"Well, if you'd keep your valuables in a storeroom instead of in a sheep, you would not only be able to find them but—"

Large and strong Samson might be, but he moved with the silent grace of a hunting leopard. Now he strode forward as if out of the air itself, Ari at his side, startling the merchants to silence. "Here, Orev—fresh meat!" Samson tossed a brace of rabbits up to Orev. "Remember those are *our* dinner, not Ari's."

Orev snatched the rabbits before the hopeful lion could maneuver into position to catch the rabbits as they fell. "Food is good, Samson. These men are here to ask you to judge between them."

Samson sighed. "Must it be now?"

Before the merchants could speak, Orev said, "They are most insistent, Samson."

"Very well. What troubles you?"

As Orev had already decided, the dispute was nothing—not compared to a girl sold into slavery, or a boy gelded to satisfy the demand for court and temple eunuchs. But he dutifully relayed the merchants' story to Samson.

The merchant routes that ran from the north to the south, the east to the west, were ardently desired by traders. A permit bearing the seal of one of the Five Cities granted a merchant access to the trade routes. The better the road, the safer and faster the journey, the more the permit cost. With enough gold, a merchant could purchase the use of a road solely for his own caravans. Which was all very well, unless a greedy clerk sold the same road to two merchants, as had happened to the two men standing before Samson.

At last Samson said, "I have heard you, and must think. Wait." He stood for a long time, stroking Ari's dark mane, staring at first the fat man and then the thin one. "I am ready to judge between you now," he said endless minutes later. He looked intently into their eyes. "Are you willing to submit to my judgment and to carry it out, no matter how foolish it may seem?"

Reluctantly, the two merchants managed to agree. "Very well." Samson straightened and said, "The road was built for all to use. It is small-hearted to deny men the right to the roads their forefathers built. Share the road as two friends should. You will find your way both pleasanter and safer."

This sensible judgment did nothing to soothe the irate merchants. When they went off, they were still quarreling. *At least they left.* Orev thanked Yahweh for this small favor.

"Why do they do this, Orev? I'm no Judge, to know the will of the Law and the Lord." Samson frowned. "And I'm still not sure how the goat comes into the matter."

"Forget the goat, or you'll go mad," Orev advised. "As for why they seek you out—it's because they think you know the answers they are too foolish to find. Perhaps it would be best if we ceded this road to the merchants, and let them work out their own quarrels. If you remain here, more men, and still more, will demand you judge between them, and no matter how you decide, there will be bitterness."

Orev hoped the argument would work. If merchants continued asking Samson to decide between one claim and the other, Orev knew it would only end in conflict. And for months, he had wished to free Samson of the invisible chains that bound him to the Lion's Path.

"Orev, I cannot leave this road now. It is trusted, safe, and only because I am here to guard it. I must stay."

"No, you must go. Samson, do you not see that the Lion's Path grows perilous—not for you but for those you would protect?" Orev knew only an appeal to what was right and good would work.

Samson rubbed Ari's plump belly; smiled as the half-grown beast wrapped its paws about his arm and began licking his hand. "But how will my leaving make them any safer?"

Grateful that Samson did not remind him that the Lion's Path had been Orev's clever notion in the first place, the harper drew a deep breath and spoke as persuasively as if he sang a new tale to a doubtful audience. "If you leave this road now, while all know it lies under your protection, it will remain safe. No one will know you have left, and it will be as if your hand still holds back the evil. If you remain, more and more will demand you not only protect them but judge between them. And you have seen how that leads only to new quarrels."

Now may Yahweh let my words sway Samson. Let him for once do what is sensible, rather than what he somehow thinks is right and honorable.

Samson stood quiet for a time before saying, "Perhaps you are right, Orev. I have no desire to sow strife. Where shall we go?"

The ease with which his friend agreed to abandon the Lion's Path left Orev feeling not only truly grateful to Yahweh but disinclined to question this good fortune. The harper smiled and said, "The road runs east to the sun and west to the sea. East would be better, I think."

To the east lay rugged hills, and desert beyond, hard traveling for any man, especially one with a crippled foot. But to the west lay the Five Cities, and peril for Samson. Since Orev had already settled in his mind that they would turn eastward, towards the hills, Samson's next words hit hard as an unexpected blow.

"West. We can visit the Jewel of the Five Cities. We shall journey to Ascalon."

For a breath, Orev could not summon words to his aid. And when he spoke, for once it was swift and plain. "Samson, are you truly mad? You can't enter Ascalon's gates!"

"Why not?" Samson said, and rose to his feet, ignoring Ari's playful swipe at the sword hanging from his master's belt. "A jewel merchant told me Ascalon prepares for a great festival, to honor a god called Hadad-Rimmon. The Sun Partridge Dances go on for seven days, he said, and there is new wine and much song and merriment. All the city rejoices, and all are welcome. I've never seen such a festival. Let it be Ascalon."

"Let it *not* be Ascalon! Samson, they will kill you there."

"Not during the Sun Partridge Festival. During those seven days, all within Ascalon's walls are sacred. Lady Ascalon's greatest foe may safely walk Her streets—"

"Did the jewel merchant tell you that, too? Perhaps he lied. Have you thought of that?"

"Why should he lie?"

"Why should he tell the truth? The Five Cities would pay your weight in silver a dozen times over to capture you, Samson, and you know it." The Five Cities still blamed Samson for every crime committed by the Foxes—or by any other thief or murderer who wasn't known and captured.

Samson's face took on the patiently stubborn expression that always meant he was about to be even more unworldly and unreasonable than usual. "The jewel merchant was no Philistine, but a man from a land far to the south. And besides, I wish to see Ascalon."

Long practice permitted Orev to reveal everything or nothing with his voice. Now he chose to speak in a calm, quiet tone. "Why Ascalon, Samson? Is there a reason you will not reveal to me?"

A pause; Orev waited.

"I have dreamed, Orev. Dreamed of a black flame hotter than the sun."

"And this flame burned in Ascalon?"

"Yes," Samson said. "It burned in Ascalon. It danced Ascalon's streets, and when I followed after it, the stones beneath my feet shone like gold."

"That is why you wish to go to Ascalon? This dream of a dancing flame and golden streets?" Orev looked at Samson's face and judged that nothing would turn his friend from this path now. But Orev knew he must try one last time. "And when did you dream this dream, Samson? You have not spoken of it before."

"What matter when I dreamed this dream? And I did not speak of it before because I was bound to the Lion's Path. Now I have been freed, and I will go to Ascalon. If you will not come with me, I will go alone."

Orev sighed. "Of course I will come with you, Samson. Very well, let us go west, to Ascalon. I've never seen the Sun Partridge Dance either."

That was how they decided to journey down the ancient roadway to the sea, leaving the unforgiving hills and traveling across the verdant plain to the coast.

To the oldest of the Five Cities, to the Pearl of the Sea.

To Ascalon.

PART TWO

Rising Moon

Samson

Even the straight road to Ascalon proved hard to walk in peace. Sometimes it seemed to Orev that Yahweh delighted in setting obstacles in Samson's path.

Still, the encounter with the prophet would not have troubled Orev, save for the warning the man gave of trouble to come. Not that the prophet Samuel realized what his words revealed to Orev—and to Samson as well. To Samuel, the words he spoke held only one meaning. But his stern rebuke betrayed more than the prophet himself could imagine.

The prophet Samuel came upon them as they rested a few hours' journey from Ascalon.

Samson dozed beneath a wild olive tree, his head resting upon Ari, who slept as hard as he played. Orev sat leaning against the tree's trunk, softly singing over the words of a new song. Only long repetitions could truly turn mere words into a song that would draw laughter or tears from those who listened to its singer.

He fell silent as a man strode across the open land beyond the road, crossed the road, and approached them. Tall and lean, using a long wooden staff to aid his steps across uneven ground, the stranger looked both poor and dour, but not dangerous. Although Orev guessed the man to be only a few years older than Samson, his stiff dignity and thin face aged him. His clothing—if one could truly call a tattered tunic and a worn goatskin cloak clothing—also spoke, silent but eloquent, of a far older man, a poor one at that. A stern expression only added to the image of a joyless fellow, too serious for his true age.

But Orev would listen to anyone, gleaning news and nuggets of gossip and information that might someday inspire new songs. And Samson would speak with anyone, however forbidding he might appear. Orev nudged Samson with his foot. "Wake, a visitor comes to join us."

"Peace and greetings, brother," Samson called. "You look weary. Sit with us now and share our meal later. I am called Samson, and my friend is Orev the harper."

"I know who you are, betrayer of vows. And someday you will know me. I am Samuel, Yahweh's servant and prophet, and I keep all the vows you so lightly cast aside."

Samson frowned. "What vows have I betrayed?"

"What vows have you not betrayed? You consort with those who worship false gods. You raise up those whom Yahweh would strike down. You claim for your own that which belongs to Yahweh only. You, whose very birth vowed you to Yahweh's service, break every law and commandment."

As Samuel recited his litany of offenses, Samson slowly rose to his feet. Ari rolled into a crouch, apparently ready to leap upon this irritating stranger if Samson gave the lion the slightest encouragement.

"I have taken no vows, nor broken any." Samson met Samuel's gaze unflinching. "Nor have I offended against Yahweh's commandments. Who are you to chide me? Look to your own honor, Samuel. If I offend Yahweh, He alone will chastise me for my transgressions."

Samuel stood nearly as tall as Samson, but Samson was not only tall but strongly muscled as a full-grown lion. Without even trying, Samson loomed over Samuel like a pagan god. Samuel glared at his rival, eyes burning hate. "Our people delude themselves that they need any more king than Yahweh Himself. Some talk of you as that king, Samson." Samuel's voice threatened; danger seemed to sting the nape of Orev's neck like an angry bee.

But Samson only laughed. "Let them talk. I'm no king, nor ever will be. You shouldn't worry so much, Samuel. If ever a god could take care of His own affairs, Yahweh is that god."

"You blaspheme, Samson."

"Well, if to tell truth is to blaspheme, then perhaps I do. Are you sure you will not eat? The bread is hard, but the honey sweet—"

Samuel seemed turned to stone in the roadway. "I will not eat. And I tell you, Samson the fool, that you think to rise high, but you will fall lower than any man has ever done." Samuel's voice sounded hollow, as if he spoke from inside a cave. "Night will take you, night will destroy you . . ."

Orev's prickling sense of danger changed to chill certainty. *Samuel is not just another man crazed by power-lust. He is a prophet. He speaks as Yahweh bids him.* The fact that Orev had always doubted such a wonder as a true prophet existed only increased the fear Samuel's uncanny voice kindled in him. Fear, cold fire in the belly.

A low growl rasped the air; Ari rose to stand beside Samson. The lion's fur bristled down his spine and his tail lashed, a quick, deadly warning.

Samuel fell silent, although he glared at the lion as fiercely as if about to accuse the beast, too, of oath-breaking and blasphemy. For a moment Orev feared Samuel and the lion would leap upon each other, a clash of deadly enemies. Then Samson laid his hand on Ari's broad heavy head, and the rage burning in the air about them cooled.

"So you lead a king's beast. Do you think to be king, Samson?" Samuel lifted the gnarled wood staff he carried, pointed it at Ari.

The lion's low growl sharpened; Ari's paw slapped the staff aside. Samson knelt and wrapped his arms about Ari's neck, urging the lion back.

"I told you no, but you will not listen. Our people have only one king," Samson said, "and we need no other king than Yahweh."

"Do not mock Yahweh or me." Samuel struck the ground between them with his staff. "I have heard men speak of you as their leader. I have heard them say you should be king and lead Yahweh's people against their enemies."

"I do not mock anyone—or any god. And I cannot stop men from speaking foolishly. But I am no man's leader, and I say a third time, no man's king. Nor do I wish to be."

Samuel spat upon the ground at Samson's feet. "Do you think your lusts count for more than that dust at your feet? I have warned you, as Yahweh bade me do. I have done with you, Samson. But Yahweh has not. Perhaps if you heed my words—His words—you may still be saved."

Ari growled, a low promise of menace; Orev and Samson stood silent as the prophet turned and strode away. Soon he was lost to their sight, the only sign that Samuel had ever been there a veil of dust drifting above the road.

When the dust no longer hung in the air, Samson drew in a deep breath. "He must be mad. Do I look like a king to you, Orev?"

Yes, Orev thought. But he said only "Our people have never had a king, and they will not suffer one now."

"No, we have no kings." Samson seemed to lay aside a troubling burden; he smiled. "Shall we eat now? I am hungry, and the honey is waiting."

"Why not?" said Orev. "If we leave soon, we can look upon the walls of the Pearl of the Sea before sunset. And I am no longer as pleased with this olive tree's shade as I was an hour since. Yes, let us eat, and continue on to Ascalon the Beautiful."

At the crest of the last hill, Samson and Orev stopped and stared down the road to the plain, to the sea-city of Ascalon. The city gleamed pearl-rich under the summer sun and filled the eye even at this distance.

"I've never seen so large a gathering of buildings." Samson stared, amazed, at the sight before them.

"You've never seen a city until now. Villages and towns, that's all. Now this"—Orev waved his hand, indicating the massive walled city set between fertile plain and seacoast—"*this* is a city. I never thought to see Ascalon. I'm glad I have."

"She's beautiful," Samson said. "Look at that wall. I wonder how—"

Orev held up his hand. "Stop. I don't want to hear how the stones were moved or the tower erected. I merely wish to gaze upon the Pearl of the Sea in awed silence."

Samson flung his arm over Orev's shoulders. "Very well, silence. But just look at the Western Gate. The road seems to lead from it into the sea itself."

"Samson, what about the word *silence* baffles you?" Orev shook his head, and Samson laughed. Orev stared down towards the waiting city. Although he had never before set eyes upon Ascalon the Beautiful, the city was far-famed; he had heard much of its importance, and its value to the Philistines.

The oldest of the Five Cities, Ascalon served as seaport and bazaar. Its harbor welcomed ships from lands known and unknown; its merchants bought and sold everything from dried fruits to rare gems. Outside the walled city, farms spread over the plains, orchards and vineyards swept up the slopes of the eastern hills, adding to its wealth. Ascalon's wine was famed from Troy to Thebes.

Nor was trade Ascalon's only claim to fame. The city itself was a marvel of strength and beauty. Ascalon's walls had been built high and deep; the gates opened into tunnels sixty paces long through the guardian walls. Towers tall as a cedar stood watch by the city gates. Lime wash turned the walls white as sea foam. Gilded horns rose from the corners of the watchtowers, as if to gore the sky.

From the hilltop, Orev and Samson could see the city within the vast walls. Houses painted red and black and yellow; long streets gay with canopies of brilliant cloth. The bazaars, Orev supposed. At the center of the city a rooftop burned red-gold under the westering sun. The flaring brightness nearly blinded him, veiled the building's surroundings in reflected brilliance.

Orev closed his eyes, waited for the sun-spangled blindness to pass. Beside him, he heard Samson inhale sharply. "Orev, do you see that? There, in the center? It seems almost a city within a city."

"A palace." Orev opened his eyes, cautious. The blazing blindness had cleared; he looked again at the city, taking care to slide his eyes away from the golden heart of Ascalon. "Or a temple. There is a great temple to a goddess there in Ascalon. She's half-fish, or so men say."

"I'd like to see this goddess," Samson said. "Which half is fish, do you suppose?"

"Which half do you think? Now we'd better find a resting place for the night. The festival doesn't begin until tomorrow's sunrise. You won't be safe within Ascalon's walls until then."

"Oh, I'll be safe enough. How would those who dwell in Ascalon even know what I look like? Come on, we want to get there well before they close the gates for the night. We'll have time to explore the city."

Orev glanced at Samson, who was eyeing the towers and gates with as much interest as if they were a beautiful woman, and then at the lion reclining at Samson's feet. "Then let whatever happens be upon your own head, not mine. And you'd better put a rope around Ari's neck. Festival or no festival, I doubt the Philistines will like having a pet lion loose in their streets."

To Orev's surprise, the guards at the Eastern Gate let them pass with no more than a casual glance and a warning from the oldest—a man whose gray hair and scarred face told his history as a warrior more plainly than words—that "If that beast claws anything, be prepared to pay well for damages."

But as the old warrior also scratched Ari behind the ears, and sent them on their way down the long tunnel into the city streets with a recommendation that they try Lalage's inn if they planned to stay for all the days and nights of the festival, apparently the warning was kindly meant. Nor did the guards seem surprised to see a lion padding along on a rope leash.

Orev's chief worry was that Samson would draw too much attention to himself, or that Ari would panic in the crowded streets. But it quickly became clear that the only eyes watching Samson were those of idle women. The golden lion pacing beside Samson drew only fleeting glances.

Clearly stranger things had walked Ascalon's ancient streets than a leashed lion.

Sandarin

The guardian in charge of the Eastern Gate had brought the news himself—news brought too late, and news Sandarin still found nearly impossible to believe. Was the man Samson mad, that he put himself in Ascalon's power? Sandarin had promptly ordered Samson seized and imprisoned, only to have the gatekeeper remind him that the Sun Partridge Festival had begun, and that no man might lay a hand upon another in anger. Sandarin demanded to know why the gatekeeper had waited almost a full day to bring this vital information to him, only to be told, "My lord prince, I did not know myself until I drank to the honor of the Sun Partridge with a merchant who asked me how it was I permitted Samson to enter Ascalon."

Furious, and knowing he could not berate the man for telling him what was only law and truth, Sandarin had hastened to the Great Temple of Atargatis and laid the news before the High Priestess, who stared at him until the Prince of the City feared she had lost her senses, refusing to heed what she did not wish to hear.

"Samson?" she said at last. "Samson has come to Ascalon?"

"Yes, as I have said thrice already, my lady Derceto—the man has entered through the Eastern Gate. He walks Ascalon's streets, unscathed and untouched! With a lion and a harper, too; the man must be mad. What are we to do? He must be taken, rendered harmless to us."

Her astonishment vanished as he spoke; when he ceased, awaiting her response, the High Priestess regarded him with irritated indulgence, as if he were a particularly foolish child. "The Sun Partridge spreads His wings over all within the city walls. You know that, my prince."

"Of course I know that! I am not a fool! But we cannot let Samson roam Ascalon, doing whatever he wills, until festival's end."

"We can, and we must. I am not a fool either." Derceto frowned, then, slowly, smiled. "We must watch, and wait. If the gods have delivered Samson into our hands, we must not offend them by violating a sacred festival."

"The gods will not bind and imprison Samson," Sandarin pointed out, and Derceto laughed, a sound that made the Prince's palm itch with the urge to slap her painted cheek.

"Of course not," Derceto replied. "That is for Ascalon's soldiers to do. Unless you wish the Temple to take charge of the matter?"

Sandarin did not. The capture of Samson belonged to the City, not the Temple. When he pointed out that Samson had entered the City's walls, not the Temple's, Derceto nodded, as if in complete agreement. But Sandarin did not trust her; given the slightest chance, the High Priestess would eagerly claim the prize for her own.

Still, unless the man placed himself into Derceto's claws, there was no law that permitted the High Priestess to demand Samson. This thought comforted Sandarin only until he reached the Temple Gate.

For there it occurred to him that a man capable of blithely striding into the stronghold of his greatest enemies was capable of any action, however mad. Samson might do anything, even try to join forces with the High Priestess. Sandarin only hoped, as he was borne back to his palace in his gilded cedarwood litter, that Ascalon's greatest goddess would favor his prayers over those of Her own High Priestess. And that the Sun Partridge Dances would dazzle the barbarian lout Samson so greatly that the man went nowhere but the nearest wineshop. Wine-drugged, Samson would be easily taken.

By the City. Not by the Temple.

As Our Lady wills it, of course. And not, Sandarin thought, remembering Derceto's mock-meek smile, *as our High Priestess wills it!*

Delilah

"Then there came the day that mighty Samson laid his eyes upon Delilah. Delilah the Dark, Delilah of the night-black hair. Delilah, who desired Samson's heart, and Samson's soul, and would stop at nothing to claim them as her prizes. She was beautiful as night and cunning as a fennec, and she filled his eyes until he could see no other. He vowed he must have her for his own, or die of love . . ."

When I look back upon that last summer Aylah and I spent together in the House of Atargatis, I see two girls, each foolish in her own way. And I see a span of unalloyed happiness that I never again knew. I thought Aylah as happy and content as I; nor did she reveal by word or deed that she was not.

We both were ordained priestesses now, Rising Moons, and much sought after for our skill in the Dance. I knew our talent pleased the Temple, and brought it much profit, too. Merchants and princes freely gave rich offerings to have the Sun and Moon dance for them.

Although we were not yet Full Moons, Aylah and I were tended as if we were images of Our Lady Herself—or as if we were prized mares from the southern desert. I laughed when Aylah called us that, one day in the baths as slaves smoothed oil of amber into our skin. Aylah did not even smile to acknowledge her own jest.

But jest it must have been; were Aylah and Delilah not the most cherished of the Rising Moons? We each now had a handmaiden whose only duty was tending to our clothing and dressing us for the Dance, and another whose task was to ensure that our faces were painted and our hair knotted and curled so that we might dance with perfection of appearance as well as of movement.

There was one more honor we were being prepared for: that of acting as the Goddess Herself in the rites of love. There were many ways to serve and to honor Our Lady Atargatis, but love was the most worthy.

Each priestess acted as the goddess at least once in her life; some were called only that one sacred time. Others found the joy in honoring Our Lady with love that I found in the Dance. Sometimes I dreamed that I might be called to love as I was called to dance, but this desire I spoke of only to Aylah.

Aylah claimed she did not care, but I believed her calm, cool demeanor veiled an inner fire. I still dreamed of the highest honor for Aylah—that someday she would stand before us in the blue and gold of the High Priestess.

I knew better than to speak of this vision to Aylah, but nothing could keep me from wishing such a future for her. Why should Aylah not be High Priestess? Was she not beautiful, fair and graceful, proficient in all the skills we had been so carefully taught? To see Aylah garbed for the Dance, glittering as the sun whose rays had been stitched in gold thread upon the tiers of her skirt, was to look upon perfection.

Although I knew I was no longer the plain, awkward-looking child I had once thought myself to be, I still saw myself as shadow to Aylah's bright beauty. She tried to argue that I had become at least as beautiful as she, but I could not yet look upon myself and judge fairly.

And Aylah's worth was easy for any to see. The pale thin girl from the north had ripened into a golden goddess. Her hair never darkened as she grew into womanhood; the silk-straight mane remained the color of spring sun, just as her eyes remained clear dawnlight blue, and her skin pale as fresh milk. All the lines of her face and body curved smooth and womanly, in perfect harmony of form.

While I— Well, as I say, I had improved over the years, but my chiefest claim to beauty remained my hair, the color of moonless midnight, its soft darkness falling in heavy waves nearly to my knees. For the rest, my eyes were dark as my hair, my skin the deep honey red of dark amber, and my slender body strong and supple as a cat's. A dancer's body. If I owned any beauty, it was too subtle to be seen beside Aylah's placid perfection.

To me, it was simple: Aylah was flawless, and I was not.

This makes it sound as if I spent hours studying my mirror, comparing myself to Aylah, but in truth, we had little enough time to brood. The Temple kept us too busy to waste the rare moments of leisure we were granted.

Although we belonged to Our Lady Atargatis, She was not the only deity worshipped in Ascalon. Atargatis held pride of place as Queen, but each season brought its own gods and goddesses, and the city celebrated their many feasts and festivals. The Great House of Atargatis watched over the lesser deities and their holy days and celebrations; our priestesses tended other gods, honored other festivals, that Our Lady might bless them with Her presence.

The most joyous of these other festivals came at the beginning of autumn, when the grapes were gathered in and the new wine was pressed. The god thanked then was Hadad-Rimmon, Lord of Wine, known as the Sun Partridge for both his own joyous lusts and the bright heady passions his gift and favor bestowed. Everyone loved the time of the Sun Partridge Dances, a full seven days of rejoicing marked by dances at every feast and every temple, dances in the city streets and along the wide road that led from the Sea Gate Tower down to the harbor.

During that intoxicating week, wine flowed more freely than water, and honey-cakes and sweetmeats were piled high at every merchant's shop and every Temple gateway for all to take freely and eat. All trade and all daily ritual was set aside, all feuds and quarrels forgotten, every stranger welcomed; the vilest criminal might walk Ascalon's streets in perfect safety, immune from capture and punishment. For seven days it was a duty, as well as a pleasure, to honor Hadad-Rimmon by indulging in sweets and spices, dance and song, wine and love.

This year I looked forward to the Sun Partridge Festival with a new fervor. For this year Aylah and I were sixteen, and already the Temple's most prized new dancers. This year there could be no doubt that Delilah Moondancer and Aylah Sundancer would be chosen to lead the First Dance and the Last Dance. To lead the First was honor enough, as it was to lead the Last. But to lead both First Dance and Last—only half a dozen dancers in the Temple's history could claim that prize.

For once I waited to hear the names the Seven Fish had chosen for the places of honor with not only a mask-smooth face but a joyous heart. For this time I knew what the Seven would proclaim. Perhaps Our Lady had murmured into my ear as I lay sleeping; perhaps it was only the vanity of youth. But I heard my name and Aylah's called, and our places in the First Dance and the Last given, without even the slightest tremor of surprise.

Beside me, Aylah drew in her breath sharply; clearly she had lacked my confident belief. Once the ceremony of choosing ended, and we all scattered to our various tasks, I caught Aylah in my arms and hugged her hard.

"First Dance and Last! Oh, Aylah—we may ask for whatsoever we desire now, you know that?"

She returned my embrace, and kissed my cheek. "It is a great honor, heart-sister. I am glad it gives you such joy."

"And you? Don't you care at all, Aylah?"

"Yes, but only because you do. And because it is a pleasure to watch you dance. For the rest . . ."

"Now do not say any of the other dancers would do as well! You know the steps perfectly, better than I myself sometimes. Tell me, what shall we ask for?" I had not exaggerated when I said we could ask for whatsoever we desired. Those who led the First and the Last Dances could claim what they wished as prize, if their dancing pleased the gods. Since Aylah and I would lead both dances, we could demand a handful of stars and Lady Ascalon would be bound to obtain the heavenly gems for us. "Come, Aylah, is there nothing you desire?"

"Our freedom." Aylah spoke so softly I could have pretended I had not heard those words.

But I had, and they sliced deep as a keen blade. "What do you mean? Are we not the Temple's most cherished daughters?"

"Oh, yes, we are that. As for what to ask for as our reward for leading the First Dance and the Last—I think it wisest to wait, and see what Fate sets in our path." Aylah regarded me steadily, her pale eyes cool as winter dawn. "Someday we may be glad to own the right to ask for whatsoever we desire. I do not think we should wield that weapon lightly, on mere gems and garments."

Samson

"But no man is without fault or flaw, no man is without a fatal weakness. Great Samson could resist any lure, overpower any foe, save one.

"Strange women, strange women drew his eye and snared his heart. And when he looked upon such women, Samson forgot what he owed to his people and his god.

"Yes, a woman beguiled him . . ."

Ascalon was the Pearl of the Sea and its women adorned it like living gemstones. Old ways still held sway in this ancient city; women walked the streets bold as men, dressed in bright garments that drew the eye. Many of the merchants in the bazaar were women, as were the artisans who shaped Ascalon's famous pottery and the perfumers who blended fragrances in demand across half the world.

Nor did Ascalon's women guard their eyes; they stared upon men as openly as men gazed upon women they desired. Samson drew women's eyes in a blatant fashion unheard of in the Hebrew villages.

At least there women had the sense to disguise their lusts behind their veils. Orev hadn't realized Ascalon would be quite so enticing; he could only be thankful that Samson seemed to notice nothing untoward—but then, Samson was the least vain of men. He ascribed much of the interest they attracted to Ari's presence, and Orev agreed that the lion did draw people's eyes.

Samson was more interested in Ascalon itself—women he could meet anywhere. The city's massive walls fascinated him, as did the system for drawing water from the spring beneath the city. He examined the huge gateway and its arch, questioning the guards about the composition and structure of the tunnel leading from the tower gate into the city streets. Orev could only hope the guards, all of whom seemed happy to converse with this inquisitive foreigner, didn't think Samson a spy.

Then there was the fascination of the forbidden: the temples of Ascalon. Dozens of small temples adorned the city, homes to as many gods and goddesses. But the chief ornament of Ascalon, and the most enticing, was the Great House of Atargatis. That temple dominated the western portion of the city, its painted walls reflecting the sea beyond it. Larger than most villages, the House of Atargatis ruled over far more than the mere worship of its goddess. Vineyards, farms, trade—the Temple controlled all those.

But what most saw was the Temple's pious ceremonies of worship—and its priestesses, women flaunting the gaudy, decadent costume of a time fast fading from memory. Bare gilded breasts, slender corseted waists; seven-tiered skirts heavy with spangles and bells—supple, dazzling women whose painted beauty ensnared all who gazed upon them.

That such women might be claimed for an hour, or for a night, by mere mortal men only seemed to add to their aura of enchantment.

Orev had been dazzled himself when he first set eyes upon a priestess walking the smooth-cobbled streets of Ascalon. The priestess had seen him staring and had smiled; clearly Orev was not the first stranger to the city who had lost the power of speech upon beholding her. Samson, too, had stared—and at him, the priestess had gazed with a clear unabashed delight.

"I think she likes you," Orev had said, and Samson had only shrugged.

"I think it is her duty to like everyone," Samson had answered, smiling at the priestess, "and I think she would be easy to like."

But when the priestess had beckoned, Samson shook his head, and she had merely shrugged and walked on. Orev had stared after her, watching the sway of tiny silver and shell charms sewn upon her flounced skirt. "She would have liked you to follow her," he'd said, and Samson answered,

"Yes. But she is not the one for me." Samson had stroked Ari's head. "The Sun Partridge Festival begins tomorrow, you said?"

"At sunrise." The merchant in the nearest market-stall offered up this information as he held out a garland woven of strange yellow flowers that turned out, when Orev touched them, to be made of cloth. "A garland for the Dance?" the man had asked, and Orev shook his head. "A garland for your beast, then?" the merchant had added hopefully, and Samson laughed and cheerfully handed over a lump of copper for a garland of cloth poppies.

"Next time, at least let me do the bargaining," Orev said, after Samson had hung the garland about Ari's neck and they had wandered on down the bazaar. "If you can even call it bargaining when you hand over whatever the merchant asks without saying a word."

"It's a festival" was all Samson had had to say in his own defense. "And the garland looks well on Ari."

Orev had given up, and contented himself with the knowledge that Samson gained wealth as easily and cheerfully as he lost it again. And there was too much to gaze upon to spend time arguing. All Ascalon was prepared for the Sun Partridge Festival. Flowers and fruit and banners bedecked buildings; at each corner men and women set in place huge jars of wine and dozens upon dozens of small clay cups.

Samson had aided in this endeavor, his strength making a hard task simpler at half a dozen corners. In return, one of the women had invited Samson and Orev—and, perforce, Ari—to lodge with her family for the night.

"You'll want a good meal and a good night's rest, for the Dance begins with the dawn," she'd said, regarding Ari rather doubtfully. "You'd better leave that beast of yours in my back shed. We run peaceful festivals here in Ascalon, you know. No lions chasing people through the streets. We leave that sort of nonsense to places like Gaza."

By which Orev had inferred that while the Five Cities might be allies, they were rivals as well. Apparently when not standing united against outsiders, Ascalon and Gaza fought like sister and brother. He doubted that Gaza really permitted lions to run free in its streets—although the woman's complaints that Gaza thought itself better than Ascalon, and spent far too much on such frivolities as new bronze city gates, rang truer.

"Lord Gaza is jealous of Lady Ascalon," she had announced. "The Great House in Gaza that Dagon has dwelt in time out of mind is no longer fine enough—oh, no, Gaza must tear the old temple down and built a finer one. They think to outshine Our Lady's Great House here. Well, they won't. Everyone knows that builders these days cannot equal those who created the ancient temples."

"Why not?" Samson had asked, and the woman said, "Oh, you know how it is. In the old days, builders took more care, more pride in their work. But what can you expect when all places like Gaza care about is what something costs? We're wiser than that here in Ascalon."

At the next dawn, the Sun Partridge danced—and so did all the city. Even Orev found himself hauled along, lame foot or no, until he could wrest himself free and steady himself with his walking-stick. And Samson—well, Samson danced happily, not caring that this festival, this Dance, honored a strange god, that such dancing might anger his own god.

Of course, the warm spiced wine the dancers swallowed at each pause in the labyrinthine Dance might have been the cause of Samson's unmarred enjoyment. Orev managed to stop draining the unglazed cups of wine after the first three, taking a sip only and flinging the rest to splash on the ground like dark blood among the broken cups. But he was older and more wary than Samson.

Even the few cups of festival wine Orev had drunk seemed to kindle his blood. By now wine-fire must flow thick and hot through Samson's body. Orev only hoped that the woman who had given them lodging was right, that Ascalon enjoyed peace, even during drunken festivals. He had no idea where the endless Dance had carried Samson—who had no malice and no sense. *I suppose I must seek him, and hope to find him before he gets into trouble again.*

To Orev's great relief, he encountered Samson only two corners away. Samson had freed himself from the Sun Partridge Dance and stood beside a booth laden with wine cups and heavy with garlands. He stared down the long street as if dazzled as men and women danced past. In one hand he held a tangle of blue ribbon and red roses. In the other, he held his long knife, its polished blade a flash of light.

"Is all well?" Orev asked, and Samson smiled.

"Yes, all is well. I have seen my future, Orev."

"If all's well, sheathe the knife before it makes someone nervous."

Samson glanced at the knife as if wondering how it came to be in his hand. He slid the blade back into its sheath and gestured towards the line of joyous dancers that had circled back, heading for the next street. "Look, Orev—see the dancer there? The one leading the Dance? She is the woman I have waited for, whom my heart has hoped to find. She is the woman who will be my wife."

A flash of midnight and silver, a chime of bells—

"Samson, she's a priestess of Atargatis. You might as well wish to wed the moon!"

"I don't care. I must have her."

"You don't even know her name," Orev said, and Samson turned and grasped the arm of the nearest man.

"The priestess leading the dance—the girl like a black flame—who is she?" he asked, and the man stared at him as if astounded—or very drunk.

"You must be a stranger from a far land, that you do not know Delilah Moondancer. Let me go now, for my wine cup is empty again." The man waved the cup in proof of this, and Samson put his hands on the man's shoulders and pushed him gently in the direction of the nearest wine booth.

Then Samson turned to Orev and smiled. "Her name is Delilah," he said, and Orev fought down an urge to pour the contents of the nearest wine jug over Samson's head.

"Very well, you know her name. But how are you even to ask for her, Samson? Walk up to the Temple Gate and demand to see the High Priestess?"

Samson smiled and flung his arm around Orev's shoulders. "You see? I knew you would find the answer. You always do."

"I but jested—" Orev began, then stopped as he realized Samson wasn't listening. For a moment, as he watched his friend stride off in the direction of the Temple, Orev was tempted to let Samson face this particular peril alone. *Perhaps a harsh enough rebuke will drive this mad fancy from him.*

Or perhaps it would not. Sighing, Orev followed after Samson. *I wish we had never come to Ascalon. O Yahweh, I know not why You have set this snare before Samson. But if it seems good to You, give me the wit to save him from such a great folly.*

The Great House of Atargatis dominated the seaward quarter of Ascalon. Its gates faced a vast square crowded with men and women celebrating the Sun Partridge Festival. The Temple Gate stood open; any who chose could walk freely into the First Court and partake of the feast being set out upon long tables that, combined with booths and wine-bearers and dancers, turned the vast courtyard into a labyrinth.

By the time they made their way across the courtyard, past belled dancers and smiling wine bearers and garlanded booths offering everything from luck-tokens to kisses and other erotic delights, Orev had grown very tired of the Sun Partridge Festival. There just seemed to be too much of everything, too freely given.

When he told Samson this, his companion merely laughed. "You complain that a festival is lavish? That people are generous? There's no pleasing you, Orev. Come, let us find the High Priestess."

Always impatient of protocol, Samson caught the arm of the first person who passed by—one of the Temple eunuchs, to judge by the man's soft painted face and the fringed skirt he wore—and said, "I wish to speak with the High Priestess of this temple. Where may I find her?"

"Are you blind? She who is Goddess-on-Earth stands there upon the steps." The eunuch pointed, and Samson and Orev turned and looked upon what Orev at first thought to be a painted and jeweled idol. Then the idol vanished as the woman moved, spreading her arms wide and beckoning with both hands. Her palms were dyed crimson, the color of a setting sun.

As if he saw nothing save that dazzling image, Samson strode across the courtyard to the Temple steps. There he stopped, gazing up at the High Priestess. Orev, following more slowly, came up to Samson in time to see the High Priestess look down at Samson, and to hear her say, "So you are Samson. And yet you dare enter Ascalon, dare enter Our Lady's House, you who are our enemy?"

So much for anonymity. I told Samson this was a bad idea. It was clear to Orev that the High Priestess not only knew who Samson was but was unsurprised to see him here. *Almost as if she expected him to come to her . . .*

"I am not your enemy. And is not the city, and this temple, freely open to all when the Sun Partridge dances?" Samson regarded the High Priestess steadily.

High Priestess Derceto smiled, a subtle curve of red lips. "That is true. Have you come, then, to feast upon Our Lady's bounty?"

"No. I have another boon to ask."

"Speak, then. What do you desire of the House of Atargatis?"

"I have seen a priestess whose touch kindles fire in my heart. She is called Delilah Moondancer. I ask that you give her to me."

A flash of darkness in the long gallery above the court; a cry slic-
ing blade-keen through the festive noises. Samson looked up and
smiled. Orev tilted his head back and saw the two girls who had led
the Dance. Midnight and midday; shadow and sunlight, their true
selves masked by paint and gems. A heartbeat later the two young
priestesses withdrew in a swift swirl of skirts, scarlet and ebony van-
ishing from sight of those in the courtyard below. Samson gazed at
the spot where they had stood watching him. Orev looked again at
the High Priestess.

She regarded Samson with cool eyes; eyes flat and opaque as a serpent's. "You wish to claim one of Our Lady's priestesses? You are bold
indeed, to come here and demand such a prize."

"I do not demand," Samson said, and turned back to gaze serenely
upon the High Priestess. "I ask."

"You *ask.*" The High Priestess's expression did not alter, but her
voice mocked. "And you think that Her priestesses are yours for the
asking, Samson of Zorah? What can you possibly offer great enough to
gain you such a prize as the priestess Delilah?"

Take care, Samson, Orev silently begged. *This woman is dangerous.* Behind
her flat jade eyes lurked greed and cunning. High Priestess or no, Derceto was not thinking of the girls in her charge, or the goddess she
served. Derceto thought only of gain.

"What would satisfy you?" Samson asked, and Derceto answered,
"What will you give, to enjoy a night with this priestess you desire?"

"You do not understand. I do not wish to claim Delilah for a night
only, to use her as a vessel for mere lust. I wish to marry her. I want her
for my wife."

For long moments the High Priestess neither moved nor spoke,
seemed turned to cold stone. At last she said, "That is another matter. I
cannot answer you now. Go, and return at sunset. I will have an answer
for you then. Do you swear to accept that answer?"

"I will accept whatever answer Delilah herself makes. If she denies me, I will go, and trouble you no more. If she is willing to be my wife, you must give her up to me. Is that a fair bargain?"

The High Priestess smiled—and Orev felt a chill slide down his spine, cold as springwater. "That is a fair bargain," Derceto said. "Now you may either feast upon Our Lady's bounty or leave Our Lady's House. At sunset you will have Her answer."

Delilah

The day of the First Dance, Aylah and I rose before dawn, that we might be ready to dance the Sun Partridge across the sky. By the time the sun burned away night's last shadows, we stood hand in hand at Ascalon's Eastern Gate, awaiting the first clash of timbrils and beat of drums. Aylah's skin was cool; she always seemed cool—but my blood raced hot, and as soon I heard the first chime of music I began to dance. We danced along the wide main street that ran straight through Ascalon from the Eastern Gate to the Sea Gate, and behind us fell in all the rest who would dance with the Sun Partridge. Some would dance the entire pattern, from Eastern Gate to the Sea and then back again; others would manage only a few turns before dropping out to celebrate the festival in other ways. It didn't matter.

I danced, and that was all I cared about.

We wove through Ascalon's garlanded streets, past shops and wine booths and people shaking rattles and beating on drums, adding to the noise of the musicians and the singing crowd. Men and women danced for a street or two and then dropped away as others joined the line. I kept dancing, sure-footed and joyous; I had spent many hours memorizing the path through the streets that we were to follow and never faltered at a turn.

Pride is a fault; I grew too confident. We led the dance through a street full of booths selling festival trinkets and sweetmeats. At the corner where I must turn next, I dipped and twirled, and nearly fell; something had caught my hair.

My concentration on the Dance slipped from me, and for a moment I paused, trapped between one turning step and the next. My swinging curls had hooked upon a booth's garland, bells and blue ribbons tangling with crimson roses. I could not pull free, and I dared not stop—

All this took less time than three beats of my heart. Then a man tall and golden as the Sun Himself shoved forward and, with a flash of bright metal, sliced through ribbons and roses, freeing me to dance on. His fingers brushed my cheek as I turned, a caress swift and hot as flame. I had no time to do more than smile at him and see him smile back before the Dance itself swept us apart.

But as I swirled away from him in the turns of the spiral dance, I carried with me the memory of his smile, and of his eyes burning the clear hot blue of the sky above us.

Delight in the Dance consumed me; I felt neither thirst nor weariness. I felt nothing but joy until the First Dance ended, back at the Eastern Gate as the sun reached the top of the sky. When I stopped moving, all strength drained from me, and I would have fallen had not servants from the Temple waited to hold us up and press goblets of clear water into our trembling hands. For once Aylah seemed as shaken as I; we smiled at each other as we tried to drink, only to find our shaking hands spilled the water down over our breasts. I had not thought I would be so tired, and was grateful to step into a palanquin plentifully supplied with cushions and with wine and sweet foods.

As we were carried home to the House of Atargatis, I summoned the strength to ask Aylah whether she had found joy in leading the dancing. "I had not expected to be either so happy or so tired after," I said, and Aylah smiled and handed me a small round cake sticky with honey and sharp with cinnamon.

"I had expected to be so tired, but I had not expected to be so happy," she said. "Yes, Delilah, I found joy in the Dance. But for once no one was watching to judge if my every step was perfect and every gesture faultless."

"Praise Atargatis for that, for I nearly ruined the entire Dance," I said, and Aylah laughed, a thing she did not often do.

"Oh, Sister, you always think you will ruin everything! You are not Our Lady Herself, you know."

"This time it is true. When we went through the street jammed with festival booths—"

"That was all of them," Aylah pointed out. "Eat, Delilah, before you faint from weariness." She licked honey from her fingers before reaching for a dish of silvered almonds.

"We had to turn a corner," I went on, "and my hair caught upon a garland. I thought I would fall—you must have noticed." I took a bite of the small cake, savoring the mix of sweet and sharp flavors, as Aylah shook her head.

"No. Eat more."

"The whole Dance would have fallen, but a man cut the garland free. You must have noticed *him*?"

Again she shook her head. "I tell you again, Delilah, I saw nothing. I was dancing, remember? And trying to keep up with *you*."

I felt oddly disappointed. "You did not see him? He was very tall, tall as a god, and golden as a lion, and he smiled—"

"Well, in that case I am sorry I did not see him—but you seem to have looked at him well enough for both of us." Then, instead of asking about the man who had saved the First Dance, she said, "For Our Lady's sake, stop nibbling like a mouse and eat! Don't waste our one chance to eat as much as we like without anyone saying we must not!"

Of course, I consoled myself as I obediently ate, I had looked upon the man, and Aylah had not. *If you had set eyes upon him, Aylah, you would not be so indifferent now!*

The stranger was the sort of man that Aylah would say no sensible girl believed existed. The sort of man all priestesses dreamed of as lover on her Maiden Night. Although I had seen him only for the space of a smile, I would never forget his kindness. His eyes were blue, bright and clear as summer sky—

"Delilah? Are you dreaming?" Aylah reached out and tugged the lion's claw token braided in my hair. "If you fall asleep now, you will be carried straight to bed—and you swore you must see the High Priestess open the Temple Court. Have you changed your mind?"

"No, I have not changed my mind. Even if you are too weary, I will go."

"To see Derceto in all her gems and glory?" Aylah smiled, and shook her head. "Well, if you are not too weary, neither am I. I will come with you, heart-sister. Where you go—" She stopped, and looked away, as if intent upon the gaudy booths we passed.

I reached out and clasped her hand; my fingers warmed her cool skin. "Where you go, I go. And I promise we will not stay long—just long enough to watch the High Priestess open Our Lady's House to all who choose to enter it."

"To all who wish a meal they need neither cook nor pay for nor clean up after," Aylah said, and I laughed.

"Who cares why they come? Does Our Lady ask their reasons? And are you quite sure you did not see the man who cut me free of the garland?"

"I do not care. I do not pretend to know what Our Lady thinks. And yes, Delilah, I am quite certain I did not set my eyes upon this godlike man who has captured your heart."

"He did *not* capture my heart. I only thought him—"

"Perfect," Aylah finished, and I flung my handful of silvered almonds at her.

"I will never see him again, so it doesn't matter what he's like. I don't want to talk about him anymore," I added with great dignity.

Aylah gathered up the almonds that had fallen into her lap and tossed them back at me, one by one. "It was not I who spoke of him first. It was not I who spoke of him again and again. It was not I who . . ."

By the time our litter was set down outside the Court of the Rising Moons, almonds lay scattered among the cushions like wayward stars. But no one scolded us. As leaders of the First Dance and the Last, we could do as we pleased—at least until the Sun Partridge Festival was over.

All the temples in the city threw open their outer courts between the First Dance and the Last, offering food and drink to any who came through their gates. The High Priestess or Priest of the temple acted as giver of the feast, so Derceto would stand as Goddess-on-Earth on the steps to the Great Outer Court, that all might look upon her and see Atargatis Herself.

I wanted to gaze upon that dazzling vision. That was why I grasped Aylah's hand and turned away from the gate into the Court of the Rising Moons. "Let us go to the gallery above the Outer Court," I said. "From there, we can see everything."

Aylah sighed, and for a breath I thought she would object again. But she only shrugged and said, "Oh, very well, if you wish it. Why not? We can eat and sleep after."

On the longest nights, during dark hours when even poppy will not grant me sleep, I still hear her saying those light words. And until the moment when I draw my last breath, I shall wonder what would have befallen us all had Aylah said no to me on that day, and not yes.

Smiling, I waved away the fussing servants, and Aylah and I walked through the corridors and gates until we reached the steps to the gallery encircling the Outer Court. The gallery was cool with sea-green tile; arched windows looked down to the courtyard below. I led Aylah to the first window, and we leaned upon the ledge, gazing at the vivid scene spread before us.

Men and women clad in brilliant festival garments had begun entering the court. Long tables had been set in seven rows across the courtyard.

On each table a different manner of food or drink had been set out, enough, it seemed, to feed hundreds. The tables were tended by Full Moons of Atargatis's House; on this day, priestesses acted as servants to whomever came asking meat or drink.

And on the steps that led from the Outer Court into the First Court stood the High Priestess of the Great House of Atargatis. At first I almost thought a statue of the goddess had been placed there, so still did Derceto stand and so perfect was her appearance. She wore the ceremonial gems and garments that only the greatest rituals warranted. Derceto glittered like a jeweled statue, and I saw awe and wonder on the faces of those who walked through the Temple Gate as they looked upon her.

"A goddess indeed," I whispered, and Aylah said, "Truly, she looks very fine." She laid her hand on mine and tugged gently. "I'm tired, Delilah. Let us go—"

But I did not listen, for the man whose quick thinking had saved the Sun Partridge Dance strode through the gate into the courtyard below. Tall, taller than I remembered, and even more brilliant than the sun; the strong midday light gilded his skin and hair.

"Look, Aylah," I said, and nodded towards the sun-bright man. "There—that is the man. The one who saved the First Dance."

Beside me, the only sound was Aylah's breath rasping the heated air, a sound that seemed to prick the skin beneath the heavy chained curls weighting my neck. I turned and stared at a stranger, as if a ghost-pale image now stood where my heart-sister had been.

"Yes, Delilah. I see." Dancer's paint gleamed vivid upon her lids and cheeks and lips, turned her face into a brilliant mask. Her eyes never left the man below as she said, "We cannot thwart our fate. I could fling myself from this window and the gods themselves would catch me up before I died upon the stones. Shall I put it to the test?"

"No!" I cried, catching at her arm—and it was then that he looked up, his eyes caught by my sudden movement, his ears by my wild cry.

Looked up, and saw Aylah standing beside me in the window, beautiful as the Lady Herself.

And I knew, deep in my cold bones, that my life had changed—changed utterly between one breath and the next.

Derceto

Few things surprised Derceto anymore; that Samson had managed to astonish her proved him a very unusual man. She had played the part of Atargatis Incarnate so many times she sometimes thought her garments could act the role without her inhabiting them. The ceremony of welcome to the Feast of the First Dance had been no different than a dozen other such ritual occasions—until Samson stood before her and asked to marry Delilah Moondancer.

She had managed to summon words to answer him, and kept her voice smooth as well-water. No one watching would have suspected that her blood beat so hard her skin shuddered, that her thoughts swirled swift and uncatchable as storm clouds. No, all those watching would have seen was the High Priestess calmly welcoming Samson, coolly questioning him, cleverly binding him to do as she bade him.

Perhaps Bright Atargatis really did answer desperate prayers.

Of course Samson would not gain Delilah—for one of his conditions would never be met. Even if Delilah were told of his desire for her, the girl would never abandon her brilliant career as Atargatis's priestess merely to become a man's wife.

But Derceto had no intention of telling Delilah. No, Samson would be told that Delilah agreed, accepted him as her husband. *And if he asks why she is so willing, I shall tell him that Our Lady ordered her to go to him. But I doubt he will ask.* Men always preferred to believe that what they wished was the gods' will.

So he will gladly accept my word that she whom he desires truly wishes to become his wife. And then he shall learn that to wed one of Our Lady's Doves is not a thing easily done. No, he must earn his bride.

If he can. For Derceto had no intention of letting Samson succeed. The man so greatly feared by those who ruled the Five Cities had delivered himself into her hands.

She could hardly believe her good fortune—once he failed her tests, and fail he would, Samson would belong to the Temple. Then Atargatis would be seen as greater than this Hebrew hero's strange god; more important, Derceto's power as High Priestess would be seen as greater than that of the Prince of the City. To Derceto, Samson was no hero. He was a playing-piece in a game, important only in his value to her opponent. The Temple must always triumph.

And half Ascalon saw Samson come willingly into Our Lady's Court, saw him petition me, saw him bow before me. Or at least saw the Hebrews' champion, the harper's favorite, the hero of a dozen songs, bend his head and leave at Derceto's bidding. No one need know what he had asked, and what she had answered—not until she had decided precisely how best to wield this weapon that had given itself into her unyielding hands.

You wish to wed Delilah Moondancer, Samson? Let us see how hot your passion truly burns. There was a song, an ancient tale, that told of a man who performed a dozen tasks to win his prize. *No need for a dozen. Three, I think, should suffice.* While the tasks must be worthy of so glorious a prize as Delilah, the goddess's stipulations must at least appear possible of achievement.

Samson

Just before sunset, Samson and Orev returned to the Great House of Atargatis. Orev expected long delay and much ritual before Samson could stand before the High Priestess and hear her answer; he prepared to wait—or to be taken and chained by soldiers.

But Temple servants, unarmed and meek, met them at the Outer Gate, and bowed before them, and led Samson and Orev through the Great Outer Court, up the stairway into the Second Court, and then through a maze of corridors and courtyards that Orev knew he could never retrace without a guide. *We are trapped here.*

Before a gate painted deep blue and inlaid with pearls and iridescent shells that formed patterns of waves, they stopped. The Temple servants bowed again and silently withdrew. Samson regarded the barrier and then glanced at Orev. "Should I open it?"

"If you don't, we might as well not have come here. Unless you're going to see reason and come away again, you might as well open the gate."

"Orev, you worry far too much." Samson lifted the bar and pushed the blue gate open.

To the harper's surprise, only High Priestess Derceto awaited them in the private garden beyond the gate. No attendants, no guards— Orev sensed something wrong in this secretive meeting. But what was amiss he did not know.

Perhaps I worry too much. Orev studied Derceto's masklike face. *But I doubt it.*

The High Priestess remained silent, waiting, and so Samson spoke first. "The sun sets on the first day of the Sun Partridge Festival. And I have come for the answer you promised me."

And now she will say no, and Samson and I will leave this city before another sunset—

"The priestess agrees to wed you," Derceto said, "and the omens are favorable."

Samson smiled; Orev stared. *I don't believe it. What is she plotting?*

"But . . ." Derceto added, and then paused, as if awaiting a reply from Samson.

I knew it. Of course there is a condition that must be met before Samson may claim his bride. And it will be neither easy nor safe.

"You are not a wealthy man, Samson. You offer nothing as a bride-price to repay the Temple for so great a loss. You will receive a beautiful wife who brings with her a dowry from the Temple and all the blessings of Our Lady Atargatis. And what do you offer in return?"

"Whatever you ask," Samson said, and the High Priestess answered smoothly, "It is not what I ask, but what She asks. In exchange for the priestess we have promised you, you must perform three tasks. When those three tasks have been completed, then the wedding will take place."

"What are these tasks?" Samson asked, and the High Priestess smiled.

"You must plow a field. You must sow a field. And you must reap a field."

That sounds simple enough. So there must be a snare hidden somewhere. Orev knew better than to speak at the moment; he waited.

"Must I wait for the crop I sow to grow?" Samson asked, and the High Priestess smiled—a pure, practiced curve of her painted lips.

"Are you so impatient? What is one season?"

"Nothing, to a goddess." Samson's voice remained cheerful, as if he merely bargained for a trinket with a bazaar merchant. "But to a man in love, a season is forever. And besides, once the Sun Partridge Festival ends, I will no longer be safe within Ascalon's walls. So I must complete the three tasks and wed my bride before sundown on the day of the Last Dance."

This sensible comment made both the High Priestess and Orev stare at Samson in surprise. For the space of three breaths, Orev thought the High Priestess had been struck mute. Samson merely waited, patient as stone, for her answer.

"Very well—we shall find a crop that may be reaped as it is sown." High Priestess Derceto sounded amused now—but neither the amusement in her voice nor the smile upon her lips went further. The rest of her face remained a polished mask. And her eyes revealed nothing.

Her bare gilded breasts rose and fell as she drew in a deep breath; light glinted from gold-painted skin. "Now hear all the terms of the bargain, Son of the Sun, before you bow your head to it. We would not have you say the Temple of Atargatis tricked a mere mortal man. Listen well, and be sure you agree to all I offer. Once the covenant is made between us, there can be no turning back. Do you understand?"

"Yes." Samson's steady good humor did not alter. "I understand, High Priestess of Atargatis. Now tell me what I must do—all of it—to gain my heart's desire."

Oh, Samson, I fear you have just delivered yourself into her claws. No woman— especially a harlot priestess of Ascalon—can be worth surrendering yourself to a demon's bargain.

Derceto lifted her hands, held them out so that the hennaed palms flashed crimson. "Hear, then, the laws that rule this bargain between the Great House of Atargatis in Ascalon and Samson the Hebrew. Samson must plow a field of our choice, using the beasts and tools we shall give him. And he must sow that field with the seed we shall give him. Last, he must reap what he can from that field."

She paused, giving all there time to think on what she had said before continuing in her strong clear voice. "If he completes these tasks, the Great House of Atargatis will bestow upon him the priestess he claims as his bride, and will dower her with a fine farm on rich land. If he does not—

"If Samson does not complete these three tasks and wed his bride before the Sun Partridge ceases dancing, he surrenders himself to the Great House of Atargatis, for Our Lady to do with him as She deems fit."

Derceto lowered her hands and gazed upon Samson. "You have heard. Do you agree to this bargain freely and of your own will?"

No, Orev thought. *No, Samson; this is a trick, a trap.* If the Temple took Samson as a slave, his life would be measured out in minutes. But Orev knew he could say nothing that would deter Samson from this mad enterprise. He could only wait as Samson smiled and said, "I have heard, High Priestess, and I agree to this bargain freely and of my own will. Shall the first test be tomorrow?"

For a moment, Orev thought the High Priestess was surprised by Samson's cheerful urgency. Then she smiled. "So impatient—well, perhaps that is a good omen. But I must consult the oracles, ask a propitious hour to begin. You will be told when we have an answer from the Seven Fish."

"When are you going to ask?" Samson said, and the High Priestess stared at him, clearly unaccustomed to such a frank response to her pronouncements.

"As soon as you leave Her courts, I shall be free to set all in motion." She rose from her cedar chair, paused. "There is yet one more condition that you must agree to. Until you complete the Three Tasks and win your priestess, you must not reveal her name to any other. If you do, you will lose all." Derceto did not wait for Samson's reply, but turned away and left the audience chamber through the carved ivory gate behind the chair. The audience clearly had ended.

"Come on." Orev touched Samson's arm. "Let us leave before you agree to anything else."

In silence, they walked out of the courtyard and through the great outer gates. Orev considered the terms of the bargain Samson had struck with the Temple; there must be trickery involved, no matter how straightforward the Three Tasks had been made to sound. *I wonder if we can find out what the High Priestess has planned? Perhaps one of the Temple slaves can be bribed—*

But what could they bribe anyone with? Samson's sword? Orev's harp? A tame lion?

"I wonder," Samson began, and Orev regarded him hopefully; perhaps Samson had realized the folly of this undertaking. They could simply leave Ascalon, forget about the priestess . . .

"Do you think, Orev, that the High Priestess would let me attend when they ask the Temple oracles the best hour to begin the tests? I've never seen fish prophesy before."

"No, I don't," Orev snapped, and even the thought of the High Priestess's expression should Samson ask her such a thing failed to lighten his mood. Rich lands and fine cities lay beyond the sunrise; Orev wished he owned the power to transport Samson to the eastern shores of the Black Sea—the farthest place the harper could imagine.

There was such a thing as being too good-natured.

But when Orev tried to convince Samson the Temple dealt in deceit and trickery, and suggested leaving Ascalon at once, Samson only said cheerfully, "You think the bargain a trap for a fool—do you think I don't know that? Have faith, Orev. Yahweh will give me the strength for what I must do."

"It's not your strength I'm worried about," Orev replied, and Samson laughed.

"You're clever enough for both of us," he said. "Stop worrying, and trust in our god. Do you think Atargatis's fish really talk?"

"I think Atargatis's fish probably make more sense then you do." Orev abandoned his efforts to persuade Samson to forsake this mad attempt to win his chosen bride. He supposed he must do as Samson had advised, and have faith. There really didn't seem to be any other course open to him at the moment.

• • •

"Now Samson had set his eyes and his heart upon a woman of the Philistines, and wished to take her for his wife. And he asked for her, and she was given to him . . ."

But not freely, at a price so high that only Samson would consent to pay it. Later Orev often wondered if Samson's priestess-bride thought the price she herself paid too high for the short span of freedom it bought her. Remembering her cool eyes and clear voice, and her sharp wit, Orev wished for her sake that she had remained in the Temple, safe.

Although that was not what she had wished for herself. As the years passed, Orev began to believe that she had known what marriage to Samson would cost her, and had paid willingly.

Even more willingly than Samson, who awaited the hour appointed for the Three Tasks with such impatience that Orev could hardly believe the time between Derceto's decree and the beginning of the first task was only the time it took the sun to rise and to set, and to rise again.

"The man Samson is to come to the land between the sea and the city tomorrow as the full moon sets and the morning sun rises. There he is to plow a hide's worth of land. If he succeeds in that, Our Lady will reveal the time and place of the next task." The soft-faced boy who brought the High Priestess's words at the next day's sunset spoke them with slow care, as if fearing to forget even one. When Orev told him he had remembered them well, the boy smiled, and then bowed and ran off.

"Well, that doesn't sound too hard," Samson said, and then, "There's no need to scowl at me like that, Orev. Do you think me such a fool I don't know there must be a snare set for me?"

"I think you too besotted with your priestess—with whom you have yet to exchange even one word—to care what the tasks are. I just hope she's worth it."

"She is. And who can blame her Temple for wishing to keep her?"

"Then the High Priestess should have just said no, rather than giving you hope. I think—"

"You think this a plot to enslave me or slay me or both. Yes, Orev, I know. Now I am going to bed. I have a field to plow at dawn. The tide will be out then."

That last comment baffled Orev; abandoning all hope of his friend coming to his senses, the harper sighed and went to bed. Samson was right in one thing, at least—they both needed rest.

Next dawn, Samson and Orev went out the Sea Gate and walked to the pen that had been erected upon the sands. Beside the pen stood the High Priestess and at least two dozen of Ascalon's warriors, well-armored and armed with iron-tipped spears. When Orev drew closer to the pen, he saw why. It held two bulls.

And not just bulls, but the Great Bulls that roamed free over Canaan's rich plains, descendants, some said, of the Sacred Bulls from Crete. Red and white, and twice the size of a farmer's ox, with horns long as a man's arm sweeping forward like sword-blades—

"There." High Priestess Derceto held her arms out, as if offering empty air. "There are the beasts you must harness. And there"—she gestured at the damp sand between the pen and the little waves teasing the edge of the beach—"there is the field you must plow."

Not only can they not plow a field, they can't even be yoked. They'll kill Samson before he can toss one of them. Orev didn't even bother to consider the impossibility of plowing a strip of sea-strand that lay between low tide and high.

To Orev's astonishment, Samson looked upon the huge bulls and laughed. "How many hours have I do accomplish this, Lady?"

"As many as you wish, Samson. But remember the Sun Partridge dances for only four days more. You must accomplish the tasks before that time, or forfeit your freedom."

"A man does that when he marries," Samson said. "A good omen, yes, Orev?" Samson clapped a hand to Orev's shoulder, pressed hard.

Obeying the silent command, Orev nodded. "A good omen," he echoed.

"A good omen indeed." The High Priestess looked down upon Samson and smiled. Her eyes gleamed flat and cold, a serpent's calculating gaze.

An omen—but a good omen for whom?

Samson smiled. "Then, since the omens are good, I will begin." Without pause, he walked forward, towards the pen; the soldiers drew aside to let him pass. Apparently untroubled, Samson unbound the knotted rope that closed the gate and entered the bull pen. Orev closed his eyes and whispered the most fervent prayer to Yahweh he had ever uttered.

Even that sounded loud against the sudden silence. Orev opened his eyes, expecting to see Samson's blood on the pale sand, blood on the gleaming horns.

But the scene before him was peaceful. As the circle of soldiers stared, the Great Bulls crowded each other, seeking closeness to Samson. They bent their massive heads to lick his hands, permitted him to stroke their thick-muscled necks.

Samson smoothed his hand over one of the great curving horns, turned to face the High Priestess. "They seem willing enough—another good omen. Where is the yoke and the plow?"

For all the long years of his life, Orev cherished the memory of Derceto's painted face in that impossible moment. *Has she even brought yoke and plow, being so certain that by now Samson would have bled his life out on the sands?*

As Samson continued to cozen the great beasts, the warriors looked to the High Priestess. Orev smiled, thinking how well this tale would weave into song. *"And even the beasts bowed before Samson, the Great Bulls that once belonged to gods. And so Samson triumphed over the evil plotted against him . . ."*

"Take the man Samson the yokes for the bulls, and the plow to harness them to." Derceto's voice sounded as if she held shattered glass upon her tongue.

So there were yokes and plow after all—well, she would not wish her scheming too plainly seen. Orev watched as two of the men pulled the yokes close to the pen's gate, and a third dragged the plow and let it fall beside the fence. Gravely, Samson thanked them and turned his back upon the bulls, opened the gate and picked up the heavy wooden yokes, set them down inside the pen. He spoke softly to the bulls again, and again they licked and nuzzled at his hands.

As Orev watched, marveling, Samson set the yokes upon the necks of the Great Bulls, led them out of the pen, and hooked their yokes to the plow. "Which hide of sea-strand must I plow?" Samson asked.

Silent, Derceto pointed at a stretch of sand close to the sea's edge. As soon as the tide turned, it would be inundated, wavelet by wavelet. The field Samson must plow with the Great Bulls was set off by a length of leather cut from an ox hide in one long continuous strip.

Not an excessively large field, but Orev could not believe that Samson could persuade those bulls to pull a plow. At least the sand was still firm, for the tide had withdrawn to its outermost limit. Derceto had staked all on a murderous delay as Samson endeavored to yoke the Great Bulls to the plow. Now there was time to spare to plow the plot of sand.

If the bulls would pull at Samson's bidding.

Samson led the bulls over to the makeshift field. There he walked back and leaned upon the plow, pushed its iron blade deep into the sand. But instead of trying to order the bulls to move forward as he leaned upon the plow, Samson walked in front of the beasts, leading the way down the field, and the yoked bulls followed.

None of those watching uttered a sound; the silence was so great Orev heard the waves sigh, and a seabird call far out over the water. Samson alone spoke, and that in soft low words to the bulls that followed him, dragging the plow, turning up the sand in uneven rows.

When all the sand within the encircling hide was plowed, Samson stopped. He offered the bulls his hands again, and again the beasts snuffled and licked him. Samson then smiled and swiftly unyoked the two bulls. Freed, they nudged Samson, who merely stroked their heads. After a moment, the bulls turned and slowly wandered off, heading, Orev supposed, for their accustomed pasture.

"I have completed the first of the tasks you set me," Samson said. "When must I accomplish the second?"

"Now, if you dare the second task." Slowly, Derceto pointed to a basket by her feet. "Sow what lies within this basket," the High Priestess said, "and as your third task, reap what you can."

As none of the watching soldiers moved, Samson came forward and lifted the basket. Holding it with care, he walked to the edge of the plowed sand. There he paused, waiting, before he pulled the lid of the basket back less than a hand's width. Orev watched, with increasing anger, as Samson strode swiftly along the crooked furrows, pouring out what the basket held.

Scorpions.

If Samson had reached into the basket to catch up whatever seed the High Priestess had given, he would have been stung with a venom that could slay a lion.

But Samson, the uncouth, untutored barbarian, had been too canny for High Priestess Derceto; he had plowed the field named by her, with the beasts she had given him. Now Samson sowed that same field with scorpions, gently shaking the poisonous creatures from the darkness of the basket into the damp, turned sand, moving quickly so the baffled, furious creatures had no chance to sting. When the basket held no more scorpions, Samson moved away from the plowed sand and the death seeded there.

He walked up to the High Priestess and set the empty basket at her feet. "High Priestess of Atargatis, I have done all you have asked. I have plowed the field you chose, I have sown it with the seed you chose. And I have reaped my own life safely from that field. I have completed the Three Tasks. When may I claim my bride? Remember, the Sun Partridge dances only three days more."

Derceto stared at Samson; Orev watched a vein throb beneath the skin of her throat. "When the omens for the wedding are favorable."

Her voice sounded harsh as a raven's. "Before festival's end. Yes. When the omens are favorable."

She turned and walked away, towards the Sea Gate into Ascalon. After a few moments, the soldiers seemed to decide they no longer need guard a stretch of sand, and soon only Samson and Orev stood by the pen that had held the Great Bulls.

"I hope the omens are favorable soon," Orev said, watching Derceto's stiff back. "I'm tired of city life."

"I too. But I have won the wife of my heart, so I am glad we came to Ascalon."

"I'll be gladder to leave it. I thought you would die here when I saw those bulls. Those tasks were meant to kill you, Samson."

Samson smiled. "I know. The Temple does not wish to part with its Dove. But truly, the tasks were not so hard after all. A little patience and care—"

"Patience and care won't turn Great Bulls into oxen. What magic tamed those bulls?"

Samson laughed. "Orev, I have known for a day and a night that I must plow with whatever beasts the Temple decreed. It was not hard to learn what I would be given—or to go to the beasts and make them my friends. Bulls are lazy, peaceful creatures at heart. Honey-cakes and soft words taught them to follow me. True, the furrows were not straight, nor deep—but no one said I must plow well. Only that I must plow the field I was shown with the beasts I was given."

"I don't think honey and soft words will win over the High Priestess." Orev remembered the flat anger in Derceto's eyes as she realized that Samson had survived the Three Tasks. "Take care, Samson. You have lived, and won not only a bride, but a great enemy."

"I know. So I think, Orev, that the wedding should be celebrated as soon as the omens are favorable, and that they must be favorable as soon as possible."

"Yes," said Orev, "and so I think as well."

"Now, how can we ensure omens that the wedding must be soon?" Samson asked.

"I don't know. Perhaps we should toss our own lots to determine the day."

Samson smiled. "Perhaps. And I think I will ask for those two bulls as part of my bride's dowry."

"And I think you are mad. Settle for the priestess, and leave the rest alone. What would you do with two Great Bulls on a farm?"

"Plow," Samson said. "What else?"

Aylah

Although she knew her heart-sister never would believe such hard truth, would laugh and try to coax her to laugh as well, Aylah lived in fear. Since she was very small, she had known herself vulnerable, her very hair her betrayer. Because of her sunlight hair, she had been thrust before the shaman who journeyed endlessly across the lands north of the Dark Sea, had heard him name her fate. She had been five years old the day she had been condemned as the Sun's bride. From that moment, she had been pampered, given meat even before her father ate. She told no one the meat turned to ash upon her tongue, its savor burned away by her fear. Someday she would be old enough to wed the Sun, and on that day, she would die in fire. When the wild men from the south rode through her people's camp, caught her by her pale hair, hauled her across a saddlebow, and rode away with her as one of their prizes, Aylah had been grateful to them. They rode far, so far she hoped the Sun would no longer know where to seek his bride. They took her far away, to a land unlike anything she had ever seen before. She was sold, and sold again, until at last she reached the slave-market in Ascalon.

By that time, she had long since ceased feeling grateful to anyone. Untame, she scratched and bit anyone who laid his hands upon her. Those who owned her quickly learned that beatings only fed her anger;

few wished to trouble themselves with so intractable a girl. Only her
hair saved her, for there was always someone who coveted her for its
gold—and always someone who sold her on quickly, once he discovered
her fierce refusal to yield.

When the plump gelded man in long robes shining with silver thread
had purchased her in Ascalon, and had her dragged off to a building so
huge she could not see beyond it, she had sworn silently that she would
never yield to those within those endless walls.

That was before she met Delilah.

Unlike Aylah, Delilah hid nothing; all Delilah thought, dreamed,
believed was given freely. In Delilah's eyes, Aylah saw not greed, but
admiration and love.

I saw the snare spread before me, yet I stepped into it willingly. Aylah would not
lie to herself, although she concealed a great deal from others. The
Great House of Atargatis was a pleasant place to live; she was tended
and cared for, treated kindly. She could have withstood that, kept her
heart guarded against the kind priestesses, the gentle life, and the sweet
goddess she had been bought to serve. But she could not resist Delilah.
Not because she loved Delilah, but because Delilah loved her.

And love draws love. That was one of the first lessons New Moons were
taught. Aylah had thought those words folly, until the day she discovered she cared for Delilah, who cared so very much for her.

Delilah never doubted, never feared. Delilah drew Aylah onto paths
that Aylah would never have dreamed of walking. Delilah's fierce love,
her serene faith, gave Aylah the courage to be, if not happy, at least content with life in the Temple, with her favored position as Delilah's sun-
shadow.

But unlike Delilah, Aylah never surrendered her trust to those who
ordered their lives. *Never trust too much—better still, never trust at all, and twice
never trust those in power over you.*

"The High Priestess has asked to see me? You are certain she did not
ask to see Rising Moon Delilah?" Aylah regarded the New Moon who

had served as messenger—a small girl full of self-importance in her task—but the child simply repeated the words of the summons. *So my fate has come at last. I knew it when I saw him in the courtyard, watched him seek me out. I can hide from the Sun no longer.*

She was glad Delilah was not with her; Delilah would be full of questions to which Aylah could give no sweet answer.

But when she entered the High Priestess's outer chamber, Aylah was surprised to see Derceto smile and beckon. "Come sit at my feet, child. I have something I must ask of you—or rather, something Our Lady asks."

Cautious, Aylah did as Derceto had bidden, looked up into the High Priestess's eyes, eyes opaque as jade. Eyes that revealed nothing. *But I can play that game as well as you, Derceto.* Aylah remained silent, waiting.

At last the High Priestess said, "You know the man Samson came to Our Lady's House—" She paused, as if uncertain how to continue.

"Our Lady's House is open to all who come with loving hearts," Aylah said. Piety could hardly be chastised. She waited again.

"Of course. And that he asked for a priestess for his wife is also no secret. And that Our Lady demanded he be tested with three tasks. I never—" Derceto drew in her breath sharply, as if distressed. "Who could have dreamed he would succeed? But he has, and now claims his bride."

Aylah knew she was expected to ask; she obeyed the silent command. "He claims me, High Priestess?"

To her surprise, Derceto shook her head. "No. And before I speak another word, you must swear you will not reveal what I now will tell you."

Aylah nodded; her skin grew cold, as if snow fell upon it. Even before Derceto spoke again, Aylah knew what would be said.

"He demands Delilah," the High Priestess said.

No. Oh, no. For once, Aylah's bone-deep control deserted her. "You cannot," she said, forgetting she addressed the High Priestess. "You cannot. It would—it would destroy Delilah."

Delilah's heart and mind were given entirely to Bright Atargatis and Her Temple; the Lady's Dance created Delilah's life. Aylah thought of Delilah stripped of her dancer's bells, her priestess's girdle, bound to one man only— *She who is Atargatis Herself when she dances, who will joyously give the goddess's pleasure to those who seek its comfort. No. No, I cannot let Derceto do this.*

"He has completed the Three Tasks," Derceto said in a low voice. "What else can I do, but honor the Temple's word?"

So that is it. And although the trap lay in plain sight, Aylah knew she would step into it, allow its jaws to spring shut upon her. "Give him another," she said. "Give him me. I ask it as my reward for leading the First Dance and the Last."

She sat there at Derceto's feet, hoping she would not be sick, as the High Priestess smiled, radiant now. Derceto laid her hands upon Aylah's smooth pale hair; Aylah remained still as stone. "I thank you, Aylah—as both High Priestess and a woman who is to you as a mother, I thank you. I had thought of this, but hardly dared ask it—"

Which of course is why you sent for me and told me all this, Aylah thought. But she said only "Better me than Delilah, for both Delilah and Our Lady's House. I will not disgrace the Temple, High Priestess. I will be a good wife to Samson. But I do not know how to say all this to Delilah, and it will hurt my heart to leave her forever."

There, Derceto. Now what will you say?

"Oh, I do not think you will be leaving her for so long as that," Derceto said. "Now listen to me, Aylah, and listen well, as if I were Atargatis Herself. There is a task She wishes done, and only you can do what is needful."

Silent, Aylah listened as the High Priestess instructed her in what she must do. *So I am to kill to please you? I wonder what Delilah would say, could she hear her revered High Priestess breaking a sacred vow, betraying her promised word, plotting murder?* Aylah knew she would say nothing to Delilah; to learn what Aylah now knew would only hurt Delilah and do no good. Nor would Aylah blindly obey Derceto's orders.

Marry Samson in Delilah's place, yes. Murder him, no. *This is my chance. At last. A chance to live my own life. A good life. If only Samson will listen to me, once he unveils the cheat, all will be well. I will make him a better wife than Delilah would.* Samson was a man, after all, albeit one from a rough, uncouth tribe. But Aylah had been schooled in the Lady's Arts; Samson might beat her at first, if he were a hard man, but once she set her lips and hands upon him, he surely would accept her in his house and bed, even if he did not forget Delilah. Aylah smiled, knowing Derceto would take that as a sign she acquiesced, would do as commanded.

Only one thing troubled Aylah: leaving Delilah. But despite her heart-sister's belief that Aylah outshone her, was more favored by the Temple, Aylah knew better. In her heart, Aylah was no priestess. She could sing every prayer, perform every ritual perfectly, dance every step precisely. But Aylah could not give herself utterly, as Delilah did. *So I will go, as the High Priestess commands, and you will remain.*

At least within the high thick walls of the Temple, Delilah's intensity was contained, her ardent passions confined to the Lady's dances.

Within the walls of Atargatis's Temple, Delilah would be safe.

Delilah

That the barbarian Samson wished to claim a priestess for his wife could not be kept secret. The tasks he must undertake to win his prize were open for all to witness. But the name of the priestess Samson had chosen—that, the High Priestess kept close. She gathered all the priestesses—New Moons, Rising Moons, Full Moons, Dark Moons—and all the Temple servants, too—in the huge public courtyard, and there told us that she saw no reason to name the priestess until Samson fulfilled the Three Tasks. And as there was little chance he could succeed, Derceto did not wish to trouble anyone's mind. Why fear a fate that might never come to pass?

But I knew; I remembered Aylah's face as she looked down at Samson, and his as he looked up. That he desired Aylah did not surprise me; doubtless he had forgotten me the moment he set eyes upon her as she followed me in the Dance. But Aylah did not desire him, had turned to ice and stone under his gaze.

I vowed that he would never take Aylah from me. And I had no reason to think Samson could plow and sow and reap what he had been given. The day the High Priestess stood before the high altar and said in a clear cold voice that Samson had won his wager—and his priestess to wife—shock chained me; I could not seem to move, even to reach out to Aylah.

When Derceto ordered that Aylah and I come with her to the Court of Peace, only Aylah's firm grasp upon my hand, tugging me to follow her, enabled me to obey the High Priestess's order.

Past the Ivory Gate, in the Court of Peace, Seer-Priestess Uliliu waited by the pool. High Priestess Derceto led Aylah and me over, waited as we bowed before Uliliu and before the Seven Fish.

Then Derceto said, "There is no kind way to tell you this, so I will speak plain truth. Samson has won his wife. I must keep my word, and bestow upon Samson the priestess I promised him. I grieve that you must lose your heart-sister, Delilah, but—"

"No," I said, not even caring that I interrupted the High Priestess.

Derceto sighed and held up her hand. "I know what you would say, Delilah, but this is not in my power to mend. The man is favored by Our Lady—or his god is greater than She in this matter." Derceto reached out and touched my forehead, softly, as a mother might. "But to ease your heart as much as I can, I call upon the Seven to reaffirm Our Lady's will in this."

Unable to speak, I bowed my head. To call upon the Seven Fish merely to try to comfort me—that was kind.

So Seer-Priestess Uliliu tossed different grains and seeds into the pool, studied the fish as they swam and squabbled over the food. As had happened when the oracle was being taken for my future in the Temple, the sun-gold Utu claimed what he wished, snatching it from the others and swirling off.

At last the Seer-Priestess lowered her arms. "The omens are plain. Sun calls to sun. Aylah will wed Samson. It is done."

I expected some sign from Aylah, but she neither moved nor spoke. *If she will not speak, I will,* I thought—but as I opened my lips to protest, Aylah squeezed my hand. When I glanced sidelong at her, she shook her head.

Silenced, I stared down into the sacred pool. The Seven Fish curved through their clear, placid world, their wide tails spread. Endlessly circling, their scales bright against the cool tiled bottom of the pool, the fish ignored us now that Uliliu had lowered her hands.

Defeated, I went quietly away from the Court of Peace, Aylah's hand holding mine to guide me. Neither of us spoke until we reached our own room. There I stepped back from my heart-sister so that I might see her face as I spoke.

"Aylah, why did you—"

"Stop you from speaking?" Aylah twined a lock of her hair about her fingers, and I knew she was about to tell me less than pure truth. Aylah would not lie to me, but she would withhold knowledge, if she thought it best. Now she stared at the pale bright hair tangled about her fingers and said, "What good would come of your words, Delilah, once the fish have foretold my future? Surely they cannot be wrong."

"I could ask your freedom as my reward for leading the Dances," I said, but Aylah only shook her head.

"Not when Our Lady Herself promised one of her priestesses to Samson. Let it be, Delilah. Please."

For a heartbeat I wanted to yank her hair away from her hands, force her to reveal what she truly felt. Then my anger passed as swiftly as it had grasped me. *She thinks it hopeless, and does not wish to make matters worse by showing her misery.*

I spent all the night praying to Atargatis for a way out of this snare. At last, as the darkness lifted to silver dawn, I abandoned the effort. *I am not a goddess, to change the future, or even a seer, to know what will be—*

My breath caught; I knew I had been answered. I shook Aylah's shoulder, awaking her. "Come and dress," I said. "We must speak to the High Priestess. I have had a—a Sign from Our Lady."

"Oh, Delilah, don't—" Aylah began, but I pulled until she rose. Then I badgered our servants until we were dressed and painted, fit to approach the High Priestess. I would tell Aylah my plan when I unfolded it before Derceto.

I was certain in my heart that I had been granted the blade to slice through this knot of wicked blasphemy. My plan would save both Aylah's shining future and the Temple's purity. When I revealed Our Lady's wisdom before the High Priestess, surely Derceto and Aylah would rejoice as I did.

"If my lady Moondancer does not remain still instead of darting about like a weasel, she will bow before the High Priestess with a face spotted blue and green. Is that your wish, Dance Priestess?" This reproof from my serving-maid Briesisat drew giggles from the other maidservants, and even a smile from Aylah.

I forced myself to cool the joy that heated my blood like new wine's fire; to smooth my face into a priestess's mask and bind my body to stillness.

I would be able to dance my delight soon enough.

To Aylah's astonishment—though not to mine, for had not Atargatis Herself guided me here?—when we stood before the High Priestess's gate and asked admittance, it was granted. We did not even need to wait for the Gatekeeper to go and ask whether we might enter, another sign to me that I had been led here by Our Lady's design.

That was the only part of the pattern that went as my mind had laid my dream-plan out before me.

The High Priestess did not receive Aylah and me in her inner throne room, but out in her garden court. Nor had Derceto garbed herself in formal seven-tiered skirt and gilded corset, nor painted her face and breasts, nor bound her hair with scarlet in the Goddess's Knot. Although Aylah and I had spent half the morning preparing ourselves to bow before the High Priestess, Derceto wore what any highborn lady might in her own garden.

A skirt of saffron-dyed linen over a longer skirt of green fringed with yellow tassels that brushed her ankles, a girdle with shell and silver luck-charms braided into the dull crimson wool. Her hair, sleek and brown as bay wood, lay down her back in a loose thick braid. A necklace of amber and ebony beads hung low between her ungilded breasts. She was cutting poppies with a silver sickle; when she saw us, she set aside blade and blossoms on the stone bench and smiled. "Welcome, my daughters. Come and tell me what troubles you, that I may remedy what I can and ease what I cannot."

For the first time, I felt that the High Priestess truly stood in place of my mother, that she was a woman with a woman's heart as well as a pure vessel of her goddess. She seemed human, caring, rather than a brilliant jewel one might admire but never love.

Derceto's smile gave me even more courage than my dream had done. Now, as she sat down upon the stone bench, the High Priestess beckoned us forward. When we knelt at her feet, she looked intently into our faces.

"You are not uneasy in your heart," she said after she had gazed into Aylah's eyes.

"No, High Priestess." Aylah spoke so softly I could barely hear her, although I knelt so close to her that our thighs touched.

Derceto then turned to me. "So it is you, our Moondancer, who needs our care. Speak freely, that I may aid you."

I sat back upon my heels and began, telling the High Priestess of my wretchedness and misery now that I was to lose my heart-sister. I could not understand how the Temple could bestow one of its priestesses upon a foreigner, a barbarian who slew men at his whim and led our people's enemies against us. *A man who makes heat dance under my skin whenever I set eyes upon him*—but that fiery truth I did not say to Derceto.

"Atargatis's will is not ours; She sees into time that will be as we cannot. Do you doubt this, Delilah?" Derceto's voice soothed, comforted. Encouraged.

I felt Aylah's foot press against mine but ignored the warning nudge. "No, High Priestess. I do not doubt Our Lady's love and wisdom. But I have had a sign from Her—"

I had a sign from Aylah, too; she swayed, seemingly losing her balance upon her knees. Her elbow tapped my side, a pressure barely felt as my leather girdle guarded my body from hip to breasts. Again I ignored my heart-sister's signal. I thought only of myself, of my own desires. My goddess had revealed a path to me, and my High Priestess smiled upon me and urged me to speak.

And I did.

"My lady Derceto, I stayed awake all this past night praying for guidance from Our Lady Atargatis. Surely She cannot wish one of her priestesses given to a stranger. Oh, I know Seer-Priestess Uliliu consulted the Seven Fish, but as night ended and dawn drew near, I heard . . . something. As if a veil were drawn away from my eyes, I saw that there are greater seers than the Seven. There is She Who Sees at En-dor. It is at En-dor that we must ask the fate of this man Samson, who demands what belongs to the Goddess Herself."

Silence. I could only hope my fervor had touched the High Priestess's heart.

"So you wish to go on a pilgrimage to En-dor? Our Lady Atargatis has demanded this?" Derceto regarded me coolly, plainly unpersuaded.

I drew in a deep breath. "Yes." My voice rang with certainty; by now I had convinced myself that I had heard our goddess's voice, rather than my own thoughts, revealing Her wish. "We are to go to the Seer at En-dor, my heart-sister and I. It is she who will unveil Samson's fate." *And Aylah's—and mine.*

Beside me, Aylah knelt silent. I saw the High Priestess stare at her, and then look back to me.

"This is a great and hard thing you ask, Delilah. And we cannot be sure it is Atargatis who sends this command to you. You know we have consulted the fish once." Derceto leaned forward and cradled my chin in her smooth hand. "Will you trust that I wish only good for you?"

I nodded, and she smiled.

"Then—since you are young, and perhaps have misunderstood your waking dream—I will consult the Seven once more. You may be there, if you wish, as may your heart-sister. But remember, Delilah, that Our Lady knows better than we who are mortal what should and what should not come to pass. If I order this done for you, child, will you grant me a boon in return?"

"Yes, High Priestess. Of course." I could hardly speak the words swiftly enough. "What must I do?"

"This time, will you accept what the Seven Fish reveal as truth?" Derceto gazed at me for so long, with such compassion in her jade-dark eyes, that I felt tears begin to burn. *She is so good, so kind. She truly acts as our mother.*

Just before I disgraced myself by weeping before her, Derceto said, "Very well. Let it be written that the Priestess Delilah and the Priestess Aylah will question the Seven once more, that the Sacred Fish may unveil Our Lady's will for them both."

"The Priestess Aylah is destined to wed the Son of the Sun—if he proves himself worthy."

Once this newest oracle of the Seven Fish had been pressed into clay and set out with the other tablets to dry in the sun, I knew I had lost the struggle. My efforts, my pleadings, had achieved nothing. For the first time, I doubted Our Lady's wisdom, and told Aylah so. Then I flung my arms around her and wept upon her shoulder; she stroked my hair, and I felt her draw a deep breath.

"You don't mean that, Delilah. You speak so only because for once Her will and yours differ."

"That's not fair! It's not true, either. The Seer-Priestess must have misread the omens. You cannot marry this man. You are Atargatis's priestess."

"If Atargatis wishes to bestow me upon Samson in marriage, who am I to defy Her will? Remember the Seer-Priestess consulted the fish twice—the second time only because you asked it, Delilah. Yet the answer remained the same."

That silenced me, and for a moment I stared, for from Aylah, I had expected a tart answer casting doubt upon the Seven's wisdom and the Temple's honor. Then my blood chilled, and I heard myself saying, "You wish to marry this man. That is why you sound so strange."

Aylah will have him, and I—I will have nothing. No, that was not my thought; it had been sent by a night-demon who had lost her way, wandered through this bright day to torment me. No again; Our Lady would not permit demons to trouble us in her own House. Tears burned my eyes, and I pressed my hands over my lips so that I could not utter words I did not even wish to think.

Aylah put her arms around me, pressed her cheek against mine. "Heart-sister, what I wish does not matter. What troubles me is that, in this, it seems that what you wish does not matter either. Don't stare so; we all know you are the Temple's jewel past price. But even you must do as the High Priestess bids. You know I have no choice but to obey."

The hours before the Last Dance fled like shadows from the sun. Counting those hours—so few, so swiftly passing—I did nothing but pace and pray. I could not imagine how I was to lead the Last Dance, knowing it would also be the last time I ever danced with Aylah beside me. I did not wish to eat, nor to sleep. Worst of all, I found I could not endure Aylah's docile acceptance of her fate; I could barely speak to her without anger, my words bitter, meant to hurt. Only my heart-sister's refusal to quarrel kept peace between us as she prepared to leave me forever.

All her mind seemed given to deciding what she might take away with her and what she must leave behind. I watched as she ignored the small jars of paint for eyes and cheeks and lips, the scarlet ribbons for her hair, the delicate glass vials that held scented oil. She gazed upon her jewels, and in the end left them lying in the Egyptian box that had been a gift from an admiring patron.

"Will you take nothing?" I demanded at last, and Aylah glanced sidelong at me before she answered. "I will take nothing I do not own and that I do not need."

"You will not take your own garments, your own bracelets and earrings?" Slow and heavy with resentment, my words fell like stones between us. "You will not take your dancing bells or your—"

"Delilah, stop. You tear yourself to pieces over nothing. These things"—Aylah waved her hand towards the small treasures she had rejected—"these do not belong to me, they belong to a priestess. After tomorrow, I shall no longer be a priestess. And Derceto has promised to send me to my husband with all that I shall need, so you need not worry."

And when I accused her of caring nothing for me, Aylah said only "You know that is not true, Delilah. Now you should eat, and rest, and ready yourself for the Last Dance."

"I cannot do it. I cannot lead the Last Dance. I won't." Even to my own ears, I sounded like a sulky child.

"You can and you will." Aylah hesitated, as if weighing her next words with great care. At last she said, "If tomorrow is to be the last time we two dance for Ascalon and for Atargatis, I wish us to dance well, and with joy. Promise me we will have this, Delilah. Please."

"A wedding gift?" As soon as the words were said, shame burned my blood. *Who now is the better priestess? I, who have fought and protested Our Lady's will in this? Or Aylah, who bows her head and does what Our Lady asks of her?* The answer was humiliatingly clear: I, who prided myself on my devotion to Atargatis and Her Temple, had proven less worthy than Aylah, who so often spoke so mockingly of both.

I bowed my head. "We will dance the Last Dance well, and with joy, heart-sister."

At least we will have that to remember. At least we will have that.

I was told, by some who watched us that day, that never before had Night and Day danced so well—as if we truly were goddesses ourselves. Perhaps it is true, for never before had I given myself so completely to the Dance. I saw nothing but sun dazzling my eyes, felt nothing but pure unthinking delight. For the span of time we danced the Sun Partridge home, guiding the god through the streets of Ascalon, I was truly happy.

After the Last Dance's last steps, my dance-engendered joy drained away. Now Aylah would be given to Samson, and I would lose them both—no, I would lose Aylah. I knew Aylah was right; it seemed that she had no choice. Goddess, oracles, and High Priestess all ordained this marriage. But that did not mean I must watch as my heart-sister gave herself to our enemy.

The Last Dance over, Aylah was taken away to be prepared for her marriage to Samson, for the wedding must take place with unseemly haste. If Samson remained within Ascalon's walls beyond tomorrow's dawn, he would be fair quarry.

I remained behind in our room when the New Moons came to lead Aylah to the ritual bath. Nor did I prepare myself for the ceremony and the feast that would follow. I ordered my maid away, ripped my garments from my body, flung my earrings and necklace and bracelets to the floor. Clad only in my hair, I threw myself onto the bed and buried my face in the pillow. Stuffed with sweet herbs and dream spice, soothing to the mind, today the pillow gave no ease.

Several times during that long afternoon girls came to the doorway and asked that I attend the bride. I ignored them all, refusing to acknowledge I even heard their words.

Then, for a time, I was left alone. The last person who attempted to free me of my selfish grief was Nikkal. She came to me and touched my shoulder. "Delilah? Look at me, that I may speak and know you hear my words."

I could not hold firm against Nikkal's soft concern. I looked up, half-hoping she had come to tell me that I had only dreamed Aylah was being torn away, that all that had passed since the Sun Partridge Festival had never happened.

"Delilah, your heart-sister asks that you help prepare her for her wedding. Will you come and stand her friend in this?"

It was my last chance, and once again I spurned the gift held out to me. "I am ill," I said and turned my head away, so that I stared into the deep blue tiles set into the wall.

For a few moments that I counted out in heartbeats, Nikkal stood there, waiting. Then, at last, I heard the rustle of linen and the chime of ankle-bells, and knew she had walked away.

As Nikkal left, Mottara, favored handmaiden of the High Priestess, entered my room, swift as a weasel. She carried a wine cup; she held it out to me and said, "Drink this; it will ease your heart, at least for a time."

Nor would Mottara listen to my sullen refusal, pressing the clay cup at me until I must clasp it or be anointed with the liquid it held.

"I don't want it," I repeated, and Mottara merely shrugged. "The High Priestess Derceto herself sent it, telling me to give the cup into your hands. I care not whether you drink or pour the Lady's gift onto the floor!"

Mottara stamped her foot, indicating she had lost all patience, and turned her back on me. Slowly, I raised the cup; beneath the tartness of wine lay another scent, a heavy sweetness. *Poppy*, I thought, recoiling a little, and reminded myself that sending me hours of oblivion was a kindness. High Priestess Derceto had not needed to extend such a favor; I must remember to thank her, later.

I even took a sip, but the thick poppy-laced wine sickened me. About to set the wine cup aside, I glanced up to see Mottara half-turned, watching me. So I took another swallow before I put the cup upon the floor beside my bed.

"Leave it there," I said, as Mottara's eyes followed the movement of my hand, studied the position of the wine cup. "I may wish to drink more later," I added, and then flung myself facedown on my pillows. After a moment, I heard Mottara's slow footsteps and the clink of her copper anklets, heard the painted leather curtain pushed aside. I listened hard, but only silence followed. Mottara had left my room, but she had not continued on across the small courtyard.

She waits outside my door. Why? Even the small amount of poppy wine I had drunk slowed my thoughts. Had Derceto's handmaiden been sent to ensure that I did not attempt to stop the wedding ceremony? As if I could—for the Temple had offered Aylah up to Samson as a prize. *As if she were a talent of silver or an iron sword—*

No, not silver, not iron. Gold. They both shine golden as the sun. I closed my eyes and saw twin pillars of fire flare up, flames dancing against darkness.

The image distressed me; even after I opened my eyes again, my blood beat hard beneath my skin, and my breath quickened as if I ran from danger. To calm myself, I picked up the cup from the floor and drank down a hasty mouthful of the soothing wine.

This time the wine and poppy juice comforted me—and it seemed to grant wisdom as well as peace. In my attempts to save Aylah from her fate, I had beseeched those who ruled my world, and been rebuffed. But there was one whose aid I had not sought with enough fervor, enough faith.

I had not truly asked Our Lady Atargatis. I had not offered enough. I understood that, now.

Now I could go before Her and beg Her aid. This time She might listen, and grant my petition.

I must form my words carefully, must truly offer Her myself. And perhaps— perhaps . . . I found myself thinking again of silver, and of sword-blades, and of hot sun. *No, no. That is no way to plead for Her favor.* My petition to Atargatis must be as perfect as my dances before Her, and for the same reason: to honor Her.

So as Aylah stood in the ritual bath while maidservants and priestesses braided her hair and bound it with ribbons, painted her hands and feet with henna, stroked perfume into her skin, and garbed her for her wedding, I lay upon my bed, smoothing my thoughts so that no more false images rose to trouble me.

For what I would do, for what I would ask, I must be serene, and brave. *I will free you from this marriage, Aylah. I swear it.*

I kept my vow, no matter that its keeping brought misery to both Aylah and myself. When it was too late, and the man she married had led her away to the world beyond Ascalon, I regretted my harsh words, my cruel withdrawal. But that repentance came later.

As Aylah exchanged the scarlet girdle of a priestess for the sky-blue

veil of a married woman, I offered myself before the statue of the goddess in the Temple's oldest and most holy shrine. There I held out my
hands in supplication and prayed to the goddess I served—prayed in
grief and anger, with a passion that burned through my bones like fire.

"O Bright Atargatis, Beloved of gods and men, hear me, I beg You.
Let my heart-sister Aylah not be bound to this man. Let her not remain
Samson's wife. Hear me, Your daughter Delilah, who implores this of
You."

I fell silent and waited, gazing into the idol's jeweled eyes. Nothing
stirred within their depths, save flickering glints, reflections of the little
flames of the lamps set in the wall-niches. Shadows cast by the lamp-
flames caressed the idol's ivory breasts, swirled over the coral scales below her waist. The scent of roses and of myrrh lay heavy in the air.

No answer. Perhaps I had not prayed hard enough, or given enough.
I tried to think what more I could offer up to gain Her aid. I should
have bowed to Her wisdom, accepted that Her answer to my plea was
"No, Delilah. This you may not have."

But I was young, and heartsore, and believed I suffered the worst
pain I would ever know. I pressed on when I should have turned back.

"O Atargatis, you who are the Morning and the Evening Star, the
Moon of all delights, I, Your daughter, beg You to listen with favor to
my plea. Star of the Sea, Lady of Love, grant my petition. Free my
heart-sister from this impious marriage, and I will do whatsoever You
require in return."

Samson

"So great Samson wed a woman of the Philistines, a woman who pleased him well. And a great feast was held, a wedding feast with many guests. A feast where many rich dishes were served and much fine wine was drunk, wine such as the Philistines delighted in.

"And the guests drank deep and the night grew late, and as the moon rose high, the guests demanded to test Samson with riddles before he might set eyes upon his new bride's fair face . . ."

There was one thing in the Philistines' favor. No people Orev had ever heard of planned more sumptuous feasts. And when it came to celebrating a wedding between the handsome hero who had succeeded in tasks a god might hesitate to undertake and the lovely priestess he had fallen in love with at first sight—well, for that occasion nothing was too rich or too fine to spread before the assembled guests.

Most of whom were Philistines, of course. Samson had sent messengers to Zorah, asking his parents to come to his wedding and to bring what guests they wished, but Manoah and Tsipporah did not come. Once Orev thought he'd spotted some of the young hotheads who longed to call Samson "leader" in the crowd of wedding guests; he hoped he was mistaken. He must have been; why would the Foxes come?

The ceremony itself took place in an extravagant pavilion just outside the walls of Ascalon. A crimson cord circled the pavilion; the cord's
ends touched the city walls, making the wedding ground part of the
city itself. The pavilion spread its blue and yellow roof over a space
larger than half a dozen of Zorah's houses. Within, blue smoke coiled
through the air, smoke heavy with the cloying odor of nard. Carpets
woven in designs of lilies and palm trees spread over the ground; tas-
seled cushions lay scattered at the edges of the carpets. Low tables held
golden bowls of fruit and silver trays of sweet cakes.

Orev wasn't sure what to think of the arrangement—better than being trapped within the city, in the event of trouble, but somehow it
seemed odd. He'd expected the wedding to take place within one of the
courtyards of Atargatis's Temple. There was no point in talking with
Samson about the matter; the happy bridegroom only laughed, no matter what Orev tried to tell him.

"Philistine ways are not our ways. Let my bride be married as she
wishes. After we are wed and Yahweh grants us children, she will forget
Ascalon."

That the bride—a priestess dedicated to her own goddess—might
not wish to marry at all seemed not to occur to Samson.

And Orev was forced to agree with Samson's argument that since he
had performed the Three Tasks set him, and been proclaimed worthy
of a priestess's hand in marriage, the Temple of Atargatis had been
more than generous. The bride's promised dowry proved to be a farm
in Timnath, a village two days' journey from Ascalon and only a few
hours' walk from Zorah. Samson and his wife would dwell close enough
to Zorah to please his parents—assuming they could accept a Philistine priestess as their son's bride.

"We shall live happy there," Samson had said. "And you, Orev, if you
grow weary of life upon the road, come and act as steward for me."

"I'm a singer of songs, not a farmer."

"Sing as I farm, then. Music makes a task sweeter."

It was always hard to argue with Samson, harder still to be angry at him. In the face of such manifest joy, Orev's worries over the whole affair seemed to fade to pale shadows.

But Orev soon learned he was not the only man troubled by this lavish and seemingly joyous wedding feast. As he and Samson entered the bridegroom's tent, a figure glittering as one of the Temple idols awaited them, reclining upon the embroidered cushions meant for the bridegroom's use until his summons to the bridal feast.

"My lord Samson?" The words, spoken in a lazy drawl, sent a warning chill down Orev's spine. As if the man sensed this, he smiled and said, "No, I have not been sent to strike down Samson—as if I could." He rose, and bowed, and all the gems hung about his neck and woven in his hair glinted bright as stars. "Permit me to present myself—Aulykaran, brother of Sandarin, who is Prince of the City of Ascalon."

"Greetings, and be welcome," Samson said, even as Orev asked, "And why is the brother of the Prince of Ascalon here?"

Aulykaran smiled. "To give the bridegroom a wedding present, of course. Why else?"

"To poison my wine?" Samson suggested, a remark so sensible that Orev stared at him in surprise.

"Oh, not I. That sort of thing I leave to dear Derceto and my beloved brother. I'd be careful what you eat and drink at your wedding feast, if I were you, Samson." Aulykaran turned his attention to Orev. "You know, harper, I don't think your friend the hero is nearly so foolish as you seem to think him."

"I don't think him foolish," Orev said. "I think him too good-natured. He keeps his temper too well-chained."

Aulykaran studied Samson intently for a moment. "Perhaps. But I would not like to be there when you unbind your temper, Samson."

"I have no need of anger," Samson said.

"Someday you will, and on the day your anger rages free, I trust I shall be far away. Now, about that wedding present—"

"You have not yet answered me," Orev pointed out. "Why are you here at all, let alone bestowing gifts upon your brother's enemy?"

"My brother's foe, not mine. I am here because a bridegroom should be given fitting gifts, and because I enjoy meddling. I also enjoy giving advice, but I find that good advice is so rarely followed. Still, it amuses me to offer my wisdom upon the altar of the gods."

Samson laughed. "I take advice, if it is truly good. Is this good advice your wedding gift to me?"

"In part. First, I shall merely mention that the High Priestess and my dear brother are most certainly enmeshed in schemes almost as elaborate as this wedding. They're up to something, but I, alas, am not privy to precisely what the two of them plot."

"And you are telling me this because . . . ?" Samson asked, and Aulykaran smiled again.

"You see, harper? Not so foolish. Well, Samson, perhaps I tell you this because a wedding should be a joyous occasion—although marriage so seldom seems to be. Perhaps because I prefer peace to taking up the sword. Or perhaps because you seem like a good man, and I meet so few. Or perhaps because your bride comes with a rich dowry and I wish to borrow a pouch of silver from you? Who knows?"

"Perhaps you just wish to cause trouble, my lord Aulykaran." This seemed the most likely explanation to Orev. "At least, you have no need to borrow silver from anyone."

"No? Samson, will you lend me what silver you possess?"

Samson unclasped a bracelet from his wrist and held it out. "Of course. Take this, if you need it."

Orev sighed, and Aulykaran laughed. "Yes, friend harper, I see he is a great trial to you." To Orev's surprise, Aulykaran took the thin bracelet from Samson's hand.

"You will have this back again when you leave Ascalon, which I strongly urge you to do the moment the vows have been said. You have been given asses and servants by the Temple?"

Samson nodded. "Yes. They wait—"

"I know where they wait, and they should wait in vain. Outside this pavilion, to the east, tethered near my own litter and my own slaves, are two strong mules and some provisions for your journey. You will know them by this bracelet of yours, for it will be tied to one of the mules' reins. Take those mules, and your wife—assuming you are truly given one—"

"I have been promised her," Samson said, and Aulykaran lifted his brows and shook his head.

"And I promise," Aulykaran said, "that you would be wise to take your bride, my advice, and the mules, and leave by the swiftest road away from Ascalon. And I wish you joy in your marriage, Samson." He bowed, and strolled out of the tent with the indolent grace of a leopard.

Samson gazed after him, thoughtful. "Do you think we can trust him, Orev?"

"This from you, who trusts everyone?" Orev considered Aulykaran's words, and his cool amused eyes. "Odd as it may sound from my lips— yes, I think we can trust him. I don't know why, but yes."

"Because although he does not like to think it of himself, Aulykaran is a good man at heart." Samson eyed the curtain covering the doorway to the tent. "How long until I am summoned, do you think?"

"Not long enough," Orev said, and Samson laughed.

"I will wait," he said. "But I do not think I care for any wine, Orev. At least, none from a vessel only you and I will drink from."

Derceto

She arrived at the wedding pavilion just as the sun reached zenith and all shadows vanished for a brief span of time. The bearers set down her gilded litter; Derceto stepped out with the grace of long practice. She stood quiet for a breath, letting those who gathered to watch events unfold gaze upon her. She was High Priestess, owed the people of Ascalon the sight of Atargatis's Vessel.

Then she walked, in slow, measured paces, into the vast wedding pavilion. The air trapped within the tent's brilliant cloth walls was hot, but Derceto ignored the minor discomfort. Sandarin awaited her, and she would not grant the Prince of the City even the small satisfaction of seeing her troubled by the heat. She paced across the pavilion, her bare painted feet soundless upon the thick carpets, to the two thrones waiting beyond the wedding fire. Incense smoke swirled in a slow dance through air sweet and heavy as honey. Derceto stepped around the wide brazier in which cedar and sandalwood and nard burned, and sat upon the throne beside Sandarin's.

He said nothing; there was no need for words between them. *We understand each other better than many who have been forty years married.*

Which was why Derceto had ensured that nothing about the wedding feast had been left to chance—or to Sandarin's interference. During the seven days of the Sun Partridge Festival, Temple took precedence over City. It was to the Temple that Samson had delivered himself, and it was the Temple that would claim him.

No matter what the Prince of the City plotted. *For I set my own plans spinning the moment Samson uttered Delilah's name seven days ago.*

Now all lay ready. Samson need only act as any man would on his joyous wedding day. *Eat and drink, Samson. Drink long and deep.* If Samson drank deep enough, he would never wake. If he drank only enough to sleep overlong, he would awake to find himself bound, the Temple's slave. *For at sunrise, festival truce vanishes with the morning mist. And if your power is stronger than that which lies in the wine, and you do not sleep at all . . .*

Why, then the guests Derceto had so carefully arranged to attend would ensure that even if Samson lived to carry his wife away from the feast, he would go no farther than the nearest bend in the road. Derceto studied the guests who crowded the pavilion, seeking her unwitting allies. They thought themselves clever, believed they had slipped into the wedding uninvited and unnoticed, rather than as her own chosen guests. *I ensured the news of Samson's wedding to Atargatis's priestess traveled far. I knew it would entice them, lure them here.* Derceto studied the crowd, her eyes seeking. Ah, there they were—a band of uncouth, ill-clad louts. "Foxes," they called themselves, sworn to Samson.

Mad foxes, keen to bite, yearning to see Samson prove himself the hero-king they demanded he be. *You Foxes wish to see Samson bring down the Five Cities.* Derceto gazed upon a slender youth—no, a maiden, despite her warrior's garb—who glared about her with angry eyes. *You wish to see Samson slay us all. How will you like watching as he bends his head before me, the High Priestess of Atargatis? As he claims a Philistine priestess as his bride? Will you follow him then, Foxes? I think you will not.*

Of all who lurked within the crowd of wedding guests, awaiting her signal—or, Derceto was certain, Sandarin's—it was Samson's own Foxes who would most long to slay him.

"Ah, the bridegroom comes," Sandarin said, and Derceto set aside her silent gloating and nodded. She took the opportunity to slant a glance at Sandarin. Yes, the Prince stared meaningfully at two men standing beside one of the many copper bowls piled high with honey-glazed fruits.

Too obvious, O Prince. And only one string to your bow—your own bought men with hidden knives, I suppose. Derceto watched as Samson strode into the tent, strong and bright as summer sun. *Now I—I have half a dozen deaths awaiting him. And while you may elude some, Samson, you cannot escape them all.*

Samson came towards her, smiling, stood before her throne and bowed his head. "I have come, Lady of the Lady's Temple, to claim my bride. And to thank you for bestowing her upon me. Your goddess is kind."

If Our Lady is kind, Samson, you will be too drunk to leave before tomorrow's sun rises. No harm could come to Samson during the days and nights the Sun Partridge danced. Even Derceto and Sandarin did not dare violate that law. But if Samson remained one moment beyond the next dawn . . .

"Welcome, Samson. The wedding feast is spread before you—now eat and drink and await your bride." Derceto gazed into Samson's guileless blue eyes, and smiled.

Samson

The wedding feast began at midday, and by sunset, when the bride was brought out from Ascalon to the wedding pavilion, almost every guest was at least half-drunk. The steward assigned by the Temple to tend upon the bridegroom had kept setting full goblets into Samson's hand; Samson had handed most of them, after a courteous sip of the wedding wine, to whomever stood nearest to him. Even so, Orev suspected Samson had consumed far more strong spiced wine than he realized.

A roar of delight arose from the waiting guests. The bride's elaborate palanquin drew near, a massive, glittering affair carried by a dozen Temple eunuchs and escorted by half a dozen priestesses. Orev watched as the bridal procession approached the wedding tent, noted the painted faces of the eunuchs, the gilded breasts of the priestesses. Suddenly he wondered if Samson were wiser than he'd thought. If there was one deed that might repulse those who called themselves "Samson's Foxes" enough to repudiate Samson as their chosen leader, wedding a priestess of Atargatis could be that feat.

For the first time that day, Orev smiled.

The bride's palanquin reached the outer circle of guests; the eunuchs who carried it stopped, and the heavy jewel box that held Samson's prize was lowered to the ground.

Two attendants—priestesses clad in seven-tiered skirts and not much else—drew back the cloth-of-silver curtains; two hands, crimson with henna and gleaming with gold chains, reached out of the palanquin. A eunuch took the bride's hands, helped her to her feet as the wedding guests uttered cries of greeting.

The bride stood motionless as her attendants smoothed her garments. All that could be seen of her were her hands and her feet; a veil of sky-blue cloth woven with gold thread concealed her from crown to ankles. Their task completed, the bride's attendants turned her to face her bridegroom and followed her as she paced across the elaborate carpets. No part of the bride could be seen beneath the gold-heavy veils that cloaked her. In the torchlight, she seemed a pillar of fire moving towards Samson.

She reached the waiting bridegroom and bowed. Samson smiled and reached out his hands to her, but she remained bent before him, while the overdiligent steward set yet another heavy goblet in Samson's hands.

"This cup you must drink—all it holds—to show you accept this woman as your bride."

Samson drained the golden cup, and the veiled bride straightened. "Does not the bride drink too?" he asked, and the steward shook his head.

High Priestess Derceto emerged from the wedding tent. The two priestesses who had escorted the veiled bride from the palanquin to her bridegroom now guided her to stand before the High Priestess.

"Here is the bride you have won." Derceto's voice carried clear and sharp through the murmur of the wedding guests. "Samson, do you claim this woman as your wife?"

"Yes," Samson answered, his eyes upon the veiled figure standing before him. "I completed all the tasks you set me, and now I claim my prize."

It seemed to Orev that the High Priestess smiled—or perhaps the shadows thrown by the torches created that illusion. "Then take her hand and she who was a priestess of Bright Atargatis becomes wife of Samson."

As Orev watched, the bride offered her left hand to Samson, who grasped it in his. Samson reached out to lift the bride's veil, but she shrank back and the High Priestess said, "It is not our custom to unveil the bride at the wedding feast—it brings ill fortune. She will lift her veil for you at the proper time. Now it is time to rejoice."

Upon these words, the wedding guests pressed forward, twining long garlands of ribbons and flowers about the new-wed pair. More wine was offered, and the musicians began a lively tune on flutes and timbrils.

The wedding guests began to dance, either grasping others' hands and circling the bride and groom or twirling about in ones or twos like maddened quail in springtime. Torches flared higher, the slaves poured more and more wine, the dancing grew more frenzied. Half-worried, half-sober, Orev shoved his way through the raucous crowd towards Samson, who sat upon a heap of cushions beside his hidden bride. For a few moments it seemed impossible to get near Samson; the crowd seemed to push Orev back, sending him into dizzying spirals, caught up by the wild dancers.

Finally Orev used his chief weapon: his harper's voice could, at need, cut through other sounds like a blade. "Samson!" he called, and Samson lifted his head and glanced around.

Seeing Orev being borne away by the movement of the wedding guests, Samson stood and beckoned. "My friend—let my friend come to me," he ordered, and Orev was at last able to make his way to Samson's side. "Orev, friend!" Samson flung a heavy arm over Orev's shoulders, tried to drag him down to sit beside him. "Come drink with us!"

Samson held a large silver cup set with lapis and coral. As he gestured, wine slopped over the edge, dark as blood in the torchlight. Orev glanced at Samson's bride; she held a smaller cup still full of wine in a hand half-hidden by a web of ruddy gold from fingers to wrist.

So she does not trust the wine. Perhaps there were other reasons Samson's new bride did not drink, but Orev seized upon that suspicion. "Samson—" He put his hand on the wine cup. "Now that you are wed, I think it time you took your bride home."

Samson stared at him, which didn't surprise Orev. But he sensed other eyes studying him; the bride seemed to have shifted, that she might face him. Or so Orev thought, for he had never seen a more heavily veiled woman. What she looked upon, what she thought, only she behind that veil knew.

Samson turned to his bride. "What says my wife? Shall we leave the guests to their merriment and go to our own house?"

Silently, she inclined her head. Then she set aside her wine cup and held out her hand, not to Samson, but to Orev. Taking the hint, Orev grasped her hand and helped her rise—not an easy task, as her jeweled and gold-threaded garments weighed heavy as stones.

Samson drank down the last of the wine and tossed his own cup aside before jumping, rather unsteadily, to his feet. "Come, then, wife. Who needs a wedding feast when a wedding night awaits us?"

Not that we shall reach Timnath tonight, Orev thought. But two sunsets from now, they should be safely at the farm Atargatis's Temple had bestowed upon the bride as her dowry. Now they had only to leave the wedding in peace—an odd thought, but then, this was an odd wedding.

"Let us leave now, Samson, and quietly." But even as he spoke the words, Orev knew it was too late for that.

For Samson had pulled his bride away from Orev's steadying hand and swung her up into his arms. "Behold my bride, friends! We leave you to celebrate our wedding—eat and drink and dance as pleases you. Fare well."

This produced cries of outrage; the wedding guests objected. The groom must not steal away the bride—"Without payment!"

"I have paid for her thrice over," Samson said, laughing. His bride lay silent and unmoving in his arms, as if holding her breath. "What more can you ask of me?"

Orev scanned the crowd of guests, and so saw one of the guests glance across to where High Priestess Derceto sat beside the Prince of the City. Derceto nodded; so slight a movement Orev nearly missed it.

"A riddle! It is the custom here. The groom cannot take away the bride unless he can answer one riddle and ask another that none of us can answer." This demand was called out by a man who sounded suspiciously sober.

Within the space of three breaths, the guests all were chanting "A riddle! A riddle!" and, to Orev's dismay, others demanded, "A prize! A prize for the winner!"

"This is not good." Orev spoke softly, pitching his voice so that only Samson might hear.

"No. I know no riddles, Orev." Samson seemed baffled rather than angry.

The guests began to quarrel over who would ask the guest-riddle, and Orev began to wonder if even Samson's canny strength could help them escape. *For Derceto there has no intention of releasing us from this wedding feast. She has planned this. Does she think the guests will slay Samson in a quarrel over these riddles?*

That seemed all too likely at the moment. The guests surrounded them now, bearing, to Orev's eyes, an odd resemblance to Samson's Foxes in their zealous insistence that Samson give what they demanded.

Just as Orev began to glance around for a weapon, one of the guests called out, "I shall ask the wedding riddle. And when Samson answers it, I shall reward him with my admiration for his cleverness." Honey-smooth, the voice silenced the rowdy guests. They turned to look at a man leaning against one of the tent-poles; willow-slender and garbed in saffron linen girdled with turquoise and copper, Aulykaran, brother to the Prince of the City, regarded the scene before him with languid eyes.

"That's no prize!" someone called out, and the man glanced briefly at the protester.

"I beg to differ; surely Aulykaran's admiration is worth more in the market than another man's gold." Aulykaran smiled, and gestured toward Samson. Each movement was graceful, slow as if he moved through water. "What says the happy bridegroom? Will you hear my riddle, O tamer of bulls?"

"I will," Samson said.

"Oh, dear—now I must create a riddle. Now let me think—" Aulykaran turned his gaze upon the wedding guests and added, "Perhaps you should continue amusing yourselves; I think slowly, as some of you already know."

Orev shot a glance over at the High Priestess and the Prince of the City. Derceto's face revealed nothing. The Prince glared at Aulykaran— a man noted for both elegance and indolence. Apparently Aulykaran desired for reasons of his own to thwart either his brother the Prince or the High Priestess. *Or both. Yes, I think both.*

Tilting his head, Aulykaran slowly closed his eyes. The pearls in his ears—sea-gems the size of a dove's egg—trembled against his cheeks. At last he said, "I have it. Now listen carefully, my savage friend—are you certain you are not too weary for this? Why not set the girl down? I believe she has feet to stand upon."

Samson glanced down at his wife, who lay quiet in his arms, and smiled. "I am not too weary. Say your riddle, man of the Five Cities."

"So you can speak for yourself, how charming. I had heard otherwise." Aulykaran slanted a glance at Orev that drew laughter from the nearest guests. Refusing to be drawn into argument, Orev merely said, "I am a harper; I speak for everyone and no one. And Samson may not grow weary, but I do."

"Very well." Aulykaran yawned, and then said, "What have I got in my pouch?" Again he tilted his head, as if in inquiry; the pearls hanging from his ears swung with the movement, caught torchlight, and glowed warm fire.

Many of the wedding guests laughed, hearing a vulgar meaning in the seemingly innocent question. Samson took the query at the common value of its words, but he, too, laughed.

"Simple enough—the answer is nothing, for you borrowed silver from me not so long ago," he replied, and Aulykaran bowed.

"You are correct, and are now the richer by my sincere admiration. You have answered a riddle; now you must ask one."

"That's not a riddle!" someone roared out in the slurred tones of the very drunk, only to be suppressed by others even drunker.

"Well, Samson?" Aulykaran asked. "You have promised to pose a riddle; now you must perform for us."

"Then I shall do as I have promised." Samson paused, and Orev only hoped his friend could think of something, and quickly.

At last Samson said, "I saw strength bring forth sweetness, and I saw sweetness bring forth strength."

"That's not a riddle either!" The outraged complaint set off another round of argument among the drunkest wedding guests. Orev ignored them, watching the High Priestess and the Prince of the City gaze at Samson. Perhaps it was no more than the shifting light, but Orev thought he saw fear shadow their faces.

Aulykaran held up his hand. "Silence, friends. I must think—and you all know how difficult a task that is for me. So while I think, you drink."

Laughter from the closest guests, and shouts of agreement. Aulykaran bowed, then regarded Samson consideringly. "I am not precisely certain," Aulykaran said, after pressing his fingertips to his forehead, ostentatiously considering the question, "but—no, that cannot be the answer. Let me try again."

There was a brief silence, then, as Aulykaran began sipping at his wine, apparently forgetting the entire matter of riddles, someone shouted out, "The answer! We must have the answer!"

Aulykaran set down the golden goblet, stared about as if astonished. "Then why ask it of me? How am I to know?" He lifted his hand, gesturing towards Samson and the bride. "Bridegroom, I yield. What is the answer to your riddle?"

"A stone lion became a hive for bees. What is stronger than a lion, and what is sweeter than honey?"

"How true. I declare Samson the victor, and free to depart with his new bride." Bowing to Samson, Aulykaran blithely ignored the glare Sandarin directed at him. The Prince of the City clearly was not pleased with his brother.

Lord Aulykaran, you are amazingly helpful; I wonder why? But Orev decided the answer to the riddle of Aulykaran's assistance could wait. Leaving this wedding swiftly, safely, was far more urgent a matter.

Samson smiled. "I thank you, friend, and now that I have answered your riddle and you have not answered mine, by your own custom I take my bride and leave you all to feast in our honor."

Aulykaran bowed. "Long life and happiness to you and your bride. Now I return to the chief delight of such occasions—the pleasure of good wine."

And to Orev's relief, most of the wedding guests joyously returned to eating and drinking. Unhindered, Samson walked out of the pavilion, his veiled bride in his arms. Before Orev followed, he looked again at the High Priestess and the Prince of the City.

This time, there was no mistaking the signal the High Priestess gave; a motion of her hand that drew obedient nods from half a dozen men and women who stood aloof from the feasting. After Derceto's gesture, those who had awaited her order mingled with the others, once again becoming mere wedding guests whose only interest was feasting and drinking.

Slowly, Orev made his way out of the wedding pavilion, thinking hard. The High Priestess and the Prince of the City plotted still—that was clear as springwater . . .

"Orev! Let us leave this place and go home." Samson caught the harper's arm and guided him to an elaborate litter—Lord Aulykaran's, for beside it were two sturdy mules. Samson's bride waited there; Samson set her upon one of the mules, a sleek gray. Bulky packs had been tied behind the saddles; Orev hoped the bundles held something useful, such as food and clothing. "Ah, the wedding gifts from Aulykaran," Samson said. "So we will reach Timnath all the sooner."

Samson helped Orev to mount the second mule, then led both away from the pavilion, towards the high road that led northeast, to Timnath. Samson had freed Ari to accompany them, and the two mules, after wary inspection, decided the lion presented no threat.

"Mules have more sense than horses or donkeys," Samson said. "See how they understand Ari will not harm them? They were a kind gift."

"Samson, why should the Prince of the City's brother bestow such gifts upon you?" Orev found this generosity even odder than the wedding had been.

Samson glanced up at him and smiled. "Orev, did you drink too much wine? You spoke with the man—he wishes only to create mischief and to avoid violence. Now let us go away from here as fast as possible."

Clearly Samson had not imbibed nearly as much wine as Orev had feared. "So you're taking Aulykaran's advice?" Orev asked.

"Don't you think it wise? It was your advice as well." Samson began striding faster, and the mules picked up their steady pace.

They traveled in silence for a time, the full moon casting enough light for them to follow the road safely. At the crest of a long rise, Samson stopped, and they all looked back.

Behind them Ascalon glowed like a pearl beneath the moon. Outside the city wall, the wedding pavilion blazed harsh, its torches warring with the silver moonlight.

"How long do you think they'll feast without the bride and groom there?" Samson asked, and turned to smile at the veiled woman sitting upon the gray mule.

"Until the food and the wine are gone." They were the first words Orev had heard the bride speak; words muted by her heavy veil. Then she said, "Lift my veil, husband. It is time you looked upon your bride's face."

With gentle eagerness, Samson gathered her wedding veil in his hands, lifted the mass of gold-shimmered cloth until she was revealed to his eager eyes. Orev could not see the bride's face, but he could see Samson's, watch as amazement replaced ardor. Silent, the bride reached up and freed her veil from Samson's grasp, flung it back to hang down behind her.

"Samson? What's wrong?" Orev's question was answered as the bride turned her face towards him. *So that is what the High Priestess planned— to cheat Samson of his heart's desire. But why?*

Samson's bride turned back to her husband. "Now you know how Derceto keeps her promises. Do you mean to send me back to the Temple?"

"Do you wish to return there?" Samson asked, and she shook her head.

"I am no longer a priestess, but your wife. Unless you repudiate me?"

Samson stared at her, and for a breath his face seemed carved of stone. Then he laughed, a sound harsh and forced. To his hard-won bride, he said, "There is a tale my people tell, of a man who labored long to win one wife and was given her sister in her stead."

"And what did that man do, when he uncovered the ruse?" She regarded Samson calmly, awaiting his judgment.

"Labored another seven years to earn the other sister," Samson said.

Orev drew in a deep breath. "Why did the Temple—"

"Trick Samson into wedding me? Because I am of lesser value than she whom your heart desired. And because there is a task I am to undertake." She lifted her hands to her tight-braided hair, pulled out two hairpins of intricately carved ivory. She held them out, flat upon her palm.

"Take care how you touch these, unless you wish to sleep forever."

"You are to slay me?" Samson regarded the ivory hairpins, took them carefully into his hands.

"That is what High Priestess Derceto ordered. The Five Cities fear you beyond reason, Samson. They live in terror of your bandit army, your ambition to rule as king over them." She glanced back down the long road to Ascalon. "I think we should go on now. Later we can decide what to do."

Samson offered the hairpins back to her; after a moment's hesitation, she accepted them, wrapped them in a length of her veil and knotted them tightly in the cloth.

"My wife thinks we should travel on," Samson said, and his voice held no emotion that Orev could interpret. "What do you think, Orev?"

I think we should not have come to the Five Cities. I think you should never have asked to wed a priestess of Atargatis. I think you should send this false bride back to her Temple and return to your father's house. But it was far too late for Samson to turn back from his fate now. So after a moment, Orev said the first words that came to his tongue.

"I think that drunken sot at the wedding feast was right, Samson. Those weren't riddles."

Aylah

Leaving the House of Atargatis proved harder than she had thought it would be. She had forgotten that she had known nothing else but Temple life since she was a small, frightened, furious child, that she would be turning her back upon all things familiar to her.

That she would no longer walk through her life hand in hand with Delilah.

She had asked that her heart-sister come to help her prepare for what awaited her, but Delilah had refused. That had sliced keen as ice through her heart, but Aylah understood Delilah's anger and pain. And perhaps it had been better this way, better that they not see one another on this fateful wedding day.

For who knows what Samson may do, once the deception is unveiled? He might beat her, or kill her. Or he might send her back to the House of Atargatis, where she would have to face the fury of a disappointed High Priestess. Aylah hoped he would do none of these things, hoped he would accept her in Delilah's stead. *And of course, he may not live to lead me away from Ascalon. I do not know what Derceto plots, but I doubt I am the only playing-piece upon her game board.*

Aylah lifted her hands and touched the pins that bound up her long pale hair. Ivory set with amber, the sharp ends deep crimson, like a bloody sunset. Henna-dyed, one might think—unless one knew the deadly truth. *You have erred, Derceto. You think me as pious, as dedicated, as poor Delilah. You think I will murder at your command.*

Well, she would not. This marriage to Samson was her one chance to escape the opulent, stifling life of a priestess. And if Derceto plotted, so did she. It had taken very little deliberation to decide who she should enlist as her ally. Aulykaran. Indolent, elegant, good-natured—and clever.

When she had revealed Derceto's plan to him, Lord Aulykaran had readily agreed to aid Aylah—and when Aylah gazed steadily at him, and asked him why he would do this, Aulykaran had merely smiled and said, "You underestimate the pure joy of meddling in other people's affairs, my lady Sun. Now tell me why you wish to disobey the High Priestess and leave behind not only a soft life and great fame, but your dearest sister." Aulykaran still smiled, but his eyes regarded her keenly, judging.

"If I had not offered to become Samson's bride in Delilah's place, Derceto would have given the task of slaying him to Delilah. If the Temple asked such a thing of her, it would kill Delilah's heart. I cannot let that happen. And as for why I wish to go with Samson—well, I am no true priestess. I long for a quiet life as wife and mother. This is my chance to gain that life."

Aylah had regarded Aulykaran, gauging how much she must offer him. "If you truly will aid me in this—help me get safely away, and Samson and his harper friend as well—you may have whatever you would ask of me." To bed Lord Aulykaran would be no hardship, especially if it ensured his cooperation.

But Aulykaran had only said, "To see Derceto's face, and my brother's, when Samson once more slips through their cat's-cradle plots will be payment enough. Now, I suppose you have the entire affair planned out, and need only tell me what my part in this entertainment is to be, while I need only follow your commands. But I do have one last question for you, Priestess Aylah, before I consent to oblige you in this."

"And what is that?"

"Have you no fear of what Samson the mighty warrior will do to you, once you unveil your face to him, and he learns he has been cheated?"

Aylah smiled. "No. The Temple has taught me well how to delight a man, and whether he truly loves Delilah or not, Samson is a man, my lord. I will please him, for I will be a good loyal wife. I will make his home happy, and I will joyously bear his children. Delilah—she is not meant to be a man's wife. She would yearn always for the Temple, and for Our Lady's Dance."

Aulykaran regarded her steadily; for once no laughter brightened his eyes. "A good answer, Priestess. Very well, I will help you—and Samson, of course. He seems a good man, and the gods know there are few enough of those in any land. Now tell me what you would have me do."

Her faith in Aulykaran's abilities had proven right. His indulgence in whatever chanced to amuse him, his dedication to pleasure and mischief, meant that nothing he chose to do seemed odd. Aylah watched from behind the heavy bride's veil as Aulykaran guided the wedding's rituals into the most harmless path.

Even the wedding riddles had been turned into mere foolish jests— and Aulykaran had carefully ensured that no one else gained the chance to ask anything more serious, more difficult to solve. *We both owe you much, my lord Aulykaran. I know it, and I think Samson knows as well.*

For she had swiftly decided that Samson was no mindless strongman. She had watched him closely and realized that, despite the endless cups he waved about, Samson actually drank very little of the overrich wedding wine. And when he had laughed, and swung her up into his arms to carry her from the fire-bright pavilion, his hold upon her was firm and steady. Nor did his breath smell too strongly of wine.

He seemed kind as well. He had carried her to the mules Aulykaran had assured her would be awaiting them, lifted her onto the nearest beast's back. Then he stood, his hands resting upon her waist, and said, "This is truly what you wish?"

A fine time to ask! Aylah had thought, as she silently inclined her head, assenting—and to her astonishment, Samson had smiled.

"A fine time to ask you, I know," he had said, and for a cold breath Aylah had feared he could hear her thoughts. "But I could hardly ask it when all the wedding guests stared at us, and your High Priestess watched you. I was told you came to me willingly. Was that truth?"

He had regarded her as steadily as if he could see through the glittering threads of her veil. Aylah had drawn in her breath deeply, calmed herself before she answered. "It was truth," she said. "And it would be wise to take me away from this place now."

She did not speak again until Samson halted, turning to look back down the long road to Ascalon. The city gleamed pearl-bright against the dark sea glittering beyond; the wedding pavilion flared, torchlight warring with moonlight. *This may be the last time I shall look upon Ascalon, the last time I shall see the Temple.* The full moon's light transmuted the Temple's rooftops from brazen gold to silver and shadow. Somewhere beneath those shining rooftops, Delilah lay upon her bed . . .

Delilah, who would not even come to help dress me for my wedding. Aylah had not expected Delilah to be at the wedding itself, of course; one glimpse of her would have ruined Derceto's scheme. *But I had hoped she would at least clasp my bracelets, pin my veil to my hair. I suppose even I am a fool at times.*

For Delilah mourned not only the loss of her heart-sister, but the loss of a man she had seen only twice. A man Delilah did not admit, even to herself, that she desired. *But I know you hunger for Samson's love, Delilah, even if you do not. Of course you would not come to adorn me as bride—to yield me to a man you yourself yearn to claim.*

Still, to leave Delilah without saying farewell— *No. I will not think of that. Delilah must remain safe, and I must . . . I must take great care what I do next.* For Aylah now played her own game, not Derceto's, and the next move would win or lose all. She drew upon the long years of Temple training to summon calm acceptance. *I must forget that I have lost Delilah, no matter what I do. Derceto has ensured that, whether I obey her or defy her. I must claim my own life now.*

When she was certain she could speak softly, her voice uncolored by fear or sorrow, she said, "Lift my veil, husband. It is time you looked upon your bride's face."

She had known that this would be the crucial moment, that all the rest of her life, and of Delilah's, depended upon what Samson did when he learned he had been tricked. This was a man who had slain many men, whose strength and power caused the Five Cities to tremble for fear of what he might do . . .

Samson stood before her, gathered up the veil that wrapped about her like silent flame. The gold woven through the cloth weighed heavily upon her; she would welcome release from the stifling burden. He lifted the veil, and soft night air caressed her face. She forced herself to breathe, to remain calm. To study the face of the man gazing into her eyes.

His own eyes shone—first with passion, then, as he stared at her, with the cold glint of fury. *Now he realizes he has been cheated. Now he may strike out, and if that is all he does, I shall be fortunate.* Unlike Delilah, Aylah had been beaten many times when she was carried across the wide world as an unruly slave; she knew how to endure blows.

But the accusation, the anger that she had expected to lash out at her, did not come. Samson said nothing, merely stood and looked upon her, and she saw the rage fade from his eyes. It was his friend, the dark lame harper, who spoke first, asking what troubled Samson. Aylah turned to face Orev, who fell silent as he, too, saw whom Derceto had given into Samson's hands . . .

At last, Samson laughed—a bit harshly, but still, he laughed. And as he spoke, telling her that she need not return to the Temple unless she wished to, Aylah listened to his calm voice and smiled. Nor did her revelation that she had been sent to be his death cause Samson to lose his temper. *He is truly strong, your Samson.* Aylah spoke the words only in her mind, wishing silently that Delilah could hear them.

For this was not a man so simple-hearted he felt neither fear nor anger. *This man is so strong he can control his own rages—as if anger and lust were unruly stallions he must curb.* She studied Samson as he led her mule along the road away from Ascalon. *You are angry, Samson, but you will not loose that anger upon me. I wish I could tell you the whole truth—that Delilah would rather die than leave the Temple. I will make you a better wife than Delilah ever could. Perhaps, in time, you will come to love me—at least enough to keep us both content.*

But now she had more important worries than whether her new husband would love her at all. *He is a man, and I can deal with a man well enough. Once I take him to my bed, he will look upon me with more favor.* When she held Samson in her arms, beguiled his senses with the arts of pleasure she had been taught . . . *You may still yearn for Delilah after that, Samson, but you will crave me as well.*

Samson worried her less than did the High Priestess. When Derceto learned that Samson still lived, that Aylah, rather than returning to the Temple, remained with Samson as his wife, her fury would be deadly. *I must warn Samson that we have an enemy venomous as a serpent and vicious as a wounded leopard. If we are to live long and happy, we must take great care. Derceto will not forget I have betrayed her.*

They traveled onward into the day, until the sun stood high above them, and Ascalon and its dangers lay far behind. They no longer walked the high road; Samson had led them across the low hills, cutting half a day from their journey. Now, at midday, he led the mules to the shade of a small grove of willows.

"Willows mean water," Samson told Aylah as he lifted her down from the mule's back. "We can let the beasts rest here."

Willow, a tree favored by Bright Atargatis. Aylah decided to take this as a good omen for what she now must do—truly become Samson's wife. *I must lure him into my arms, take him into my body, and I must do it in daylight, not in darkness.* Samson must not be given the chance to lie with her and pretend he held another in his arms. *You must see me, Samson. Me, not Delilah.*

So while Samson tended to the mules, Aylah went over to Orev, who stood staring at the small spring bubbling between the willow-roots. "I ask a favor of you. Will you leave us alone here, Samson and I, until the shadows lengthen again?"

Orev lifted his eyes to gaze upon her face; Aylah regarded him steadily. "Do you think to make him love you?" the harper asked at last, and she shook her head.

"I think to be his wife. He cannot possess Delilah, and he cannot forget her. But that is no reason he and I should not be content together. Will you do as I ask?"

"I have a new song I must practice, and for that I need to be alone. Beyond that rockfall should be far enough." Orev untied his harp from the pack and began to walk away, slowly. Just past the willows, he stopped and turned. "Samson has a soft heart," he began, and Aylah smiled.

"I know," she said. "Do not trouble your own heart over this, Orev. I am not the woman he dreamed of, but I am the woman who can make him happy. Now go and practice your art, and I will remain here and practice mine."

Orev stared at her, silent, and then did as she asked. When he was out of sight, Aylah studied the willow-grove and selected a spot well-shaded by the flowing leaves, where moss grew thick as lamb's wool. There she spread her wedding veil upon the cool ground. And when Samson walked towards the willows, she held out her hand.

"Come, Samson. Come and rest for a time. Please, do not refuse, for I need your help. It took six handmaidens to dress me, and I cannot free myself of these stifling garments."

She had been right; Samson was but a man, after all. And if he wished he held Delilah close against his heart instead . . . *Well, that I am too wise to ever ask, and he is too kind to ever answer.*

Good marriages had been forged of less precious virtues.

. . .

That night they camped on a low hillside, and Aylah lay quiet, pretending to sleep, so that she might hear what Samson said to Orev
when he spoke freely. She had to listen carefully, for Samson kept his
voice soft, and the night wind sighed, half-concealing words. But she
heard Orev praise her, pointing out her virtues to Samson, who bade
him be silent.

"For I know what you try to do, Orev, and it is kindly meant." Samson spoke without either anger or joy. "But I am not a fool, no matter
what you sometimes think, and I know I must be content with what
Fate has given me now."

"She is beautiful," Orev murmured.

"She is better than that," Samson answered. "Aylah is kind and
clever, and has a good heart. She will be a good wife to me."

A pause. Then Orev said, "Tell me you will let that suffice. Tell
me—"

"Tell you I have forgotten Delilah? No, Orev. I will not tell you
that."

"Then promise you will not go down into Ascalon after her. At least
promise that."

"I promise that I will not seek Delilah out in Ascalon. And I promise I will be a good husband to my wife Aylah. But I will promise nothing else."

"You still think to win the other, then." Orev's words fell heavy on
the night air.

"I think I must thank Yahweh for the gift of Aylah, and I think that
if He denies me Delilah now, there is a reason. Go to sleep, Orev. We
still have a long walk before us tomorrow."

When Samson came and lay beside her, Aylah waited until his
breathing slowed. She turned and slid her arm around his waist, pressed
herself against him. As he slept, she gazed up at the night sky, dark as
Delilah's hair, and vowed again that she would make him happy.

Even though neither of us can ever forget Delilah. Aylah wished she had some power to make Delilah forget Samson. Perhaps time would fade passion. But even if it did not . . .

My choice for us all is better. Now Delilah need never learn the truth about her beloved Temple. Now she will live the life she was born for.

And so will I.

Samson

When they crested the last hill and looked down upon the farm that had been given as Aylah's dowry, Orev sighed inwardly. Even he could tell the land that now belonged to Samson and his bride hadn't been tilled or tended in at least a generation. *I wonder if even Samson can plow and sow and reap a harvest here.*

As if he had heard Orev's thought, Samson said, "The land rests, and the house and outbuildings can be repaired. A fine dowry for you, wife."

Aylah smiled. "All that is needed is a roof on the house, and perhaps a new wall. Truly a generous dower, husband."

Already Samson and his substitute bride had grown comfortable with each other. Now safely away from the Temple, Aylah spoke freely, jesting with Samson as if she had been married to him for years instead of days.

At first, Orev had worried that Aylah, accustomed to the pampered, indulged life of a priestess in Ascalon, would prove a curse rather than a blessing. But she had shed her elaborate wedding garments when they first stopped to rest at the willow-spring, and the bridal gems as well. When they moved on the next morning, they traveled not with Aylah, Priestess of Atargatis, but with Aylah, Samson's wife.

Orev watched her walking beside Samson, admired the strength and power in her steady strides. That she had been one of the Temple's dancers showed in every graceful move. Apparently she was incapable of awkwardness. She had unbound her hair and plaited it into two braids that fell to her waist. Her pale hair glowed against the blue linen gown that covered her from neck to ankles, and its long sleeves hid the serpent tattoos coiling about her arms. Sturdy sandals protected her feet from the hard road.

Now where did she acquire such suitable garments? One might almost think she had planned her escape from the Temple, truly wished to be a humble farmer's wife.

"Are you tired, wife?" Samson asked. "If you are, you must ride your mule."

"For the honor and profit of the Temple, I danced long hours, danced until my feet bled. Walking will not tire me." She gazed down at fields overgrown with nettles and wild grass. What had once been a tidy small orchard stood between the fields and the house; here, too, the weeds had grown thick and heavy among the almond trees. Orev thought there were other trees as well, apple and cherry and lemon, perhaps. All the trees were so neglected Orev could only hope some still bore fruit.

"It looks very pretty—from here," Aylah said, "but I know nothing of farming, or how to judge whether this land is good or ill." She paused, added, "Although I think . . . ill."

"Oh, there is nothing here hard work won't mend. Let us go down now and see what needs to be done," Samson replied.

"Everything," Orev said, and knew the others did not hear. *Ah, well, this proves Aylah spoke truly about one thing, at least.* For it seemed clear enough that the Temple's ruler had not expected Samson ever to set eyes upon the farm that had been given as Aylah's dowry.

An hour later, Orev learned that, while Aylah seemed placid as a desert pool, her wit was as keen as his own. They reached the farm, and while Samson tended to the mules, Orev and Aylah walked slowly over to inspect the house. Or, rather, the remains of the house.

"Do you know what I don't understand?" Orev asked, and Aylah turned her winter-dawn eyes upon him, waiting. "Clearly the High Priestess did not expect Samson to live to see what you brought as your dowry, and so any wretched plot of land would do. But this farm belongs—"

"Belonged," Aylah corrected.

"Very well, belonged. A farm belonging to so great a temple—why has it been left to rot? Where is the profit in that?"

"That is all you do not understand? Then you are a fortunate man indeed, Harper Orev." Her voice held no hint that she jested; her face remained smooth as a dancer's mask.

"Fortunate, but still unenlightened. This farm poses a greater riddle than any offered up at your wedding." Orev smiled, and to his delight, Aylah smiled back.

"The answer to this riddle is simple enough. The farm was an atonement offering after the man who owned it killed his wife and children, and was himself slain by her brothers, who then gave the farm to the Temple. Since murder had been done here, and the land stained with blood, the farm must lie fallow and untouched for seven years."

"And have seven years truly passed, or has the Temple given Samson cursed land?" Orev asked, and Aylah glanced slantwise at him.

"Truly seven years have passed. You cannot think the Temple would act in an impious manner?"

Before Orev could answer with laughter, Aylah turned to greet Samson, who strode towards them.

"Home at last," Samson announced when he stood beside them, gazing at the farmhouse. The building might be halfway to collapse, but Samson ignored its faults. Smiling, he turned to Aylah and swung her up into his arms. She smiled back—already, Orev saw, she found it hard not to smile when Samson did—and slid an arm around his neck.

"Wait, Samson, and I will unbar the door." Orev stepped forward, but Samson shook his head.

"No need for that." Samson strode forward, pushed the door open with his foot. The heavy wood door wobbled, then seemed to twirl like a dancer before it fell backwards into the house. "I'll need to mend that," Samson said, and carried his bride over the threshold—and the door—into her new domain.

Orev followed, and looked around at the empty dwelling. A large roofless courtyard was flanked by the wings of the house. Ancient bricks formed walls that needed plastering; the stairways to the second floor and to the roof had few steps free of holes. Orev decided to let Samson be the first to ascend them. *Land and house not touched for seven long years. Let us see how you conduct yourself now, priestess-wife.* An uncharitable thought, but the urgent pace of the journey had wearied Orev; his lame foot throbbed, and pain flashed like lightning up his leg if he stepped wrong.

Samson set Aylah upon her feet. "Well, it was once a stout enough house. But those stairs need shoring up—see where the bricks have shifted? The side wall must be rebuilt, too. And the roof must be repaired, and the beams sag. And—"

"And forty other things need mending," Aylah said, "but not now. Now I must see if the kitchen-yard still exists, or if the oven and fire pit, too, must be rebuilt."

"Oh, if they are gone, that is easily remedied." Samson flung his arm around her shoulders, and the two of them disappeared into the rooms beyond.

Orev moved outside to the nearest spot in which he could sit in shade. *Well, Samson seems happy enough, and the lady, too. I wonder—* A crash from within yanked his attention back to the neglected house. "Samson?" he called, cautious. The house could easily hold traps for Samson and his bride . . .

Samson appeared in the doorway. "Some old wine jugs fell over, but they were empty anyway," he said. "Orev, why don't you come in and sit down in comfort? There's a stool, and a bed frame."

"I don't suppose the bed ropes are strung?"

"No, but that's easy mended."

"There's no bedding," Orev pointed out.

"Well, no. But my wife gives you her permission to unpack the garments and cloth sent with her and use them as you will." Samson disappeared into the dimness of the house once more. There was another noise, this one harder to identify until a pair of squirrels fled out the door, chattering bitter complaints. The next sound rang clear—Aylah's laughter. It was the first time Orev had heard her laugh.

The first time but not, Orev trusted, the last. The graven image Samson had carried off from Ascalon had softened with each step they took towards the farm, and a new life. *She becomes more woman and less priestess as each moment passes. Perhaps this mad marriage of Samson's will bring him joy after all. Perhaps he will forget the dark one, Delilah—and let this one make him happy.*

Aulykaran

The day was hot, and Aulykaran already half-bored when his brother strode onto the rooftop garden. Aulykaran was proud of that garden, a paradise upon his own roof. Usually, of course, the garden was a quiet paradise . . .

"I don't remember inviting you," Aulykaran said, setting aside the roll of papyrus. Fresh from Egypt, and supposedly a catalog of earthly delights that would make Atargatis Herself blush, the book was far tamer than most of the scribblings on the city walls.

"I'm the Prince of the City," Sandarin pointed out.

"Yes, Brother, I know. I also know you never come to me unless you want something. Do tell me; it's far too hot for riddles."

Sandarin frowned, and Aulykaran smiled, knowing he'd reminded his brother of the total failure of the competing plots against Samson at the hero's wedding to the priestess. Not even Derceto's admirably persistent attempts to poison Samson's lion—symbol, some said, of his powerful god, Yahweh—had succeeded. Aulykaran's favorite eunuch at the Temple had kindly sat with the great beast during the wedding and fed it with meat Aulykaran had provided. *I wonder if Derceto believes the power of Samson's god prevailed, saving both him and his ridiculous pet?*

"I ask only the simplest, most pleasant of favors," Sandarin began, and Aulykaran raised his eyebrows. "Delilah Moondancer's Maiden Night falls soon, and you will be the man who claims it."

"I will, will I? I assume you're paying?" For all that a priestess's Maiden Night supposedly belonged to any man Bright Atargatis led to her, the truth was that the Temple selected a Rising Moon's first man very carefully. Among the requirements was a substantial offering to the Temple. "And why? Do you think the dancer will babble all Derceto's secrets? Or even that she knows any of them?"

Sandarin's face took on the pious expression that warned Aulykaran his brother was about to lie to him—which was only what Aulykaran expected. "Of course not," Sandarin said. "But for so important a Rising Moon, and on so momentous an occasion, I wish to honor Our Lady by—"

"Bribing me to be her first," Aulykaran finished. "Not that I object, you understand—especially as you'll make the very generous offering to the Temple—but unless I know what you hope to gain by this, I won't do it."

"You will." Sandarin already sounded querulous; knew he had lost the argument.

"No, Brother, I will not. It's your quarrel with the Temple, not mine." Aulykaran regarded his brother through lowered lashes and yawned. "That's one reason. Another is that you ask me to labor, and you know I never work. And for a third—"

Sandarin glared at him. "I am the Prince of the City—" he began again, and Aulykaran sighed.

"Yes, Brother, I know." Clearly his brother intended to be difficult today. Sandarin was Prince of the City of Ascalon, held in his hands both riches and power—and yet this prize did not satisfy him . . .

"You aren't listening! Have you heard a word I've said to you? You'd think being offered the chance to claim the Maiden Night of Ascalon's finest dancer would at least interest you."

"Well, of course it interests me." Aulykaran loved beauty almost more than he loved his own indolent way, and when Delilah danced, she became Beauty Incarnate. "But what interests me more, at the moment, my dear brother, is how you intend to persuade the Temple that I am Our Lady's Choice for Delilah's Maiden Night. The last time Derceto gazed upon you, she did not seem overpleased with you. That, by the way, is my third objection to this scheme."

"You will persuade her," Sandarin announced.

"Oh, I will, will I? I doubt mere words will serve here—how much are you willing to pay, Brother, for this favor? And why, by the way, do you care who is granted the gift of Delilah's initiation into the Lady's sweetest Dance?"

"Women like you. You'll please even a virgin priestess."

"Ah, and you think Delilah will be so enthralled by my touch that she will become your spy in the enemy's camp? Or to be more accurate, in the enemy's Temple?" Aulykaran laughed softly and shook his head. "You're wrong, Sandarin. Delilah Moondancer loves Bright Atargatis more than she will ever love any man." He considered the matter, weighed the potential for becoming ensnared in his brother's schemes against the undoubted pleasure of doing as his brother asked. "Still, as you shall pay for it, I'm certainly willing to wait for her in the pleasure booth."

"That's all I ask," Sandarin assured him.

"All you ask at the moment, anyway," Aulykaran said. "Still, for me to own the Moondancer's Maiden Night will be amusing—for me and for her—and I'm sure you'll get around to demanding repayment in some form or other in your own good time."

"So you'll do it?" Sandarin said, and Aulykaran sighed.

"I know I'll regret this—eventually—but yes, Brother, I will do it. Now go away and let me think how best to approach the Temple on this delicate matter."

After his brother had, most reluctantly, left—for Sandarin wished to argue until Aulykaran agreed with him—Aulykaran picked up the Egyptian scroll once more. Slowly unrolling the scroll, he contemplated his brother's latest scheme. *Now what advantage can Sandarin possibly gain by*

purchasing Delilah's Maiden Night for me? Not even for himself, which might make some
sense—no, he wishes the Temple to squander such a treasure on his useless younger
brother . . .

Ah, I see.

Sandarin could hardly believe so pious a priestess would act as in-
former, no matter how much she might favor Aulykaran after a night
spent with him. But Delilah was one of the Temple's treasures, her
Maiden Night a great prize. Squandering that prize upon Aulykaran
would ensure that Derceto could not use it in any scheme she might
cherish. To thwart Derceto, Sandarin would pay almost any price.

For once, Aulykaran thought his brother had been almost clever.

Delilah

I did not see Aylah again for half a year, and then it was none of my doing that brought about our meeting. Looking back upon that half-year after my heart-sister had been reft from me, I see that Derceto made certain I had not even a heartbeat of time to miss Aylah or think of the man who had won her, or to grieve, or to think for myself. Derceto charged Nikkal with my care, and also ordered that I study under each teaching priestess who had even half an hour to spare for me. Every moment of my day was filled, from Dawn Singing to the Sunset Prayers; my teachers worked me hard, and I fell into my bed each night so weary I could not lie awake and brood.

Then, as suddenly as the extra lessons had begun, they ceased. When I asked Nikkal why, she smiled and laid her hand upon my cheek. "Because, Delilah, it is time to prepare you to become a Full Moon." Nikkal smiled again. "Don't stare so—you must have known it would soon be time."

Yes, someday, of course. Some far-off day, long seasons away. My blood suddenly beat swift and hot beneath my skin, with delight or with fear I could not tell. I closed my eyes, to summon serenity, and the image of a sun-gold man dazzled against the darkness. I refused to acknowledge the image, swiftly opened my eyes again to banish it.

"Now?" I said, and Nikkal laughed. "Yes, now. You are more than ready for this honor, Delilah."

I did not feel ready; I felt awkward and alone. I had always thought to ascend the steps of Our Lady's service with Aylah, attaining each new rank together. And although I had been trained well in all the arts a Rising Moon might be called upon to perform, and thought myself mistress of the skills that would be demanded of me, I still felt unprepared, not good enough. Fire danced light-footed across my skin; bees seemed to murmur in my ears, dizzying me. Between one breath and the next, I summoned and then discarded half a dozen different responses, none of them worthy.

I managed to keep my voice steady as I asked, "When will I be called?"

"At the next full moon, you and the others who are to rise with it."

The next full moon was only seven days away. "I cannot," I said. "I am not ready. I will disgrace myself and our House. I—"

"Softly, Delilah. Do not torment yourself with such thoughts. You will be ready, I promise you. The full moon rises in seven nights, and by the time it does, you will be perfect." Nikkal put her arms around me and held me close. I laid my head on her shoulder, listening as she said, "I know you wish Aylah here to walk beside you, but we each follow the path marked for us by Our Lady. Aylah's road lies before her, and yours before you, and they are not the same. You have courage and skill, Delilah. Do not deny yourself or your strength."

Seven Rising Moons would become Full Moons once we had offered ourselves in Our Lady's name, and for the short days before the next full moon, we prepared for the ritual. Our days were spent in the baths, where keen-eyed handmaidens watched over us as we soaked in warm asses' milk to soften our skin. They then poured cool water over us before they scrubbed our skin with crushed almonds mixed with honey. After, we sat with cups of tart pomegranate wine and watched as the

Full Moons most skilled in the arts of the Lady of Love revealed their secrets.

The Day of Choosing began with another bath in water sweet with rose and cassia. The bath servants washed our hair, too, drying it over incense burners so the heady fragrance of nard and myrrh clung to it. Scent was stroked over our throats, the curves of our elbows, the creases between hip and thigh, the backs of our knees, the soles of our feet.

Then began the intricate process of painting our eyes with malachite and lapis, of gilding the nails on our hands and feet, adorning our cheeks and the tips of our breasts with carmine. Our feet and hands had been tinted with henna the day before; now the patterns of spirals and stars glowed red as sunset.

After the painting and gilding, handmaidens skilled in dressing hair took command of the preparations. Our hair was divided: some gathered and bound with scarlet ribbon at the nape of the neck in the Goddess's Knot, the rest spiraled down our backs in long curls. Then we were garbed as Rising Moons for the last time.

And then Nikkal came to lead us to the Court of Peace, for the High Priestess's blessing. I hung back, reaching for Nikkal, seeking comfort against the wild fears that rushed through my blood.

I cannot do this. I am not ready. What if the man does not please me?

What if I do not please him? I will offend Our Lady Atargatis. Why must it be this full moon?

"There is no need to trouble yourself over this, Delilah." Nikkal gently kissed my forehead. "Do you think you are the first girl to make this offering? The first to submit to the Goddess's Choice?"

"But—"

Nikkal put her fingers over my lips. "Be silent. All will be well. Trust me. " She waited, watching my face, until I slowly nodded. Then she smiled. "Good. Now breathe slowly and deeply; summon calm, let peace flow through your body. Come, for the others are as fearful as you, and all need the comfort of the High Priestess's blessing."

We stood upon the steps facing the Great Outer Court, seven Rising Moons still as graven images. In our hands, each of us held the end of a scarlet cord. The seven cords led down the steps, into the court. There the cords had been so laid down that they seemed tangled, an impossible sealed knot. Then the cords separated again, leading out into the street beyond the Temple Gate. We who stood upon the steps could not see where the ends of the cords rested—nor would it matter if we could. The carefully laid labyrinth of cord in the center of the court-yard ensured that no one could tell which priestess held which cord until the man who picked up the other end in the street coiled it back to the priestess who held it in her hands.

Only then would she look upon the lover Our Lady had ordained for her.

Using every trick I had been taught to remain calm, accepting, I waited upon the smooth tiled steps. I tried to think of nothing, not even to wonder what man would follow the thread to my feet. But my mind and heart were willful; I dreamed of a man strong as a lion, sweet as honey—

No, I ordered myself. No, I will not dream of Samson.

We waited, all seven of us, as the minutes stretched long. Waited, and hoped the man who had paid to catch up the scarlet cord that led to each of us would be pleasing. But we knew that the choice was Our Lady's, not ours. I glanced down at the serpents beneath my skin; after this night, the black lines would be shaded in with blue. Someday, if I proved worthy, the sea-dark blue would be adorned with red and gold. I tried to think of that, and of nothing else.

At last a man walked through the Outer Gate, gathering up his cord as he came forward. I could sense the other Rising Moons doing as I did—vainly attempting not to stare, slanting our eyes to see who had been first chosen.

Tall, slender, and moving with the languorous grace of a weary panther, he coiled up the scarlet cord with a careful grace that seemed almost mockery. He made no pretense of confusion when he reached the mass of overlaid cords, merely rolling up the one that was his as easily as if it were the only one in the courtyard.

With elegant deliberation, he finished his task, stopping before me. For a heartbeat, all I could think was that I was first to be chosen. A good omen.

Lord Aulykaran held the ball of scarlet cord that led to me. He smiled, and winked at me, and I could almost hear Aylah's drily amused voice saying, "But Delilah, did you think the Temple would not find you the proper man for your Maiden Night? With the offering he must make to be given *you*?"

I held out my cupped hands, and Lord Aulykaran let the ball of scarlet cord roll from his hand into mine. I closed one hand around the ball of cord and reached out with the other to Lord Aulykaran. He took my hand in his, and I led him into the Temple, and then up the steps along the wall to the roof where the pleasure booths had been built. The full moon would witness Our Lady's Choice.

No priestess ever forgets her Maiden Night. I was twice blessed; I knew the man Our Lady chose for me, and I also knew him a master of pleasures.

I had danced at many feasts given by Lord Aulykaran, and knew him to be hard to please, but generous to those who did please him. I knew he sang as well as a master harper. I knew he favored pearls over any other gem. I knew many women would eagerly pay to lie with him, if they could.

We climbed in silence, walked across the roof as the full moon shone above the eastern hills. I chose the booth farthest from the stairs, and led him into it.

The booth was created of standing screens intricately carved from cedar. Cushions stuffed with lamb's wool and feathers covered the floor.

There was no roof; we would be able to watch the stars and moon as they soared above.

I pulled the spangled curtain that served as door and turned to Aulykaran. *Be calm,* I commanded myself. *You know him; he knows the Lady's Dance better than any man in Ascalon.*

"For Our Lady's sake, sit down, Moondancer," Aulykaran said. "Just watching you think so hard exhausts me. And you are a goddess tonight, so you must sit that I may sit as well."

Something in his voice set me at ease; so many people had spoken to me with honey-voices today that Aulykaran's tartness came as a relief. I smiled, and sat down, gathering my tiered skirt carefully.

Aulykaran promptly lowered himself to the cushions, reclined upon one elbow. "There now, isn't that better? And you have such an enchanting smile, sweeting, that I could do nothing all night but bask in its radiance."

I tried to answer in the same light, confident tone. "Are mere smiles a proper way to honor Her? This is my Maiden Night, Lord Aulykaran. Bright Atargatis has led you to me."

"Ah, is that who she was?" Something in the way Aulykaran spoke reminded me of Aylah; too mocking under a mask of perfect compliance. But his amusement, his easy assurance, gave me courage. With each word he spoke, my worry lessened.

"Of course. Who else?" I set my hands on the knot of my girdle and untied it, silently blessing the hours spent learning to accomplish this task in the dark. I set the girdle aside and said, "I have unbound my girdle. Now you must aid me in offering up my maidenhood to Our Lady. If you are not too fatigued, of course."

"No," Aulykaran said, "I am not too fatigued."

Despite all my lessons, the reality of the Lady's Dance surprised me. I had expected nothing, the first time, save that I would no longer be maiden. But my submission to Her gained me more than I deserved.

Lord Aulykaran proved everything I had heard of him to be true.

Whether he believed or not, he was a true servant of the Lady of Love. And he opened me to a force stronger than sword-blades.

As the full moon poured down silver light, Her power flared through me, and I understood at last. I was only a vessel for Our Lady Atargatis; I need do nothing but surrender myself to Her, and She would use my body as if it were Hers. That was what happened when I danced for Her. This act of devotion was no different.

Yet even as I yielded to Our Lady's divine pleasure, I longed for something more, although I did not know what it was I sought. Lord Aulykaran offered gentle guidance and exquisite sensual indulgence. And I was grateful to him for these gifts, even as I yearned to surrender to a man who would kindle delight and joy within me, rather than merely appease my body's urges.

On my Maiden Night, I lay in the arms of the most skillful lover in all Ascalon, a man who awoke my body to its power and granted me the key to carnal wisdom. Yes, I lay in Lord Aulykaran's arms, opened my body to his, accepted all he had to offer. I claimed the Goddess's promise as I drank rapture from his lips, arched and shivered against his practiced hands. And as I closed my eyes, and imagined another cradled me in his arms, coaxed ecstasy from my willing body.

On my Maiden Night, when all my heart and soul and mind should have been dedicated to Our Lady's worship, to utter devotion to Her, I lay in the arms of the man She had chosen for me—and dreamed that another man's hands stroked me, another man's lips caressed mine. Beneath the moonsilver light, I lay in Lord Aulykaran's arms, and dreamed I lay with Samson.

After my Maiden Night, I knew my true worth to the Temple. I was sought after not only for my dancing but for my ability to grant Our Lady's pleasure. Neither of my skills came cheaply; few men could afford Delilah Moondancer. Lord Aulykaran was one who could, when he chose, make sufficient offering to the Temple to claim me for a dance, or for a night. I liked him well enough, enough that rumor named him my favorite. I suppose he was; there were even times I lay with him and did not close my eyes and dream that another man embraced me.

I tried to forget I had ever looked upon Samson, just as I tried, when I danced, to forget that I now danced alone. Only in memory did Aylah mirror my steps, playing Sun to my dark Moon.

I did not think I would ever again see either Aylah or the man who had stolen both my heart-sister and my heart. But I was wrong, for the gods love best to toss men and women like dice to summon their futures.

And so I, just as I believed I had fought and won my battle, accepted my loss and gained serenity, I saw Aylah again—and again the bedrock beneath my feet melted into water and flowed away; again I struggled to balance past and future.

The year had turned; winter passed away and it was once again New Spring, the Month of Roses. To celebrate that festival, the smaller temples and the Groves asked the Great House of Atargatis in Ascalon to send the Goddess to bless their rituals. The Temple sent priestesses to carry the presence of Atargatis to Her worshippers.

The ceremony of choosing took place in the open Temple, before the public altar. Two deep bowls, one of alabaster and one of jade, waited upon the altar's smooth-polished marble. The jade held small tiles upon which were written the names of the Groves and temples; the alabaster held the names of priestesses of our House. The High Priestess drew one tile from the jade bowl, and then one from the bowl of alabaster. That was how the priestesses were chosen for the Groves. By lot, and by chance, and at Our Lady's will.

This season, my name was called, a thing I had known might happen. I had been chosen to act as Goddess at the Grove in the Vale of Sorek.

I had never left Ascalon before, so the journey to the Valley of Sorek enthralled me. Although I traveled in a litter, the cloth-of-silver curtains were tied back so that I might be seen by the common folk. Or, to be more truthful, so that they could look upon a priestess from the Great House of Atargatis.

Their eagerness to see a priestess from Ascalon mirrored mine to see the land beyond Ascalon's broad walls. Never before had I seen a place not surrounded by walls of one sort or another. But on the road, the land flowed ever onward, endless under the arching sky. And nothing seemed to remain motionless. Men and women worked in the fields, tending the ripening crops. Others led donkeys laden with wood or fodder along the verge, pausing to yield the road—and to stare—as my procession passed by them.

I was carried past fields rich with early wheat; each breeze sent the wheat quivering, as if the field were the coat of a great golden beast. Later we traveled between olive groves, and the trees' leaves danced to the slightest shift of air, changed from green to silver as they turned.

Of all the strange beauty I saw along the way, I liked the flowers best. I had not expected to see splashes of scarlet in the sown fields; I had not realized that poppies grew among wheat and rye and barley. As we passed a field luxuriant with more poppies than grain, I rang the bell hanging from the litter's frame. When the porters stopped, I stepped out and went to the edge of the field. I stooped and picked double handfuls of poppies, and only when I carried my prize back did I see the looks upon the faces of the older priestesses and the handmaidens who rode in an ox-drawn cart behind my litter. Some looked appalled, some merely annoyed.

"Remember always that you must think before you act, Delilah." I could hear Nikkal's gently chiding voice as clearly as if she stood beside me. Heat stronger than that caused by the sun flashed over my cheeks; I should have asked one of the handmaidens to pluck flowers, if I desired them. Still, I was to be Goddess of the Grove and they were not. Smiling, I walked back to the cart.

"A gift from Our Lady's bounty," I said, and handed poppies to the two priestesses and the four handmaidens sitting in the cart. "Take these and remember that She grants us beauty and joy—and that I thank you for aiding me during this New Spring."

This drew smiles and murmured thanks; I took the rest of the poppies I had gathered and went back to the waiting litter. Once the procession moved forward again, I spread the poppies in my lap and marveled over their color. So vivid, so dazzling. No paint could achieve this beauty.

Entranced by the scarlet petals, I wove the poppies into a small wreath. I held the circle of flowers in my hands, then set it upon my head like a crown. What more suitable adornment for Our Lady's priestess than Her flowers, after all?

When we arrived at the Sorek Grove, I soon learned that any worries I might have were as nothing compared to those of the Priestess of the Grove. As soon as my litter came into view, she ran out of the small house outside the Grove, calling in delight, "Oh, you have come at last! Praise the Lady!" She dashed up, all her hair and skirts flying, and grasped the silver curtains. "A thousand blessings upon you, and you are staying for all the days and nights of the festival, aren't you?"

She stared at me with brown eyes as huge and soft as a fawn's. The Priestess of the Sorek Grove was a young girl, not a woman; her breasts were still only promises for the future. And she was plainly overjoyed to see us arrive from Ascalon.

I smiled and stepped out of the litter, and kissed her upon the cheek, as my sister-priestess. This was only proper, since as Priestess of the Grove, she and I were of nearly equal rank. Indeed, she held a somewhat higher honor, although I did not think she would invoke her status and insist on taking precedence.

"Greetings, Sister," I said, controlling my urge to wipe the smudge of dirt from her cheek. "I am Delilah, Full Moon in the Great House of Atargatis in Ascalon the Beautiful. I am honored to be chosen to serve in your Grove this New Spring. What is your name?"

"Delilah?" The little priestess's eyes grew round as full moons. "Are you the one who dances? Delilah Moondancer?"

Heat burned my face; I felt oddly mortified by this child's awed delight in seeing me. But I would not hurt her heart, so I smiled. "Yes, I am Delilah Moondancer. But you still have not told me what you are called."

"Oh—I am sorry." Her cheeks blazed red as the poppies I had picked along the road. "I am Atirat, Priestess of the Sorek Grove. I bid you welcome in the name of Our Lady."

I could not imagine how this child had become Priestess of the Grove, but I did not ask. I bowed and murmured the proper words acknowledging her welcome. I only hoped there would be a place for all of us from Ascalon to eat and sleep and, most important, for me to properly garb myself for the festival.

When I learned there was another there at the Grove who aided Atirat, I gave silent thanks to both my goddess and hers. Although no priestess, Donariel proved a good, steady woman old enough to be my mother. She looked me over carefully, and then escorted us to the hastily woven house of willow those of us from Ascalon would call home for the next few days.

After she had shown us where we were to live, Donariel asked to speak with me, and when I said, "Of course; shall it be now?" she relaxed and almost smiled.

"Will you walk with me, and show me something of the Grove?" I asked, and as we walked from the willow-house across the smooth ground to the Grove itself, Donariel told me what I needed to know.

"You are twice—no, thrice—welcome, my lady Delilah. I will tell this short and straight, for I know you must walk the Grove and also need rest. Our Grove Priestess is the daughter of the last priestess who ruled this Grove. Atirat was raised to follow her mother as Grove Priestess, but her mother died a year ago, and although Atirat is past twelve, you can see she is a child still. That is why we sent to Ascalon, begging a priestess from the Great House to come. Atirat cannot be Goddess-on-Earth."

"No," I said. "She is far too young, even were she trained in the Goddess-on-Earth's duties."

"Had the Great House of Atargatis not sent you, Atirat would have insisted on carrying out her duty as Priestess of the Grove. But now she need not, and for that I thank Bright Atargatis, and Her Temple, and you."

"Don't forget to give thanks to Sweet Asherah as well," I said, and was pleased to hear Donariel laugh.

"I will not forget. Now here is the gate to the Grove. Return when you are ready, and you will find a good dinner prepared for you."

I thanked her, and watched as she walked back towards the little houses. I, too, was glad now that I had come; no child could become Goddess-on-Earth. That Atirat had been willing to try did her credit. *She must have been terrified. Well, now I shall be Goddess here this festival, and Atirat need not fear. Someone must send a priestess to teach Atirat, and to aid her until she is truly of age to be Priestess of the Grove.*

I must tell the priestesses who taught the New Moons, when I returned home to Ascalon. So thinking, I walked through the arched willow gate into the Sorek Grove.

There was little about the Lady's Grove in the Vale of Sorek to differ it from any other goddess-grove. A gate of willow and silver led into circles of trees planted long ago and lovingly tended: olive, willow, pomegranate. The Sorek Grove was not large—only three circles of trees and half a dozen pleasure booths set among them. But the image of the goddess on the gate had been newly painted, the old statue of Her at the center of the Grove freshly polished and gilded. When I entered the Grove, I walked down the path to the statue, and bowed, and laid the poppy-crown I had woven at Her feet.

Help me act well in Your name. I had dreamed all my life of acting as

Goddess-on-Earth. *Aid me, Bright Lady, to do honor to You and to Your house in Ascalon.*

I had thought the exhilaration of acting for the first time as Grove Goddess would burn forever as one of my brightest memories. But while I cherish that brief time even now, a lamplight warm against dark dreams, its brilliance faded even before I returned to Ascalon. For on the third day, when I had finished the final blessing of the Grove, I walked down through the trees to the river. And there, beside the river Sorek, I met a woman walking along its bank towards the Grove. She paused when she saw me, then came forward, moving with calm, easy grace, until we stood facing one another at the river's edge.

"It is good to see you again, heart-sister," Aylah said.

After the first loving greetings, I stood back, holding her hands, and stared at Aylah. "Half a year has been forever," I said, and then, "You've changed."

She smiled. "Only my garments, Delilah. I am still just as I was when I lived in the House of Atargatis. But we make an odd pairing now, do we not?"

She was right; no longer did we form one brilliant image of Sun and Moon. We had been called each other's mirrors when we danced together. But as I looked at what Aylah had become, I slowly began to see how different we truly were.

I stood there in all the glory of a priestess, a Full Moon of the Great House of Atargatis. Curled and knotted hair, painted face and gilded breasts, cinched bodice and seven-tiered skirt, scarlet girdle and anklets hung with silver bells—unless I moved, I could be taken for a statue, an icon rather than a living woman.

But no one would mistake Aylah for anything but a mortal woman now. Sun had gilded her skin, turned her face the hue of wild honey. Her bright hair hung in two long braids, the ends bound with leather. A skirt of undyed linen fell to her ankles; over that she wore a tunic woven in blue and white stripes. The tunic's sleeves covered all her arms from shoulder to wrist, hiding the serpent tattoos she had earned when she became a Rising Moon. She wore a veil, too, a simple length of sky-blue cloth. The veil lay draped about her shoulders; she had pushed it back off her hair when she saw me at the riverbank.

In only one thing were we alike now. Both of us stood barefoot on the sun-warmed ground. Yet even in so simple a thing as that, we differed. My henna-tinted feet glowed rose-red. Aylah's were brown from sun and dust.

"Well, Delilah? Have you seen enough to scold me for yet?"

"Oh, Aylah, I would not scold you—" I began, and she laughed.

"Of course you would; you always did. And you always wanted me to look like the Queen of Heaven, and I— Well, I prefer to be comfortable. I always did."

I looked at our clasped hands, felt the strength and hardness of hers. "Oh, Aylah, I am so glad to see you. How did you know I was here?"

"Because everyone for a dozen villages around knew the Great House was sending Delilah Moondancer to be Goddess-on-Earth here in the Sorek Grove before you even left Ascalon. Such news flies faster than a swallow. But you must have known I would come, Delilah. Timnath is but an hour's walk. Our farm is just beyond the village."

For a heartbeat I could say nothing; Aylah drew in her breath sharply, and before I could gather words, she said, "So you did not know? Or did you not wish to know? Did no one tell you that this is the Timnath Grove? Or that the farm that was my dowry from the Temple lies near Timnath?"

"I—I knew the Temple dowered you when—"

"When I married Samson. You need not slink around the words, Delilah. It is no shame to marry."

"No, of course not. But for the Temple to give you—a priestess—to such a man . . ." *A man with strong hands and a sweet smile. A man bright as the sun itself.*

"Samson is a hard man to say no to," Aylah said.

"Because he wanted you for his bride, not one person—not even the High Priestess—could say 'No, Samson. You may not have her'?" I tried to keep my face smooth, a proper priestess's mask. Once I had shared all my dreams with Aylah; now she must never learn I still desired a man I could never possess. Fear that I would betray myself made me speak sharply, my voice harsh, as if I hated both her and Samson. "Why didn't they tell him no? Why set him tasks? Why give him such hope? Why risk you?"

Aylah looked at me with what I realized, with a shock, was amusement—and pity. "Oh, Delilah, you never change! To you the world is so simple—black or white, yes or no, false or true. They set Samson tasks because they thought he would be killed before he completed the first."

"But he was not killed." I still did not understand how he had succeeded. "Was his god truly stronger than Atargatis?"

Aylah shrugged. "Perhaps—or perhaps Samson is cleverer than his enemies. And perhaps Atargatis wished him to triumph. Did you never think of that, Delilah?"

I felt heat flood my face, and was thankful for the paint that covered my cheeks. The carmine hid the sign of my shame. *It is true; I never thought of that.* But Aylah, who had always seemed to doubt, had owned more faith in Bright Atargatis than I, Her avowed servant. If Atargatis chose to bestow Aylah upon Samson, who was I to question Her plan—I, who in my grief and folly had asked too much of Her?

"You are right, Aylah." *Not what I desire, but what Our Lady desires.* "If Atargatis Herself wished to grant Samson's prayer—"

"Then you would stand here now, not I. They did not tell you, did they, those who rule Our Lady's Temple?"

"Tell me what?"

"It was not I Samson desired as his wife, Delilah. It was you."

I gasped and pressed my hand to my mouth, just like any silly girl in a harper's tale. "Me? He wanted to wed *me*? Then why did he take you instead? And why—"

"Why did the Temple offer up me, and not you?" Aylah laughed and regarded me with the patient tolerance of a mother for her child's follies. "Oh, Delilah, how can you be so wise and so foolish at once? Do you think the Great Temple spends years training one such as you to be priestess, to dance before Our Lady, to draw gems and gold from men's hands into the Temple's treasure-store, only to waste her in a marriage to anyone? You always believed me more beautiful, more graceful, more favored than you—for you loved me, and your heart rules you. But you were always wrong, Delilah."

As I stared, trying to summon words to answer, Aylah held up her hand. "No, let me finish. You must listen and believe. The Temple's eunuch bought me only because the Prince of the City's servant thought to buy me, and Derceto and Sandarin loathe each other. Who was I? A girl from beyond the North Wind, with no skills and no graces, and nothing save yellow hair as my dower. Had I not been your heart-sister, do you think I would have become a Rising Moon, or been chosen to dance? And your mother is wed to an Ascalon merchant of rank and wealth; the Temple would not choose to offend a generous benefactor."

Me. He had wanted me, desired me for his own. Me. For a heartbeat I felt again his hand on my hair as he freed me during the Sun Partridge Dance . . .

"But if Samson wanted me, why did he accept you in my stead?" I kept my voice soft, smooth. I would not reveal my thoughts, I would *not*. I tried to forget that Aylah had always seemed to know what I truly felt, no matter what I said, or how.

"Samson took me because the Temple tricked him, Delilah."

"How tricked?" I heard myself ask, and Aylah said, "A bride goes veiled to her wedding."

"And when he lifted your veil, I suppose he did not notice—" Anger clawed my bones, growled beneath my words. I do not know what cruelties I would have spoken, but Aylah silenced me by pressing her fingertips to my painted lips.

"He is simple and good—not simpleminded. Please, Delilah, listen to all I must tell you."

Despite my long years of training, I found myself struggling to regain calm. "Aylah—"

"Wait. There is one thing more. If there is anything you wish to say to me about my husband, heart-sister, say it now and I will listen, and say not one word in return." She looked at me, her eyes steady, as if she awaited attack.

Cold slid through me like a serpent. A hundred angry words battled to fling themselves at Aylah, to strike down her happiness. *Why should she be happy? Why should she have him, while I—* "No," I said. *No, I will not say these things. I will not think them. I will banish them from my heart forever. I will let Aylah be happy with the life she has chosen.*

At last, when I had imprisoned those wild, sickening words of accusation and desire, bound them with silver chains and locked them away in an ivory casket, I said, "No, heart-sister. There is nothing I wish to say to you about Samson. And yes, I will be still, and I will listen well to what you must tell me."

Aylah looked keenly at me, then said, "First, you must understand that Samson never lies, and he does not easily see deceit in others."

I drew in a deep breath. "He does not lie, he trusts too much. I understand. Now tell me," I said, and Aylah revealed all that had passed between the Sun Partridge Dance and the day Samson had carried his priestess-bride through the gate into her new home.

High Priestess Derceto herself had instructed Aylah in the deed she was to accomplish, and how she was to carry it out. That was when, Aylah said, she learned she was being given in marriage to a man who had triumphed in the three impossible tasks assigned him by the Temple, a man who had labored long and faithfully—and successfully—in the belief that he would be granted Delilah Moondancer as his bride.

"I was afraid, then," Aylah told me, "for who knew what a man so greatly deceived would do? But I was more afraid of Derceto and what she would do to me if I refused than I was of Samson. And indeed, I wished to do as she ordered me. Part of what she ordered, anyway."

"What part?" I asked. Oddly, I felt nothing, neither grief nor joy nor even surprise, at Aylah's revelations. Perhaps a corner of my mind had always known there was something amiss in the entire affair.

"The wedding." Aylah slanted her eyes at me, gauging my reaction. "I wished to be married, Delilah. I love you dearly, sister of my heart, but I am no true priestess. I longed to escape the Temple walls. This deception gave me my chance."

As I stood still as a painted idol, refusing to acknowledge the pain these words gave, Aylah spoke on in her soft, careful voice. "I was afraid Samson would know at once I was not the bride he had been promised, but Derceto had me adorned so heavily the gold and gems and embroidered silks hid my form."

Yes, that would have been necessary to carry out the deception. While Aylah and I were of the same height, she was full-bodied, womanly, while I still remained slender as a desert hound, all my curves created by dancer's muscles.

"Your hair?" Mine flowed like black water down my back; hers glowed like sunlit honey.

"Braided with black cord, tight-bound so that not a strand escaped. And then there was the bridal veil; I was covered by so long and so thick a cloth that he could not see my face, or the color of my hair. The High Priestess told me to keep the veil on until I entered Samson's home as his wife—and if I could, to keep it on until he lay with me. Samson told me that the High Priestess told him it was an ancient custom, that a man not see his bride's face until the marriage had been consummated."

"And did you keep the veil on until the morning after?"

"No. I lifted my veil for Samson as soon as we were out of sight of Ascalon."

"And when he saw you, when—" For the first time in my life, I found it hard to summon words.

"When he realized he'd been cheated by the Temple? He stared at me, and then he laughed and said that he should call me Leah."

"Why?"

"There is an old tale his people tell, of their first fathers and mothers. One man, named Jacob, fell in love with one sister and worked many years to earn her bride-price. But on their wedding day, her father sent her older sister, hidden under a heavy veil, to wed Jacob. Jacob was less fortunate than Samson, for it was not until the next morning, after he lay with her, that he saw his wife's face and learned that he had not married his beloved Rachel, but her sister Leah. He married Rachel, too, in the end, after working to earn another bride-price."

"Samson laughed? He was not angry?"

"Bitter laughter, but yes, he laughed. And he is rarely angered. He was not best pleased, that I will grant—but I begged him not to send me back to Ascalon and the Temple. He listened, and then said that if the Temple valued me so little, I might as well remain his wife. He did ask why I had been given instead of you, and I told him what I told you. He still desires you, Delilah—he is too kind to speak of you, but I know he has not forgotten the woman he wished to wed. He knew it would be deadly folly to return to Ascalon, to try to claim you there. But you are here, close—only come with me now, and Samson would gladly take you to wife as well. We would be together again."

For one treacherous heartbeat, I longed to tell her yes. *Yes, I will put my hand in yours and—and what? Walk away from Our Lady, from the Dance?* I held out my hands to Aylah. "We can be together once more. Come back with me. Come back to the House of Atargatis, where you belong."

She shook her head. "I never belonged there. Now I am free of that place, and shall never look upon it again."

A pang lanced my heart; Aylah no longer cared for me and for what we had shared. Aylah the Priestess, Aylah Sundancer, had vanished. Aylah my heart-sister had abandoned me.

"So you have forgotten me and all we shared? You do not even wear the amulet I gave you." Since the day we had exchanged talismans, our sister-tokens had been knotted into the ends of small braids behind our left ears. I still wore the one she had given me, the lion's claw a ghost-weapon nearly hidden by my black hair. To remove the amulet, to lay it aside in my jewel box, would be to admit I had lost Aylah forever. But Aylah no longer wore the coral fish I had given her in exchange.

She smiled. "I no longer wear it braided into my hair, for I am no longer a priestess of Atargatis, and wish those I now live among to forget I ever was." Aylah reached to her neck, pulled a thin cord from beneath the tunic that covered her from throat to knees. The amulet I had given her the day we became avowed heart-sisters hung upon the cord. "You see? I wear it still." She regarded me steadily. "But even if I did not, I need no token to keep you in my heart, Delilah."

She let the little coral fish drop back beneath her gown. For a moment I thought she wished to speak, but she only looked upon me with an odd expression of loving sorrow.

"Aylah? What is wrong?"

She hesitated, then shook her head and smiled. "Nothing."

Nothing you wish me to know. Never had I been able to either coax or force Aylah to say anything she did not wish to reveal, but I knew I must try. I held out my hands, and Aylah laid hers in mine. "Something troubles you," I said. "Tell me. Please, Aylah, you must tell me. Perhaps I can help."

"No, Delilah, you cannot. Please let it be."

I stood as tall and straight as the Grove Goddess, made my voice heavy with self-importance. "Remember I am a priestess; you may confide in me safely."

That brought a smile to her lips, as I had hoped. "I have no more to worry me than any woman who carries her first child."

This news drew an answering smile from me—as doubtless she had hoped. "You are with child? Oh, Aylah! Is . . . your husband . . . pleased?"

"How not? What man does not dream of his sons?" Aylah smoothed her hands down her blue linen garment, revealing the lush rounding of her body.

"So you pray the child you carry is a boy?" I asked, and Aylah let her dress fall loose again and laughed softly.

"It would be better if the first is a boy. Then my husband's father and mother will praise my name and call me blessed, for his people prize sons above all. And perhaps they will then be able to recall my name when Samson takes me to Zorah to visit them."

"And so if your child is a girl, they will berate you?"

"Oh, they will berate me whatever I do; they do not think me fit to be Samson's wife. But they will greet a first daughter as proof I am fertile enough that they may hope for boys next. So all will be well."

Placid and soft with contentment, Aylah's voice stroked the air. I looked upon my heart-sister, and wondered when and how the Temple dancer had been tamed; the priestess of Atargatis banished. Suddenly fearful—of what, I did not know—I reached out and grasped Aylah's hands.

"Come with me," I said again, although she had already refused my plea that she do so. But an odd urgency forced the words from me. "Come back to the Temple."

"No, Delilah. I cannot return there. And besides—" She stopped, and her eyes slid away, did not meet mine. "I am not like you, heart-sister. For all the days I dwelt in Our Lady's House, I was looked upon only as something rare and strange, something they could raise up and display as—as if I were another idol of ivory and amber. And not for who I am, or for what I can do, but for my face, and the color of my hair. They valued me most because you loved me. I have not the skill nor the calling to be a priestess of any god or goddess."

"You do. You *do*." Fiercely spoken words, as if I could claim Aylah for my own once more, bring her back to the safety that lay behind the Temple gates.

Aylah merely shook her head. "No, I do not, and the High Priestess and all the senior priestesses of the Great House knew it. I am not like you—you are passion and faith; you are a true vessel of Atargatis Herself. But I am none of these things. For myself, I have always wished for a quiet life. For a husband, for a home. For children who will not be taken from me. That is what I want, Delilah. Even if the Temple would take me back now, I would not go."

"Of course it would take you back. Why not?"

Aylah hesitated, as if weighing what she should say and what she should not. At last she said, "Forget those words; I should not have spoken them. Remember only that I am content as I am."

"How can you be? You could have been High Priestess in Ascalon!"

"No, I could not. But then, I never wanted to be High Priestess. That was your dream, Delilah. Not mine."

There was no bitterness in her words, only clear strong truth. For half a dozen heartbeats, there was only silence between us. Then I forced myself to make an effort to speak calmly, to speak kind words. "So you are happy. I am glad."

She smiled then, the close, secret curve of her lips that so resembled the smile on the image of Atargatis that stood in Ascalon's Temple. "So am I. And when you, too, are happy, Delilah, I will be happier still."

"I am happy." At least, I thought I was. Was I not a priestess ordained, and the Temple's pride as Dancer Before Our Lady Atargatis? Yet at Aylah's words, something stirred, uneasy, beneath my heart. I closed my eyes for a breath and banished the strange emotion. My future stretched before me as set and immutable as the ancient spirals in the dancing-floor. I knew who and what I was, and how each day, each month, each year would pass. I would not listen to a small still voice that asked, *Is that enough, Delilah? Is that truly all you desire of life?*

Aylah regarded me steadily with her moon-pale eyes. "If that is true, I am glad of it."

A priestess learns to wear a mask; I smiled back at Aylah as placidly as if I felt nothing more than pleasure at seeing her once more. "Then be glad, heart-sister. And come to us at Our Lady's House when your child is born, that the goddess may bless you both. And perhaps—"

"No, Delilah. My child will not serve in Atargatis's Temple. And I do not wish to wait. You are a priestess; give me the goddess's blessing now."

There was an urgency in her voice that I set down to the fears many women suffer as they await their children's birth. But I said only "Of course." It was my duty, after all. I would have done it even for a stranger, or an enemy, who asked for such a blessing.

So we embraced as friends, and then, as priestess, I called down Our Lady's blessing upon her and her unborn child. When the blessing had been spoken, Aylah smiled, and kissed me.

"Here." Aylah drew the cord over her neck; she reached out to me and took my hand, pressing the token against my palm. "Take this, to remember that I will always hold you in my heart, beloved sister." And then, as I stared down at the little coral fish cupped in my hand, Aylah said, "Be happy, Delilah. Remember that now is all the time there is." Then she went away again; the rites of the Full Moon are not for women already carrying the goddess's greatest blessing.

I shall always be grateful that we parted sweetly that day, with no hard words to lie forever between us in the Land Beyond the Sunset. For that was the last time I saw my sister Aylah.

High Priestess Derceto summoned me months later to tell me news of Aylah. She did not put her arms around me and weep with me, as Nikkal would have done in her place. Derceto merely told me in plain words that my heart-sister had died, and how. She said nothing of Samson, only that men he had wronged had burned his fields, and his gardens, and his house, with his wife and child inside it. They piled brush and dead wood before the door and across the windows, so there should be no escape.

Aylah and her newborn daughter died in fire.

Samson

It is not an easy thing to give up glory for sweet dull days. Aylah had been a famous temple dancer, had swayed her body before princes who had thrown gems before her gilded feet. Now she lived as a farmer's wife, unadorned and unlauded. She swore herself content—even happy. Perhaps she truly thought herself so; Orev didn't know. He only feared that one day Aylah would wake and look at what she had become, and think upon what she had been, and regret her choice.

And if she did?

Orev could think of half a dozen tales spun from a woman's change of heart—and none of them ended happily. But warning Samson would be useless, and speaking upon such a matter to Samson's wife worse than useless.

For the wrong words might transmute Aylah's sisterly fondness for Orev to dislike. And whether she complained of him to Samson or whether she did not, such ill-feeling would poison the peace of Samson's home.

I would have no choice but to leave, to set my feet upon the road again. And perhaps I should; I grow lazy and slow-witted here.

But he was loath to leave; he could tell himself that Samson needed a steady, sensible friend to aid him, but Orev knew that for a lie. He simply did not wish to leave the warm comfort of the home Aylah had created, into which she had welcomed him as she would an older brother.

And with both Aylah and Samson insisting he remain, Orev found it easy to push away the knowledge that this halcyon life could not endure. Samson had too many enemies—and too many so-called friends who were even more dangerous to him. The Foxes still roved the hills and the roads, killing and plundering, with Samson's name their battle-cry. Samson now refused even to speak with those who claimed to be his Foxes.

"For if you will not obey me when I tell you to let men travel the roads in peace, there is no other word I wish to say to you. I wish only to tend my fields as my wife tends her garden." That had been his final avowal to Enoch and his fierce band when they had run eagerly to Samson's farm, ready to claim him once again as their true leader.

"It is that Philistine woman who weakens your heart, when it should be strong against our enemies." Beriah, vixen among the Foxes, slid her hand over the hilt of the dagger strapped against her hip. She stared at Aylah, who gazed back unflinching.

Samson put his arm around Aylah's shoulders. "Speak soft words to my wife, or do not speak at all. Now leave my land and my house, and do not return until you will obey my orders as you always swear you long to do. And if I see any of you hunting on this road that runs past my dooryard, I shall slay you myself."

The Foxes had slunk away in anger and in doubt. Many cast slantwise glances back at Samson. Beriah hissed to Enoch, "The Philistine bewitches him. Free of her..." That was all Orev heard before the Foxes slipped past him, into the small orchard behind the farmhouse.

He repeated the words to Samson and to Aylah, who looked at each other; Samson smiled and shook his head, and Aylah shrugged. "What they say is of no importance," she said. "My husband's father and his mother do not like me either, but I cannot change the hearts and minds of others."

Samson put his arm around Aylah's waist and spread his hand over her rounding belly. "They don't like you because they don't know you.

When our child is born, my mother will come running soon enough, and she will learn to value you as I do."

"Yes," Aylah said, and reached up to lay her hand against Samson's cheek. "All will be as it should be. Now I must go to my own work, or you will have no dinner."

Orev followed Aylah through the house, out to the oven and the fire pit behind the kitchen. "You are troubled," he said. "Do you know anything that would be better shared?"

She did not protest, or claim herself at peace with all the world. Instead, she gathered up the meat wrapped in palm leaves and laid it on the bed of smoldering coals at the bottom of the fire pit. For a moment she stared down at the waiting fire. "Yes, I am troubled, Orev. Samson thinks everyone as good as he is—and as sensible. But men are not good or sensible. And I know how bitterly his people resent me, as if I had stolen him from them." She turned and looked at Orev. "How much longer do you think either his people or mine will permit us to live in peace?"

Orev wished he could lie, could sing up a comforting tale of patience and long happy years. "I don't know."

"Not long, I think," Aylah said. She touched her fingers to her thickened waist; her eyes seemed to stare into a future only she could understand.

"Aylah—" Orev began, only to be interrupted as she swung around, pulling off her veil and flapping it at the yellow dog that had followed Samson home one day and now—with her brood of half-grown pups— guarded the farmyard.

"Get out of there! Leave that alone, you silly dog! Stop her, Orev, before she burns her paws."

"If she does, she'll stop," Orev pointed out. By the time he'd helped Aylah chivy the dogs out of the kitchen-yard, stamped out burning leaves, and salvaged what remained of the meat, the sense of foreboding had lifted. Surely, when enough time had passed, both the Hebrews and the Five Cities would see that Samson was neither hero nor danger.

In time, Samson and his wife would dwell in peace with their children and, in the fullness of years, with their children's children.

And no man shall remember the names of Samson, the farmer, and Aylah, his wife.

And that was as it should be.

And that was how it was, for a time. Samson settled easily into a farmer's life, traded the highborn mules for a flock of sheep and another of goats. As if trying to repay with sweetness now the pain that would come, the seasons turned, and a year after her marriage to Samson, Aylah brought forth a daughter—her labor so easy that the midwife Samson had brought muttered of witchcraft. Aylah laughed. "No witchcraft, old mother, but Our Lady's blessing. Give me my daughter."

Like any new mother, Aylah forgot what she had paid in long months of waiting and hours of pain when she cradled her infant in her arms. And like any new father, Samson marveled at the strength of his newborn daughter's grasp.

When the child was seven days old, Samson told Aylah and Orev that he would travel to Zorah, to tell his parents the news.

"And to bring them back with me, that they may name the child. So have all ready to greet them—and do not do the work yourself, my wife. Rest, and hire girls from the village to cook and clean."

"As if those girls would do anything right, except giggle," Aylah said as she and Orev watched Samson walk away down the road. Once Samson was out of sight, she kissed the top of her daughter's head and set her in a sheepskin-lined basket. "Watch her for me, Orev. I have work to do. And don't tell Samson I did the cooking. Someone must do it, after all. I don't want his parents thinking he has married a useless wife."

Samson had left the farm in Aylah's competent charge before—and relied, as both Samson and Aylah assured him, on Orev to protect her and the land from danger. Orev accepted this as the meaningless kindness it was; a lame harper would deter no one. On the other hand, the mere sight of Ari and the dogs dozing in the dooryard of the farmhouse often sent even peaceful travelers circling far to avoid passing the gate. *Appearance is all, for the lion is far gentler than sweet-faced Aylah!*

Never before had there been trouble when Samson went away, to find a lost calf or lamb, or to aid someone in building a house or a wall or a well. Orev had no real reason to think this time would be any different. Only an unease of spirit, caused, he supposed, by the malice the Foxes had not hesitated to display, disturbed him.

And unease of spirit, however troubling, was not a true warning. Orev soothed his mind by telling himself that Samson would be gone for only three days. He could not tell if Aylah worried; her face was always smooth as cream. Aylah tended her babe, and Orev practiced a half-formed song. Ari slept in the sun, flat against the hot earth, a living carpet. Two days passed in that tranquil fashion.

Then the Foxes returned, accompanied by other bands of men who believed as the first Foxes did: that force would win the prize they sought.

As predators do, the Foxes appeared at sunset. Orev had been lazing by the door into the house—"Pretending to practice your new song, but really waiting for me to let you rock the baby to sleep," Aylah had said and smiled, and carried the fussing infant into the house to feed her. With great effort, Ari had roused himself and padded after her, hopeful; the lion knew Aylah was the giver-of-food.

Orev smiled and set his harp aside. The evening was too calm, too beautiful, to waste on any task, however worthy. Clear blue light shadowed the land, deepened as the sun fell lower into the west. Streaks of red and gold stretched out from the setting sun until the western sky blazed fleeting glory. Shadows darkened . . .

And moved. Beneath the trees of the orchard, along the road past the farm, men lurked. And as the light dimmed, the shadowed men moved forward, towards the farmhouse. The farm dogs began to bark, warning of intruders. As the first came close enough for him to see their faces, Orev recognized Enoch and Ichavod. *The Foxes. This is not good.* Orev pushed himself to his feet and called Aylah's name.

The urgency in his voice brought Aylah swiftly to the doorway, the babe still sucking at her breast. She looked past Orev, and drew in her breath sharply.

"Let me speak to them," Orev said, and Aylah nodded and pulled her veil over her daughter, as if to hide her from evil eyes.

But it was too late for calm words; the Foxes hunted.

"Keep your mouth closed, harper," Enoch said. "There is nothing you can say that we wish to hear."

"We have come to burn away the wickedness that holds Samson in bondage," Ichavod declared, then turned and beckoned, and flames blossomed against the shadows. Torches.

Orev reached out and grasped Aylah's arm. "Come," he said, and began leading her away from the house, hoping to circle around the pack of men converging upon it. Aylah followed, sure-footed and graceful, and for a dozen steps Orev thought he had succeeded. Let them burn the house; Samson would rebuild.

Then Aylah stopped, and Orev found himself facing a dozen men—and Beriah. "Leave now, harper, and live," Beriah said. "This"—she gestured at Aylah—"this evil must die, that her spells die with her."

"If you touch her, Samson will surely slay you all." Orev kept his voice steady, hoping quiet sense would sway those who had come to kill.

Beriah only laughed, mocking him. "Samson is not here to interfere. We only do what is right. We will free him from this sorcery."

How did they know Samson was gone? Orev looked past Beriah, saw Terach, the boy who yearned to sing great songs. "You, Terach—is this the deed you wish to honor with your harp and your voice? How a band of armed men slew one woman and her babe?"

Terach stared and opened his mouth as if to speak; Beriah shoved him back with her elbow. "Don't listen to him, Terach; he's tainted with her corruption. You have a choice, harper—leave or die with her."

Orev had never thought himself a brave man; pain was a faithful companion, not an honor he had sought. But now he heard himself saying, "I will not leave her. Either let us pass or you must murder one of your own people, as well as Samson's wife and child."

He put his arm around Aylah's waist and began to walk away, and for three steps, all was silence. Orev dared hope his calm words had won their lives, soothed the Foxes' anger. He did not see which man hurled the stone out of the darkness. He only felt the pain as the stone hit, pain that made him stagger against Aylah, his weight pushing her forward. And that was all it took to turn the waiting men into a huge mindless beast. A beast with but one urge.

To kill.

Never afterward was Orev truly sure what had happened, or how. He remembered Aylah thrusting her child at him, and brutal hands tearing the infant away. He remembered blows that sent him to the ground, remembered clinging to the earth as the mob rushed past, carrying Aylah and the child along with it. He remembered the smell of smoke and the sound of fire eating walls and roof.

He did not remember hearing Aylah scream. He told Samson, later, that he thought she and the child had been killed before the house burned around them.

But he was never sure, and to the last night of his life, he dreamed of Aylah dancing in fire hotter than the sun.

When he roused enough to look upon the world again, night had passed and gray dawn revealed what the Foxes had done. The house had burned, and the fields that lay beyond it. The orchard had not burned. But there was little else left.

The farm dogs had fled, but Ari had not. The lion lay sprawled flat upon the earth before the house, and even from where he sat, Orev saw that dried blood stained the beast's golden coat. Orev struggled to his feet and hobbled over to the lion's body. Flies rose buzzing from the spear wounds in the lion's side and from the gash across the great beast's throat. But fat and lazy though he had been, Ari had done his best to guard Samson's home. Bloody cloth and a strip of flesh remained trapped in the lion's closed jaws. Orev hoped that Ari had fatally injured at least one of the Foxes. He stooped and set his hand on the lion's mane, then forced himself to turn to the house.

All that remained was a smoldering pile of ash and charred wood. He knew he would find nothing—did not wish to find anything. But he also knew he must look. The roof had burned away and the walls fallen in; Orev supposed the house in which she had been so content served well as Aylah's funeral pyre. He refused to think of the child, so small and soft and golden. *The daughter went with her mother. That is what they both would have wanted.*

Samson will return. Samson will avenge this wickedness. Samson will— Orev found himself weeping. Some deeds could never truly be avenged. And when Samson returned, Orev would have to tell him what had happened, and see the light die in Samson's eyes. Orev did not know if he could endure that. But he knew, also, that he must. He owed it to Aylah and her unnamed daughter. And to Samson himself.

And to the Foxes. Yes, Samson will repay their evil deeds.

Even that thought did not comfort him. But it gave him a reason to endure, and to face Samson without shame or guilt.

That would have to be enough. Later, Orev knew, he would find himself twisting words, creating a new tale out of this grief. *Because I am a harper, and all harpers weave songs out of all that happens for good or for ill. But I will sing that song later. Not now. Later. Much later.*

Delilah

After Derceto told me that my heart-sister and her daughter were dead, and how they had died, I sat in my room as if my body had turned to stone. I did not move even when Nikkal came to comfort me; when she put her arms around me, I felt nothing. I could think only that Aylah had foreseen this, had warned me. And that I had done nothing to save her from the cruel fate she had suffered.

"Delilah?" Nikkal stroked my cheek, smoothed back my hair. "Delilah, speak, weep, anything. You must—"

"There is nothing I must do now." My words fell cold into the air between us. "I did not act when I could have saved her. Now it is too late."

"Delilah, you are not Atargatis Herself, to say what will and what will not happen. I know how you loved Aylah, but—"

But I ceased to listen. I did not wish to hear Aylah, my heart-sister, spoken of as if she no longer existed. Worse, as if she had never lived. *Oh, Aylah, I love you still. One does not cease to love just because the loved one dies.*

I do not know how long Nikkal remained, trying to console me. Nor do I know how I came to be in my bed, but when I awoke, I lay beneath a soft wool blanket, and one of the Temple maidservants stroked my face with cool rose-scented water. Beyond her stood a plump man in a robe of white linen spotted with red; a cap covered his hair, and from that cap red leather lappets dangled, framing a round face that seemed oddly ageless. A wide leather collar hid his neck. I could not imagine who or what he was until I felt movement as a warm weight upon my legs shifted. A moment later I found myself staring into soft brown eyes. The dog sniffed my mouth, then turned to look at the waiting priest.

"Ah, she wakes. Milchienzeek's mercy is boundless." The priest smiled and motioned with his fingers; the little dog curled up in the curve of my arm and began to lick my chin, quick warm strokes of its soft pink tongue.

So someone—perhaps the High Priestess herself, for had she not sent her own wine to ease my pain?—had been concerned enough to send for one of Milchienzeek's dogs to aid me. A consort of the god Dagon, the goddess Milchienzeek was patroness of healers; dogs belonged to Milchienzeek, for She had created them, incarnate vessels of divine love. Her temple was small, compared to those of other gods, but Milchienzeek and Her Thousand Dogs were well-loved.

Although all dogs belonged to Milchienzeek, those bred by her temple were the most precious to Her. Small sleek animals, white as cloud save for their soft ears, which were red as new copper, the temple dogs had healed many when all else had failed. Milchienzeek's priests refused no one who begged aid of Her dogs for any illness of body or of mind.

I supposed Derceto had meant only kindness in sending to Milchienzeek—but did she truly think even a goddess's dog would make me forget that Aylah lay dead, and her child with her? I closed my eyes and said, "I am well. Leave me now, both of you."

A pause, then the little sounds of the maidservant gathering her bowl and clothes, of the dog-priest turning away. I lay still as stone, realizing only when I heard the whisper of air as the curtain fell over the doorway that the dog remained at my side.

The dog ceased licking my cheek and began to nudge me with its cool damp nose. When I did not move, the nudges became more insistent. I opened my eyes and began to push the little animal away; refusing to be rejected, the dog ducked under my hand and pressed against me, licking my fingers.

To force the dog from me, I set my hands upon its sleek body. I intended to lift it off my bed and set it upon the floor, but the dog gazed at me with brown eyes filled with such compassion I could think only that the last time I had seen such loving eyes had been when I said good-bye to Aylah in the Grove at Sorek.

No. When she said farewell to me. *"Be happy, Delilah—"*

My heart had been stone since the moment Derceto told me of Aylah's death. Now that stone shattered into a thousand blade-keen shards; at last I wept, long and silently, as Milchienzeek's dog huddled against me and licked the hot salt tears from my face.

Samson

Since Orev could think of nothing else to do, he took his harp and his walking-stick and left the still smoldering ruin of Samson's farm. He walked north, on the road to Zorah. He did not hurry; what need? At noon, he met Samson and his parents walking south.

When Orev saw them, he stopped and waited as Samson strode towards him. Orev had rehearsed many ways in which to tell Samson that his farm had been destroyed, his animals killed, his wife and new-born daughter murdered. Now he saw he need say nothing. His face and revealed all Samson needed to know.

"I'm sorry." Orev's voice came out hoarse as a true raven's.

Samson said nothing; he ran past Orev, heading to what had been home only a day ago. Orev, Manoah, and Tsipporah were left to follow, as Orev slowly told Samson's parents they would never see their first grandchild, and why.

By the time Orev and his parents arrived at the ruined farm, Samson was staring at the pile of charred wood and clay that had been the farmhouse. His hands and arms were dark with ash. He stood silent as Orev told him what had come to pass at the farm in Timnath. Orev spoke quickly and plainly, as if that would lessen the pain. The quiet broken by the warning barks of the farm dogs. Orev leading Aylah and the babe through the encircling Foxes. "I thought we would walk safe away. Then someone threw a stone. And then—"

And then the killing frenzy as the Foxes tore Aylah's babe from her arms. Tsipporah began to weep, her sobs the music to which Orev told the rest of the tale. Of the stones, and the fire.

Orev told how he had come back to the world to find the house a burnt-out pyre, and Ari dead. "I think he savaged at least one of them. He had a bloody cloth clenched in his jaws." Then Orev stopped, and the only sound was Tsipporah's weeping. Manoah put his arms around his wife. *Ah, you reviled your son's wife when she lived, but now— Well, what good man or woman would not sorrow over so dreadful a death?*

Samson said nothing for a time. At last he looked at Orev, and his sky-blue eyes seemed cold and hard as stone. "They knew I was not there, those who call themselves my Foxes. They knew I was not there. How did they know I was gone, Orev?"

The harper stared, wondering why he had not thought to ask that question. Never, never would the Foxes have dared attack Samson's wife had Samson been there. "I don't know."

Samson rose to his feet. "Someone told them, and someday I will know who. Now I ask you to take my mother and my father back to Zorah. I am going out, to walk upon the hills. If you love me at all, do not come after me."

Samson was gone all that day and the next night, and the day and the night after that. Then he returned to Zorah, bringing with him a lion-skin. Ari's. Cautiously, Orev asked where he had been.

"Hunting." That was all Samson said, and Orev did not dare ask anything more.

Samson was never quite the same after he returned. To some, he seemed even more the rash, reckless hero of so many lying tales. Samson tanned the lion-skin and wore it as a cloak; tribute and reminder. He still smiled, but his smiles no longer reached his eyes.

To Orev, it was clear that something of Samson's sweetness had gone forever, burned from his heart. Perhaps that part of Samson had vanished to seek his wife and child, to tend their ghosts. Or perhaps their deaths had killed something in Samson, the trait that had let him look upon an unfair world and merely laugh and happily go his own way.

For all the trouble that amiable tolerance had caused, Orev discovered that he missed the old Samson, the one who never scowled or angered.

This new Samson— Orev was not sure the Samson who now lived could be trusted to chain anger, to act out of kindness and good faith.

PART THREE

Full Moon

Delilah

Now I know it is not easy to create one of the Lady's priestesses; to rear a girl to be both tender as new fleece and hard as new iron, clever as a fennec and docile as a dove.

Those who ruled the great House of Atargatis in Ascalon believed they had formed me into such a creature. Had they not trusted utterly in their power over me—their sublime confidence that no matter what transpired, my heart and my will belonged only to the Temple—never would I have been sent against Samson as a weapon.

As my heart-sister Aylah had been.

When High Priestess Derceto sent for me, a full moon's turn after Aylah's death, it was the last time I had no thought other than to prepare myself, to obey. I permitted the handmaidens who had been set to watch over me to comb and curl my hair, to lace my body into the stiff leather bodice, to drop the seven-tiered skirt over my head and tie its gilded cords about my cinched waist. At last, fittingly painted and garbed, I walked through the Temple gardens to the High Priestess's courtyard.

The Gatekeeper let me pass at once, and I walked, proud and graceful as I had been so carefully taught, across smooth marble stones to

the alabaster bench where the High Priestess sat. The willow tree behind her cast shadows over her, shadows that slid across her body like
pale serpents. Beside her stood a richly clad man: Sandarin, Prince of
the City, Consort to Lady Ascalon.

I stopped before High Priestess Derceto, folded my hands over my
breast, and knelt. My body knew how to move with grace, whether I
cared to or did not. And I did not; I cared for nothing, now that Aylah
was forever gone. I did not care if I made the proper obeisance. I did not
care why the Prince of the City was there, or why the High Priestess
had summoned me. I bent my head, and waited, silent.

Derceto set her crimson-tinted fingers beneath my chin, lifted my
head until she could look into my face. Before she could speak, the
Prince said, "*This* is the girl? You would risk the Moondancer, when you
have lost the other already in your vain attempts to rid us of that man?
Choose another, Lady Derceto." He sounded impatient, angry.

"This is the girl," Derceto said in a voice smooth as cream. "And it
must be Delilah Moondancer, and no other. Our Lady's Children have
foretold it."

A pause, then Sandarin said, "Then I suppose we must send her, as
you and the Seven agree so well." His agreement sounded grudging.
"Let us trust Our Lady's Children know what they ask. Have her
stand."

When I rose to my feet, Prince Sandarin walked around me, looking
me up and down as if I were a slave in the open market rather than a
highly valued priestess in the House of Atargatis. But High Priestess
Derceto did not rebuke him. She smiled as he frowned.

"She looks nothing like the other priestess you gave him," he said at
last. "Are you certain she can beguile him?"

"Oh, yes, she will beguile him. She has been chosen by Our Lady for
this task."

"That's what you said about the last one," Sandarin told her, and
suddenly my blood beat hard beneath my skin, creating a roaring like
wild waves in my ears.

The last one . . . the last one— The last one chosen had been Aylah, my heart-sister sent to slay my heart. I had hated both Aylah and Samson; twice hated Samson for seducing Aylah away from the Temple, away from me and to her death . . .

Derceto smiled. "This time it is true."

Her words echoed through my pounding blood. *This time it is true. This time—*

"What task?" I asked. The words came of themselves, and my voice sounded very far away.

Derceto turned to me, hesitated, then spoke slowly and solemnly, as if choosing her words with great care. "A heavy task, yet one that will ease your heart, Delilah. The man who caused your heart-sister's death still lives, still plots against us, still roams free and happy. You will trap him for—"

"For the Five Cities," Sandarin said, cutting across Derceto's careful explanation.

Samson. They want me to bring them Samson. He wanted me, not Aylah, and now they think I will lure him back. Back for what? Another attempt to kill him with an unfair test of Three Tasks? My blood seemed to slow, beat hard and cool beneath my skin. Aylah had been right, always. Derceto had lied; lied to Samson—and to me. *And to Our Lady? Atargatis, Lady of Love, summoned Samson, set me before his eyes. Derceto denied us that love.*

Now it was Sandarin's turn to smile at me. "And this time we will have him, and there will be no mistakes. You must succeed. Not like—"

No mistakes. Not like—Aylah.

Aylah, who had died in fire—because the High Priestess and the Prince of the City had sent her to Samson in my place. *Samson wanted me, not Aylah. If I had been sent with him, would I now dance upon the wind as dust and ash?*

Suddenly I wondered who had told Derceto of Aylah's death, why and how she had known exactly who had slain Aylah and her child. I remembered Derceto saying, "They piled brush high around the house." How had she known that? What witness had told her?

And where was Samson, when men had come out of the shadows carrying fire and death? *Far from his home, for otherwise no man would dare harm Samson's wife, his child.* Had Samson been there, either Aylah and her daughter would still live or Samson himself would be dead with them.

Men Samson had wronged had burned all that was his, Derceto had told me. But Aylah had told me of a man who valued justice above all, who used his strength to aid those weaker than he. So what men had he so wronged that they would murder a woman and her newborn babe when Samson eluded them? *Or was it Aylah's death they sought, and not Samson's?*

"Delilah?" Derceto's voice called me back; her eyes regarded me keenly. "I know this is hard for you to hear, but you must. I promise you the prize you seek. Only have patience now, and listen."

Sandarin laughed, a sound abrupt and harsh as a jackal's cry. "Is this the faithful, dutiful priestess you swore will be our true sword-blade against Samson?"

Derceto twisted, supple as a weasel; glared at Sandarin. "And I ask you, too, to be patient a little longer, Prince. Delilah will do what she must, never doubt that. She will bring us Samson."

Both Prince and High Priestess seemed very far away, their voices echoing so that I barely understood their words. I listened to another voice, one only I could hear. *"Even if the Temple would take me back,"* Aylah had said, and now I understood. Aylah had failed, and Derceto did not accept failure as an offering. *Failed, and died for it. Died because she would not betray Samson to the Temple—*

Anger burned hot through my bones; I longed to speak. But for once I did as Aylah herself would have bidden me. I kept my face smooth and my lips closed. I waited for the High Priestess and the Prince of the City to reveal their lies, their deceit; to condemn themselves out of their own mouths. I remembered Aylah's fond, rueful tone as she had said that Samson never lied . . .

Derceto smiled, and patted me upon my cheek. "You are a good girl, Delilah," she began, and if I had been a cat, my fur would have stood on end. Something coiled, serpent-sleek, beneath the High Priestess's smile, her caress, her soft warm words. All those were false, as false as the painted face she displayed when she acted the part of Goddess-on-Earth.

But I thought of Aylah, and of Samson, and bound my rage and fear, forced them to obey my will. I could not command a smile, so I lowered my gaze as if too honored to look upon the High Priestess of the Great Temple.

"I try to do as Our Lady wishes." My voice whispered mouse-meek. Men forget that a mouse is cunning as well as timid. "You said a heavy task. What is commanded of me?"

"Come, sit beside me." Derceto put her arm about my shoulders, guided me to the alabaster bench beneath the shimmering silver-green leaves of the willow tree. Prince Sandarin followed; I found myself sitting between them, as if they were guards and I a prisoner.

Be silent. Say nothing. Let them speak, let them hone the blade themselves.

I knew that when they looked upon me, they did not see the Delilah who was a girl with too quick a temper, a girl graced with the gifts of dance and of faith, a girl who had lost her beloved sister. They saw no deeper than the paint upon my skin, and so did not see the woman whose heart desired a man she could never claim. *A man who loved me from the moment our eyes first met, who dared the Three Tasks that he might win me.*

Samson saw my heart, saw Delilah the woman.

The High Priestess and the Prince of the City saw the priestess Delilah, the Full Moon who existed only to serve. And not, as I now knew, to serve Our Lady Atargatis—*Her* bidding I would do gladly.

She would not demand that Her loving servants play the parts of whore and murderess. Nor would She sell us into bondage. *You are love itself, Bright Lady. You would not deny me Samson.* Atargatis Herself had sent Samson to me, a gift of love from the Lady of Love. But deeds the goddess would not stoop to beg, Her highest acolytes did not hesitate to demand.

"Delilah, there are things I must tell you that it will pain you to hear," Derceto began, "but you must hear them. For what your heart-sister began, you must complete." She paused, clearly awaiting some answer from me.

I nodded, and she smiled at me and called me good and obedient and brave. I merely waited, watching as the Prince of the City jumped up to pace back and forth behind us like a bored leopard.

Then Derceto said, "There is much you do not yet know, Delilah—"

"And she never will unless you tell her." Prince Sandarin owned far less patience than I. I saw High Priestess Derceto glare at him; if eyes were blades, he would have been stabbed to the bone.

"Some things take subtlety, Prince. The girl already mourns her heart-sister; she must be gently handled." Derceto turned back to me, laid her hand upon my cheek. Then she began to explain, subtly and gently, that Aylah had been chosen by Atargatis to rid the land of Samson, enemy of Our Lady and of the Five Cities. That it was Atargatis Herself who had imbued Samson's heart with desire for Aylah—so great a desire that the Three Tasks did not discourage him.

Samson is no enemy of Our Lady's. I remembered every word Aylah had spoken to me, that day we met in the Grove. And Aylah had spoken of a man almost too sweet-natured, too honey-hearted, to wish harm to anyone. A man who had honored an unwanted bride as greatly as if she had been the true choice of his heart—

"Now I will confide something to you that may sound evil, but sometimes it is necessary to do evil to gain a greater good." Derceto paused, and I nodded again. "It seemed to us that no man could survive the Three Tasks, and that Our Lady, in Her wisdom, had chosen this way of ridding us of Samson's evil."

Only with time did I truly savor Derceto's cleverness; to mix true with false, creating a new truth she wished me to believe. I enjoyed turning her own trick against her, later.

"But Samson completed the Three Tasks." Words I would never before have uttered leapt from my lips, as if Aylah spoke through me. "Did Atargatis change Her mind?"

Derceto eyed me sharply, but I simply stared at her wide-eyed, as if awaiting enlightenment. "Even Atargatis Herself cannot control all things." Derceto's voice was too carefully pious. "Samson's trickery and his god's ill will prevailed in the Three Tasks, and it is not for us to question Her."

No. Samson prevailed because Our Lady saw into his heart and knew him for a good man. A man Aylah loved. A man who was kind to Aylah even though he had been deceived into taking her when his heart desired me—

Prince Sandarin stopped pacing and rounded on us. "Which is why we gave him that priestess. And let us hope that you do better at carrying out Ascalon's will, and Bright Atargatis's will, than she did."

Hearing him speak so, as if Aylah had no name, no value, save as a playing-piece in his game, chilled my skin. Aylah had been right; she had been nothing to City or Temple but a useful tool. *A tool discarded when it no longer fit their hands.*

"Delilah will do what Aylah did not." Derceto laid her hands over mine. "Aylah failed. Perhaps Samson beguiled her—who knows what magic he may possess? But you will not."

"What did Aylah fail to do?" A heaviness oppressed me, a sense of impending storm. Suddenly I remembered Aylah saying, *"I wished to do as she ordered me. Part of what she ordered, anyway."* And I remembered my sense that there was something Aylah would not say, some evil she did not wish me to know . . .

She was to murder Samson. The answer fell into my mind, heavy and sickening as an overripe peach. *That is what Aylah concealed from me, why she was so certain she could never return home to the Temple.* All that had shadowed Derceto's words like relentless ghosts formed into certain knowledge. *The Three Tasks were to have killed Samson. When that failed, Aylah was to murder him. Now Aylah is dead and they will send me to entrap him, because Derceto knows Samson wanted me all along, and will take me now without question.*

"There is no easy way to say this"—Derceto swiftly looked at the Prince of the City, her fierce eyes demanding he remain silent—"so I will say the words plainly. Aylah was to be Atargatis's weapon. She was to slay Samson, but—"

"But she failed." Prince Sandarin strode around to stand before us. "Now the High Priestess here tells me you won't fail us. Is she right?"

Fearing to speak, lest I begin screaming curses at them both, I pressed my hands to my mouth. *Say nothing yet, say nothing until you are calm.*

"One thing more, Delilah. You must know that no matter what promises he may make, what vows he swears, Samson hates us and our gods. He demanded Aylah leave all that was precious to her behind, forbade her to carry anything from the House of Atargatis into her new life." Pain shadowed Derceto's face—or so I would have thought, had I not met with Aylah in the Grove near Sorek.

"Take this." The High Priestess set something small and cool in my hand. "Look at it, if your heart weakens, and remember."

I stared down at the twin of the coral amulet I had given Aylah. The amulet she had still worn when we met at the Grove. The amulet she had placed into my hand, that I might remember her love always. No one in the Temple knew I now held both our sister-tokens in my keeping. What Derceto offered me was a copy, a copy that must have been made before Aylah left Ascalon as Samson's wife. Not a sister-token, but a lure to entice me, gain my willing aid in her plots.

Aylah's ghost whispered to me, telling me evil it hurt even to hear. *"When I did not slay Samson, Temple and City schemed to bring him to their killing ground. Who revealed to my enemies that Samson had left us alone, unguarded, I and my babe?"*

The Temple had betrayed Aylah, condemned her for her failure to commit murder. Aylah the beautiful, the sun-maiden. Aylah the sacrifice, who had always known how she would die. *In fire.*

As the High Priestess and the Prince of the City smiled at each other, I stared down at the false token in my hand. The little fish burned fire-bright against my skin. I closed my fingers over the amulet. *Yes, Derceto, I will look at this, and I will remember. I will remember that Aylah died so I would be willing to lure Samson to his own death.*

"Priestess Delilah? I asked if—"

"If I would fail." Calm, I raised my eyes to the Prince of the City. "I will answer your question now, Prince. I will not fail."

"You will be richly rewarded," Sandarin said. "The Five Cities will be grateful, and generous. You need not slay him yourself, if it proves too difficult—some say the man has his god's protection against blades and poison. Kill him if you can, and if you cannot, find out how he may be taken. Deliver Samson to us, and you may ask anything you choose."

Almost, I said that I needed no reward, but I saw the greed in Derceto's eyes and merely nodded. Let the Prince think what he would; let Derceto believe she would claim for the Temple whatever riches the Five Cities offered. I did not care.

Derceto was false, the world she ruled illusion. All I had loved, Derceto had torn from me. All that Our Lady had given, Derceto had destroyed.

My heart-sister. My joy in the Dance. My first bright desire when I looked upon the man Atargatis had sent for me.

All gone, and in their place, truth. Now I knew what I must do. *I will avenge Aylah, quiet her ghost.* A cold vow, set in the scale beside a hot desire to lay my hands upon Samson's skin. *I will claim Samson, for he is mine.* Unruly passion, burning sudden and fierce as summer wildfire. Aylah herself had begged me to be happy. I forgot that she had also begged me to be cautious, distrusted fierce bright loves.

Our Lady sent him to me. Derceto cheated both the Bright Lady and me. Suddenly I saw Samson's face again, as he had looked up and seen me gazing down from the window. Bright as the sun, his eyes wide with pure awe and desire—

I would avenge Aylah's death. And I would claim Samson as my own, for whatever span of time Our Lady allotted us.

After I left the High Priestess, I wandered, apparently aimlessly, through the corridors and courtyards. I let tears spill, wiped them with my fingers, smearing kohl over my cheeks. I did not care what path I set my feet upon, for there was no place within the Temple that I could trust.

At first I had thought to go to the Court of Peace, seek truth of the Seven Fish. Then I thought of the avid gaze of the fish as the Seer-Priestess dropped seeds into the dark water, of their gaping greedy mouths . . . I clenched my fists; the twin amulets dug into my left palm. The Seven Fish revealed nothing, nothing but what the Seer-Priestess wished us to know. *False. All false.* Always, always Aylah had doubted— and she had been right. The fish were useless—

No. Not useless. Swift as the fish after seeds, the words flashed through my mind. *Think,* I commanded myself. *Think as Derceto thinks. What is an oracle but the revelation of what the Temple wishes us to know?*

Suddenly I remembered my desperate, foolish plea in the days before Aylah had been bartered to Samson: that I might ask the Seer at En-dor what the future truly held for Samson. I had not been given the chance to learn what awaited us all, for Derceto had already decided what was to happen. But now—

"Now Derceto needs you. And you can tell her anything you choose, Delilah." For a breath I thought Aylah stood close to me, that her voice whispered tart wisdom into my ear. Perhaps her ghost had come to me in truth, drawn by my love and grief; I never knew, for I dared not risk even a glance behind me, lest she vanish. And it did not matter, save to my heart, whether Aylah's ghost spoke or whether my memory had summoned my heart-sister's calm ability to pluck sense from passion's tangled web.

Derceto needs me, so I can ask whatever I desire. And she will grant it. So long as the High Priestess must have what only I could give, I could ask anything. I opened my left hand and stared at the two coral fish. By Atargatis's Mercy, no one but I knew that Aylah had come to the Sorek Grove, that she had spoken her heart to me. That I knew she had still worn the sister-token I had given her.

So Derceto had told a foolish, unnecessary lie—a lie that served only to prove her evil. I did not need Aylah's sister-token to remind me of our love, and nothing Derceto said would make me act as a trap for Samson. But Derceto need not know that I would never betray the man who had been kind to my heart-sister, who had fathered her daughter. The man my heart knew Atargatis had sent for me . . .

I will tell Derceto that only at En-dor shall I learn how I may beguile Samson, how I may lure him into the snare the Five Cities prepare for him. But that was not what I would ask of the Seer. I had my own desires that I wished fulfilled; my own future that I wished revealed to me. And I could safely ask whatever I wished, for no one ever knew what passed in the Seer's cave save the petitioner and the Seer herself.

Unless the man or woman who had sought to know what only the Seer's gift could reveal chose to speak of what had been asked and answered, it would remain forever lost in the smoke that stained the walls of the ancient shrine. Derceto would know only what I chose to tell her.

And she will believe you, Delilah. Tell them what words you wish them to hear. Order them to do what tasks you wish to have done.

For the first time, I understood that the fear the Five Cities suffered rendered them vulnerable. Just as pride and arrogance led High Priestess Derceto to look upon all of lesser rank as mere players on her game board—and blinded her to their loves, and their hates, and their ambitions.

Fear, and pride. Two fatal weaknesses.

Fear and pride will force Derceto and the rulers of the Five Cities to believe all I say the gods ordered me to do. Fear and pride will bring them begging to my feet, pleading to grant anything I say the gods have asked.

Fear, and pride—my new allies.

Any tale I choose . . . Silently, I spoke to the only one in all the Temple whom I could trust. *Bright Atargatis, I vow by Your Love that I will free my heart-sister and her daughter. I vow I will unbind their ghosts and release them from the night winds into Your care.*

When Derceto's chief handmaiden came in search of me, seeking to know why I had not come to Sunset Prayers, I was lying upon my bed, weeping. I heard the rustle of cloth as Mottara pushed aside the curtain, the clink of anklets as she slipped into my room. I refused to move, to acknowledge the handmaiden's presence. After a few moments, she slunk off again. I waited, but no one else came, either to chide or to comfort.

I rose, and wiped the tears from my face. No one had come to light the lamps, but that did not matter. I did not need light to comb a lock of my hair smooth, to braid Aylah's amulet into it beside the lion's claw token she had given me. The false token, the one Derceto had given, I bound with a red thread and hid among my lesser jewels.

Let Derceto see and hear only that I wore a coral fish beside a lion's claw—a good omen, a sign I would be the weapon the Five Cities demanded. Derceto needed good omens now; she would believe it so because she wished to believe. Yes, and she would willingly grant what I would ask of her.

This time when I told Derceto I must go to En-dor, to find wisdom there, she would agree. And if she did not . . .

If she did not, I would say I could do nothing without consulting the Seer at En-dor. *And Derceto will believe me, for it will be the truth.* To learn what I must do to gain what I most desired, I knew I must ask at En-dor.

My journey to En-dor was the second time I left my home in the Great House of Atargatis, traveled beyond the walls of Ascalon the Beautiful. Unlike my first excursion, when I went to act the Goddess at the Sorek Grove, I did not gaze about in wonder and joyous anticipation. This time, I studied the landscape I was carried through, noting the twists and turns, marking where the road ran straight and safe, where tumbled rocks or tangled bushes might conceal danger. The way from Ascalon to En-dor was long, and I felt uneasy in my bones. During the day I suffered forebodings to which I could not put names. At night, when I slept, I dreamed that I walked the road alone.

I was not alone, of course. As was fitting, I traveled in a litter, es-

corted by a dozen Temple guards and accompanied by two handmaidens twice my age. No one with any sense would hinder us upon the
road—or so I was constantly assured once we left the highway that ran
along the seacoast and turned inland, heading north to the hills below
the Sea of Kinneret. I listened to the guards as they talked among themselves, gauging the risk of one route over another; they were not easy in
their minds about this journey. They spoke of the danger of foxes,
which seemed odd to me, for what danger could foxes be to an armed
band of men?

"Have you not heard of Samson's Foxes?" Bodar asked, when I questioned him. Bodar commanded the Temple guards escorting me, and as
the High Priestess herself had given me into his care, Bodar treated me
with more respect than my rank alone demanded. When I shook my
head, he explained that bands of men roamed the hill roads. "Brigands,
claiming Samson as their leader."

"Do you not believe he commands these robbers?" I knew Samson
would never condone the deeds the Foxes committed in his name.
Aylah had called him kind and lenient, and almost too truthful.
And I had my own memories of Samson: freeing my trapped hair
the day I led the Sun Partridge Dance; standing patient in the Temple
courtyard waiting on the High Priestess's pleasure; smiling up at me
where I stood watching—such little things, to claim my heart forever . . .

No, Samson would never lead such wanton killers as the Foxes. But
I wished to know what others thought of Samson—truly thought,
when no one stood nearby to judge every unwary word. "Why do you
doubt?" I asked Bodar now. "Is not Samson the greatest enemy of the
Five Cities?"

Bodar hesitated, as if trying to decide what I wished to hear. At last
he said, "Perhaps he does lead them. Or perhaps he once led them and
no longer does so. Many now call themselves Samson's Foxes. Easy to
claim, my lady priestess."

"Yes," I said, "easy to claim." Then I thanked him and withdrew to think over what he had said. Many Foxes now, all proclaiming Samson as leader. *He never ordered such crimes; he has not an evil drop of blood within his veins. But I know who would order any evil if it gains her what she wishes. How would these Foxes know when to strike at Samson's home?* Someone had sent the Foxes that knowledge. Derceto. With one stroke, the High Priestess punished Aylah's failure and gave Samson a reason to take revenge. *She laid all blame upon Samson, created out of nothing a madman who robbed and killed, who ravaged farmlands and destroyed peace.*

Fear now traveled the high roads; Samson's shadow, silent and deadly. And who would believe that shadow truly belonged not to Samson, but to Derceto?

All my life I had heard the Seer of En-dor whispered of as the most powerful of all those who Saw Beyond. I had envisioned a rich shrine, beautiful and imposing; I had imagined She Who Saw decked with gems and garbed as richly as a goddess.

Instead, at the end of my journey, I faced an uneven path that I followed to a narrow opening in a rocky hillside. Just outside the cave sat a small girl setting white pebbles in a circle; she looked up as I slowly approached, and then pointed to the dark doorway.

"Am I to go in?" I asked, but the child simply went back to playing with the white pebbles. I looked behind me down the path; large tumbled boulders hid my escort from my sight. I could go back or I could enter the cave. I drew a deep breath and stepped forward, into darkness.

I never did see the cave clearly. Even when my eyes adapted themselves to the dim light, I could make out only the banked fire on an ancient stone hearth, and the figure of a woman crouched beside the smoldering wood. Smoke permeated the air, rich and bitter; laurel burned in the fire, or myrrh. Smoke and darkness embraced me, oddly comforting. I was safe here, as safe as I had been while I grew in my mother's womb . . .

"Did you come to stand forever in my doorway? Come in or go away."

The Seer's voice held no emotion, nor did she turn to look at me. I stepped carefully forward, until I stood beside her. Neither young nor old, nor half-mad from the burden of great power, the Seer seemed no more than any mortal woman. Now that I stood close, I saw that she sat cross-legged, and that she had laurel leaves piled in her lap. As I watched, she took a handful of the leaves and dropped them onto the slow fire. Flames hungrily ate the leaves, sending even more smoke surging upward.

"Ask your question, Priestess," she said.

"You know—" I began, and stopped. Of course the Seer knew why I had come. Why else, but to learn my future? Doubtless she knew who I was, and perhaps even why I stood here now.

"You are here. Ask." She tossed another handful of laurel leaves upon the hearth. Smoke swirled through the cave, and with each breath we drew its heady power into our bodies. "Ask, Dark One. What would you know?"

I had thought hard and long on this; had formed the question I would ask She Who Saw with the care of a seal-carver etching an image into flawless crystal. I had repeated the words a dozen times a day as I journeyed here, until I knew my petition by heart, knew it as well as I knew the prayers to Atargatis. *Reveal to me how I may avenge my heart-sister and her daughter. Show me how I may unveil Derceto's evil. Show me the way to my future with the man my heart desires.*

But now I remembered nothing.

And into the smoke and silence, I heard my voice speaking words that were not my own. "I would know Samson's fate."

The words seemed to swirl upward into the smoke; I longed to breathe them back in, but it was too late. The question had been asked— and I longed to know what future awaited Samson. *His fate is mine, now.*

The Seer nodded, and held her hands over the smoky fire. "Show me Samson. Show me the Son of the Sun."

The smoke coiled, darkened; the Seer keened as if mourning a child. When she spoke again, her words echoed against the stone surrounding us. "The Son of the Sun. Bound by a woman, he will destroy a god. Night comes when the Sun dies. Go now, Night's Daughter. It is not yet time for you here."

Then silence. At last I realized the Seer had left only her body here; her spirit walked among the ghosts of past and future. She would say no more to me now.

En-dor not only granted me an answer I did not yet understand, but unbound a power I had not known I possessed. When I returned to Ascalon, to the Great House of Atargatis, and bowed before the High Priestess before looking straight into her lying eyes, I knew that Derceto feared me now. *She is afraid I will learn the truth, all she has done to bring me to this moment.* Derceto would do anything to keep me her willing weapon against Samson. *Oh, yes, I can now ask whatsoever I desire, and it will be granted.*

"Well, Delilah?" Derceto asked. "Did the Seer at En-dor reveal what you must do?"

"Yes, High Priestess. Everything I must do was revealed. Grant what I ask, and I will do what must be done."

"Ask," was all she said, but it was enough.

I smiled, and began to speak. "First, I will need your blessing, High Priestess. And then I will require jewels and fine garments and a cook who can prepare rich dishes well. And I will need a house, a house in the Valley of Sorek..."

"The Valley of Sorek," I had decreed, and so it was there, in that lush wild garden, that the Temple's trap was set.

Of the lands that belonged to the Temple, I chose an extravagant, frivolous pleasure-palace that lay upon the southern bank of the glittering River Sorek. Beyond the gilt-edged wall surrounding the house, fields of poppies spread bright as blood. A grove of pomegranate trees

shaded the southern wall, and the small cinnamon-sweet roses of Da-
mascus grew in the sheltered gardens.

Opulent as a queen's court, lavishly painted and tiled and gilded;
whatever clean beauty the dwelling might have possessed was hidden as
completely as a priestess behind her painted mask. No one offered any
objection when I stared at the sun blazing on the gold-tipped elephant
tusks arching above the courtyard gate and said,

"This one."

Those two words set the Temple's plan, my plan, into motion. I neither knew nor cared who dwelt within the river-palace, or where they
would go, now that I had claimed this property for my own use.

Nor did I think the Temple cared overmuch. I had chosen as I had
been expected to choose—a palace that was a treasure in itself, whose
riches would dazzle princes. A mere man would be overwhelmed. But I
knew Samson would not be dazzled; Samson would see the palace for
what it was. A snare.

But the snare was not crafted to catch Samson, but his enemies—
and mine.

I knew I must take care, for Derceto was no fool. I must seem to
work wholehearted to do Derceto's bidding. There are many ways to
seduce a man, to bend him to the Lady's will. Knowing myself watched,
I began with the most obvious. Derceto expected me to offer myself to
Samson, to seduce him with my body. So that was how I would begin.
As long as the High Priestess believed me to be wholly her creature,
Samson and I would be safe together.

Safe to plan our vengeance against those who had sent Aylah to her
death.

The palace I had chosen had been created for pleasure alone. A summer
dwelling rich with open colonnades and latticed windows, it had gardens planted to reveal their beauty at certain times, or in certain light.
There was a Moon Garden, in which only white flowers grew; by day
the garden seemed dull, lifeless. But it came alive by night. When the

moon rose full, the white flowers glowed in its silver light like pearls, became mirrors of the moon.

But the Sun Garden was my favorite. There every flower glowed yellow as sunlight: day lilies and narcissus and iris, bright little suns against the cool green of their leaves. Just to stand within its brightness warmed my heart.

Much of the house had been built of cedar, and the sharp clean scent of that wood underlay the extravagant perfumes of frankincense and nard. Many of the walls had been painted with scenes of pretty women dancing or handsome men hunting. On the wall of one of the long open colonnades, blue monkeys picked pale yellow crocuses.

Sometimes it seemed to me that not even a handspan of the palace's walls had been left unadorned. What was not painted was set with tiles of brilliant red, blue, and yellow. Exuberant, finely carved patterns swirled over cedar pillars. Gateways were inlaid with silver, or with lapis, or with ivory. So much of that precious material adorned the palace that the dwelling had been named for it: the House of Ivory.

I liked the name; it reminded me of the Ivory Gate at the heart of Our Lady's House. And in spite of all the hatred and cold anger I felt for the High Priestess, I still loved Bright Atargatis. I had lost my heart-sister, and my trust in the Temple, but not my goddess. That faith, at least, I still possessed.

Samson

"Like a panther Delilah hunted Samson; like a serpent she beguiled him. And even Samson, stronger than a hundred men, was weaker than one frail woman . . ."

To the end of his long life, Orev never forgot how the dark dancer had claimed Samson's future as if the days of his life belonged to her by right. Delilah had used no guile to ensnare him; no wiles to keep him. She had merely waited, patient as time, until Samson came to her.

The news that Delilah Moondancer, priestess in the Great House of Atargatis, had left Ascalon to dwell in the ivory palace in the Valley of Sorek traveled swiftly. When the tale reached Samson's ears, he said,

"I go to the House of Ivory. Do you come with me, Orev?"

A chill slid through Orev's bones. "Don't, Samson. There is nothing there for you."

"You're wrong, friend harper. You heard her name. Now they have sent her whom my heart seeks."

"They've sent a trap, Samson."

"Yes." Samson shrugged. "That's a small matter."

"It will be a great matter when the Philistines take you. They'll chain you to a rock out in the harbor and leave you there for the fish to feast upon."

Samson laughed—but his laughter was no longer the joyous sound it had been before he lost wife and child to fire. "You worry too much."

"And you don't worry enough. Forget about Delilah. Do you think those who rule Ascalon's Temple have sent her because they believe they owe you another wife?" Orev knew speaking so brutally carried risks; he counted on Samson's innate honesty and inability to lie even to himself.

For a moment Samson closed his eyes, shook his head as if to banish cruel memories. Then he said, "No, I think as you do—that the House of Atargatis has sent another weapon against me." He gazed down the river valley to the west, as if he could see the House of Ivory before him. "But I told you, it doesn't matter. I go to meet my fate. Come or not, as you choose."

She stood waiting within a window, as if she knew not only that he would come to her, but when. Samson strode through the garden as if he had walked its path many times, and stopped, looking up at her.

"I am here," he said, and she leaned upon the window's ledge, gazed down into his eyes.

"Wait," she said, and withdrew into the shadows behind her. A few moments later she came out to him, moving cat-soft, cat-supple, into the sunlit garden. She wore nothing but a skirt of blue-green silk sewn with peacocks' eyes and a scarlet girdle knotted about her hips; the girdle's long tassels fell almost to her ankles. A small coral fish upon a golden chain lay between her bare breasts. Samson reached out and laid his fingers gently upon the coral amulet.

"You wear Aylah's charm."

"Yes." She lifted her hand, curled her fingers over his. "The High Priestess gave it to me, so that I might always look upon the amulet and remember how my heart-sister died." She pulled away, held up her hand, the coral fish resting upon her palm. "Look upon it now, Samson. What do you see?"

Samson looked, and something changed in his face; the sun darkened. "I see truth," he said. "What do you see?"

"I, too, see truth." Delilah had tilted her hand and let the amulet slide back down between her breasts. "Come in to me, and we will share our truths. I have waited long days and nights for you, Sun of my heart."

No, Delilah had needed nothing to ensnare Samson—nothing but herself.

Delilah

At first I was uneasy with him—I, Delilah Moondancer, Full Moon of Atargatis who had been the Goddess for a dozen men, felt fear coil beneath my heart. For this time I was not acting as Our Lady; no goddess used my body as Her own. Now, with Samson, I was only Delilah, a woman he desired and who desired him.

I felt lost, afraid, as if all my hard-learned skills had vanished. Would I please him? Would he think me a poor substitute for Aylah? Aylah, whom we both had loved, in our different ways . . .

So when I beckoned Samson into my bedchamber, I trembled as if I were a maiden again, and he the first man I had ever seen. When I took his hand, his warmth seemed to burn my cold skin. It took no great wisdom for him to see my heart-sickness.

When I sat upon the leopard-skins that covered the bed, and urged him to lie beside me, he merely sat next to me and put an arm about my shoulders. He touched my cheek, gently, and I flinched as if burned. "Do not tremble so," he said. "You need not fear, I shall not force myself upon you. I thought you wished this, but if you do not—"

"I do," I said, and then, willing myself to tell at least some truth, "But I fear I will not please you."

Samson laughed, softly. "It is I who should fear I will not please you—you, the most desired priestess in Ascalon."

"Only because Aylah chose you over the Temple." I longed to know if he favored his memories of Aylah over me; I knew I should not ask. Whether he said yes or no, I would hate him for it. So I did not question him—not then. I drew a deep breath, felt the false amulet lying warm against my skin. "Samson, there are things I must tell you—"

He slid his fingers down my throat, between my bare breasts, touched the coral fish. "And things I must tell you. But must they be said now?"

My skin burned where his fingers had traced a path. "No." My heart beat so hard I could only whisper my words. "No. Later will be time enough. Later."

After that, we did not speak; there was no need for words between us. At last I held my golden hero in my arms, and I forgot all else. And for once, as I lay with a man, I was only Delilah, and not a vessel for my goddess. I shall always be glad that I remembered to lay wreaths of poppies and roses at Her feet each morning, that I gave thanks to Her for Her gift of human love.

But when the first hot swift rush of passion eased, we talked, Samson and I—talked until the sky darkened, and then through the cool deep hours of night. It seemed we had known each other always. And we spoke most of Aylah, whom we both had loved, and who had loved us.

That first night I told him everything I knew from Aylah, and from Derceto, and from my own wounded heart. Being Samson, he neither raged nor struck out at me. Instead, when I ceased speaking he asked only, "Is that all you know, Delilah?" Without waiting for my answer, he reached out and slid his fingers between my skin and the coral amulet. "My friend Orev calls me too trusting, but you are far more innocent than I."

As I stared, Samson closed his fingers about the coral fish; with one swift tug, he snapped the thin chain that held it about my neck. As I touched my throat, Samson studied the coral amulet, then set it upon the cushion beside us. He put his hands on my shoulders. "Listen to me, Delilah, and although I am no harper, I shall tell you a story."

"And I shall tell one in my turn." I looked at the amulet Samson had torn away; reached up to touch Aylah's true token hidden in the Lady's Knot at the nape of my neck. "Tell yours first, Samson."

"Who gave you that, Delilah? Oh, it looks like the sister-token you gave to her, it is a fine copy—but it is not the one Aylah wore."

I smiled—or, rather, I bared my teeth, as if I were a hunting cat. "The High Priestess Derceto gave me that amulet with her own hands. She said you forced Aylah to abandon all that bound her to the House of Atargatis."

"Your High Priestess lied." Samson gazed steadily into my eyes. "Aylah told me—"

"I know what Aylah told you, Samson. For I spoke with her in the Sorek Grove, when you two had been half a year wed and she carried your child beneath her heart." I drew a deep breath; there would be no retreat from what I must say now. "I know the High Priestess lied, my love. I know how she deceived you, tricked you into wedding Aylah—"

"When I had asked for you?" He touched the little coral fish, stared at it as if it could summon back the past. "I know Aylah went to Sorek Grove to see you once more. Tell me what Aylah said to you at the Grove that day, Delilah."

He did not look at me and spoke soberly; I knew what he asked of me was important. Slowly, that I might speak only what Aylah had indeed said to me, I repeated what I remembered of my heart-sister's words. "And then, at the last, she asked me to call down Our Lady's blessing upon her and the child she carried."

"And that is all?"

I sifted the memories of that day again, then nodded. "Yes, that is all."

"Then I shall tell you what Aylah did not." Samson moved away, reclined upon the carpet at my feet, so that he might gaze up into my face. "She was a tool, yes, but not merely a bride to stand in your place. Your Temple never intended to lose her forever.

"Your heart-sister . . ." He looked at my fingers touching coral fish and went on. "She was commanded not only to wed me but to slay me. Aylah told me all before we reached our home in Timnath. Your High Priestess gifted her with hairpins filled with venom. Upon our wedding night, Aylah was to pierce my skin with those pins. I would have died before morning."

"Yes," I said, "I know. The High Priestess herself told me." I remembered again Aylah's eyes refusing to meet mine when we spoke at the Sorek Grove. She had not wanted me to lose my faith in the Temple and those who ruled over it. *Oh, Aylah—you were kinder and wiser than I.* Slowly, I reached into my braided and coiled hair, unbound the Lady's Knot, and shook my hair free. I claimed the true amulet from its hiding place and held it out to Samson.

"This is the true sister-token I once gave Aylah. She gave it back to me when we met in Sorek's Grove, that I might remember her always. Will you take it from me, Samson?"

He gazed down at the little fish lying upon my palm, red coral against honey skin. "I would cherish it, Delilah. But will you not regret giving it up to me? I know what Aylah was to you."

"And still is. I need no token to summon her memory." The true token would be given, as it had been before, with love. "Besides," I said, "I have the other, the false token the High Priestess gave to me, when she told me you had caused Aylah's death. When she sent me to murder you." I paused, waiting, but Samson revealed no surprise. Well, only a true fool would not have suspected me, after the Temple had already sent one woman to kill him.

When he said nothing, I smiled, and held out the coral fish to him. The true amulet I would give to Aylah's husband, whom I also loved. The false amulet I would keep, to remind me always that the High Priestess, the Goddess-on-Earth, had lied, and had sent my heart-sister to her death. "Take this token, with both Aylah's love and mine. You can bind it in your hair."

"You set it there," he said. "Your fingers are cleverer than mine."

And so with my fingers I combed out Samson's sun-bright hair and braided the coral amulet into the soft golden mane. As I tied the final knot, I bent forward and kissed the hollow between his neck and shoulder. "There," I said, "now you are bound to me."

"A willing prisoner," he said. "Sun and Moon—"

Fear sliced my heart, and I swiftly laid my fingers over his lips. "Do not say it, my love. It is ill luck." All I could think was that once Aylah and I had been Sun and Moon together, and Aylah had burned, as if consumed by the Sun she had been called.

"Then I will tell you something sweeter to the ear," he said. "Your hair is like summer night, and your breasts like full moons."

"Now, perhaps. But what of when I am twice as old as I am this perfect day? My hair will dull, my breasts sag. What pretty words will you have for me then, when the years have changed me?"

"Everything changes, Delilah. You battle against Time itself. Against Life itself. You cannot win." He smiled at me. "And you a priestess of the Lady in Ascalon!"

"You mean I should know better?"

"I mean you should believe life's truth."

"Oh, I know the truth." I rolled over; my hair slid like midnight serpents across his sun-kissed chest. "Samson—" I hesitated, for what I wished to say to him was treason thrice over, and blasphemous as well.

He stroked my hair, coiled it into circles that burned dark against his skin. "Speak, Delilah. A trouble shared is a trouble—"

"Known to all the world within a month." I sat up, my movement pulling my hair away from his body. Thus far we had spoken with a passionate caution, chosen each word, each tone of voice, with great care. "Not tonight, my love. I will tell you, but not tonight. Will you trust me, and wait?"

"I trust you, but why wait? Come away with me now." He took my hand, laced his fingers through mine. "There is nothing to keep you here."

Desire burned; desire to leave pain and grief behind, to follow him to world's end. But I could not abandon my ghosts . . .

"Delilah?" Samson's voice seemed to come from far away. "You summoned me here for more than a night's passion. Will you not tell me why?"

"I will, I swear I will. But we have time—from full moon to full moon, before those who sent me lose patience."

"And send armed men against me instead of a woman."

"Yes," I said. "Give me seven nights, Samson. Seven days and nights for us. Then—"

"Then it will be time to speak of what lies ahead." His voice sounded hard as stone. I looked into his eyes and saw that he, too, lived with ghosts.

"Yes. But until then, we are free." Of course we were not; all we possessed was the illusion of freedom. But for that short span of time, illusion was enough.

I longed to know all I could of Samson, and I had no shame. I asked his friend, the harper called Orev, to tell me all that Samson himself would not. It was from Orev that I learned how Samson wished only peace, how he had tried to guard the roads for travelers, even those unknown to him. From Aylah, I already knew how Samson loved women, was kind even to a bride he had been tricked into accepting. But to hear from Orev of Samson's care for strangers, for the weak and helpless, human or beast, gave me an odd pleasure.

"You love Samson well, do you not?" I asked, and Orev said, "He is both the brother I never had and the son I never shall have. He is unlike any other man I have ever met."

"A mighty warrior," I suggested, and Orev laughed.

"Only because others claim him to be so. Samson is no warrior.

What he loves best to do is build, to create useful things from wood and stone. He has no desire to rule over others or to gain great riches."

"He lacks ambition? He, who could be a king among his own people?" I waited, as Orev frowned, choosing carefully what words he next would speak to me.

"Once Samson was a man of peace who would not choose a king's glory over long happy days. Now—" Sorrow shadowed Orev's eyes. "Now I do not know. Which would you choose, Delilah?"

"Neither," I said. "I choose justice for the dead."

"No matter the price?"

"Whatever the price is, I will pay it."

Orev smiled, but his eyes still grieved. "I fear Samson is willing to pay it as well. Remember, Delilah, that the gods laugh at mortal plans."

They were sweet, those few precious days I spent with Samson in the House of Ivory. For seven days we thought of nothing but each other, did nothing but play at love all day and all night. Aylah had been right: Samson had been formed of sunlight, and once no shadows had darkened his mind or his heart. Once he had been unthinkingly happy, as I had been— and for this short span of time, I wanted that happiness back for us.

I enjoyed teasing him; we would lie by the round pool at the heart of the Moon Garden, where all the flowers bloomed white, and I would tell my stories and beg him to tell me his.

He never wished to; he was the least prideful man I ever met. "There is little to tell, Delilah. I have done nothing that any other man might not do, if he chose. You should ask Orev, if you wish to hear tales of great deeds."

I smiled; it was easy to smile at Samson. "That is not what I have heard, Samson. I have heard . . ." I shrugged, letting a veil slip away until the smoke-soft cloth barely clung to my breasts. "Oh, I have heard many tales of you. That you slew a lion with your bare hands. That you slew a hundred men with only an old bone as weapon. That you carried away the great gates of Gaza. Because of a woman, of course—a harlot, was she not?"

Here he laughed. "I have never lain with a harlot, and as for the gates of Gaza, I have seen them. A man might hammer out the hinge-pins, but the gates are taller than two men, and thick bronze covers the cedar. It would take a god to carry them off." He paused, then said, "Or a man with a cart and stout oxen to draw it."

It was that tale that sparked a plan in my mind; Samson knew how to make wood and stone do his bidding. I, too, laughed, softly; how like Samson to think of the way a thing might truly be done by a mortal man. "A cart and oxen? What true hero uses such poor things?" I asked, and he smiled.

"I am no hero, Delilah—nor am I god-begotten, which I have also heard said of me. I am only a man, with as many faults as any other man. You are a priestess, so I am sure you will believe what I will tell you of how my mother conceived me. Unless you would rather listen to Orev sing it?"

"No, I would always rather hear your voice, and of course I will believe you. I know you would never lie to me." Of course he would not; never in all my life did I meet another man so pure of mind and heart.

"Listen then, and I will tell the tale as I was told it—and as my father was told it, and all those who dwelt in our village heard it."

It was a common enough tale: a plain good man wed a girl for her pretty face. The years passed, and the pretty girl had no children. This was a hard thing for her to bear. A barren woman was reckoned worthless, a man without children reckoned cursed.

"No sons to carry on a man's name, to care for him and his wife in their old age—yes, that is a curse."

"No daughters to carry on a woman's name—that too is a curse," I added, and waited to hear what he would say, remembering Aylah had told me his people valued sons far above daughters.

Samson only twined his fingers in my loosened hair; the dark strands formed a net about his hand. "Well, we agree that children are a blessing," he said, and continued with the tale of his miraculous birth.

His father Manoah did not berate his wife for her barrenness, nor did he set her aside. But he prayed hard and long for a son.

"My mother loved my father dearly, and longed for a child as much as any other woman. And one day an emissary from Yahweh appeared to her and told her she would bear a son. Well, she found that hard to believe, but nevertheless she ran and told Manoah what had transpired.

"My father doubted, and prayed to Yahweh to reveal the truth to him. And my mother went out a second time, and met again with the angel, who again told her she would bear a son. And again she ran and told this to my father."

"And what happened?" I asked. I leaned my head against Samson's chest, heard his heart beat slow and strong.

"What happened? A moon's turn later, she told my father she was with child. She also swore the angel had said that she must eat only the best food, that no wine nor unclean thing must pass her lips.

"So goes the tale: an angel of the Lord appeared unto her—and lo, my mother conceived and brought forth me." Samson laughed, a low, oddly rueful sound. "That is the story she has told so often she must think it truth by now. But I think it only half the truth."

"Only half?"

"How is it that my father's seed should quicken within her womb only then, when it never before did so?" He shook his head; his hair swayed across his back like wheat stirred by summer wind.

"What, then? Did your god's messenger bring your mother more than hopeful words? Many heroes are god-gotten."

He hesitated, then took my hands. "If I tell, you must swear you will tell no one."

"I will not utter a word of any secret you may tell me, my heart. I will swear it upon anything you desire."

"Your promise is enough."

"But should I not vow it upon some sacred object?"

He shrugged. "If your promise is faithless, will a sworn promise be worth more? You have said you will keep what I reveal to you close. That is vow enough for me."

"You are too good, Samson. Remember all men are not so pure."

"That is their business, not mine."

"And what is yours, Lord of the Sun?" I tried to keep my tone light, as if I merely played with words.

He turned his hands over so that mine lay in his palms like waiting doves, honey-soft against his hardened skin. "To live. To laugh." He bent and kissed the centers of my palms, his lips warm against my skin. "To love."

Tears burned behind my eyes. *Oh, Samson, do you think either gods or men will grant such freedom to any mortal?* Aloud, I said the first words that fell into my mind. "Did your mother love your father?"

He smiled. "She loved her husband. As for my father—I do not think she ever even saw his face. I think she went to the Lady's Grove on the full moon, and lay with whoever laid red roses at her feet. The angel of the Lord said only that she would conceive a son. How—that was her riddle to solve."

"How like a man, to load all into a basket and set it into a woman's arms to carry!" I exclaimed. But the tale made sense. How else would an Israelite come by that sun-gold hair, those summer-sky eyes? His father must have traveled far to reach the Ascalon Grove. Achaean, perhaps, or from even farther north.

"Perhaps my father still doubted that an angel of the Lord had appeared to her; perhaps he believed every word. He has always treated me as if I were his true son. And you, Delilah? Who lay with your mother in the Grove to get you?"

"I never think of it." Now I wondered why I had not. And now I did not wish to waste the precious time I had been granted. I knew that, after a month, Temple and City would want what I had been ordered to bring them: Samson.

I felt sorrow drag at my skin; Samson ran his thumb over my lips. "You look ready to weep, my heart. What troubles you?"

I drew a deep breath and put my hand over his, pressing his palm against my cheek. "The time for love-play is over. It is time I told you all the truth, Samson."

"What, that the Temple set you as a snare before me? A blind man could see that."

"But you do not know why I consented to act as bait in their trap," I said, and Samson smiled.

"Because you love me beyond reason, of course. You see? I am no more humble than any other man."

Above us the sky arched, a deep endless blue; the sun gilded all its light brushed. We had gone out of the House of Ivory, down to the shore of the Sorek. There we sat in silence for a time, watching the river-water ripple past like spangled silk.

Then Samson said, "I love you, Delilah. I have loved you from the first moment I saw you, all ebony and gold and with your hair caught by a wreath of roses."

"Love? I am one of Atargatis's Doves, Samson. Can you love a woman who has been Atargatis Herself for other men?"

He did not answer at once; I liked that better than if he had blurted out his reply unthinking. "Yes," he said at last.

"Truly? And can you love me only? I have heard that you lust after all women, Samson."

"And if that is truth, do you blame me for my desires?"

"Not I. But you are pledged to your people's god, are you not? I have also heard that your god does not smile upon men who run after women not of your own tribes."

"Say rather that my people's Judges do not smile upon such men. Truly, I do not think Yahweh cares, or He would have chastised me for my actions long since." Samson reached out and caught the edge of my veil. "Since Yahweh made all the world, He made women as well as men. And since He is Lord over all the earth, He knows He created women to be loved."

I laughed again; laughter was my strength, my refuge. "So your god's name is Yahweh? What does that mean?"

Samson smiled; sunlight stroked his hair, drew bright gleams from his sky-eyes. "It means—oh, Lord, the One. The God."

"What a foolish name." I chose a pearl from the gilded basket I had filled with sea-gems, tossed the pearl into the Sorek, slanting my eyes to see what Samson thought of this mad extravagance.

Rather than looking shocked, or chiding me, he smiled again and plucked a handful of pearls from the gilded basket. He flung three into the river, carefully aiming to land in the fading ripples created by the pearl I had flung, as if to give it company.

"From water they came, and to water they return," he said. "Now, Pearl Beyond Price, tell what your Atargatis's name means."

"Lady of Heaven. Star—" I began, and Samson laughed.

"What foolish names," he said. "I have traveled far, Delilah, and all the gods and goddesses are called Lord and Lady, Sun and Moon, Father and Mother. Their names mean God. Or Goddess. Don't frown at me, Night-Hair. One should be glad to learn truth."

"I know enough truth to last me a dozen lifetimes." My words sounded bitter as vinegar; for all our love, our happiness veiled grief and anger unappeased. *Oh, Aylah, heart-sister. How could they have sacrificed you, and for nothing, nothing.* Tears pressed hot behind my eyes.

Samson reached out and set his fingers against my cheeks, his touch gentle as a morning breeze upon my skin. "Don't weep, my love. Come with me. I will take you away—"

"As you took Aylah? I would be no safer than she." I wished the words unsaid the moment I uttered them, but it was too late. Tears slid hot and wet down my face. Samson stroked away my tears; I opened my eyes to see streaks of malachite and lapis gleaming vivid upon his hands.

"Something eats your heart, and it is not only Aylah's death," he said. "Tell me. It is time. We cannot lie to ourselves any longer, my love."

I drew in a breath that shuddered through my body. I knew I stood upon a spindle's point, that the words I next spoke would spin whatever future I desired. I could say anything, or nothing. Or I could speak the truth, the truth we had both promised each other that first day Samson came to me in the House of Ivory. Always, beneath our sunlit love, ghosts and darkness had waited.

Still I hesitated, knowing what I must say would stab Samson's heart. But Aylah's ghost whispered on every breeze, watched from every shadow. I owed her justice. And I owed Samson truth.

"The Temple ordered Aylah slain, Samson. And it was those calling themselves Foxes who killed her."

For a time he remained silent, as if he had not heard me. Then he glanced down at his hands, rubbed his fingertips together, smearing the green and blue eye paint he had wiped from my cheeks. At last he said, "Do you think I do not know who killed my wife and child? But who sent them—that I did not know. How is it you know this, Delilah?"

"I learned it from the High Priestess herself, and from the Prince of the City, too. I do not know why your Foxes should do Derceto's bidding, but—"

"I know why." Samson's voice was so low I could barely hear the words. "The Foxes sought to turn me into a weapon against the Five Cities."

"As the Temple sought to turn me into a weapon against you." My mouth tasted bitter; I swallowed hard. "You are right. The time for love is over, Samson. I have sworn to avenge Aylah and her daughter. Will you aid me?"

He looked at me steadily, as if judging my strength. "You should blame me as well as your High Priestess." Samson looked straight into my eyes, accepting that I would hate him for what he next would say. "I left her alone, with only Orev to watch over her and the child. I knew she was troubled, fearing the Temple would punish her for failing to do as she had been ordered. I should have listened to her."

"Yes," I said. "But you are not to blame for the evil others do. You did not slay Aylah and her child. The Foxes killed them, with Derceto's aid, and the City's. And we shall make them pay for what they have done."

He looked down at the ground, as if he found answers there. Perhaps he did, for after half a dozen breaths he lifted his head and looked into my eyes. "I, too, have vowed to avenge them. When I looked upon the ashes of my house, I heard Yahweh tell me to wait, that in time I would have justice. But when, and how? I can hunt down the Foxes, but others, too, are guilty."

Now. The time to speak is now. I drew a deep breath and began. "Listen, my love, for at last I have a plan . . ."

A plan that Samson's own tales had given life. Stone loved Samson; he could set his hands upon it and it would work happily to his will. The new Great House of Dagon in Gaza had been built of stone— built, so Samson told me a master builder had claimed, poorly. They had built upon a foundation that would not hold, with stones that awaited only the right touch to free them to fall. To crush, and kill.

The Five Cities feared Samson, longed to enslave him, to destroy this great hero utterly. "They wish you forgotten, Samson. You forgotten and your people despairing."

"Your plan, beloved?"

Love flowed through my blood, forbidden fire released. How could any woman breathing not love him? Even though I lay naked in his arms, when I spoke, his eyes remained upon my face; he heeded my words.

"Listen, sun of my heart—this is a reckless scheme, a dangerous one." I put my hand over his mouth, silently forbidding him to speak yet. "The new Great House of Dagon is to be dedicated at the next new moon. The Lords and Ladies, the High Priests and High Priestesses of the Five Cities will be there to honor Dagon. They will stand by the great altar there. If you can bring down that part of the Temple then, it will slay those who plot against you, who sent Aylah to her death, and her daughter with her. But—"

He lifted my fingers from his lips, kissed the palm of my hand. "But to do that, I must be there, in the Temple, on the day it is dedicated."

"Yes."

"And I am too well-known to go as a worshipper of Dagon."

"Yes," I said again.

"There is another thing, Delilah. How long will your High Priestess wait for you to accomplish your task? Already we have dallied here half a moon."

"And yes a third time." A full moon glowed when I first took Samson in my arms; soon it would be moon-dark. "I have delayed, sent word that you have some secret to your strength, your power, that I must beguile you into revealing what will render you helpless. That I have cozened the secret from you three times, only to find you lied to me."

He laughed. "And she believes this?"

"She dare not disbelieve. She wants the glory of claiming you for her Temple, just as the Prince of the City desires the glory of defeating you. We will cheat both, and award the prize to Gaza. I will go to those who rule the Five Cities, and the Great Houses of the gods, and tell them that Dagon claims you for his own. That you must be displayed in His new Great House on the day it is dedicated."

I leaned back and gazed up at Samson. "And then—"

"And then I, their sacrifice, shall give Dagon more than he ever thought to receive." Samson smiled; for a heartbeat he seemed all sun and lion. I could believe a god had fathered him.

"Is it a good plan, my sun of all men? Tell me, is it pleasing to your god?"

"He is a god of hard justice. Yes. Tell me, my queen of night, is it pleasing to your soft goddess?"

I thought of Aylah, who had sung Her prayers and danced before Her altar. Aylah, who had not truly believed, but had done her best to do Her honor. Aylah, who had lain with Samson in the Lady's Dance, and borne a daughter, proof of Her favor . . .

"Yes, I think it is pleasing to Atargatis."

"Then we must hazard all on this toss of the gods' dice," Samson said.

And after? Once Samson had fled Dagon's Temple, leaving Derceto and Sandarin dead—what then for us? I was Atargatis's priestess; I still loved Our Lady, and the Dance. But I loved Samson, too. A treacherous longing to be his and his only possessed me. *Later. I will think of that later. There will be time for us later.*

So I smiled. "So I must beguile your secrets from you, Samson, sun of my heart, sun of all men. Tell me—tell me—tell me—" I kept chanting those words until he stopped my mouth with his. I thought I heard echoing laughter.

But it was only the River Sorek, its waters rippling joyously as they carried the pearls we had cast into it down to the endlessly laughing sea.

Samson

"Now it came to pass that because of the woman Delilah and her wiles, great Samson was taken by the Philistines, taken and bound with great fetters of brass. And because the Philistines feared great Samson so, his eyes were taken from him, the Philistines put out his eyes and set him to grinding in a mill, that all Gaza might mock him who once they feared above all men . . ."

"You're going to do *what?*" It was the third time Orev had asked the question, and somehow the answer never changed. The only explanation his mind provided was that Samson and his Moondancer priestess had both sacrificed all their wits to some hitherto unknown deity.

Samson regarded him with a serene compassion that made Orev long to strike him. "We are going to play the Philistines' game—"

"But with our laws, not theirs." Delilah Moondancer finished Samson's sentence as easily as if they had been twenty years wed.

"Whatever game you plan is too dangerous to play at all," Orev said, and wondered why he bothered to speak. Neither Samson nor Delilah heeded a word he said.

"I have made a vow." Sparks flew upward from the hearth fire, reflected fire in the priestess's midnight eyes. "I swore before Atargatis Herself that my heart-sister and her daughter will rest quiet."

Samson laid his hand over hers. "And before the pyre that had been my home and Aylah's, I swore to Yahweh that my wife and child would be avenged—and I heard Him promise I would do so."

As Delilah twined her fingers through Samson's, Orev stared at the two of them, trying to summon words that would act as pure water, would wash away this mad desire. At last he said only "Those are fine words. But how do you intend to achieve these vows? Those who burned the farm, slew your wife and child, slipped away like vipers. How will you find them now?"

Samson and Delilah looked at each other; she nodded, and he turned back to Orev. "The ones who held the torches, the ones who set my home ablaze—I will kill them, and gladly, when next they cross my path. But those who placed the torches in their hands and sent them to murder my wife and my child—*they* must pay for that."

"But Samson, my friend, how do you think to find such powerful and ruthless men?"

Delilah laughed then, soft and low and bitter as poisoned honey. "You Hebrews—men, always men. Do you think a *man* devised such a plot against my lord Samson? It was High Priestess Derceto who wove this web of deception and death."

"Even if what you say is truth—no, I do not doubt you, but perhaps you do not know all the tale—how can you touch her?" *Let my words have power, let me guide these two back to common sense, away from this madness—*

"Because I am Delilah Moondancer. Because when I dance, men throw gold beneath my feet. Because Derceto believes all are as venal and corrupt as she is herself." Delilah stared into the fire; flames danced shadows over her face and hair. "That Samson is a good man who does no harm but what he must—that she would not believe."

"It is all simple, Orev. Delilah was sent to lure me to her, to render me powerless, that the Five Cities may take me prisoner. They wish to display me as a prize, to show that they are stronger than I. And that their many gods are stronger than our one." Samson smiled, a wolfish grin so unlike his constant tranquil good humor that a chill touched the nape of Orev's neck.

But that swift unease vanished as Delilah began to speak again, replaced by dread heavy as a stone upon his heart. For she spoke of High Priestess Derceto's scheming with the Prince of the City of Ascalon, and the attempts already made to capture Samson.

"But they failed, all failed, and why? Because Samson's god favors him, and because—"

"Because those who tried to take me can think only in the paths they have already learned to tread. Change frightens them. Nor do they understand that a man may summon power from lifeless stone."

"And Derceto thinks me still her obedient playing-piece. So when I send word that I have won Samson's heart, and know how he may be easily taken, I will be believed. They think him half-god, you know, that there is some trick to his strength, his skills. Did not they see at his wedding that the drugged wine did not even lull him?"

"That's because he drank less than a mouthful of it," Orev pointed out, and was ignored.

"And I have sent word that ropes cannot bind him, that poison is powerless to harm him. But now—now I shall say I have discovered his secret." She leaned her cheek against Samson's shoulder, twined her fingers in his long sun-bright hair. "I know just what I shall say. Did you know, Samson, that if your hair is cut off, you will become as other men are?"

Samson caught her hand and kissed her palm. "Clever Delilah. Is she not the wisest of women, Orev? No, don't speak yet—let me tell you the rest of it."

The rest of their mad scheme turned upon the fact that Derceto, High Priestess of Atargatis's Great Temple in Ascalon, would attend the dedication of Dagon's Great House in Gaza at the next new moon. For one brief span of time, all those whom Delilah and Samson hated would stand together by the altar in Dagon's Great Temple . . .

"Which as you know is the newest of the Great Temples, and builders now are nothing. Compared to those who built even two generations ago, they are only children playing at making bricks. Do you remember the master mason I once spoke with upon the Lion's Path? He told me then how Dagon's Temple was made—and that it could not stand if the earth shook."

"Samson, you are not a god, to make the earth tremble at your will. What does it matter how well or ill Dagon's Temple was built?"

"It matters because I have listened to how Dagon's Temple in Gaza was made, and looked at the drawings of how its stones are set and its lintels braced, and I tell you, Orev, I can bring down the arch over the altar whether the earth trembles or not."

Orev looked into his friend's fire-shadowed eyes. "So you will let the Philistines capture you and take you before Dagon? Samson, *think.* Why should they do so foolish a thing? They fear you greatly—you're more likely to be thrown down one of the prison-shafts and left there to rot."

Even as he spoke, Orev knew no words of his would dissuade Samson, or Delilah either. But he had to try.

"No, they will not. The Lords and Ladies of the Five Cities wish to see Samson for themselves, see that he has been taken and serves them as a slave. And where better to display their prize than in Dagon's Great House? I will tell them that Dagon demands this. So they will keep Samson safe-prisoned until the Temple is dedicated. All the Great Ones will attend the rituals in Gaza; Derceto will be there. Once he sets his hands to its stones, Samson will know how to destroy the Temple. With Atargatis's mercy, none of the innocent will suffer; only the guilty will perish. And Samson and I—"

"We will be free," Samson finished.

For a moment, Orev hoped they were jesting. But a glance at their faces told him they were not. *They mean to do this. Are they—*

"Are the two of you mad? You'll both be killed. That won't help your dead, or the living, either."

Samson smiled, draped his arm over Orev's shoulders. "We won't be killed. Only those who have done evil shall die. Who knows better than I how to move stone? And we have Yahweh's own promise that I'll succeed."

"And the Lady's. *'The Son of the Sun will destroy a god.'*" Delilah's night-eyes glittered bright. "The Seer at En-dor saw it."

"You *are* both mad," Orev said. "You do know that, don't you?"

"Not mad, but resolute," Samson answered. "Delilah has designed the plan well. Trust me, Orev, we have thought long on this. And we accept the risk we run, the price we may have to pay."

But you don't think you will have to pay it. The two of you truly think this scheme is god-blessed. That you will succeed, and live— Orev stared at his friend and at the priestess who stood beside him. Samson's work-hardened hand curled about Delilah's small, soft one; their fingers coiled in a lovers' knot.

So that is how it is between them.

Pain chilled Orev's heart. That the two sought this wild justice for his wife and her vowed sister was risk enough; that they truly loved as well could prove fatal. In Orev's experience, few things were as danger-ous as love. Better to dance upon a bed of hot coals than to trust love to make all right in the eyes of He Who Made the Sun and Stars.

But Orev's long study of human nature had also taught a cool, dis-passionate truth: those in love would listen to no one and nothing save their own hearts. The only thing he could do for Samson and the priestess Delilah was to wait until they needed his help—and hope that his aid would be enough to save them from disaster.

Seeing the dedication burning in their eyes—Samson's the blue flame that danced above a forge's coals; Delilah's a cold fire dark as shadowed stars—Orev doubted that anything could stop them, or that his love for both could change one breath of what would come.

But he could pray, and hope.

Hope was all he had, now.

PART FOUR

Dark Moon

Delilah

When I went before the rulers of the Five Cities, I garbed myself as
Priestess of Atargatis. I knew I faced a hard task; the words of a Full
Moon of Bright Atargatis would carry more weight than those of a girl
garbed as a dancer—even a much-famed dancer.

I stood before them all and told them, calmly and quietly, that I had
gained the answer they so desired.

"I asked Our Lady for aid, and She granted my plea and petition. I
know how you may take Samson prisoner, what will make him as easy
to capture and bind as any other man. But Atargatis asks something in
return for this favor."

I waited until the Lady of Gath—always the most impatient—
demanded to know what Our Lady asked in payment. No hint of emotion troubled my painted face as I answered. For all any of them could
tell, I recited words about which I cared nothing.

"Our Lady and Mother, the Star of the Sea, Bright Atargatis, revealed to me the arts by which I lured Samson and seduced his secrets
from him. But She also said that Samson belongs to the gods, that Dagon Himself demands Samson be given into the keeping of Dagon's
Great House in Gaza. Dagon commands Samson be displayed before
the altar when His new Temple is dedicated at the next new moon, that

all may see Dagon's power and Samson's weakness. Therefore, while Samson may be taken, he may not be harmed.

"So you must swear to me, swear upon the most holy altar in the Five Cities, that Samson will not be harmed. No blade, whether of iron or bronze, may touch his skin. No club, whether of wood or of stone, shall break his bones. No flame may burn his flesh. If I do not have your oath on this, then Samson may pillage your caravans and lay waste to your lands until the stars grow cold and Our Lady Atargatis will not lift a finger to stop him."

Without hesitation, they swore upon Atargatis and upon Dagon that every word I had spoken would be heeded and obeyed. After the rulers of the Five Cities had consecrated this vow, and Derceto had burned their offerings on the high altar of Atargatis Herself, I told them how Samson would be rendered harmless.

"You all know he has sun-hair, long and bright. This hair is dedicated to his god, Yahweh. When I, a priestess of Atargatis, cut the hair from his head, Samson will become as all other men. Then you may safely take him, and carry him off to the Great House of Dagon in Gaza."

On the day Samson and I had decided upon—when only half a moon-turn remained before the dedication of the new Great House of Dagon in Gaza—we sat in the bright Sun Garden of the House of Ivory. I had cut his long hair, carefully, and held it in my hands. We waited, silent, for the forces of the Five Cities to come through the Sun-Gate at the hour appointed.

His hair was soft as sunlight, and as warm. I looked down at the bright mass of his hair, sun-fire in my hands. "Beloved," I began, and then stopped, for I heard the creak of leather and the jangle of metal. It was too late now to say anything at all.

A dozen warriors burst in, then halted, cautious, spears and swords ready. They might have been hunting a great lion instead of one un-armed man. But when I smiled, and nodded, they rushed forward and seized Samson. They regained their rough courage when Samson remained still as stone, feigning weakness, while I twisted the locks of his long soft hair in my hands, as if flaunting his loss before his eyes. He remained still as they bound him. Thus far, the scheme Samson and I had woven followed the pattern we had laid out with such care.

But we had staked all on the Lords holding to the vow I had extracted from them. I had formed the oath carefully—but not carefully enough.

No iron blade bit into his flesh, no club broke his bones, no fire burned his flesh. Those who ruled the Five Cities kept the letter of their oath. But they violated its spirit. The heavy-set man who had borne in the chains to bind Samson now lifted a small object wrapped in crimson silk from his belt. He unfolded the silk, revealed two silver hairpins. The pins shone bright as stars and had been honed to deadly points.

No blade, no club, no fire. Only a woman's hairpins, the final betrayal—

"No," I said, but no one listened, and if they had, they would not have heeded me. Samson's eyes gazed into mine. "We have not lost yet, Delilah. Have faith, and wait."

He spoke so softly only I heard. His courage gave me the strength to do one last thing for Samson. I forced myself to smile, and to whisper, "Beloved."

My smile was the last thing his eyes ever saw. I prayed to the Lady of Love that it might be some small comfort to him in the darkness.

The warriors took Samson to the Great House of Dagon in Gaza. The Temple servants took me back to the Great House of Atargatis in Ascalon.

I did not know where Orev was taken. Only later did I learn that he had slipped away, knowing he could be of use to his friend only if he remained free, and followed Samson to Gaza. I looked only inward, seeking oblivion. I could not bear to see even memories.

I remember very little of the next handful of days. I remember the sickly sweet taste of poppy syrup; I remember lying upon embroidered cushions in a closed litter. I remember swaying shadows, and cool hands upon my face. And I remember the scent of bitter spice, and High Priestess Derceto saying, "You have done well, Delilah." The words echoed as if I lay in a cave with walls of stone.

After that, I remember nothing. I slept for three days, refusing to wake.

But I could not sleep forever. I opened my eyes at last, and saw that I lay in my own bed, in my own room. I was home again in Our Lady's House. And, just as when I had mourned Aylah's death, a priest of Milchienzeek stood beside my bed, and one of that goddess's little dogs lay with its nose cool against my neck.

Absently, I stroked the dog's smooth white coat. Outwardly comforted, I used those moments to remember what had brought me back here, and to think what I now must do.

I must still play the game. I must not reveal by word or glance that I care whether Samson lives or dies. I must trust his faith in his own god. His last words to me still echoed in my ears:

"We have not lost yet, Delilah. Have faith, and wait."

"You wake at last," the priest said. "That is good. Milchienzeek is kind."

"How long have I slept?" I was horrified to hear the priest say that I had lain asleep for three days. But I betrayed nothing; I patted Milchienzeek's dog one last time and then stretched and sat up.

"My thanks," I told the priest. "But there are those who need your Lady's dogs more than I." I smiled; it took all the strength I had. I turned my eyes to the handmaiden who sat beside the doorway and was twice glad I had used caution in my first waking moments.

For the handmaiden who watched over me was Mottara. The High Priestess had again sent her own most loyal servant to tend upon me.

To spy upon me, to weigh what I say, and how I look when I say it. I hoped Mottara was disappointed when I smiled at her also and said, "You may tell High Priestess Derceto that Delilah Moondancer has returned. Tell her, too, that I await her next command—and my next dance."

Mottara rose to her feet and bowed. "I shall do as you ask, Priestess." As she pushed aside the door-curtain, I added, "And send Pehkah and Japhilit to me. I wish to bathe and dress."

Mottara inclined her head—perhaps to hide the fact that she suddenly seemed to have set her teeth into a bitter fruit. "As my lady Delilah orders." Before I could issue any more commands, Mottara slipped past the curtain and let it fall closed behind her.

The priest of Milchienzeek was kinder; he seemed truly pleased I had woken well and happy. "The blessings of Milchienzeek the Kind upon you, Priestess of Atargatis." As if it were part of the blessing, the dog licked my hand. Smiling, I thanked both priest and dog, and they, too, went away. For a few moments, I was alone.

But I was too wise and wary to think myself unobserved. I had learned much since the day Samson had freed my hair in the Sun Partridge Dance. Now, the only person I trusted here in the Great House of Atargatis was myself.

So although I wished to weep until my eyes burned, to drink poppy syrup until I fell again into the comfort of nothingness, I did neither. As if I did not see the vial of poppy lying upon the mother-of-pearl chest, as if I felt nothing but relief at my return to Our Lady's Temple, I stretched again. Then I yawned and lay back upon my pillows, awaiting the arrival of the servants I had ordered Mottara to send to me.

And, hardest of all, I smiled. Whoever spied upon me would see only a young priestess haughtily rejoicing that she had succeeded in the task assigned her. A girl eager to claim the rich reward she had been promised.

And I shall claim that reward. But not here, and not today.

Today I must wait, and smile.

And have faith—and wait.

Samson

"*From Delilah's soft arms they dragged mighty Samson, Samson whom a woman's wiles had rendered helpless as any other man. The Philistines took him, and bound him, and because they feared him and his god so greatly, they put out his eyes—but even a blind man may see truth, and his god.*"

Later, when he grew tired of conjuring reasons that mighty Samson permitted himself to be captured by mere Philistines, Orev added words to please those who listened.

"*From Delilah's soft arms they dragged Samson, Samson whose hair she had shorn, rendering him helpless as any other man. For Samson had been vowed as a Nazirite before his birth, and he drank no wine and ate no unclean thing, nor did a blade ever touch a hair on his head. But the woman Delilah beguiled him, and Samson at last revealed that his power lay in his uncut hair . . .*"

Harper's privilege, the creation of that iron vow—for those who listened wished to hear of a hero, a man unlike other men. And after all, those words held half a truth. Had not Delilah persuaded the rulers of the Five Cities that Samson might be easily taken if only his glorious mane of hair were shorn like a lamb's?

"*Rejoicing, the Philistines bound Samson with fetters of brass; rejoicing, they bore Samson to Gaza, to the Temple of Dagon. And there in that vile Temple, they bound blind Samson to grind grain for the Temple, thinking to mock him and bring him low.*"

"But Samson trusted in his god, and Samson bowed his head to Yahweh's will. And Samson ground grain in Gaza, and awaited Yahweh's word . . ."

The Philistines took no chances; they might have blinded and bound him, but clearly they still feared Samson. A full fifty warriors of Gaza guarded the ass-drawn cart in which Samson had been chained. No one was permitted to approach the cart the warriors surrounded.

Orev did not even try to do so. He merely followed Samson and his jailers along the road to Gaza. No one seemed to object; what danger could a lame harper pose to fifty armed men, after all? Nor did Orev cherish hopes of freeing Samson; he knew it to be impossible.

And he feared more for Delilah's safety than for Samson's, at the moment. The Foxes had already slain one of Samson's women, and would delight in slitting Delilah's throat. Still, it would take a few days for the news of Samson's capture to travel the length and breadth of Canaan. Gaza was two days' journey from Sorek Vale at a swift pace, and Samson's captors moved swiftly, clearly eager to hand their charge over to others. Orev felt reasonably certain that the overconfident fools who called themselves "Samson's Foxes" would not hear what had be-fallen until Samson was prisoned in Gaza—and Delilah safely returned to her Temple in Ascalon.

He was half-right; by the time the prisoner's escort was only a day's march from Gaza, Orev glanced aside, his eyes drawn by movement. And there they were, the Foxes, watching the Philistines from the un-tended land beyond the road. Orev recognized the twin brothers Dawi and Golyat—no one could mistake their red hair. Now the harper scanned the sides of the road as he walked, knowing that more of Sam-son's self-proclaimed allies must stalk him and his guards. A mile on-ward, Orev spotted Achbor and Enoch. Perhaps the rest of the Foxes lurked out of sight; Orev didn't know.

What I do know is that if they try to rescue Samson now, all he has suffered will be for nothing. The first thing Gaza's warriors would do if attacked was cut Samson's throat. Better a dead lion than one who escaped. *I would not wish to be the captain who must tell the rulers of the Five Cities that he let Samson escape now.*

Apparently even the most reckless of the Foxes understood this, for although the Foxes gazed intently upon the Philistines and the captive Samson, they did not move. Orev felt their eyes upon him as well, and breathed more easily only when the watching Foxes were far behind them. Another danger to Samson's mad plan averted.

Orev continued grimly on after Samson and his watchful guards. *Perhaps I should have called the Foxes down to us. A clean death for Samson might have been better than whatever lies ahead.* Orev lacked his friend's faith in the plan concocted in the House of Ivory. But whatever awaited in Gaza, Orev would not let Samson face a dark future alone and friendless.

The first thing Orev discovered was that it was easy enough to see Samson—for his captors had set him to pushing the mill that ground grain for the Great House of Dagon. Half the city came each day to watch and to jeer; Orev was simply one more curious onlooker. If Gaza thought to debase Samson by making him labor as would an ox, the plan failed. For Samson seemed to notice nothing, ignoring the insults; obedient, he pushed the bar that turned the millstone until he was ordered to stop.

It was harder to meet with Samson privately in his cell—but far from impossible. An offering to the guard upon Samson's door bought time alone with the blind hero.

Waiting was hard—only seven days remained until the dedication of Dagon's Temple—but Orev forced himself to patience. *I must not seem too eager, must not draw attention to myself.* But patience did not come easy, for Orev had learned something that doomed Delilah and Samson's plan— even had Samson still possessed eyes to see.

Three days after Samson had been set to turning the mill, Orev bribed his way into his friend's cell. Even after so short a time, the guard was accustomed to men and women wishing to visit the famed slayer of a hundred men; Orev's request held little interest for him. The guard merely closed his hand over the silver ring the harper gave him and then unbolted the door and held it while Orev stumbled his way down a short flight of stairs. As Orev reached the bottom, the door swung shut, leaving him in darkness.

"Samson?" The name echoed against the cool stone walls of the cell.

"Orev? What are you doing here? Are you mad?"

Orev followed the sound of Samson's voice, his hands reaching out, questing. A few steps, and he touched Samson's arm. "Am *I* mad? You are the one who's imprisoned in Dagon's Temple."

"Yes, Orev, I know. Have a little faith." Despite his blindness, despite the heavy collar about his neck and the chain leading from the collar to a ring in the stone wall, Samson did not sound either desperate or dismayed. "Tell me, where is Delilah? Is she well?"

"She dwells once more in the Great House of Atargatis in Ascalon. She is hailed as a heroine, and a rich reward has been bestowed upon her. She is the High Priestess's darling now, they say. Samson—"

"Do they?" Samson laughed, the joyous sound echoing uncannily against the cell's stone walls. He grasped Orev's shoulder and pulled him close. "Well, soon comes the great feast honoring Dagon, when the priests dedicate this ill-made temple. All the nobles will be in the Temple, as will the rulers of the other Great Houses of the gods and goddesses of the Five Cities. They long to see me brought low before them all. Now, upon the day the Temple is dedicated, I will be displayed before the altar as a prize won by their god, just as Delilah told them Dagon demanded—"

"Samson, be silent!" Orev used his harper's voice to command obedience. "Listen and heed. Your plan won't work now. Do you know what they're going to do? They're going to chain you to the pillars by Dagon's altar. The chains are hanging there now. Chains of iron, Samson. Chains even you cannot sunder." The last chance of success had vanished when those chains were forged.

For long moments, the only sound was Samson's breathing echoing in the darkness. At last he said, "I understand."

Orev let out his own breath, his tense muscles relaxing. Apparently Samson would for once in his extravagant life be sensible. "Good. We still have four days. The Foxes are lurking somewhere near Gaza. I'll find them, and they can free you before you're bound to Dagon's Temple."

"So those who burned my wife and daughter wish to save me now?" Samson laughed again, a sound ringing harsh against the stones, then he spoke with quiet power. "Then our plan still holds good. The chains will make it easier to fulfill my task. Yes, Orev, send the Foxes into Dagon's Temple. They, too, must be there. But tell Delilah that she must not come here now. Tell her nothing more. Tell her—tell her I love her, and I will meet her in Ascalon, after."

Samson wants me to lie to Delilah? Samson wants me to lie— Orev struggled to find the words that would convince his friend to abandon the deadly scheme. "Samson, are you mad? You are blind now, and weak from turning the grindstone. You cannot do this. Even if you could—"

A clink of chain against stone; Samson reached out and laid his hand on Orev's shoulder. "Of course I can. Turning the grindstone has only hardened my body, and I don't need eyes to sense where a building's weakness lies. I shall pull down this Great House of Dagon and destroy those who destroyed my family, as I swore I would. Yes. All will be as Delilah and I vowed."

"Samson—" Orev began, only to have the man ruthlessly ignore him.

"You need do only one thing: tell Delilah what I have said to you, that I can still bring justice down upon those who have done evil. Tell her I will avenge our dead. And tell her I say she must not be near Dagon's Temple when the Temple falls. Nor must you."

Orev shook his head, forgetting for a moment that his friend could not see, even had there been a lamp to light the prison cell. "Samson, you cannot. Listen to me; I will think of another plan to free you from bondage—"

"Even you cannot do that, Orev. But for once, you can do as I bid you and not argue. Go to Ascalon and tell her whom my heart loves what I have said to you."

Orev tried once more, offering Samson's heart's desire. "Samson, let the Foxes rescue you before the last day dawns, no matter the cost. You can escape. You and your Delilah can live in peace—"

"And you have always called *me* mad." Samson reached out to touch his friend's arm. "No, Orev. Even if the Foxes could save me, and even if Delilah and I could find a place we could live safe and free, I will start no war—for that is what my escape would bring. Disaster to our people. How many times must I say that we cannot win a war against the Five Cities? Or that there is no reason for such battles?"

"And you think bringing Dagon's Temple crashing down upon you better? Assuming you can do it. If the pillars hold, all you've endured will be for nothing."

A pause, then, "That is as Yahweh wills. I have sworn to do this thing, and I will do it. Now go, and tell Delilah we have not yet failed. There is ample time for you to reach Ascalon before Dagon's Temple is dedicated—and you and Delilah must stay there. Neither of you must be in Gaza on the day they drag me to the Great House of Dagon to mock me before all the people and offer my suffering up to their false god. I would not condemn you to die with me."

Delilah

"Now Delilah had given great Samson into the hands of his enemies, into the hands of the rulers of the Five Cities. And they filled her hands with gems and gold and silver, and she went away laughing . . ."

Returning to Ascalon, dwelling once more as a priestess within the Great House of Atargatis—I had thought those would be hard things. But I was wrong. I had lived all my life in that Temple; my body moved instinctively through the rituals required of me. I think very few noted that my heart had changed.

Certainly Derceto did not. Before her, I became a false Delilah, one whose only wish was to claim the rewards promised her. The day I awoke back in my own bed, I began to play a part, to be what Derceto wished to see when she looked upon me. That was why I asked at once to see the High Priestess and why, when she granted that request, I demanded the reward the Five Cities had promised me.

"For I have done all asked of me, and more. May I not claim what is due to me?"

When I asked that, Derceto smiled; the taut planes of her face softened, her rigid stance eased. Clearly she had feared I'd fallen into the same trap as had Aylah, become tainted by love for Samson. My words reassured Derceto that I still belonged to her.

"Of course, Delilah. Think upon what you most wish to have, and I will arrange the matter myself." The High Priestess laid her hand upon my cheek. "All will be as promised. Now let us rejoice that you returned safely, and all will be as it was—as if nothing ever happened to take you from us."

I bowed, and thanked her, and walked away smiling. High Priestess Derceto had believed me; me and her own lies. There was nothing else I could do now. Nothing but wait, as Samson had bidden me.

"Have faith, and wait."

As if nothing had ever happened.

At first, I thought I would at least have some word from Orev, but soon I realized that, even if Orev came to Ascalon, never would he be allowed to speak with me. So I stopped hoping for even that much consolation. I would not speak of what had passed during the days I had beguiled Samson—but that was set down to my credit. I had acted on Lady Ascalon's behalf, the glory not mine, but Ascalon's. To my other virtues, I now added modesty.

Nor would I listen to tales of Samson's ordeal as Dagon's slave. I had done with him, I said. I had set a honey-trap for a fool, and caught him through his own folly. He was nothing to me now.

"Have faith, and wait."

But I had paid a price for the success of our desperate scheming. I could no longer dance. Oh, I could sway my body to the music, I could move my feet in the proper steps. But the joyous fire no longer burned within me. When I danced before Our Lady, I knew that what I offered now only grieved Her.

No one else seemed to notice anything amiss—save Sharissit. The Dance Priestess gazed long at me after the first time I danced again, and I slid my own eyes away from the deep sadness in hers.

I tried not to care. The new moon drew ever nearer; the new Great House of Dagon in Gaza would be dedicated only a few days hence. And Dagon's great prize, Samson, was to be displayed before the high altar, that all might see the power of the Five Cities—and the weakness of the Hebrew god.

Once again I begged that I might come before the High Priestess—this time, I sent word that I would ask a boon of her. Her reply was swift: yes, Delilah might come before her and ask.

I smiled, and thanked the little New Moon who had carried my message. The child stared at me wide-eyed, and for a heartbeat I saw myself through her eyes: the Priestess Delilah, who had conquered over Samson. A Full Moon of Atargatis. A glory to the goddess's House. My mouth tasted sour, suddenly, and I could not meet the New Moon's shining, eager eyes. Silently, I sent the child away again. Then I called for my maidservants and began to prepare myself to confront High Priestess Derceto.

I took as much care that day as if I adorned myself to act as Goddess-on-Earth. When I was ready, I looked upon myself in the smooth circle of my mirror, to ensure that nothing of the woman I had become lay revealed. I saw only a priestess's face, a perfect mask. Delilah Moondancer stood once again ready to do as she was bidden. *As if nothing had ever happened . . .*

I set the mirror aside and went to perform the next steps in the deadly dance I had begun the day I looked upon Aylah's sister-token lying on High Priestess Derceto's open hand. The next moves should be simple; I reminded myself to beware the snare of pride.

So when I knelt before Derceto, I became a true suppliant. What I asked of her, I desired so greatly that I let tears well into my eyes—a flaw that only perfected my plea. "You go to Gaza, to the Dedication Festival at the new Great Temple of Dagon. I beg of you, take me to attend upon you there."

She gazed at me with those opaque eyes I had once thought so kind, so holy. "Will not the sight of the man Samson pain you, Delilah? You need not go only because you think it will please me to see you so strong."

"That does not matter; I must go. I must see him humbled less than a slave. I must see him again that Aylah may truly be avenged." Then I remembered that I need not beg, that I could claim this as my right. "Let this be my gift for leading the Sun Partridge Dances." Dances I had danced long ago, when I thought I knew my future. "Now I know why I never asked for it before."

Each word true; I waited, untroubled. If Derceto would not take me in her entourage, I would walk to Gaza myself. Gaza lay only half a day's journey south of Ascalon; I could walk the road easily. But it would be simpler and safer if Derceto would grant my request. She continued to study my face, said at last, "Very well, Delilah. You may accompany me to Gaza." The High Priestess smiled, as if indulging a daughter's whim. "And if you change your mind—"

"I shall not," I said, and then thanked her with all proper ceremony and went away, to wait until the time came to travel to Gaza.

To Samson.

•

Gaza was not the gem among cities that Ascalon was; strength, rather than beauty, was its domain. The Great House of Dagon reflected this difference—Dagon's new temple dominated the city of Gaza rather than graced it.

I barely noticed, for all my heart and mind was fixed upon the coming ceremony: the dedication that would sanctify the Temple of Dagon and complete Samson's dishonor before the nobility and priesthoods of the Five Cities.

As Dagon was the patron of Gaza, all other gods and goddesses owned lesser temples. The arrival of High Priestess Derceto of the Great House of Atargatis in Ascalon—along with two dozen attendants and lesser priestesses—strained the resources of Gaza's temple to Bright Atargatis to the utmost.

That, too, I cared nothing for; the Gaza temple might bed me down upon a heap of straw and I would not object. My goal was Samson, not comfort.

For the next three days, I played my part to perfection. Delilah, Priestess, Full Moon of the Great House of Atargatis in Ascalon. Delilah Moondancer, incarnation of the Bright Lady Herself. Delilah, heroine who had beguiled and conquered our great enemy, Samson.

A simple role to play, for all who dwelt in the Five Cities wished to believe what had already become a harper's song. If I had told those who bowed before me and begged my blessing upon their heads that I plotted to destroy not Samson, but an evil in our own Cities, a corruption in our own Great Houses of the gods and goddesses, I would not have been believed.

Already I was Delilah, lure and snare; Delilah, betrayer of Samson. Who would not believe that of me now? Did not Samson, he who had prowled the high roads, who, the stories claimed, had stolen a virgin priestess from her temple, who had burned half Canaan in his rages, now labor as a sightless beast of burden in Dagon's mill? And had not Delilah's wiles condemned him to such an existence?

I did not argue with those who praised me for my courage and cunning. Garbed and gilded until I seemed an idol rather than a priestess, I stood before the image of Our Lady in Her House in Gaza from midday until sunset for each of those three days. In Atargatis's name, I accepted the thank-offerings laid by the grateful, and the curious, at my feet.

Derceto watched me, and seemed satisfied. By neither breath nor movement did I reveal my true feelings. I did nothing untoward; I did not even try to learn if Orev, too, stayed in Gaza. For those three days, I was the most pious of any priestess in all Gaza. I turned all my thoughts to Bright Atargatis. I knew that She would not betray me— nor, with all my will focused on Her, would I betray myself to those who watched.

On the third night—the night before the ceremony that would dedicate the Great House of Dagon to the service of its god—I did nothing I had not done each night before. Maidservants stripped away the garments that marked me as a Full Moon of Atargatis, washed the kohl and carmine and gilt from my skin. Two handmaidens unbraided my hair, unbound the red ribbon that confined the Goddess's Knot at the nape of my neck. I stood quiet and waited as they combed out my hair, as they admired the sheen of its raven's-wing black in the flickering lamplight.

I smiled, and gave no hint that every drop of my blood demanded that I hurry, hurry—that I must hurry or be forever too late.

When the maids had done with me, and I was alone, I forced myself to wait another endless span of time. When I had silently recited all the prayers to Our Lady from first dawn to sunset twice, I knew I had waited long enough. I rose from my cold bed and began to dress in my plainest clothing. Even that was of too fine a linen to pass unnoticed, but a dark cloak veiled me from eyes to ankles. Now if I were seen on the streets, I would be only another poor woman; a shadow among shadows.

The man who guarded Samson's cell did his job well—by which I mean he knew how and when to accept tangible thanks for favors. Since I did not even try to haggle over the price, the matter of entry to Samson's cell was easily arranged.

As for the rest—well, that was my affair. The guard's part of the bargain was to open the door twice: once to let me enter and once to let me leave.

"Go on in—more fool you. Do you think you're the first woman come to lie with blind Samson?" The guard spat upon the ground, shifted so that he might tie the gold chains I had slipped into his outstretched hand into a fold of his tunic. "Don't think I'll give these back when you don't get what you want of him. You've paid to enter his cage, and that's all. The rest is up to you, but I warn you, he's stubborn as a wild ass. Oh, never fear, he won't hurt you, either. He's either a coward or a simpleton—I don't know why he was feared so."

"Because men are even greater fools than women are. I have paid you; let me pass."

He tugged at the knot to make sure the gold was safely bound, and then nodded. "As you wish, lady. Never say Yaddu failed to keep his part of any bargain. And when you've tired of teasing the man, call my name and I'll let you out again." He slid back the iron bar and pulled the door open. "I'll wait here if you like. Most of them give up in less time than it takes me to drink a jar of beer."

I walked past him, paused in the doorway to darkness. "Do as you please tonight. I will not call until dawn."

"It's seven steps down," the guard said. "I can't give you a lamp. Light is forbidden—and the man's blind anyway."

"Thank you, Yaddu." Courtesy cost nothing, and after all, the man had not needed to tell me the number of steps. Then I stepped through the doorway. I waited until the door closed and I heard the bar slide back into place before I reached out to touch the chill stones and walked down the stairs, counting each step. At the last, I paused again; I could see nothing. Not even shadows eased the blackness before me.

"Delilah." Samson's voice whispered against the stone walls.

"Where are you?" I said, and reached out.

His hands caught mine. "Are you mad, to come here?"

"No madder than any of the other women who wished to lie with you—dozens of them, if the guard is to be believed." Of all the words I had thought to say to him, I had never thought that I would jest, or that he would laugh. How could I have forgotten that he laughed so easily?

"How did you know it was I?"

"By the way you move through the air. By the scent of your skin. By the very sound of the breath you take." Samson began to pull me towards him, then stopped, holding me off.

"What is the matter, Samson? Fear not, for I have paid the guard enough to spend all this night with you." Even knowing he could not see me, I smiled. "We will not be interrupted, beloved."

"I—am not very clean," he said, and for a moment I did not know if I would laugh or weep.

"I do not care," I said, and flung myself forward into his arms.

When my hands touched his body in loving exploration, for the first time I was glad we met in darkness. I cared nothing about the dirt matting his shorn hair or the rank scent of his unwashed skin; it was the half-healed wounds, the feel of his bones sharp beneath his skin, that I could not bear.

When the first rush of passion faded, I lay cradling Samson in my arms, savoring the feel of his body against mine. I stroked his nearly bare head; his short-cut hair rasped my palm. "I liked it better long," I said, and Samson laughed, softly.

"It will grow again. Now stop trying to hide your reason for coming to me. You must not risk yourself like this. Did Orev not tell you I said do not come here?"

"I have not seen Orev since—since the day you were taken. And it would not matter if I had. I came because I could not live if I did not see you. And to tell you that tomorrow is the day you will be taken to the Great House of Dagon and chained between the pillars before the high altar, that all may look upon you and mock you and your god. The priesthood of Dagon's Great House will be there, as will the High Priestess of the Great House of Atargatis in Ascalon."

"I know, beloved. And I tell you what I told Orev when he came to speak with me—that they may mock as they please, but my god will laugh as theirs falls into a pit of their own digging. By the favor of Yahweh, I shall have my chance to destroy evil."

I touched his cheek. "Did you not hear me, my love? You will be chained. Now you cannot—"

"Now I cannot destroy Dagon's Temple and live." There was neither anger nor fear in Samson's calm voice. "But I can still topple its stones."

"No." My bones turned cold as I understood. "No, beloved. Wait. Let them display you, let them mock you. Then later, I can ask to—to be given you as a slave. Then we can—"

Samson put his fingers over my lips. "Then we can what, Delilah? Live in Ascalon with you as priestess of Atargatis and me as your blind slave?"

I grasped his wrist, pulled his hand away from my mouth. "We could go far away, to another land. We could live—"

"No, my heart, we could not. Your Temple and City would hunt us to world's end." Samson stroked my hair. "I have had long hours to think of nothing but those iron chains. I know what I must do. Now you must promise me something, Delilah."

"Anything," I said.

"That you will not be there, in Dagon's Temple. Nor will Orev—he did not come to you in Ascalon?"

"No. Or if he did, he was not permitted to speak with me, or even send a message."

"I should have thought of that." His fingers touched my cheeks. "Don't cry, beloved. Listen. Orev must still be in Gaza; sometimes I think I hear his voice, pretending to jeer with the others. He foolishly watches for a chance to free me. You must promise to find him, and to flee Gaza with him before tomorrow's ceremony."

I lay silent, remembering that a heartbeat ago I had sworn I would do anything he asked.

"You promised, Delilah," Samson said. "You and Orev must go; leave the rest to me. Remember our plan, beloved."

"A foolish plan," I said. "We were mad to even dream it might succeed."

"It will succeed—but there is always a price, Delilah." For a moment Samson sounded like Aylah's echo, his words crystal-hard truth. "We were foolish only in hoping to gain the gift we asked without offering anything up in thanks for so great a favor."

"Then we both will pay that price."

"No. You promised me you would do anything I asked of you, Delilah. I ask that you live. Suppose you conceive a child this night? Would you condemn her to death before she even draws breath?"

"Suppose I do not conceive a child? And even if I do, perhaps we will have a son, not a daughter."

"No. Our child will be a girl." Samson spoke with a certainty that made me close my lips over objections and arguments. "We will have a daughter, beloved. A girl to live in love, and in laughter."

There was so much I longed to say to him—a lifetime of words that would remain unspoken between us. At last I said only "Let it be as you say, beloved. Now let us give my goddess and your god as much aid as we can in conceiving our laughing daughter."

As I had vowed to the guard Yaddu, I did not call for the cell door to be unbolted until dawn. The last hour of the night I had spent lying awake, staring into darkness as Samson slept in the circle of my arms.

During that silent hour, I had given thanks to Our Lady—pure thankfulness for Her kindness, a prayer unalloyed by any taint of demand or desire of Her. I had called upon all the skills the Temple had inculcated in me, used the arts of passion to fuel the durable fire of love itself.

Now is all there is— For the first time, I truly understood what that meant, and how to use that hard-won knowledge.

Now is all there is. Freed from the bonds of pain and loss, for those few precious hours, we created paradise within a prison cell.

For during that last dark night, love alone was enough.

Wise for once, I slipped out of Samson's cell in the elusive moment of half-dawn. Between darkness and daylight, I walked unseen through the streets of Gaza, my cloak giving me the look of a shadow, a shadow soon to be burned away by the light of the rising sun. I kept my promise to Samson; I did not return to the guest-chambers in Gaza's Temple of Atargatis. Derceto would seek me in vain today.

But I did not seek out Orev, and I did not leave Gaza. As the sun climbed above the eastern hills and the sky's light transmuted from deep blue-black to silver, I made my way to the stairs leading up the city

wall. A gift to the guard at the bottom of the stairway gained me permission to climb the stairs to the top of the wall—to greet the rising
sun on this auspicious day, I said.

Like the wall encircling Ascalon, Gaza's city wall was wide enough
for three chariots to drive side by side, and high enough that when I
stood upon the smooth-set stones I could see across all the city. The
new Great House of Dagon loomed, a great flawed beast, at Gaza's
heart.

I walked along the wall until I reached the next gate tower. There I
pressed myself into the corner where tower and wall met. My cloak
seemed to melt into the dull reddish brown bricks and stones that
formed the tower and the wall.

A shadow on the wall, unnoticed among all the rest.

Or so I hoped, and with good reason. Today all eyes would be
turned to the Great House of Dagon, all attention focused on the dis-
honored ritual within a temple built upon a debased foundation.

*"Set enough pressure at the right spot, at the right angle, and the temple pillars cannot
stand. The Master Builder washed his hands and abandoned the job rather than deceive
with shoddy work disguised to seem strong and true. I can bring Dagon's House down,
Delilah. All who plotted such evil against those we loved will be destroyed."*

If the Master Builder spoke truth. If Samson stood chained in the
proper spot. If those we hated did not flee safely from the falling temple.

If and if and if . . .

I stared at the gilded fish painted upon the Temple roof. And no
matter what else happened, Samson would die. Even blind, Samson
might have escaped the falling Temple. But chained to Dagon's altar, he
was doomed.

Yet I knew what he would say to that, as clearly as if he stood before
me and spoke the words.

"I will be with you, beloved. Never doubt that."

How, my love? I could not even enter Dagon's Temple and go with
Samson in death. I must live, for I owed Samson a life. I must cherish
mine until our daughter was safely born.

· · ·

I stood all the morning there, watching and waiting. I knew Samson had desired me to leave Gaza after I kissed him good-bye in his cell, but I could not. I must see what befell with my own eyes. I had begun this dance of my own will; it was my duty now to tread the deadly pattern to its end.

By midmorning the Gaza streets were full with people moving towards the Great House of Dagon like a bright river. For this day of dedication and triumph, those who dwelt in Gaza had donned their most festive garments.

The priests and priestesses of other gods and goddesses moved through the streets in solemn procession. The crowds parted for them; I saw the crimson and gold of the palanquin in which High Priestess Derceto was carried as if she herself were Bright Atargatis.

As the sun stood overhead, the streets lay quiet, almost empty. The Great House of Dagon had swallowed them all.

Still I waited. I knew I would hear nothing of the dedication—not with half the city between me and the Temple. But I knew when Samson was brought before the people, displayed like a prize of war, for the roar of triumph swelled like a heavy wave through the air.

Then silence again, silence heavy as stone itself. The Great House of Dagon seemed to shudder . . . and then there was sound again, an odd grinding, as if the Temple's bones shifted and broke.

Even where I stood, I could hear screams. Then a monstrous roar, as the Temple roofs fell in upon the Great Inner Court, and the walls followed, first the walls closest to the Inner Court, and then the others that circled them, the stones crashing down faster and faster. A pillar of dust rose up from the mass of fallen stones.

The howl of shattered stone ceased. The screams still echoed over Gaza—few voices now, and fewer with each breath that passed.

I looked upon the ruin of Gaza's Great House of Dagon, and knew that Samson had been right. I should not have stayed to watch—and to listen.

· · ·

I think I was the only person that day—man or woman—who walked slowly through the dust-filled streets of Gaza. All about me people ran, either fleeing the ruin of the Great House of Dagon or hastening towards it to aid any who might survive. There were others, too, men who grasped the day's tragedy as a chance to snatch whatever goods they could lay hands upon.

I walked past them all until I reached the Temple of Atargatis, where High Priestess Derceto and her entourage had stayed while awaiting the dedication of Dagon's Great House. The doorkeepers rushed up to me, gasping and pawing at me. "Priestess Delilah—you live! All the others are dead, buried beneath Dagon's Temple. Praise Our Lady that you live—"

I suppose they kept speaking, but I ceased listening. Pushing aside any who tried to grasp me, to weep over me, I went through the Temple until I came to the rooms allotted those who had come with Derceto from Ascalon. There I began, slowly, to set the few things I would need to carry with me into a small carved chest.

Necklaces, bracelets, anklets, earrings—goods I could barter for my keep. A pair of sandals, a linen shift. A mirror . . .

Don't be a fool, girl. What need have you for a mirror now?

For a breath I did not know the voice, then I remembered. The Seer at En-dor spoke in just such husky, sardonic tones.

What need now? The words echoed as I lifted the mirror and looked into the shining disk.

The woman who looked back was a stranger. Atargatis's Dancer, Delilah the Full Moon of Atargatis, Delilah the Priestess—that girl was gone.

Just as Samson the Son of the Sun was gone. Now I knew he had vanished even before the stones of Dagon had fallen upon ruler and captive alike. The Sun-Lord had ceased to exist the moment Samson had yielded, bent his neck before me like a suppliant before his goddess. All that had been left then was a man. A man like other men. A fool.

So I told myself, striving fiercely to believe. *A fool, no more than a fool. That is what love does. Breeds fools. Fools like Samson, hero of the Israelites.*

Fools like you, Delilah. The words fell cold into my mind. Cold as stones.

Cold as your heart should have remained.

But I had burned hot, not cold; I had led him in a dance that ended not in life but in death.

As if in a dream, I heard him laugh once more, laugh and whisper, *"Love me, my goddess-on-earth. Love me, my queen of night."* And my voice teasing. *"Never. Never, never. Tell me, my sun of men, tell me your secret. Tell me . . ."*

A game we had played, thinking we both could win against City and Temple. Against life, against death itself.

"Tell me, tell me . . ."

The laughter of ghosts echoed; the laughter of two young and foolish children who had thought that the gods would dance to their bidding. That whatever madness they desired would come to pass . . .

"Tell them you have discovered my secret, Night-Hair. They will not know until too late that I have discovered theirs."

A great shudder racked my body; I buried my face in my hands. Crimson hands, stained bright with henna. Bright with blood . . .

No.

I forced myself to raise my head, forced myself to bend and look upon my image in the silver mirror. Delilah. Delilah the temple dancer. Delilah the Lady's servant.

I knew Samson would never blame me for what had befallen him—never in this life or the next. If I summoned his ghost, I knew he would say that I had done only what he himself had asked of me. But I blamed myself. I seemed to hear my name echoing through the Courts of Time: Delilah the heart-taker, the heart-slayer; Delilah the heartless.

Delilah the betrayer. Delilah, who sent great Samson to his death . . .

Yes, that is what I was. It is what I am. It is what I shall be. Always.

If only that had been true. If only I had never loved— I laid my crimson-stained hands over my stomach, swore upon my daughter's growing heart that she should be wise, be free. Never would she suffer the pain I had suffered, the pain I now endured, the pain that would walk with me to my grave, and beyond.

For now that it was too late, I knew what I had wagered, and what I had won. And what I had lost forever.

I had betrayed everyone and everything dear to me. Samson. Aylah. The Lady Atargatis Herself.

The woman in the silver mirror stared back at me, her eyes glittering silver-bright. *All I do now, I do for my daughter. And for his.*

Staring into the mirror, I lifted my hands from my body, raised them to my hair. Slowly I withdrew the ivory pins that imprisoned the tight-coiled strands, until my dark soft hair fell unbound down my back, slid over my cool skin to my knees. I looked for one last time upon Delilah in all her shining glory. Then I reached out to my dressing table and took up the waiting knife.

The horn handle warmed to my touch; the bronze blade shone mirror-keen. For a moment I closed my eyes, seeing my heart's desire as he had stood that first day, fair as the sun, powerful as love itself. *Goodbye, beloved. And know that if I did not carry your child within me, I would join you now.*

But I had been entrusted with that duty, and I would not fail him again.

Wait for me, sun of my heart. Wait.

And then I opened my eyes, and lifted the new-honed knife to my midnight hair.

Orev

"And the Philistines chained mighty Samson before the altar of Dagon. There Samson called upon his god, and his strength returned to him fourfold. And Samson pulled upon the chains with which the Philistines themselves had bound him, pulled Dagon's Temple down upon all those gathered within its dark stone walls to mock Samson and Samson's god . . ."

The dust had settled after a day; the screaming and the searching both had ceased. The Great House of Dagon lay broken, a mass of shattered stone at Gaza's heart. No one seemed to know what should be done now, for both the Lady of the City of Gaza and the High Priest of the Great House of Dagon had vanished, their bodies crushed beneath the huge blocks of stone that were all that remained of the Temple. More, most of the noble families of Gaza had lost their leaders when Samson brought down the Temple, as had the guilds. Until aid came from others of the Five Cities, Gaza could not help itself. There was no one to give orders—and if there had been, there were few left to follow them.

Children and slaves. That is all Gaza has left. Orev sat upon one of the fallen stones and gazed at the devastation before him. *Perhaps someday I shall transmute this horror into a song,* he thought, and heard a part of his soul mock, *"Perhaps?" Even now you struggle to grasp the right words to convey the noise as the stones ground against one another, and the way the dust turned men to ghosts, and the way the ground trembled from Temple to the city wall.*

The harper's curse: to see all that happened, for good or for ill, as the stuff of songs.

Yes, he would remake this tragedy as a song. *But not today.* Today he would grieve, and wonder why he remained here, staring at a pile of rock, a temple that had become a tomb.

Then he saw her pick her way across the uneven mound, lithely, as if the ruins were a dancing-floor. Orev rose slowly to his feet.

The movement caught her attention; she paused, then walked carefully over the stones towards him. When she stood before him, she let the dark veil she wore slide back enough for him to see her face. For a moment he hardly recognized her; then he realized that for the first time he saw her face without the witchery of malachite and kohl and carmine.

The painted mask had vanished utterly, stripping the priestess away and leaving only the woman. Her eyes were dry. Priestess or woman, Delilah would not weep before him.

"Samson kept his vow." Delilah's voice revealed none of the pain and grief she endured. "He is dead, Orev."

"Along with many others. Yes." Orev wondered if Aylah would have wished so many killed to avenge her and her child. The Five Cities had paid dearly for the deeds of a dozen people. But that was not a question he wished to ask.

"But he is not lost to us." Delilah smoothed a hand down over her body, rested it upon her stomach. "I went to him, the night before he brought down Dagon's Temple. I carry his child, Orev."

Absolute conviction burned in her dark eyes; Orev said softly, "That is a great blessing, then."

"Yes. We were given all we asked."

Orev longed to put his arms around her, to make her weep away her bone-deep anger and grief. But such comfort was not his to give, nor would she accept it. *She did what she must, as did Samson, and neither flinched from paying the price demanded for what they desired.*

"If you carry Samson's child—" Orev stopped, silenced by Delilah's burning gaze. He began again, taking care with his words. "You must know that any child of Samson's will be born with enemies waiting to ensure its first breath is its last."

"Yes. But no one living knows of this, save you and I. No one will ever know. I will make sure of that."

For a few breaths neither of them spoke. They stood in a silent world of stone and dust.

"What will you do now?" Orev asked at last.

"I will walk until I find a Lady Temple that does not offer fealty to any of the Five Cities, and there I shall wait until his daughter is born."

"Perhaps you bear his son, instead."

"No." The certainty in her voice silenced Orev for a moment.

"And then?" he asked.

"And then I shall raise her until she chooses for herself what she will become."

"And then?"

"And you, Orev? What will you do now?"

Evasion. She does not wish to tell me. He studied her more closely, reached out and wound his fingers in the edge of her dark veil.

"There is nothing more to say." She turned away, and the veil, trapped by his hand, slid down, over her shoulders, floated free into the dusty stones.

She made no sound, only curved back to face him. Her body still held the grace of dance. But Orev did not think she would dance again. That, too, was gone. Cut away by grief, as sharply as a blade had cut away her shining midnight hair. A widow's mourning.

She looked into his eyes, waiting, and Orev realized he would say nothing. For there was nothing to say, except good-bye.

Delilah

The last day I saw my daughter—Samson's daughter—was upon her seventh birthday. That day I bathed her and rubbed her honey-hued skin with oil of roses and myrrh; combed her fire-bright hair with a sandalwood comb and then stroked it with a square of silk until the unruly waves gleamed like a sunlit sea. Then I wrapped her gem-perfect body in scarlet linen and led her to the Temple. At the gateway into the Outer Court, I stopped, suddenly afraid—I, who had faced down the Prince of the City, who had deceived the High Priestess Derceto, who had gone boldly to Samson in the prison below the Great House of Dagon.

It had been long years since I had owned the right to come and go freely in the Great House of Atargatis in Ascalon, since I had danced before Our Lady Herself. As I hesitated, my daughter looked up at me, puzzled. "Why do we stop, Mother? You promised I could go and live with the goddess Atargatis."

"Yes," I said. "I promised you that." I looked at the time-paled serpents coiled from my elbows to my wrists, blue shadows beneath the skin. *Once they gleamed vivid as lapis. Now*— Now the serpents faded more with each passing moon, symbols of my betrayal of all I had once held dearer than life.

"Mother?" My daughter tugged my hand, summoning me back from a time long gone.

I knew myself bound by that past, those hot memories of love and passion and hate. *But our child will not live chained to my sorrows, to his fate. She will live her own life, not ours.*

That was why I had promised to surrender her into Our Lady's keeping. The day I first cradled her in my arms, I had vowed our daughter would live unshadowed by the past. Even then, I had known I could not grant her that freedom. And as she grew, I realized that his laughing daughter belonged to a laughing mother, not a mourning one.

So I told her tales of Atargatis and Her love, of the Temple and the goodness and kindness found within its walls. Every night before she slept, I sang to my daughter of the happiness of dwelling among sisters, of how Our Lady was mother to all. I whispered of the joy I had known when I had danced within Her loving embrace. I taught Samson's daughter love, not hate. And my heart rejoiced when she asked when she could enter the House of Atargatis, to dance for the goddess as I had done. I knew she would be safe and happy there. But I did not know how hard it would be to give her up, even to a better Mother than I could ever be to her . . .

She tugged again at my hand, her fingers warm and soft within my grasp. This time I let her lead me on, into the Temple.

No one stopped me as I walked with my daughter through the outer courts. No one spoke to me. I might have been a shadow passing among them, or a ghost. My feet knew the path to follow; my hands remembered how to set themselves upon the Ivory Gate. The Gate yielded, and I did what I had once vowed I never would do again. I walked of my own will through the Gate, into the heart of the Temple's world, into the Court of the Goddess-on-Earth.

There, in Our Lady's House, I gave my hard-won child into the care of the High Priestess herself. Under High Priestess Nikkal's rule, the Great House of Atargatis offered love and trust, safety and happiness. One good had come of the evil I had caused seven years ago: now the

High Priestess and the Prince of the City fulfilled their duties to Ascalon the Beautiful as joyful partners, rather than as rivals. Nikkal had always been kind as well as pious, and Aulykaran a good man beneath his pretense of being an indolent fool.

Nikkal looked down at my daughter, and smiled. "She will be beautiful, Delilah. Our Lady favors her."

I looked at the High Priestess's face, and then at my daughter's. "If Our Lady truly looks upon her with favor, let her bestow happiness upon her rather than beauty." I would not curse my daughter with that double-edged gift. I did not wish that for my Sun-Lord's child.

"You must trust the Mother of us all—" Nikkal began, and stopped as my laughter etched acid in the sweet-scented air.

"I trust Her. But She can no longer trust me." I lifted my hands and pulled out the copper butterfly pins that held the sky-blue veil over my hair. I had never let it grow long again; I kept it shorn, like a new widow's.

"Here." I knelt and laid the pins at Nikkal's feet. "An offering to your goddess." Then I let the veil drift over my daughter's head; the sheer cloth slipped down and she caught it with a swift, sure grasp. "Remember me, my dove."

I rose, and Nikkal set her hands upon my daughter's shoulders. "I will take her to the Court of the New Moons myself," the High Priestess said, and I nodded my thanks.

But my daughter did not yield at once to the gentle guidance of Nikkal's hands. Now that the moment of parting had come, she hung back; I knew she had just realized that where she now went, I could not follow.

"Mother?" It was both plea and question.

I summoned a smile from my past—such a smile had deceived princes and priests. It had even, when I had looked into my silver mirror, deceived myself.

"Go with the High Priestess," I said. "And do not forget all I have taught you, Zhurleen. Be happy."

• • •

As I left the Great House of Atargatis for the last time, I remembered words I had spoken before my child had been born: *"Until she chooses for herself what she will become."*

Easy words to say. Now that I had given my daughter into the keeping of Our Lady, I could only hope that she would indeed be happy. In the House of Atargatis, she would live and grow in love and laughter. Perhaps, someday, she too would dance . . .

I had done my best for my daughter—for Samson's daughter. Now it was time to pay all my debts. Samson's god and my goddess had granted all we had asked of them. That we had been fools was no fault of either Atargatis or Yahweh.

I turned and looked back through the Temple gate, into the Lady's joyous house.

And then I set my feet upon the road to En-dor, where my future and my past awaited me.

Epilogue
The Gate of Horn

The strangest hour of his life came long years later, when Orev sang of Samson before the king, in the king's new palace in Jerusalem. The king had sent for him, and had him brought into the court, where Orev bowed and the king, noting Orev's lameness, called for a stool and bade the harper sit before him.

"Harpers all are brothers," the king said. "I have heard you are a great song-master. Sing for us."

Orev studied the king, gauging the man's temper as he would that of a blade, before asking, "What shall I sing, Brother Harper?" He knew the answer already; what song would a new king of Israel ask for but that of the Sun of Yahweh?

"Samson," said the king. "Sing us the Song of Samson."

Orev looked at the king, and at the golden lions adorning the king's throne, and then at the woman who sat, another adornment, at the king's feet. Saffron linen so fine it seemed like sunlight stroked her supple body; a net of pearls trapped hair crimson as summer sunset, hot as the heart of fire. She slanted her painted eyes at him, regarded him with amused interest. Midnight eyes, like her mother's; laughing eyes, like her father's. *"Out of strength, sweetness; out of bitterness, laughter."*

For a moment the years dropped away like a faded veil. *"Are the two of*

you mad? You'll both be killed. That won't help your dead, or the living, either." His last
desperate effort to hammer sense into either hero or priestess.

*Samson smiling, draping his arm heavy over Orev's shoulders. "Who knows better
than I how to move stone? And we have Yahweh's own vow that I'll succeed."*

"And the Lady's. 'The Son of the Sun will destroy a god.'" Delilah's night-eyes glittering fever bright. *"The Seer at En-dor saw it."*

So young, both of them, and so certain, and so wrong. And yet—it
had happened just as the angel and the oracle both foretold. Or had
there been an angel? Hadn't that been just a village tale? *I am too old; I
have lived too long. No one will remember me, but they will live forever young, the sun-
hero and his night-love . . .*

"Brother Harper?" The king spoke gently, as was proper to an elder
song-master, yet with a hint of impatience. Courtly manners, but he
was still a king speaking to a wandering harper, after all. The sea-
gemmed woman sitting at the king's feet laughed, softly, and flirted her
long dark eyes at Orev.

Strength and sweetness both. Orev smiled back, remembering what Delilah
had named Samson's daughter. *Zhurleen. Laughter.*

"I crave pardon, my lord king. I am old; my mind drifts. But my
songs do not." He set his fingers upon the harp-strings, and began.

"Once there was a man who loved a woman so greatly that he died
for it." *Yes, I am an old man, and this may be the last time I ever sing of them. So this
one time I shall sing it as I wish, for the sake of truth, and for their laughing daughter.*

"Listen and heed, and I will sing you the Song of Samson and
Delilah . . ."

AFTERWORD

The story of Samson and Delilah is endlessly intriguing to artists and authors. As a story, it's got everything: sex, violence, love, and betrayal. It has been the subject of paintings, operas, novels, popular songs, and movies—and over the centuries, the story of these doomed lovers has acquired layers of significance not actually found in the Bible. The original story is in Judges 13–16, and Delilah herself appears only in Judges 16:4–20.

The Book of Judges covers the period before the Hebrew kings, a time when Canaan was ruled by the Philistines and the Hebrews were struggling to claim its land. Although the modern word *philistine* means "a crude, uncultured person," the Philistines were actually cultured, artistic, and wealthy. They would have been quite happy to live in peace with the Hebrews, but the Hebrews considered Canaan a land promised to them by God and intended to have it. The time of Judges was one of growing conflict between the Hebrews and the Philistines, and Samson is one of the key figures in that conflict.

Samson, like Gilgamesh and Hercules, is a hero in the archaic, classical sense: a man of possibly supernatural origin and of superior strength, who acts as he is compelled to by forces beyond his control. The items and actions associated with Samson (among them the supernatural elements of his birth, the incredible strength, the mighty rages, the lion-skin garment) make this clear. And he has a very odd name for a Hebrew, for Samson does indeed mean "Son of the Sun."

According to Judges 13:5, Samson is to be raised as a Nazirite, one who has taken holy vows or, as in Samson's case, had them taken for him by his mother before his birth, and "he will begin the deliverance of Israel from the hands of the Philistines." As a Nazirite, Samson is supposed to abstain from wine, women, unclean food, touching dead bodies, and cutting his hair. (Except for not cutting his hair, Samson violates these strictures pretty freely in the biblical account of his life.) Also according to the biblical account, Samson is amazingly attracted to Philistine women. His wife's a Philistine (Judges 14–15), and after judging in Israel for twenty years, he goes off and spends the night with a Philistine prostitute in Gaza (Judges 16:1).

It's easy to see why Samson is the Philistines' worst nightmare. He's a charismatic hero who takes their women, burns their fields, and slaughters their men—and he can unite the Hebrews against the Philistines. So the Philistines come up with a scheme to ensnare Samson, using as bait a woman with whom he's fallen in love: Delilah.

And it came to pass afterward, that he loved a woman in the valley of Sorek, whose name was Delilah. (Judges 16:4)

Although she's usually referred to in popular culture as a Philistine, the Bible never identifies Delilah as such. We actually know nothing about Delilah beyond her name—a name whose meaning is generally given as "weak" or "languishing," from the Hebrew root *dal* (weak or poor). But when I began the research for my story, it seemed far more likely to me that the root of her name was the proto-Semitic *lyl* or *lil*: night. Since names in the Bible are often used to convey meaning about those who possess them, and Samson is the Son of the Sun, it makes more internal sense for Delilah to be the Daughter of Night than the Weakling.

The Philistines see a chance to render Samson harmless to them, and offer Delilah eleven hundred pieces of silver from each of the Philistine lords if she'll learn the secret of the Hebrew hero's great strength and reveal it to them. The amount offered is huge, a veritable king's ransom, and a hard-cash indication of how much the Philistines fear Samson. The stage is now set for Samson's downfall. It's clear he trusts Delilah, because three times she asks what will render him helpless, and three times he tells her a jesting lie, and three times she tries the method he told her—and it doesn't work. Yet Samson seems totally unaware that Delilah could be up to no good.

So naturally, I asked myself *Why?*

In popular culture, Delilah is considered the ultimate wily seductress-spy, using almost inhuman cleverness to learn the secret of Samson's strength. But, as a number of analysts of the story have pointed out, Delilah doesn't use any extraordinary covert means to learn the secret of Samson's strength. No, after asking three times and getting three false answers, what she does is nag Samson until he tells her the true answer:

> *And she said unto him, How canst thou say, I love thee, when thine heart is not with me? thou hast mocked me these three times, and hast not told me wherein thy great strength lieth. And it came to pass, when she pressed him daily with her words, and urged him, so that his soul was vexed unto death; That he told her all his heart.* (Judges 16:15–17)

Realizing Samson has finally told her the truth—that cutting his hair will make him an ordinary man—Delilah waits until he's asleep and calls for a barber. With his hair shorn, Samson is easily taken captive by the Philistines, and Delilah disappears from the pages of the Bible.

Delilah is regarded as one of history's great villainesses, the woman who destroyed the great hero Samson. But that's the Hebrew point of view. To the Philistines, Delilah would have been a great heroine, saving them from Samson's rages.

To a novelist, this conflict and contradiction is irresistible. And there are so many questions the story raises. How did Samson meet Delilah? He obviously loved her—but what were her feelings for him? Did she betray him in exchange for riches? Or did she have other reasons for her actions? What did she feel when her lover was blinded and imprisoned?

Did Delilah know her own heart?

Samson "told her all his heart." An enemy revealing too much to a sultry spy? Or a man opening his heart to the woman whom he truly loves—and who loves him?

So there you have my Delilah's dilemma, as the Sun's Son and Night's Daughter dance, forever joined in our minds . . .

As eternal enemies? As eternal lovers? Or . . . as both?

ACKNOWLEDGMENTS

With grateful thanks to those who read and commented on the various and varied drafts of this book: William Ahlbach, Ellen Bushyhead, Ginny Collins, Dawn Cox, Pam Curry, Bonnie Edghill, Rosemary Edghill, Ginger Garrett, Haley Elizabeth Garwood, Roberta Gellis, Sarah Johnson, Nicole Jordan, Michael Kourtoulou, Cynthia Miller, Myra Morales, Michelle Moran, Patricia Myers, Tamara Myers, Laura Ottinger, Laura Pilkington, Diane and Dr. Maurice Rawlings, Niloufer Reifler, Marge Root, Virginia Saunders, Dora Schisler, Ron and Jenny Stone, Gloria Edghill Wenk. (My sister Bonnie and my friend Dora get bonus points for promptly pointing out that lions don't purr. In case you care, the largest cat that purrs is the cheetah. And Diane—thanks for all the extra Philistines!)

As always, the St. Martin's crew is wonderful, with special thanks to my editor, Nichole Argyres, and her assistant, Kylah McNeill. Ditto to my agent, Anna Ghosh, as well as to my copy editor, Susan M. S. Brown, and to Steve Balyeat, creator of gorgeous Web sites.

This list wouldn't be complete without adding the outrageously great Cecil B. DeMille, whose 1949 *Samson and Delilah*, in glorious Technicolor, is one of the all-time wonderful biblical epics, with some amazing costumes only equaled in magnificence and inaccuracy by those worn by Lana Turner in the equally fabulous *The Prodigal* (1955).

An even greater debt is owed to my mother and father, who loved old movies almost as much as they loved books, and introduced me to both.